THE BRIGHT HIGHWAY

THE **BRIGHT WAY**

A NOVEL

NICK CRAWFORD

ISBN: 979-8-9988266-0-3 (Paperback)
ISBN: 979-8-9988266-2-7 (Hardcover)
ISBN: 979-8-9988266-1-0 (eBook)

Any references to historical events, real people, or real places are used fictitiously. Names, characters, and places are products of the author's imagination.

Front cover images © Shutterstock.com
Book cover design by *the*BookDesigners and Levi Lack
Book design by *the*BookDesigners

ROUND LOGIC
www.nick-crawford.com

For Mama Lady, Veronica Child,
Mateo's Book Club, and Kristie Dickens.
Your lights are unequaled. Par ya Lum sakar.

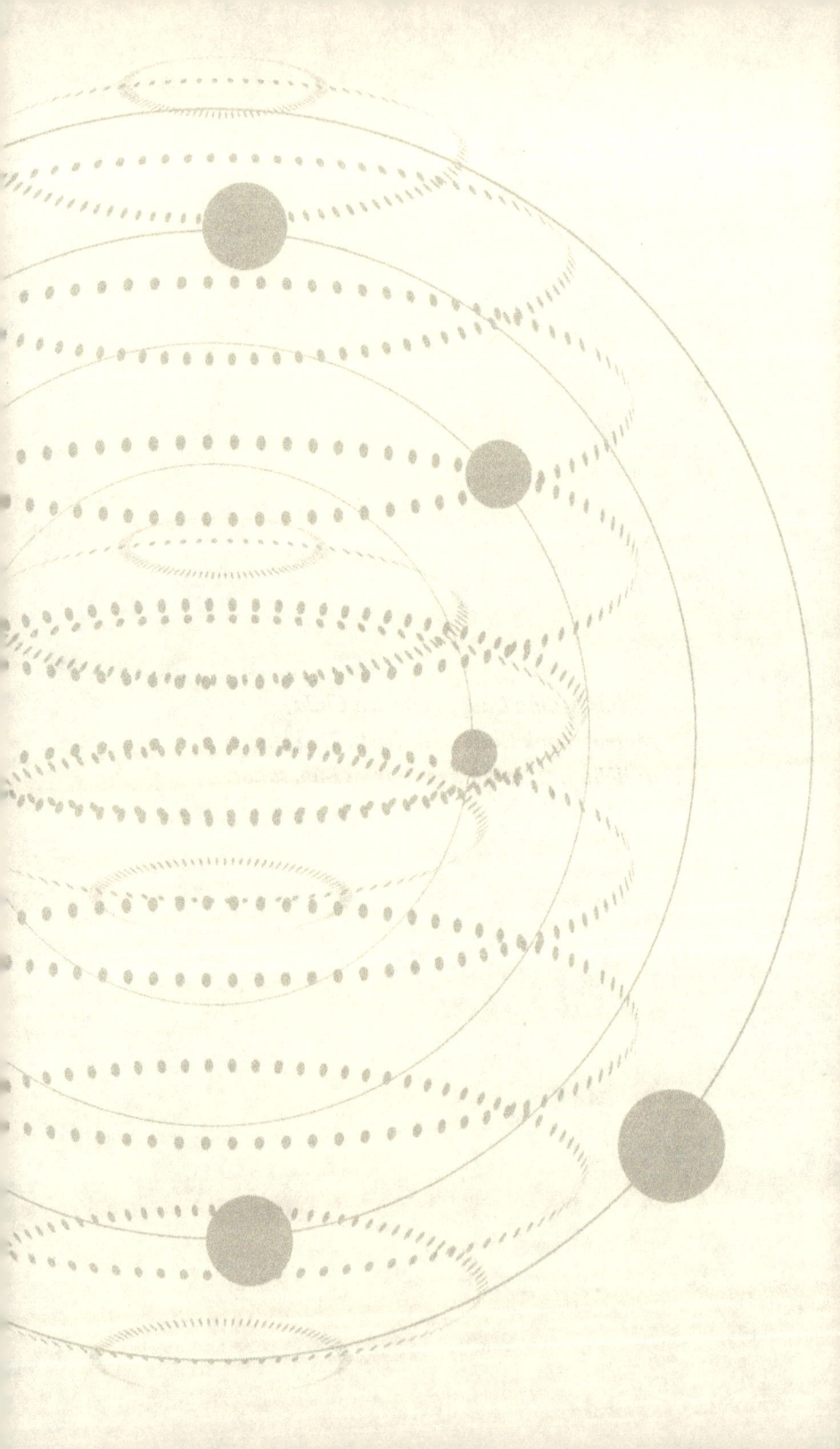

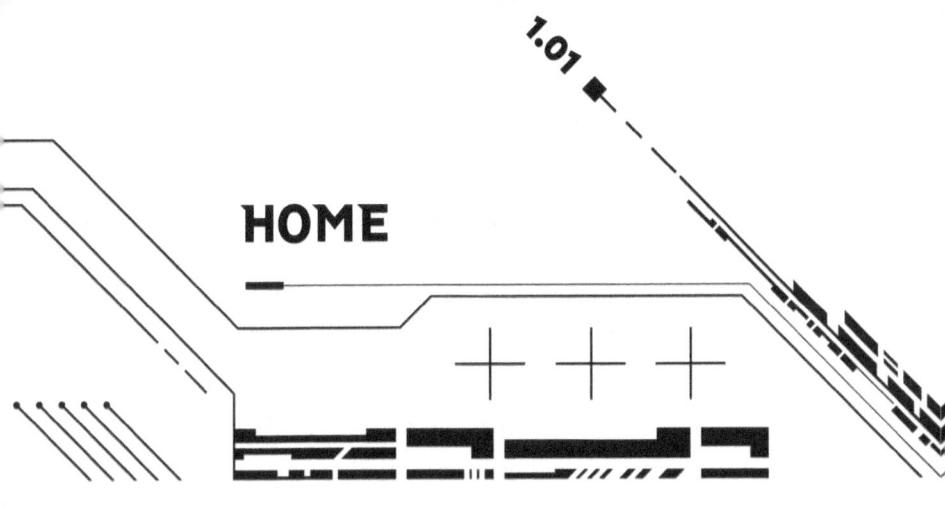

HOME

When I was a kid, I used to dream about outer space. Feels strange to call it that today. Almost makes it funny. Infinite galaxies to explore, endless worlds to dominate, and somehow the reachers came straight to Earth.

Maybe that ain't the right word either. Dream, I mean. Back then, they felt more like memories. Reversed recollections of some distant time, some inevitable future along the black beyond. I had my own little fortress by the hayloft window where I'd snuggle up tight on moonless nights and just drift away—a midnight ghost, steaming up through dusty rafters and wide Texan skies until I could see it all. This whole shadowed world. One vast silhouette where all the oldest, greatest mysteries were collapsing without due fanfare, without any of that storybook romance or neon action we'd all held in our hearts and limited minds—an entire planet still wet with despair, reconfiguring itself to match its worst, its coldest day. And I just watched. I just floated up there until it all came true. Not a wide-open outer space but an infinite threat. An endless quiet to be feared. Yeah. I saw all this darkness back

1

before I knew a damn thing about the reachers—back before they killed my daddy and I quit dreaming altogether.

"Codes."

I lean us away from the shuttle window, listening carefully for her next whisper. That was strange. She sounded nothing like herself. Sounded tired. Sounded like a dying man.

"Hey, buddy."

I spin us around in the narrow window seat, knocking our sturdy knees against a broken tray table. Or maybe we just broke it. I don't remember seeing all those plastic pieces on the floor when we buckled in. The dying man doesn't seem to care. He stinks like unbrushed teeth, and he is leaning—practically sitting—on the aisle seat's armrest with a strange sense of ease, like this is his living room and we're the one intruding.

"Travel codes." The shuttle conductor nods to our left wrist, probably mistaking our wetgen band for a common Rettag. I do have an old R-6 smartwatch somewhere in my duffel, just in case I need to call ahead or check my feed for new instructions. Haven't worn it in years. Pretty much became a paperweight after we . . . after *she* and I got together.

With spiking annoyance, the conductor starts to ask again—but finally sees us completely. Finally recognizes my *uniform*. He stops himself there. Stops every muscle in his face just like that woman did in the dock this morning.

That slender woman we bumped into. She was fine as hell and hard to miss, but I didn't see her right away. I smelled her. One errant whiff of something citrusy in the civilian orbital dock. Without stopping to think, I tracked her perfume around a blind corner, and wham—we were all arms and elbows.

Her sharp nose flicked across my chin. Her sleeveless shoulder nestled real neat and sweet against my uniform—against *our* chest—and she was quick to laugh, God bless her. She was smiling up at me, saying she was so sorry, touching our arm while I just stammered all stupid-like. Then her eyes met mine.

She went real stiff and quiet after that, like any normal person might if they sniffed your broken wind in a closing elevator, or like I've heard some X-tier reachers do when they catch you thinking something nasty—something patriotic—but I was two inches from this lady's face, and I could see that she was no invader. Her eyes were brown as muddy water, and her ears looked perfectly natural, openly displayed beneath a tight French braid. Come to think of it, most of the girls I saw in the dock this morning were wearing their hair the exact same way. Saves time getting through security, I guess. Spares you the embarrassment of getting mistaken for one of them.

No wonder she went so stiff. I'd thought it was me that did it to her, my stupid speechless face. But I get it now. She touched *her*. Just a friendly squeeze, expecting plain cotton or the hairy meat of a human wrist. She must've had no earthly reference for the alien texture she found instead.

The conductor finally remembers to salute. I quickly nod, and he continues down the aisle. "Codes. Have your travel codes ready," he mutters, sneaking one last glance at my rare gunsuit as she relaxes against my skin, as her solar scales begin to shimmer like a prismatic fish in a galactic sea. He would keep his eyes to himself if he was able to hear her *whispers*, if he ever heard how casually she just recommended his violent death.

As I turn us back to the triple-pane window, I try to remember how long we've been in orbit. *Eighty-six*, she whispers quickly. *Months*, she clarifies. Sounds about right. It's easier than sin to get lost up here, all of humanity stretched out beneath you, no recreation outside the occasional reacher pod scorching through your sector, only to be atomized seconds later once your targeting simulant locks and fires. If the logs are right, I'm the only gunner this year to be promoted from the patrol. Never thought I would be. Never thought much about it whatsoever. For most gun pilots, that's the appeal. Isolation. Ten thousand klicks between you and whatever podunk bullshit you escaped.

The flames of reentry take that cue, flashing hot and unexpected, snatching the angst from my young face. Younger than it should be. Hardly aged a fucking day. I'm nose to nose with my reflection for the first time in seven years, and nothing's changed except my eyes. They're strobing white and blue, broiling in the observation glass with inhuman heat alive behind them. No. That ain't me. Tell me that ain't me. Only reachers shine like that.

A shudder of turbulence breaks the flames. The shuttle systems finally recalibrate, smoothing our trajectory into a more gradual descent. My fiery twin is suffocated just as quickly as he was born, giving way to a rapid onslaught of forgotten terrestrial hues. She clenches our chest tightly, reminding me to take a breath. I am unable to comply. A bitter twist of sunken memories is cocktailing in my throat. A crowded blue world is rushing up to drink me down. My eyes recoil to the heavens, but our starry view is gone, completely shrouded by the hazy, stifling ceiling of the Earth.

A transparent sphere materializes there, rippling in our atmospheric wake like a giant polished marble. I gaze hysterically, swallowing the fire in my lungs, drowning in the unexpected symptoms of post-traumatic stress. The hallucination vivifies. The imagined marble flickers quickly between ghost and solid mass. I blink a dozen times, but it only grows clearer. She *whispers* once again. Not a reminder at all, I realize. A warning.

A subtle shockwave rolls the shuttle. Less than turbulence. Just a nudge. The conductor pauses his collection, glancing upward for a moment, but none of the passengers seem to register the disturbance, let alone spot the reacher pod as it escapes the shuttle's jet stream. It hangs there perfectly still, undisguised, before it darts off with blinding agility, soaring beyond the Earth's horizon between two beats of my racing heart. A Y-tier rogue, I'd bet my skin on it. The deadlier reachers always seem to come in quicker pods. Or maybe it's their minds that make 'em quick. A better sync between invader and machine. Either way, we're lucky the nearest cannon sim didn't ash us all the moment it de-cloaked.

I exhale. She relaxes.

I force my eyes back down, bravely facing the barrage of rising clouds. I shouldn't blame myself. If a soldier's pride is every step in the marathon of his career, it's only natural for him to waver when his marching orders call him home.

Old Dallas County comes into view. When I was a kid, we used to call it something else. None of that matters anymore. Local borders lose their meaning once you learn the scope of things. Earth is just an island in the ocean of the cosmos. And this ocean's rife with strangeness, drifting closer to our shores.

1.02

My vomit bubbles on the tarmac. I haven't seen it yet, but my nose and ears assail me with their best guesses. An acrid updraft, fizzing like small voices. My digestive refugees.

Gingerly, I twist us away from the stench I've made, prob-ing blindly at the white-hot pavement, scorching my fingertips like I'm crawling in frying oil. I save my breath for fresher air, finding none of it behind us. Instead, the stink of dirt and dust smothers every entrance to my skull. Everything but my eyes. I blink for the hundredth time and still see no proof of it. A deeper black than should be possible. A world so apparently empty yet so terribly loud. I hear several different conversa-tions from the crowd forming around us, sounding like shouts in my hypersensitive ears—like Christ almighty slipped and knocked the entire planet to maximum volume.

Leaning back, I rest our forearms against our thighs. Our knees press deeper into the cauterizing blacktop, but my bare hands respect their sacrifice. Her cool exterior is a godsend. As I caress her, she tugs randomly at my digits. A unique sen-sation. It's like being pinched by fleshy sequins, like the suit is searching just as blindly.

Pondering that, I guide one hand slowly back to the tar-mac. The pavement feels warm this time—and only slightly. A shadow near summer's end. The pain in my fingers fades just as quickly, like my nervous system un-flipped a switch. False alarm—the Earth ain't actually on fire. But it may be worse than that. *She* hasn't whispered since we landed. So many curi-ous questions from the shuttle crowd, so many small voices in each other's ears—but hers has left me. It's not the world that's off its axis, it's just us. Somehow, we've been desynced.

"Easy there, friend."

I jolt at the sound of another man. Somewhere above us. Or behind.

"Breathe easy there, cowboy." There's a deafening crunch of gravel as he kneels at my three o'clock. Way too close.

"I'm fine, I just—I was on the shuttle." I rise quickly, wiping the froth from my chin, completely forgetting the larger population at our feet. The stranger catches hold of us as we slip backward then sharply sideways. We skate like the shit-faced Olympics before his balance finally wins out.

"Easy, goddammit. Easy!" His hands slip in tightly around our waist, clasping in a practiced wrestler's grip. That stops us quick. We could dislocate his shoulders with minimal effort. We could elbow his lungs through the back of his shirt. Luckily, we do neither. His strange audacity makes us a statue.

"My eyes," my voice betrays me. "They—there's something wrong with my suit."

"I know, cowboy. Just take it easy."

He knows? I turn my wooden gaze instinctively toward his grip. Maybe he's wearing gloves, but I don't think so. I don't hear anything like chafing leather or crinkling latex. No musty smells or plastic odors. As a test, I allow our arms to relax, settling down against the stranger's muscular forearms. She tugs lightly, mindlessly at his flesh. If he notices, he doesn't seem to care.

He's quick to release us, though. Takes a few steps backward in the gravel—my own private avalanche at every footfall. He says, "Tell me your name," and he's already unzipping something near his waist, rummaging through it like a purse.

"Hayes. Emmett Hayes."

"Call sign?"

I notice more disembarking passengers, lingering at the edges of my remaining senses, exchanging spooky guesses and conspiracy theories. Someone's Ret-tag chimes distinctly, starting a video broadcast. Maybe we'll go viral.

"Tell me your call sign," the stranger commands this time.

"Daydream, sir." Our posture straightens automatically.

Our feet slide closer together as I realize this may be an officer we're dealing with. Could be a liaison sent to collect us.

An amused little snicker escapes his nostrils. Hard to interpret that. Usually, she would advise me right about now, whispering something like: *deceiver, terminate.* Or: *strange odor, terminate.* Not always useful intel, but her absence remains unsettling. So does this stranger. A cicada takes flight thirty meters to the south. I hear rush hour traffic crawling half a klick beyond that. But every time this man stands still, he seems to vanish—as though his very existence is being masked.

"Alright." He zips his fanny pack closed. Crunches more gravel as he steps closer, thankfully speaking softly. "Open your hand."

I comply instantaneously. Just desperate to end it, I'll tell myself later. A presumed lawful order, honestly, but my pride takes two paces back. He turns my hand gently and drags soft bristles against my palm. Paints something there. Feels like a cream. Then I hear the brush flip, reversing direction, dragging air between his deft fingers. Delicately, he lowers the other end of the tool to the slathered cream. There's a quick pinch of static just before it reaches my skin. And now I realize what's been done.

Like a thousand hatching spiders, their first instinct is to scatter. An itching heat spreads toward my knuckles. Programmed chaos. Microscopic metal life. Maybe he chose not to prick me as a time saver, or out of some respect for my dwindling ego, but the alternative point of entry sets a high standard for future nightmares. By the thousands, they rush to the tips of all five digits, nano tendrils dashing madly. Under all five fingernails, they scurry, burrowing through my cuticles to their new home within my veins.

"Sorry, cowboy, no fresh needles. But you—"

We lunge in his direction. He avoids us with ease, chuckling good-naturedly. We'll knock that smile down his throat if we can find him.

"Alright, cool it, hoss," he laughs. "It's a war crime to engage non-combatants."

A medic, of course! That's painfully obvious now. His mistake for clarifying; no fear of rank after that. "Your word against mine." We backhand the open air. His lack of laughter tells us we came close. He must be holding still and watching careful now. We kick the gravel, trying to stir him, but no movement echoes back. He's a clever bastard, that's for sure. But he's got no chance against us here.

There, she finally whispers.

My left hand feints, the other snatches, catching his collar in a fist. I'm surprised by his body weight as both his feet come off the ground.

The civilians gasp in startled terror, and I begin to wonder if I've grabbed some mute stranger by mistake. That's when I feel something sharp and cold against my wrist. My teeth begin to itch, and I taste something like old pennies beneath my tongue. Not the flavor I was expecting. I hadn't even realized my taste buds were numb. As the light returns to my blinking eyes, I look downward and see why. My vomit is full of blood. And I don't have the usual kind, not after years of cosmic radiation. Even after its communion with the dirt, it's almost black. A deep hickory oil change. My eyes flick up from there to the gathered crowd, and they all flinch backward. One of the kids begins to cry.

But that cold, sharp thing decides to bite me, causing my fist to reflex open. The medic nimbly returns to Earth, and, between his fingers, a steel scalpel glistens that same sickly color. I check my wrist, seeing one deep, precise cut just below my thumb. She *whispers,* and I know the wound will be closed within the hour.

"Daydream, huh?" The medic fixes his collar, studying me with his blue-green eyes. He's got more than a decade on me. Could be forty, forty-one years old. Two inches shorter but a clear muscular advantage. Probably a combat medic despite his somewhat stylish civilian attire. He also has an odd metallic knob on his right shoulder like an off-kilter epaulet. "I guess Nightmare was taken," he finishes his quip.

It makes me laugh in a stupid way, mostly out of embarrassment for overreacting—and for ruining his unusual shirt. But I wipe my mouth and spit in the mess, trying to sound as rough as I used to be. "Sorry 'bout that. Never fucked with nanos before. Never desynced neither."

"Really?" His blue-greens shine with a new curiosity, set in a face that seems oddly familiar to me somehow. Terribly familiar. "Never once?" he asks.

"No. But I've been off world for quite a stretch."

For the moment, he doesn't seem to hear me. He becomes entranced by her resync process, all her bright color patterns rippling with vigor again. "Well. I beg your pardon there," he says, finally lifting his eyes from her. "Still working out some kinks; I may have fragged you by mistake." He taps the back of his neck as he speaks, then crouches to scoop his nano-tool off the ground—looks like a paintbrush at one end, a cattle prod on the other—but I'm more taken by the unnatural thing that he just indicated.

It's some kind of arachnoid implant at the top of his spine—an embedded steel cube with metallic legs piercing the flesh where his neck and skull connect. It's entirely solid, but I seem to see something inside it, something like a flicker of captured hellfire. And she starts to tighten in a disturbing way—an involuntary clenching, restricting my airways. It's making me hot.

Making me feel like any second I might just—

"It's only supposed to affect Luminarans," the medic continues, hopping back to his feet.

My panic passes just as quickly. I shake my head, feeling a little dizzied, almost like I lost a few seconds in time.

"Never thought to test it on a G-1." He drops his nano-tool back in the med bag around his waist and zips it shut, not seeming to notice how nearly I just came to losing control.

"A G-1?" I blink a few times, already feeling a migraine coming on.

"A skinner," he clarifies. "Haven't seen a first-generation suit since . . ." he trails off as though suddenly remembering his good manners. "Well, let's just say, all the new boys wear synthetic." He smiles somewhat awkwardly and looks away.

So do I, glancing downward just as a breeze animates the hairs along my knuckles. She counts each strand automatically, instantly, down to where they vanish beneath her at our wrist. Her photosynthetic skin is dancing, too, just as lively in the wind, far more enchanting.

"Don't worry 'bout the nanos," the medic says, drawing my attention back to him. "Soon as you're clean, they'll self-dismantle. Just a little extra protein between sun baths." He winks, patting our shoulder as he passes, again with no discomfort at her inhuman texture.

"Didn't know I was dirty."

As an answer, he just makes that sound my daddy used to, that little laugh when he had nothin' nice to say. "If you're heading to Cooks, I'll give you a ride. Bus won't be here for another couple hours." Without even pausing for my response, he scoops up my duffel and tosses it into an ancient gasoline jeep parked on the gravel. I hesitate to follow, but he waves me onward with familiar impatience. "Giddy up now, cowboy. I got shit to do." He hops over the driver door, ignites the engine, then throws an Old Dallas adage over his shoulder. "The world don't quit when you stand still."

1.03

The old jeep is like a lullaby—tuned to a melody I know well. The suspension squeaks, and I hear my daddy's rugged voice, cool and quiet like calloused hands on a Marlin 336. The medic downshifts, pushing gas to pass an automated semi-trailer, and I hear Grandma Logan, mumbling her curses until its drone-like hum fades into the wind. Everything was *'lectric* to that woman. She mistrusted silent machines. If she'd lived to see her grandson in a gunsuit, or an exocannon, or half the incredible things in this fucked up world, she'd have dropped dead all over again. Instead, I drop my thoughts of both of them.

My eyes fall shut. I pretend to remember what it's like to dream. Seven years since I did that, since I slept at all, but the instinct remains among a few others, rising intermittently, grasping persistently at the remnant strands of my human soul. I laugh sometimes, thinking back on those first few orbits, reliving the fear of cold starvation in that quiet cockpit sized for one.

I spent two weeks in my cannon before I even realized what was missing. I remembered the word, but its sensation had faded to an impalpable definition. The way a virgin might imagine sensuality, I would never truly feel hunger again. Only thirst. And a constant sinking feeling whenever the sun can't reach her scales. I've read most of the slurs cooked up for gunners on the net, but only one makes sense to me—the one most folks have now adopted. On Earth, they call us *stems*. Thousands of branches to fill the forest high above their dying world.

I twist our wrist to check the wetgen. Condensation levels rising as we push through open air. Some Texan engineer must be ecstatic to see how far his work has carried—an atmospheric water generator smaller than a playing card. Though pride in proving science is like the celebration of new math. It was all there before we found it, before we even thought to look.

In these thirty-odd years we've had with reacher tech—since back when their first marker appeared and we were all too fuckin' curious to shut it off—we've accelerated beyond all prior expectations, beyond all imagined timelines of innovation. But there's an increasing resentment baked into every finding. With each new feat of reverse-engineering, we're reminded of one hard truth. We are not pioneers. At best, we're an iteration—chimpy children crafting crude toys from the discarded scraps of a discarded tribe.

That's what the reachers must be, after all. The refugees or banished convicts of some overpopulated world. Luminara—or whatever the sentimentalists are calling it these days. All we know is they follow the markers wherever they appear. Seven-thousand-year-old beacons summoning seven-thousand-year-old pods, each dispensed like excess waste from some civilization beyond our view. Assuming time dilation at near-light speeds, they could be far, far older. Inconceivably ancient vessels, designed to surf the galaxy for any fresh and familiar land. That's why they look somewhat like us. Just the same evolutionary math playing out on a distant planet—or the exact same planet, if you buy into any of those junk environmental feeds. Our unborn heralds from a tortured future. More like some batshit mirror dimension where humans devolved into alopecic psychic scavengers. If the reacher world is not dead at all, if it's still advancing in some distant galaxy or cloaked somewhere nearer within our own, then I am thankful not to sleep. Next time these rogues come to my doorstep, I'll be waiting with open eyes.

"How long they had you up there?" somebody asks, a bit too loudly for my liking. His voice is familiar, Southern and rough, a lot like mine used to be. He could pass for a grown-up version of my old buddy, Roosevelt Hall.

The stranger clears his throat a little louder, and I turn to him with some annoyance, some confusion. I see the medic, sitting there in the driver's seat, one eyebrow raised uncertainly, waiting for me to reply.

"Oh, you mean us?" I ask abruptly, one finger pointed at our chest.

The medic's eyebrow twitches higher. Then he snorts an honest, subdued laugh. "Pretty good guess, cowboy, yeah." He glances around at the empty jeep and open highway. "But I think you just answered my question."

"Oh. Yeah." I look down at our lap, gliding a nervous thumb over her scales. "I enlisted with the United Territories out of Houston. I was, well, that's where I was living back then." I hear Logan's growling shouts inside my head, the harsh snap of a sorghum stalk against my ankles. I lift my eyes back up and speak to the medic properly. "I joined up a few months before Chicago. This is our first liberty since then."

His head cocks slightly, much like his eyebrow did before. "Chicago. You don't mean The Storm?"

I've never heard someone call it that, but his tone is unmistakable. Certain news leaves lasting scars—flashes of where you were when it happened, which net stream you were pulling when that red banner hit your feed. Of that particular catastrophe, I have no such memory.

The same night that all those people died, a part of me was lost as well. I woke up for the final time, wrapped in a cosmic skin not quite my own. Somewhere between my penultimate dreams, a second mind had set to work, filling gaps, enhancing senses, removing the defects of my genus, hardening my skin and blood against radiation, calcifying my bones against density loss—rewiring my brain. My illiterate limits melted away as *we* became encyclopedic, something between hillbilly trash and the endless feeds of the planet's net. A damaged reacher pod obliterated Chicago, and the extraterrestrial embargo went into effect. The five great nations of the United Territories became de facto arbiters of the Earth, but my only recollections of that time are her first whispers—her first brutal thoughts fusing eerily with my own.

"Yeah." I pick up the medic's hanging question. "We were still merging when it happened. They pushed the program through right after that. The first orbital gunners."

"Merging?" he asks.

I start to answer, but she *pauses* me. A sudden trepidation. I turn to watch the stranger for a moment, and I finally see what he's just done. His voice was curious, even indifferent, but his eyes don't match that tone. The medic knows all about the merging trials, of course he does. He's not asking about that; he's baiting me toward something else.

Us, she whispers. *We,* she insists more urgently.

I watch the stranger. I replay what I just said to him. I think back on all the pluralities I've already let slip today. I remember that derisive sound he made, my daddy's sound, right after that new slur spat over his teeth. *Skinner.* That's what he thinks of us. Something less than human. Even less than reacher. As I watch the medic's clever, conceited eyes, I feel another Southern instinct start to turn. I gather sand to draw a line.

"Tacticity training," I finally answer, keeping my attention distantly forward. "The first suits and cannons were designed for satellite defense. Asteroids, Taurid meteors, international ballistics. Way before the ZA embargo. That's why we're symbiotic, not synthetic."

His eyes change again. His ears seem to widen hungrily.

"They called it training," I chuckle darkly, "but it was more like a final fitting. A solar suit for each recruit. Usually took about six days—to merge completely." I raise my naked hand. Her scales shimmer from our wrist to our padded toes. "For us, it took three weeks."

The medic twitches. I let him simmer in his derision. I pray to God he gives me a reason to lay my hands on him again.

"That makes me lucky." My eyes drift upward, even though the OP station is on the other side of the planet now. "That still puts me years ahead of those who never rose at all."

I milk that skyward glance, staring performatively at the clouds, getting ready to react to whatever ignorance he emits. But she *reminds* me it's more than that. Not just an act to rile him up. I see three faces from the gunner logs. Three names. Michael Sapp, Bryce Jimenez, and Jakey Mead. I feel myself twitch this time. I remember looking down at that colored list an hour after our merge completed. Thirty-two IDs. Mine was still yellow, not updated yet. Below that, twenty-eight names were brightly green. All tac survivors, already dispatched to orbital cannons. I scrolled back up and saw a gunship assigned to my name as well: EX-129. That was the finest moment of my adult life. Adult as far as the UT knew. In truth, I was two months shy of seventeen. I remember laughing as I scrolled down the rest of the log. I giggled like an idiot until I finally saw those three IDs listed in red.

Every cadet signed DNRs when we entered basic. Mike and Bryce thought it was hilarious. *Welcome to the UT Forces, please initial here in case of coma.* But Jakey and I were terrified. Like me, he wasn't exactly academic. Not much of a reader beyond his own last name. So, I made him trade me. I signed his deck, and he signed mine. That way, it wouldn't be legit. If the UT ever tried to pull his plug, I'd show 'em this forgery right here, and that'd be the end of it. He'd have my back, and I'd have his. We shook hands on that. Six months later, they all died while I was in the merge. Instead of dispatched gunships, their dropdowns read: *Equipment Failure, Solar Dome 4.* I checked the data center; the UT never even checked their DNRs. No need. All three of them burned alive.

"And there were endless empty eyes," the medic mutters to himself.

My eyes drop from space to meet his own. But he doesn't turn. His blue-greens drift vacantly over the highway, gathering a harshness in the tanned lines above his nose.

"Blinded by the freest worlds," he continues distantly. "Betrayed by those who knew the light." It sounds like scripture the way he says it. Like the words on the grave of a murdered foe. His faraway eyes flick to me suddenly, like the eyes of a dog that's done its dance. Waiting eyes, hungry eyes, disappointed eyes, realizing I have no treats to give. That harshness doubles in his brow. He hocks and spits out his open window. Drags his knuckles across his lips. His eyes glaze forward, as though he's riding in the jeep alone.

"I don't catch your meaning." I truly don't. No clue in hell what he just recited, and that makes it even worse—like he just spat on Jakey's grave, and I'm too dense to recognize it.

Wait. Not safe. She protests my arriving thoughts—sends an unexpected cooling wave over our shoulders and down our back. But I'm way too hot to be pacified. My country blood sings a nasty song.

"I don't know if you fragged me back there on purpose," I continue. "I don't know if those nanos were what you said they were or if Cooks is even in this direction. I don't know your fuckin' name, slick." The jeep thumps over something dead in the road, and the medic readjusts his grip on the wheel. My eyes find his medical bag. My hands plot rapid violence. "But whatever choice you think I made, whatever line you guess I crossed by puttin' on this suit, I can tell you somethin' now and only once. I'm an Old Dallas boy. If you can count your sins, I'm not right for you, friend. We won't match, not even close."

For a moment, nothing happens. The suspension squeaks and another electric simulant rig hums past us on the right.

Then the medic makes Daddy's sound again, even louder, twice as fearless. The thinnest smile arrives above his chin. "None of us choose, cowboy. Not even once before we die." He signals left to the traffic bots then smoothly merges from the highway. An unmarked tunnel comes into view. The kind you'd miss if you weren't looking. The kind you're supposed to miss. "But so long as we're making friends," he says, "I'd be real glad if you called me Prich."

He watches me all the way inside, a subtle sign of won respect, of unbroken sand. His eyes seem to smile with their own light as we both vanish into darkness.

1.04 ■- -- ——————

A timid stench catches in the wind. A wet underarm stink like onions rotting in the sun. It wafts right over the medic, but he's too unmodified to notice. Not too polite, I'm sure of that. It floats like a cloud I can almost see. The color of pickles, the clumpy texture of bad milk. It hits me like the summertime in Georgia. It makes me sneer. My disgust is obvious, but the poor kid in the booth has no idea why.

"Uh—yes, sir. You need directions?" the young gate guard stammers in a trembly voice, forcing his eyes back to the medic, Prich.

"Not today." Prich snatches his entry pass from the boy's loose grip. The kid hardly notices, already staring at my suit again, gawking at our strange chest and all the cosmic colors there. A gust of wind kicks up, and she drinks deeply, pulling moisture through the wetgen in a flurry of rippling scales.

The moron jolts, sending his hand down to his sidearm. He stops just short of it, and the whole thing becomes one hideous flinch.

I hear the medic's laugh for the very first time. Bold and unrepentant, head thrown back. The boy stumbles backward into his booth as though that rudeness has bowled him over. With lowered eyes, he presses his thumb to a fingerprint scanner and mumbles into an intercom:

"One coming through dock six." A prolonged buzzing accompanies the slow descent of the fortified gate wall. We all sit there together for a spell, waiting for the heavy gate to sink between a thick gap in the pavement. Prich carries on laughing all the while. He cackles freely as his anachronistic jeep lugs us onward into Camp Cooks.

I'd mistaken him for some kind of bigot, or even worse, a pacifist, one of those loud, self-righteous shits who thinks the Orbital Patrol is inhumane, one of those squishy sissies shouting *Protect Luminaran Lives!* from the perfect safety of their gated condo. A safety built by the patrol. But I was wrong about the medic. As we cruise through the UT Forces' southern base of operations, I realize he's not the peaceful sort at all. He is the imp of chaos.

It's another medic who notices us first. She stops deer-eyed in the road, a full box of uniforms in her arms. Prich giddily punches his horn, and she pries her eyes from us just long enough to make the safety of the sidewalk. A passing infantryman follows her gaze and nearly gives himself whiplash. I see others in my peripheral, turning and whispering their fears. Not a single one of them sees me looking back. They only see *her* and her strange dance as she makes a partner of the wind— her hypnotic shine that somehow looks the way the nicest voices sound. Sweet vocals of home and more precious places. At least, that's how she looks to me.

The medic snickers, and I begin to hate his fuckin' jeep, this damned wide-open antique thing. She *whispers* something to me, but I'm in no mood to understand. A gnawing sense of loss begins to war with my ambition, a more than subtle yearning for the cannon I'd called home. Black and endless, I'll admit, but it was mine. My high vantage of this terrestrial decay. My private refuge from this hot, expanding dread.

She *whispers*, and I can almost hear her clearly. Clear enough to spread my stubborn lips into a smile. She's right, as always. It was *ours*.

1.05 ▪— – — ━━━ ▀▄▀▄▀

I take one last look at the old jeep. Parked askew in a perfect row of its autonomous descendants, it is defiantly obsolete. A precious artifact from a world that thrived on passion.

As we make our distance from it, various detections of life ping at the edges of my mind. My eyes follow these creeping signals to our feet. Fresh cut grass, prickling and tickling toward my memories of home. That farmhouse on the dryland. And that distant shack—that crooked cabin at the northern shore of Shiloh Lake. The weeds were ambitious there, high enough to hide a holstered pistol. These few worms and wriggling things would be struck dumb by the macrocosm their vast cousins hold in the wild.

"Alright, so—" The medic cuts himself off to step out of my way.

I step out of his way in the same direction, and we almost have our first kiss. Someone should hang a bell on this bastard.

"So, just keep on straight ahead," he continues, smiling. "Another hundred yards in that direction and you'll hit Cuba's office. He's expecting you."

"Cuba?"

"The captain. He's commanding Zero X, units one and two."

Zero X. That's the first time I've heard it spoken. It almost looked like a typo in my feed.

RELIEVED UNIT: ORBITAL PATROL

ASSIGNED UNIT: OX-1

Like the perfect toy on Christmas day, that little riddle kept me faithful. I even dove into the net a few times during peak debris, trusting the autosims to watch my sector while I scrounged the boards for leaks. I was terrified to query post lest I became a breach myself, but I never found a thing—no mentioning whatsoever of the unit Zero X.

"Goddamn, they named you right." Prich derails my train of thought, backing away, finally putting some distance between us. "Daydream!" He throws my call sign to the sky, laughing like a drunk in one of those pre-invasion westerns, laughing without looking back, without any semblance of a goodbye. An unexpected pinch hits the inside of my gut. I turn us away, trying to focus on the directions he left us with, but that old ache decides to linger. I see that old shack above the lake, that total quiet when it was over—when Daddy bled and died.

I shake my head to dull the feeling. I shake again, sharper, and that lost time vanishes completely, fades back down to nothing at all.

I can't seem to remember how we got here. I feel fresh cut grass beneath our feet. That makes me think of the unruly northern trail to Shiloh Lake, but she nudges us forward with a *whisper*. I listen to her, stepping slowly, wondering why my eyes are damp and where the medic has run off to. Someone should hang a bell on that bastard.

1.06

His skin is a deeper ebony than I'd thought was humanly possible. Even seated at his desk, I can tell he's half a head taller than I am. Twice as broad. In a gunsuit, he'd be something unimaginable. A reptilian gorilla.

But it's his eyes that stop me. They remind me of the net, because I've only ever seen them there. One of them, I mean. The left one is real, a black-brown African hue. Human. But the right one is designed. A pre-regulation relic from back when reacher fever had its hold. Not that hypnotic husky blue, though. None of that cosmic, electric zeal that mesmerized us in the early days. No. The captain's false eye is yellow, clean and clear, with a perfect black pinhole at its center. Like a panther fucked a falcon. I bet he lights a match from four thousand meters. With a rail rifle, maybe six.

"It is *ooba.*" He speaks, and I feel his voice beneath our feet. Deep as an earthquake. He stands up, and I realize my mistake. He's a full head taller.

"I'm sorry?"

"Cyrus *ooba.*"

I have no idea what he's saying. But as he reaches to shake my hand, his name plate catches in the light.

C. Uba

"Oh. Sorry, I um—my escort had a little fun with me, I think."

The captain watches us with humorless eyes—until they flick suddenly to our chest. Our arms. Measuring. Evaluating us like any weapon on a rack.

I blink and he's making eye contact again—so fast I almost flinch. Microfont data begins to scroll down his panther pupil, written right to left from my perspective, likely invisible to anyone else. It's a language I don't recognize, but she whispers a hint about the content: *You.*

"Emmett Hayes is documented as a G-1."

I cringe, hearing the medic's echo between my ears. *Skinner.* "Uh. Yes, sir. I'm a first-generation gunner. Original trials, pre-Chicago."

"The Storm was more than seven years ago." Uba's false eye seems to zoom, analyzing somewhere near my left cheek. "You are too young. Who are you?"

"Emmett Hayes, sir. We—I'm a bit older than I look."

She sends a wave of colors across our chest, as though to supplement my claim. His left eye tracks the show, but the falcon stays with me, more microfont arriving.

"Call sign."

"Daydream."

"Exo tag."

"OP-129."

"Assigned unit."

It sticks in my throat. His jaw tightens, and I imagine many versions of our death. "Zero X. Zero X, fireteam one. Sir."

His expression does not change. But his shoulders turn subtly, instinctively toward combat. He's not wrong to be cautious. Even an X-tier rogue could probably get this far. Mind wipe a few patrolmen. Pull some logs from an unknown breach. OP suits are just watered-down replicas of old reacher tech anyway, and she looks shit-all like a synthetic. On top of that, I get the feeling that panther eye has never led him astray. I bet he trusts it the same way that I trust her. Maybe it's the only reason he's still breathing. Maybe pride doesn't move him at all. Only the enemy.

Finally, she *whispers*, and I remember what I need. "Pardon me, sir, but is that—is that Somali?"

His head twitches in recognition. More microfont scrolls. She helps me see.

"No, excuse me. It must be Bemba."

His face does an odd thing this time, like it's forgotten how to emote surprise. Instead, it settles somewhere between aggression and incontinence.

"My daddy did two tours in Sub-Sahara. He was a sniper for the Commonwealth," I lie completely, recklessly. But she *whispers*, and I see a page on the net from eleven months ago, some post I scrolled by absently. Hardly a second of our history is frozen behind my eyes. She holds it, and I recite: "Njeleleniko. Nshaishibisha ukulanda iciBemba. Sir."

His laughter is not the violence I expected, but it's just as immediate. The warmth of some distant homeland comes alive in his human eye. "Few men do, these days," he responds. "But it sounds natural on your lips. Ee. Mwaiseni."

"Thank you, sir. Uh, shani." I bow slightly, hoping that means the same thing in Zambia that it does everywhere else, hoping my daddy doesn't spit on me from heaven.

The captain's face says my gesture is not quite right. He doesn't fully believe my story, but he's too piqued to care—too busy rearranging all his war pieces, outlining distant scenarios where this new weapon may lend an advantage. "Alright, Mr. Hayes. Very good. Let me see your tag." He motions to my duffel and retakes his seat behind the desk. I pause, wondering if I mentioned my R-6 was in my bag or if he just happened to guess lucky. I decide it's neither. The sharp geometry of that right eye makes me think he's never been lucky once.

"Once you are cleared, I will show you to camp," the captain continues. "Set you up outside the wetroom, close to Chiba."

"Excellent. Thank you, sir." I unzip my duffel, digging inside it for my Ret-tag, hoping it's still holding a charge after all these years. "Chiba. Is that the operation sim?"

He half smiles at my bad guess. "Taiko Chiba landed two nights ago. When she clears tac, she will be OP-401, the first cannon pilot of generation four."

"She's a gunner."

"She was going to be. Now she is mine."

The suit *whispers*, and I feel my head droop slightly. Because

I know she's right. His human eye already told me. That gleeful gleam I misinterpreted. Intercepted. We're not the weapon that has him so excited. We're just here to sharpen it.

I mask my disappointment, finally handing over my R-6. "If you don't mind me asking, what exactly is the mission here, sir?"

Cyrus Uba's panther eye flicks from my tag to me again. All camaraderie vanishes. Thoughts of the enemy seep between us, quickly blackening our brief fellowship. I can almost hear my anus clench.

"The same as always, Mr. Hayes: *Defending the Earth!*"

I jolt us in a hideous, fearful way. Our back straightens. My chin levels. Our heels come dutifully together. No question of rank this time. "*Extending humanity!*" I countersign. She follows my reflexive shout with a dismissive *whisper*, a subtle pinch of disappointed shame. But the captain nods with firm resolve. Some mutual respect returns.

And my damaged pride stacks that much higher.

1.07

She reminds me of an old film. Or an Italian fairy tale, I guess. That one where the teenaged maiden is cursed and raped, and they all live happily ever after. Her narrow eyebrows are pinched together, twitching unpredictably, like she's working her way through complex math, like she almost has it. If she is that close to completing tac, her skin doesn't seem to know it. Christ, I've never seen anybody alive who looks like this. Thankfully, the sealed incubator glass keeps Taiko Chiba's dying stench contained.

"So," the captain shatters the silence with his deep voice, "is this normal? Or have I made a mistake?" He straightens his shoulders. Clutches his wrist down by his waist, the way hardened men do when bad news is coming.

"Tough to say." My attention drifts from Taiko Chiba's face to her G-4 suit. The first of its kind. A radical departure from the scaled-back G-2s and G-3s, which looked more like astronaut unitards. This prototype cuts much closer to mine. In fact, it goes further. Below Taiko's chin, only her two thumbs and trigger fingers are left exposed. The suit is skintight everywhere else, even cradling the base of her skull. She's like Achilles in reverse, held by her hair bun and dipped in engine oil. Except that ain't oil. It's simulated life on a scale I've never seen. A relative galaxy of silicon. Billions of minds hived into one. Trillions maybe. No wonder she can't sync with this inky mess. Those high-tech demigods at Dallas Dynamics made an entire suit out of nano sims.

"Honestly," I take a cautious step back from that black science, "I've never seen somebody transported while they're still in tac. Doesn't seem safe. Even in the domes, one in ten cadets are apt to—" I turn left, expecting to see the captain's furrowed brow. Instead, I see Jakey Mead. I see hope and fear and friends on fire.

I keep turning, trying to disguise the anxious shaking of my head. I blink my eyes and clear my throat, then speak again without facing Uba. "She—she'll be alright. If she's as clever as you say, I like her chances."

The captain watches me awhile. He keeps his silence, and I remember Grandma Logan's final words. I told her she'd get better. Promised her we'd find a nicer shelter, probably even get picked for housing soon. She used the last of her strength to pull me in with her bony fingers. Made sure I heard her throaty whisper: *Liars need fools. Fools need hope.* Then she closed her eyes forever to prove that I was both.

"You should have that stretcher come take a look." I glance back to the captain, relieved to see he's returned to Taiko. "Prich, I think his name was. Sorted me out on the tarmac. Knows his shit."

"At the shuttle clinic?"

"No, I mean my escort. The medic who drove me in."

"Hm. I will have my office look him up."

Whatever attention I briefly held, it's clearly lapsed. His panther eye is locked on Taiko's sickly skin, measuring vitals, souring his mood. He mutters some Bemba profanity, then double taps the viewing glass. The gurney legs fold back up beneath her cylindrical container as it retracts into the mobile incubator's main body. The warm glow of artificial sunlight streaks out between its cracks, tickling the few places it lands near our waist and elbow. The light tastes thick like concentrated sugar.

Uba cuts our snack time short, already marching back through the medical curtain. Reluctantly, we follow him into the wetroom's hot, hanging mist.

I mumble my own curses as the muggy atmosphere washes over us. She *whispers* a warning about the wetgen, and I feel heavy, overly quenched. If Taiko's nanos function anything like our scales, she'll be an extra bloated corpse whenever they roll her through this stupid room.

Apparently, Captain Cyrus Uba is made of different stuff. He seems to linger here, slowing his pace in the jungle heat. He acts as though this weren't a humid hell but some rare oasis to be relished. He lifts his chin to face the misters, and I envision

Zambian rivers. I imagine the thrill of a perfect kill, some wild beast draining on his back. I begin to realize how much further than I the captain must have come. Not for pride. Perhaps not even for himself. I begin to realize I'm going to scream if he doesn't hurry up—but Uba swats the tent flaps open, and I chase him gratefully out into dry Old Dallas.

1.08

"When she awakens, her bunk will be here, whichever one she prefers. Her personal items will arrive tomorrow."

I peek into the room the captain indicates. Several vacant twin-sized bunks are aligned in rows along the wall. Like the railroad infirmary from an even older film, I sense more spirits here than soldiers saved. Taiko Chiba will fit right in.

"You can have the officer's quarters. There, behind the kitchen."

I look past the couches and community space to the small kitchen area on the back wall. An old microwave, an electric stove, and a brand-new humming refrigerator stand by, awaiting orders. A basket of fresh fruit and roasted almonds sits on the countertop, reminding me of the humanity I've traded.

"Hm?" Uba turns to me like I just said something out loud. Shit, maybe I did.

"All looks great. Thank you, sir." I set my duffel down behind the couch as though I'm ready to settle in, as though I don't miss my quiet orbital cannon whatsoever.

The captain nods, then turns his body toward the exit. "Dinner is served at 18:00. Tonight, we will be at chow hall two, near the east gate."

"Thank you, sir. But I should mention, we um, I mean gunners aren't actually able to—"

"I understand." His panther eye flicks briefly to the fruit basket. The irrelevant kitchen. "Still, I would like you to join us tonight. As an introduction."

"Oh. Of course. Yes, sir."

He nods again. Pulls the front door open, ready to leave.

"An introduction?" I stop him once more. "To the rest of the unit? To Zero X?"

He holds there in the door frame, allowing thin heat waves to wriggle around his silhouette—a heroic aura to fit the fiction of his physique. "To the ones who created it," he clarifies with some disdain. For me or them, I'm not quite sure.

Before I can try another question, he strides forcefully into the sun.

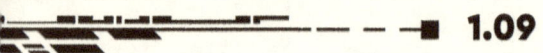 **1.09**

She shakes my hand, and that seems like pretty good proof to me. I pose for another photo, attempting to smile like sane people do, but I'm not sure why I waste the energy. It's confirmed: none of this is real. Just one expanding episode of my psychotic deterioration.

"Madame President—"

"Ms. Zhurov—!"

"Madame President—"

"Sergeant Hayes!"

My eyes snap to the fourth photographer, and his manual camera blinks a few dozen times. Flashes like exocannon fire, like that reacher's eyes at Shiloh Lake.

Release. A whisper calls my attention down to the Russian president's trembling hand, to the discoloration around her knuckles.

"Oh—" I end the handshake, and Varvara Zhurov grunts behind a false, political smile. Her nearest bodyguard takes a cautious step forward, but she turns him away with a careful look. I see a rolodex of FSS assassins behind her eyes as they meet mine.

"Strong. Good." Grinning, she pats our back. Her head tilts slightly after that, and she swallows deep inside her throat. We are incapable of sweating, but she pulls her hand away like we're soaking wet. Gives it a shake down by her waist to erase the heebie-jeebies.

She walks away, and for one short moment, I'm ecstatic to be finished. Then Norway's Aksel Knudsen hurries forward to replace her. We do the same terrible dance, but this time I'm careful to spare his precious fingers.

After the camera shutters cease and Prime Minister Knudsen steps away, I look down beyond the railing, down to the busy chow hall floor, to all the enlisted men and women with splats of protein mash on their recycled trays. For seven years I've looked down at them, but now they're finally looking up, up at us and all these masters, these illustrious lords and heads of state, we and these five pillars of the Earth's defense—China, Russia, USA, Indi-Arabia, and The Scandinavian Alliance—the daring founders and main enforcers of Zero Addition.

Down below, I see PFCs with bright young eyes and two first lieutenants who couldn't care less. I see a major general, slighted by his exclusion, and a sergeant major who may have lost too many men in the emancipation of Taiwan. He watches Li Qing-Nan, muttering battle-forged curses between each spoonful of rationed grits. I see the indecipherable eyes of the combat medic who asked me to call him Prich.

"Hayes." The captain summons me back to the executive deck. Rishi Saleem, bravely representing the tenuous Saudi/ Indian war council, stands to his left. But a much more powerful wide-hipped woman has just arrived on the captain's right. She glides two steps forward, and I am starstruck. She shakes my hand with a friendly touch, a respectful glow in her hazel eyes, and I feel warmth behind my ears. She says she knows what I have given. She understands the science well enough to acknowledge my great sacrifice for this nation, no, for this planet. I say *thank you, ma'am*, and I do my duty. The best photos of the night are won by President Mia Guerrero of the United States.

As she goes, I glance back down to the gallery of fighting men. Unsurprisingly, the medic has already vanished, or perhaps was never there. Just another figment of my condition, my unraveling—

"Captain Uba. Thanks for the invite. Means a lot."

I turn just in time to see another firm handshake at the stairs. It's nothing special. Nothing different than the greeting Uba just gave to the other leaders. That's what stuns me.

"Of course. Thank you for making the time." The captain greets the medic as though he were an equal—or something more—some financier well beyond the chain of command. He shakes the hand of this high-society man, who now sports gold-rimmed aviators in the neck of a brand-new silken shirt. His face is clean, no longer smudged in dirt and grease. That metallic knob that was on his shoulder now hovers obediently near his right ear—a personal simulant of some kind, powered by a technology I've never seen, at least not on Earth. The captain points that fancy stranger in my direction, and I ruin all fifty photos with Prime Minister Saleem.

That just makes Prich smile like he did back in the jeep, back when all my stupid guesses led me to lies. He said *non-combatant*, from which I deduced he was a medic. But he's clearly a man of a different science. He's—oh, dear God. I'm a fuckin' fool. This man is—

"Calvin Prichard." He shakes my hand, grinning wide and satisfied. "Lookin' good, cowboy. This your parade attire?" He nods to the only uniform I've worn for the past seven years.

"Oh. Funny." I barely get the words out. Amidst Prichard's clever chuckles, she *searches* our memory, finding eleven hundred different results. I don't bother checking a single one. I'm amazed I didn't recognize him. If we hadn't desynced, there's no chance we could have missed this. A curious coincidence to consider, but for now, one thing is certain. My mysterious escort is Malcolm Calvin Prichard Jr., the prodigal son of Corsicana, just a hop and skip from my hometown. Some say they welded these counties together to better match his techno-kingdom—and they may be right about that—but it was the rising cries to reclaim the old ways that moved the needle in the end. To separate this spit of Texan dryland from all the big cities overrun by reachers, they renamed this rural district as Old Dallas. It's not legally humans-only, but the locals keep it close enough.

"Hope you don't mind my little game this mornin'." His blue-green eyes dip somewhat affectionately as he leans closer, bringing his voice down to a whisper. "Figured you and I could start on our best feet without all this fancy context in our way. Damn good to meetcha, 129." The co-founder of Dallas Dynamics squeezes our shoulder without any revulsion, without any strange reaction whatsoever.

"Yeah. Absolutely. Mr. Prichard, sir."

"Prich, I told you. Just Prich, if we're still friends." He winks, then gets on his way. I watch him begin to mingle with a few scattered officers and politicians. He's wearing a Ret-tag I've never seen before. I guess that tracks. His company invented them—reverse-engineered from the microscopic camera systems found on all reacher pods. Wonder if he's still peeved about Retcon Computers—or the ghostly echo of that place—a tech company more like a corporate nation, diced up in the antitrust crises, then devalued to shit when private data became the gold standard. Only their infamous military subsidiary, Dallas Dynamics, survived the purge. One lucky break, I always thought.

Aside from selling four billion Ret-tags in under fifteen years, Mr. Prichard's little company is also responsible for the modern rail rifle, the ongoing warp drives project, and the dark energy cannons in our exosphere that I've been piloting my entire career. A reverse-engineered arsenal of galactic tech, and our best bet against the invaders who brought it here to begin with. The very teeth of the great embargo, known best as Zero Addition.

Oh, yeah. And he personally created the OP gunsuits, every iteration from us G-1 skinners to the nano-synthetic prototype that is now eating Taiko Chiba alive.

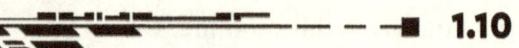 **1.10**

"Yes, very good, but why is this even necessary?"

"The Orbital Patrol?" Captain Uba clarifies.

"No," Saleem rolls his eyes. He delicately sips his wine at the other end of the long dining table, making everyone wait for his royal wisdom. "The patrol is vital. No man east of Mecca can argue otherwise."

Varvara Zhurov scoffs in the seat beside us, disgusted by his phrasing or something older, something cold and sharp she never puts down. She roughly massages her damaged fingers as though her bones deserve a lesson.

"I am speaking to efficiency," the prince continues, eyeing Zhurov carefully before he addresses the wider group: "Why send soldiers to babysit machines? Why waste millions on rare materials and tacticity domes just to create and train these . . ." He gestures in my general direction but finds no tasteful conclusion to that sentence.

His pitying eyes are followed by Scandinavia's Knudsen, Li of China, Captain Uba, and all the others, I assume. My eyes still haven't lifted from the bluefin tuna rolls expiring on my plate, these 6.77 ounces of extinct aquatic life that some private chef's private server just dropped in front of me like any box of chicken nuggets.

Rishi Saleem continues his diatribe on waste. "I simply see no reason for Indi-Arabians to make a sacrifice of this kind when programmed simulants control the cannons 99.9% of the time. Why should I disfigure any more of my recruits to offset a rounding error?"

"That rounding error accounts for three thousand human jobs." President Guerrero sounds devastated by his callousness. "Are you volunteering to discharge them? Brave pilots like Sergeant Hayes who have sacrificed so much?"

"We could repurpose them?" Aksel Knudsen sounds uncertain, perhaps shrugging his pouted lips. "The captain has already begun this, has he not?"

I look up from my tuna plate just in time to see a twitch in Uba's cheek. His human eye seems to travel to the wetroom, to Taiko Chiba's rotting flesh.

But an impatient grumble of Mandarin obscenities draws my attention to the seat beside him. "President Li would like to know what is the status of the Zero units," Li Qing-Nan's interpreter enunciates hastily, stepping up beside his seated ruler.

Zhurov laughs this time, one reckless syllable in the poor manservant's direction. She mutters a few words in her own tongue, and her armed bodyguards chuckle in shared contempt.

"Yet another waste of useful men," Saleem segues back to his initial rant. "Cyrus Uba, Zayd Aswad, Magar Volkov." He says that last name in Zhurov's direction, finally earning some eye contact. "These are masters of their craft. These are our best and rarest, all thrown together in an untested operation. We should stick with airstrikes, keep our distance, and make use of drones whenever possible. There is no reason to waste men this way. The reachers do not deserve them!"

"Why not 100?" a new voice asks.

A strange silence takes the room. Nobody turns immediately, but slowly, surely, the heads of state all swivel in this direction. They all look just past me to the table's end, where M. Calvin Prichard sits with one leg strung over the other, happily chewing a chunk of tuna.

"You got some figures I ain't privy to, or was that more of a metaphor?" Prichard washes his bluefin down with some bourbon, then smiles pleasantly in Saleem's direction. A disguise I've seen before.

"I'm sorry?" The prince sounds slightly more baffled than perturbed.

"You said the sims get it right 99.9% of the time. I'm just wondering where that specificity comes from."

Before responding, Saleem searches a few other faces around the table, like a pirate captain sensing mutiny. "I meant no offense, Mr. Prichard. In fact, I was touting the perfection of your designs."

"The near perfection." Prichard raises his tumbler again, sipping slowly, watching the prince.

"Well. You come closer than most, sir, but nobody is perfect."

Knudsen and Guerrero quickly chuckle at Saleem's joke, eager to let the tension fade. Knudsen even leans forward, opens his mouth to—

"No human is perfect," Prichard corrects. "Humans write the sims. So, no sims are perfect. That's your view?"

Saleem clenches his jaw as the quiet returns. He sets his wine glass down without drinking and gestures humbly to Calvin Prichard. "I must defer to the expert in this matter."

"Smart man," Prichard laughs genuinely. The other leaders mirror him, taking especially large sips of their various drinks. All except for Zhurov, who continues to watch him with suspicion. Similarly, Captain Uba's false eye tracks something subtle, something small and round, rising from Prichard's shoulder toward the ceiling. "Think I'll do the same," Prichard concludes to Saleem. He shifts slightly, directing his next question elsewhere. "How often does an exocannon misfire?"

"Never," the quick answer comes.

All attention shifts from Prichard to me. For a moment, I don't understand why. I wonder whose voice that was just now that sounded so much like mine.

"You sure about that, Sergeant?" Prichard turns to his right, studying me in the seat nearest to him. "You've never seen an exo miss its target, not even once?"

"I have not." I feel my lips move this time, but the words seem to get there without passing through my brain. Captain Uba brings his panther eye back down from the ceiling and watches me closely. Seems to wonder why I'm speaking so freely.

"You ever seen a pod get through the grid?" Prichard tugs me back to him with a tilt of his head—with something else I can't explain.

I catch the words this time. Because they're almost a lie. Because of what I saw in the shuttle this morning, that cloaked pod that trailed us through the line. Still, I feel compelled to satisfy him. I feel his intentions in our bones.

"If a pod gets through the stems, that means I didn't see it, sir."

Uba makes one of Daddy's sounds on the other side of the table—that conflicted grunt I never quite deciphered before he died. I see something like chastisement in his natural eye—in the other, something like respect.

"So, the sims are perfect." Prichard shrugs. "Prince Saleem is correct; we don't need the pilots."

"He's wrong." It comes out as a gasp. I start to tremble, desperate not to say any more. Because these next thoughts are true. These are the ones she helps me forget. I try to look away from Prichard, but he keeps me somehow. I can barely blink. My eyes get hot with rising tears.

"Why is he wrong, Sergeant Hayes?"

"Fuck—"

Someone gasps audibly at my profanity, Guererro or Knudsen, I can't tell which. Something tinks lightly between my tuna rolls, and I notice wetness on my cheeks. She finally *whispers*, but it sounds so far away, a distant voice in a cavernous well.

"It's alright." Prichard touches our back. His bare skin feels like the tarmac did, a searing iron against her scales. "Just help us understand, then we'll move on." He glances cutely at Saleem. Holds his nose in the bed he's made. "If the simulants never miss, if the cannons never misfire, then why do we need you?"

I feel dizzy, and the air is thick. I grasp at the table to remain upright.

"Sergeant." His wrestler's fingers pretend to console us, pretend to help us while they squeeze tighter. "Why do we need—"

"We keep the logs." I look into his eyes. I stare into his blue-greens and let it all go.

"Logs?" He pretends not to know. "What logs do you—"

"Scatter logs and collateral hits. One entry for every skin."

Prichard withdraws with some true surprise. He subtly taps the custom Ret-tag on his wrist, and I see that small, round thing float back down into view. It's his personal simulant, recording video in our direction—waiting for something.

"Every skin?" Saleem asks from across the table.

Prichard turns to the prince, but I do not. I stare at his simulant, hovering there, and I see reacher corpses, tumbling limbs amidst hot wreckage, already freezing over. "When they're ejected clean, we call them skins. There's a lot of moisture. They don't look clothed."

Saleem makes a face in my peripheral, a colorless expression before he looks away and covers his mouth.

"We take pictures before they hit atmo. Describe their features, sex, and age."

Captain Uba shifts loudly in his seat, and that should be enough—a strong signal for me to be silent now. But she *whispers* again, and something breaks inside us. She *whispers* incessantly, and I see a face in total darkness, a bald silhouette concealing light.

"They go without turning." My voice sounds strange. I stare at Prichard's simulant, the relative size of a reacher pod in our reticle before we lock and fire.

Captain Uba slowly begins to stand, moving a hand to the

holster on his hip. One of Zhurov's bodyguards takes a half-step forward, not trusting that movement, doing the same.

And that bald silhouette turns behind my eyes. Twists just enough for obscured light to scatter through. I see the eye of a woman. A shadowed face and contorted mouth.

"They go without turning, and so shall we."

"We?" Prichard finally asks. He searches my eyes excitedly, but it's too late.

The shadowed woman sees him, too.

The table's fine mahogany splinters into shards between my powerful, spasming fingers, sending tuna, ceramics, and chunky wooden missiles in every direction. Zhurov's wine glass explodes in her face, and her bodyguards do their duty quick. She's pulled out of her chair, and I'm dead to rights before the other leaders can suck enough air to scream.

"Call them off!" Uba's pacifier whines, electrifying two stun rounds in its twin chambers. "Call them off before it kills them!"

For a moment, I wonder what he means. I look around in a shuddering daze, wondering if his English is failing in the adrenaline bath, wondering what just happened and how I got here. Then I look down at the jagged hole in the fine dining spread beneath me. I see the inhuman way my hand is dancing. Like that old film where the hate-soaked demon lives in the warrior's vengeful arm, I see her scales dancing wildly in this windless room. Rippling battle-red, hot with intent, she *whispers*, and I know that she must try. Before he escapes, she must try again.

"Wait!" I shout.

Somehow, she *ignores* me. *Controls* me.

Our forearms become violent blurs, reducing both body-guards' aimed pistols to shattered pieces. She spins us up out of our seat, making a fist with my dancing hand, punching the taller Russian's bones into his heart. His feet leave the floor, and his partner's shoulder leaves its socket as we yank him closer. Our whirling heel makes bullets of his teeth, and he follows them all into the air. We spin with that momentum, two rotations, almost three, until we land on all fours atop the table—directly in the captain's eyeline.

But we're looking past him at our true target. We're hot for that accursed man alone, for that disgusting thing alive in his neck, that nasty science that made us sick. She feints us left then dodges right with inhuman speed—

The captain's panther eye beats us there. Both stun rounds hit our chest, and we thud simultaneously with our Russian victims to the floor. They lie still and extremely dead, but the electrified rounds make us convulse. My neck cranks involuntarily, pressing my cheek against the floor. Our five brave leaders' screams and gasps finally arrive as they stumble backward over their chairs. Their mouths and eyes are gaped in horror, I assume.

I can only see Prichard now. He crouches down into my blurring view just as his simulant docks stealthily on his shoulder. I see that his eyes have changed at last, not lit with dismay but dissatisfaction.

He expected us to be faster.

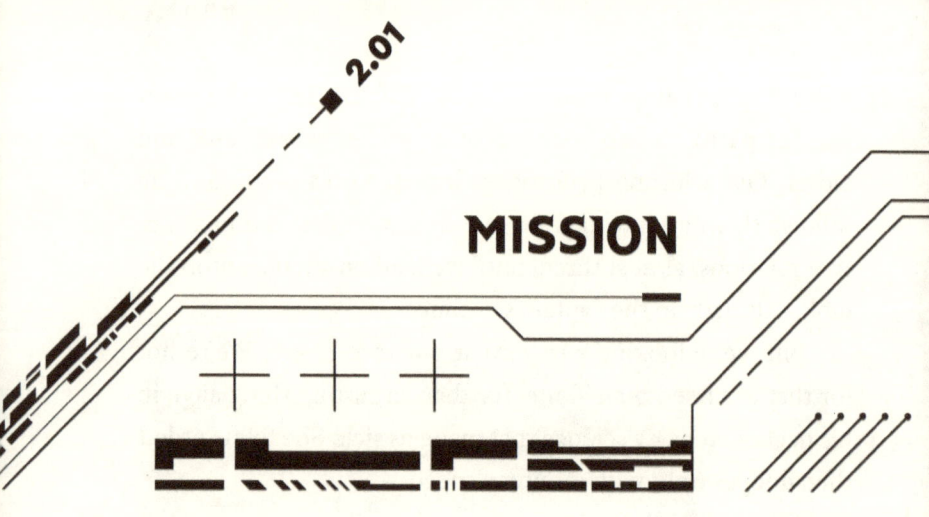

MISSION

I hear Ignacio's keys jangling at his waist, and I know it's finally time. He's standing up from his wooden chair in his small kiosk around the corner, and I can already plot his footsteps down the block. It's all in the sound. Not his usual hustle to the admissions gate. Not his pigeon-toed tip-tap to the urinal or his duck-footed shuffle to the bathroom stall. This time, he's coming on slow. Like he'd rather not come at all. Like he's scared. Every time I hear this sound, I know Ignacio's coming for us.

He'll usually draw out every step, taking a few extra sips of coffee, realizing his belt buckle isn't quite as centered as it could be. He'll stop at one of the empty cells outside his kiosk, just to be sure he didn't see a rat in that dark corner there. He'll do a radio check, then wait in the hall for Hank or that other guard who reeks like chew to lazily squawk back. Sometimes they don't respond, so he'll retreat to his station until they do. *It's protocol*, he mutters, thinking I can't hear him at this distance, through all these layers of cement. *If that freaky stem dries up, it's on them!*

Ignacio regularly concedes to all these fears and more, all to avoid pressing a single shower button on the wall outside our repurposed bunker. But he already misted us this morning, and that doctor they sent was a one-and-done. That's how I know it's time. That's why he's slower than he's ever been, why his heart is thumping so high in his thick neck. The shower button must seem easy compared to this, almost safe.

"Solitary One. Radio check."

"Solitary Two. Check good," Hank responds clearly and quickly this time.

But I hear Ignacio still standing there, clutching the radio with his sweaty fingers. He idles in the steel and concrete hallway outside The Hole where we are kept. His shuffling feet make fearful music, and I have no doubt the day has come. Ignacio's worst nightmare is coming true. He's moving again now, handling the archaic iron keys, probably hoping ours has gone missing, praying he can call in sick tomorrow and make us somebody else's problem. But he finally finds it, and I hear his heart skip twice.

"Solitary One—opening Prisoner One."

"Solitary Two—proceed with caution," Hank chirps back even quicker, really on his game today.

We are seated on the bed just as we have been for sixteen hours. Previous record was twelve, but I've been feeling much more settled-in this week. Isolation isn't exactly torturous to us. But now it's time to try our legs again. As I rise, we receive a few closing afternoon rays from the barred and bulletproof skylight five meters above our shoulders. I hear Ignacio trembling, finally raising his heavy key to The Hole's analog, double-reinforced lock. He sounds terrified, and I don't blame him. Not today.

It's finally time to free the monster from its cage.

As the first lock falls and Ignacio begins cranking the secondary, I imagine that scrawny gate guard from eleven days ago. I relive all the double-taking faces from our drive in with Calvin Prichard, all the horrified stares as we were wheeled out in a restrictive jacket from chow hall two—my right hand still painted warm with Russian blood. I can see the news washing over Camp Cooks. Two men dead on the first day that it arrived. That G-1 they called down. That skinner. It moved just like a reacher, they'll say.

The secondary thuds in that satisfying unlocked way, echoing down the harsh cellblock and back again. She *whispers*, and I hear it, too—a strange muffling around Ignacio, as though the metallic echo hit two soft walls on either side of him. A confusing sensation. Adding to that, the heavy door swings backward much more quickly than it should, almost like it's being pulled by a strong hydraulic arm.

I see Ignacio in the widening gap near the first lock. He's fleeing backward, not touching the door, not pulling it at all. Then two eyes float forward through the darkness, one mostly white, the other yellow, as Captain Uba steps much too quietly into the sunlight of my cell.

"Mr. Hayes." At the sound of his thumping voice, I snap to attention, not just baffled by his presence but by the massive steel door still swinging open behind him. "I apologize for the delay. President Zhurov made some . . . inconvenient demands."

The heavy vault door to The Hole finally connects with the hallway wall. I sense another specter in its weighted, compounding reverberations—a person-shaped gap in the air, rounding the corner now. A ghost to be sure.

Still striated with death at the edges of her visible skin, still shrouded in the spindly black veins of a demon borrowed from hell, Taiko Chiba steps into the light. The sickness in her eyes is enough to flinch me out of posture.

"Be still," Uba commands. I obey with an unnatural precision. "Look at me," he says, and my head turns on its own. I hear a small voice in the depths of my subconscious, a distant moan like some part of me has been broken and compelled.

In Uba's human eye, I see surprise and fascination. I see unease and the beginnings of regret. But his jaw tightens. His shoulders realign with his allegiance to the Earth. "Very good. Now follow me."

He turns sharply, almost silently, and I finally take notice of his attire. His boots are different than before. Lighter, more form-fitting. The material is oddly smooth, no straps or loose threads to create incidental sound. His entire combat suit seems to have been redesigned for speed and stealth, painted in a light-swallowing black. The only stitch of flair is the emblem on his skintight right sleeve. It's an embossed pair of letters almost like a cattle brand—two capital D's interlocking in a bold red font like cyberpunk graffiti.

And something else. Something I don't notice so much as feel, something at the top of his spine, perfectly flush with his dark skin. A more refined version of that arachnoid implant Prichard had, beckoning to us with its own shallow, distant voice.

The captain's implant whispers, *follow*.

And we obey.

I've been imagining this moment. Ever since that update hit my dropdown in the logs—*Orbital Patrol, Corporal* → *Special Operations, Sergeant*—I've been embarrassingly desperate, not just to meet these sturdy faces but to learn my place among them. I'm finally standing at the very tip of the UT Forces' sharpest spear, and my special office is revealed. I am a mannequin. A disposable human shape for the Dallas Dynamics spring collection.

"It was actually a happy accident." Calvin Prichard crosses the modest chapel's wooden stage, clasping his hands in front of his chest. "I started to put the pieces together in my first hours with Sergeant Hayes. Not quick enough, of course." He bows his head for those two Russians I eviscerated—three seconds of silence before he grins at his small audience again. "You see, it all comes back to this suit." He turns, gesturing to us like brand-new tech at a product launch. "As I reckon you've all heard by now, Sergeant Hayes is an Orbital Patrolman of Generation One. Pre-Chicago."

Thirteen sets of human eyeballs roll in our direction; fourteen, if you count the captain's mismatched pair. I see hidden wounds within their faces, secret fears and oaths of vengeance in their clenched knuckles and tightening jaws. I was summoned for my rare costume, my lame guinea pig happenstance. These enlisted men and women were chosen for their skills. They've survived the canopies of Sub-Sahara, the electric skies of the Yellow Sea. They've fought and clawed their way to prideful places in this twin unit, Zero One and Zero Two, the first special operations forces of the United Territories for Zero Addition.

"Before the embargo, this field of research was not quite so problematic," Prichard explains with a guilty smile, "but I was just middle management back then, so please direct your litigation to Retcon Computers." He pauses for polite laughter, but the hardened crowd gives him none. Doesn't seem to faze him. He goes on smiling through the combative silence, subtly turning to check my reaction, almost like there's something there I missed. Some inside joke between old friends.

In my attempt to avoid his eye contact, I connect with someone even worse. Basking in the tinted sunlight beneath the western stained-glass window, Taiko Chiba suddenly flicks her swirling eyes to mine.

I flinch away, shaking my head, trying to forget who she once was. I pretend I never dragged the net for her data story or sped my way through her private feed. Her accolades are mystifying. No way she could be that sharp—not half that smart if she ended up like this. Then again, it almost fits. A subspace junkie of the highest caliber becomes the first simulated human. Not by design but desperation. She'd be just another red name on the tacticity logs if Calvin Prichard hadn't worked his magic. Just like I'd still be in solitary or on the chopping block, if he hadn't found a way inside my mind.

"It's a good thing, though," Prichard smiles. "That narrow timeframe between innovation and regulation is what makes the G-1 uniform so special. In fact, this early prototype that Sergeant Hayes still wears—that his thirty-one fellow recruits once wore— was not manufactured anywhere, technically. It was grown."

The front two pews seem to wriggle from that phrasing. A few unsettled murmurs rise from the units, paired with disbelieving faces and disgusted scowls. I don't take much notice of them, myself. I'm still snagged on a different word. Sounded like he just said those gunners *wore* the uniforms, implying somehow they took them off.

"A chimeric blend of genetic marvels found on Earth. Photosynthetic sea slugs, the mimic octopus, a few variants of acoustic bats." Prichard cups a performative hand to his ear, listening carefully. "Basically, my best Frankenstein's guess at recreating Luminaran travel gear; I'd wager some of you know the science." He waves his hand at that old news, then scratches his neck apprehensively. "But there is one last little wrinkle in this suit that I've kept under my hat for quite a while. Never thought I'd admit it willingly, but I have it on your captain's word that what I am about to say will never escape these hallowed walls."

This time, the entire room seems to lean forward in anticipation. Even Uba twitches slightly, shifting his weight from the large double doors at the chapel's entrance.

"To put it plainly, there was some human testing. Not on living subjects. Just genetic samples. A few oral swabs donated by yours truly." Prichard clicks his tongue, leading into more uncomfortable hesitation. "Following that failure, a few of these first prototypes were also given what I called a blood bath. An overnight soak in donated plasma, erythrocytes and metabolic tissues. A big bucket of blood." He shrugs, watching the crowd of humanity's best killing machines, before he turns to check my eyes again. "Donated by reachers."

Somebody giggles horribly in the back corner of the furthest pew—a strange combination of shock and delight, duplicated in stereo. I see identical faces there, seated side-by-side. She *whispers* their names and designations: Chuck and Derek Bugg. Navy boys, both promoted to PO3. New-century twins, if I had to guess. Cloned from donor DNA or some lonely father without a bride.

Excluding that reaction, the crowd seems evenly disturbed, not by the common slur that Prichard used but by *our* existence. I'd be right there with them, but I'm too busy tumbling internally. The man said *wore*, and I saw their faces. Mike, Bryce, and Jakey. They died in a fire, and I moved on. But did they really? Why? Because Calvin Prichard was playing God? What about the others? Twenty-seven men and that brawny woman from northern Norway. Anka. Or Alta, I can never remember. We shared a tacticity dome, but she was gone when I woke up. Everyone was. Are they still up there? Were they truly able to retire? After seeing those three red names, after the G-2s filled the skies a few months after our small class, I just moved on. I just—

"Nod if you're still listening, Sergeant."

Prichard's signal chip *whispers,* and I obey. The crowd watches but doesn't seem to realize what they've just seen.

"Raise your left leg," Prichard commands again.

I do as he says, and they begin to understand. They begin to sit upright with rising eyebrows and slackening jaws.

"Tell me what you're thinking."

"I'm afraid we're the only—" With terrible effort, I bring my mouth closed. I turn my twitching eyes to Malcolm Calvin Prichard Jr., and his perfect smile starts to get us hot and red all over again.

"You see? The infamous Luminaran reach is just a signal—heightened brainwaves occurring naturally in their species. And my Spider Byte, patent pending," Prichard turns, tapping his upper spine where the signal chip has burrowed itself under his skin, "is designed to jam that wavelength. A near-perfect defense against their psychic attacks and apparently a powerful back door into the heightened sensitivities of these old G-1 suits. So, yeah. Sergeant Hayes is what you might call a reacher radar. You can relax now, cowboy."

I drop our leg and straighten our back, doing my best to take in air, doing everything I can to keep *her* from losing it again. The crowd makes more scattered sounds, some in amazement, most in obvious discomfort.

Army Specialist, Zayd Aswad, sneers contemptuously to that effect. He's seated dead center in the front row, so it takes no special effort for me to hear him as he twists his scarred jawline toward Sasha Carter and mutters one of the foulest string of insults to ever penetrate my Christian ears. He's clearly speaking Sasha's language. The Senior Airman swallows a turbulent burst of laugher but not nearly well enough. In seconds, his infectious fits and titters have spread halfway across the disaffected room.

Prichard watches the dissenting units for a moment. He sees the crowd wholly rejecting the apparent climax of his presentation, and the subtlest humiliation twitches in the corner of his showman's smile. Just once. One quick flicker before he chuckles lightly to himself, dropping his eyes to the uneven floorboards beneath his designer cowboy boots.

"Shit, I know what y'all are thinkin'." Prichard wags his finger. "Best defense is a good offense, sure sure. I mean, who needs a radar when you got a goddamn rail rifle, am I right?" This time, he anticipates their silence. He nods knowingly, hungrily, pursing his lips into a tight line. "Yeah. I bet all you hard boys would much rather hear me say somethin' extra spicy like, I don't know: Daydream, eliminate the shortest person in the room, or—"

Her scales are red immediately. My eyes are already tracking First Lieutenant Faye Thompson. One hundred sixty-three centimeters from her heels to her scalp, 11.7 meters between her knees and center stage.

In one whirling movement, I kick Prichard's unused stool into the air and snap two of its legs from the base. One of them is sharper. I catch it, allowing the dull one to fall to the stage, turning thirteen bloodthirsty faces in my direction.

"Hey!" In a flash, Zayd Aswad draws his custom knife from its rear sheath. Close combat specialist. Eleven confirmed kills. Minimal threat. But Sasha Carter stands up, too, reaching for his sidearm.

My right hand takes Prichard as a human shield. My red gaze returns to Faye. She's wearing body armor, densest at the sternum. Twenty-three hundred newtons required to fracture her skull. I aim for her throat. Our left arm readies the impromptu spear, and—

"Stand down!" Uba roars. His Spider *stings us* from across the room, and we fall to our knees, gasping for air, trembling as fresh epinephrine surges through my roasting brain.

Prichard coughs painfully, shaking his head, using the microphone stand to stay upright. *She* was choking him. Incidentally perhaps. Or just made to look that way. Crushing his windpipe to keep him from canceling the kill command—and to take him with us.

"Very good," Prichard wheezes, then clears his damaged throat again. "Not so mad at Zhurov now, are you, Captain?"

"Enough!" Uba marches down the center aisle and leaps up onto the stage. To my surprise, he approaches me first, helping me stand upright again. He has no obvious reaction to the crawling texture of the suit, only seeing me inside it. He holds my eyes until I nod that I'm okay.

Prichard takes a nervous step backward as Uba offers him a very different expression. Without looking away, the captain speaks to his men, "Holster your weapons."

Zayd and Sasha obey with reverent speed, not hypnotized by alien chips but by the thunder in his voice.

"This is my briefing. Not your sales pitch."

"Yes. An unfortunate slip of the tongue." Prichard rubs his throat uncomfortably. "But you must admit, the combat potential here is quite—"

"You will be silent now." Captain Uba turns his muscular back on M. Calvin Prichard, and I feel like I'm ten years old. He looks out at his twin units before addressing them in a sober tone, "Varvara Zhurov has no trust in Emmett Hayes. Nor does Li Qing-Nan or Rishi Saleem. They all requested his termination."

I receive that news like sharpened ice. I feel their many eyes on us again.

"So, I gave them my guarantee." Uba taps the Dallas Dynamics tech in his upper spine. "You will wear them, too. For protection from the enemy. For our overseers' peace of mind."

The crowd stirs with disappointed murmurs, threatening to protest.

"Or you will be replaced," Uba clarifies.

The murmurs sort themselves to silence.

"But you will not give orders to this man." He points to us, and I feel strange, like how I did when Daddy died. "He does not belong to you. You do not belong to yourselves." His dimorphic eyes scan the silent faces, landing ultimately on Taiko's. I see that shame in him again. Hotter now, innervated with a repentant call. "I think you know why."

"YES, SIR!" Their united lungs bring tears to my eyes. I stiffen our stance and await the next chance to prove my devotion.

"Because our mission is what?"

Fifteen fists strike fifteen chests. "DEFENDING THE EARTH!"

"I said what is our mission!"

Thirty boots leave marks on the floor. "EXTENDING HUMANITY!"

Her chastising *whispers* drown in the bacchanal of our fraternized sound.

2.03

I was wrong.

The hovership slows dramatically, and I hear Sasha's encrypted chatter inside my helmet. Before I can blink, everybody hops to it, condensing their rifles, priming their sky legs, double-checking munitions and tightening straps. It's easy for them. It should be after all our dummy jumps. There's no reason for me to still be sitting here, twitching in my harness, thanking *her* for our empty bladder, but I am, so now it's confirmed. I was the wrong man for this work. The last goddamn gunner they should've called down.

To my credit, I've been damn convincing these past few months. Led the unit in strength and conditioning checks. Blew the eye-and-ear doctor's fucking mind. Set new UT Forces records in man tracking and hand-to-hand. Came out of Cyrus Uba's special training looking like the inhuman super soldier he expected me to be. But I was playing with cheat codes. Without this suit, I would've been lucky to survive, let alone graduate. In firearms tac, I was dead last. My bushcraft and land-nav assessment was borderline special needs. If I couldn't smell the captain's aftershave, couldn't hear his accelerating heartbeat as

I walked right past his woodland camo, I would've failed the track completely. If it wasn't for *her*, I never would've been promoted in the first place. I'm not a fighter. I'm the dumbest kid in class. I've just got one hell of a helicopter mama doing all my homework for me.

"LZ, one hundred meters. Clear hatch," Sasha informs us from the cockpit.

Six superior men and women all start moving faster, locking helmets, lighting visors, checking clasps and strapping gear.

"Comms check," Uba transmits to us next. Five positive thumbs inform the captain he's coming in clear. Everyone except for—"Hayes?"

I flinch, then quickly show him my thumb, too. I can muster that at least, a single trembling digit. Uba nods in confirmation but keeps his eyes on me—still seated, still belted to the fuselage, visor HUD still dark, short rifle still extended and horizontal on our alien lap.

Deep in my throat, I taste a combination of bitter shame and sweet relief. At least, the captain can see it now. Connie Clark follows his eyes, and I can tell that she sees it, too. She always has. I may have the inhuman senses, but she can detect weakness. When the hot shit comes, she knows whose back to press hers against, and it sure as shit ain't mine.

She nudges Aswad's helmet with her own, and now he sees us, too. He leers at us just like he did at our undressing on that chapel stage, at our attempted murder of Faye Thompson back before she earned the honor of commanding Zero Two.

Like I said, there's some relief. Because now the captain will correct us. He'll give the order and make it simple. I'll obey because we must. Just one quick whisper from his chip, and we'll unbuckle. We'll make swift work of our jump prep, just like the rest of them. Any second now, he'll—

"LZ zero. Hatch is hot. Hatch is hot."

The captain hears Sasha's signal, and he quickly spins away. Without any interest in my ineptness, he squares his broad shoulders to the rear hatch as it rattles open. Clark and Aswad do the same. Alec Shankman, Miles Yang, and even young Danny Diaz fall in line behind them, leaving just one Hayes-shaped hole in Zero One's jump formation.

I watch the resolute backs of my brave siblings, and I feel wrong all over again.

"Go light three."

I rip my seatbelt in a sudden rush to get it off.

"Go light two."

I tap my visor, and the heads-up-display kicks on and ready.

"Go light one."

I twist and lock my rifle down to flight size just as the jump light flashes green.

"Go light go. Go light go. Go light go."

Uba embraces his falcon half, vanishing into the Kansas morning sunlight. Clark and Aswad jump out behind him, pair formation, always together. Shankman does a backflip, filling all our helmets with his dumb whooping. Old man Yang does it by the book, rifle perfectly centered, spine perpendicular to the earth. And Danny-boy thinks he's going without me, but I sprint and make him the rotten egg.

I click my sky legs together twice, and they ignite just like we practiced, cold propulsion coning down around our shins and soaring feet. Danny stands there startled in the hatchway, but I'm not looking back anymore. I'm a stem become a rocket, launching down to our first call, the first official manhunt of ZA spec ops Zero One. Though I've become much fonder of the moniker making waves around Camp Cooks, the unofficial codename we've adopted in this new active effort against our invaders. Slowly, surely, widely, our admirers have begun to call us:

The Reacher Hunters.

 **2.04**

Concrete pebbles and shredded heifer silage disperse in tidy circles beneath our sky legs as we harrier down onto Caitlin Powell's farm. In every direction, there's fermented maize and alfalfa grass, scorched and spoiled amidst the rubble of a severely shortened tower silo.

"Woof." Shankman grimaces, pinching his nostrils closed.

Yang shakes his head but chuckles lightly in agreement. Aswad simply spits. He walks over to the captain with Connie Clark lockstep beside him. Uba's already looking up at the demolished silo, likely taking heat measurements with his panther eye, confirming the pod's crash trajectory.

I breathe deeply, taking in the stench of cattle fodder, thicker than I've ever smelled it. A reminiscent trigger. A raw reminder of those peaceful years on the southern dryland, back before our nameless town got swallowed up by grand Old Dallas. Back before that violence found us, the four of us were living well, by country standards. Me, Logan, Daddy, and . . .

She *whispers*, and I feel something like soft hands on the center of my back. Not our back, distinctly mine. As though she's nudging me onward, beyond some mental roadblock. But I—I must've just miscounted. I'm sure I meant the *three* of us. Three generations of Hayes in that drafty farmhouse by the barn.

Thankfully, a distant sound draws my attention back to the Powell farm. I shake my head once, trying to dismiss that confusing whisper. I turn carefully, listening again, catching just one soft syllable from somewhere behind me. A kitten's purr in a nervous wind.

Shankman and Yang don't seem to hear it. They greet Danny-boy as he finally harriers down, landing in the bed of a classic truck. It may have been red in a prior life. Now, it's mostly browned from rust and sun decay.

Clark and Aswad maintain their duet, flanking Uba closely as his huge body crouches to a knee. He studies a smoldering chunk of concrete, then scoops a small soil sample with a collection tube. It self-seals as he slips it safely into one of the many pouches on his belt.

I hear the wind's purr again and turn my eyes in its direction—back toward the long dirt road and the parked tractor at the very distant end of it. Two people there. Kids maybe. Like ants at the edge of my visible horizon. One looks like a boy, standing on the massive rear left tire. The other one is taller, a girl on the tractor's roof, waving her arms at us, shouting something at the top of her small lungs. If I had the captain's eye, I could probably read her lips. Instead, I turn one ear to the wind and wait for that purr to arrive. I repeat exactly what I hear into the comms:

"South. In the corn. Further south."

Uba pockets a second sample as he rises to his feet. He follows my eyeline down the road and watches the children for a moment, briefly covering his human eye. From the children, he turns due south, settling on the endless wall of corn just beyond the demolished silo. He lets his human eye see again.

"Yeah, I'm on it. Target confirmed," Sasha pipes in from

the hovership, still cautiously maintaining the high altitude we jumped from. "Two hundred meters south of LZ. Smoking drones now."

In the distance, directly above Uba's eyeline, two small scout drones start flashing red lights and trailing smoke as they hover in a guided circle. Our tactical vultures.

"Copy that." Uba turns in his own slow circle, connecting eyes with Aswad, Clark, Shankman, Yang, Danny-boy, and myself. I think I feel a low-Richter earthquake, but it's just my thumping heart. Uba says, "Zero One. Rifles free."

And we all unlock and extend our rifles. Popping stocks, sliding grips into place, engaging hot sights. The captain's long rail rifle hums with an electric thirst that makes me shiver. Shankman lets out a little whistle, and Danny-boy jumps down from the rusty truck bed. Clark checks for loyalty in Aswad's eyes, and he firmly taps his helmet to hers in acknowledgment.

The captain patiently inhales, lets it out even slower, then looks back to the long, high wall of corn. "Tactical columns. A1, B2."

We fall into formation, two staggered lines.

"A1 good," Yang enunciates clearly.

"B2 ready," Aswad grumbles.

I crouch our knee to the dirt and look over to B2. Shankman winks from third position and blows me a sloppy kiss.

Uba takes the lead between both lines, eyes still forward on the wall of crops. He twists his boot in scattered silage, then readies the unit with one raised fist. The fist becomes two pointed fingers, and just like that we're marching.

Zero One toward kill or capture. Straight into the corn of Caitlin Powell.

2.05 ■— — — ———————

I thank God for the daylight. I praise the UT Forces for active comms. I send a curse to Calvin Prichard for his unsettling Spider Bytes.

Damn things make me itch. Not in my neck. I'm the only one without an implant. It's deeper than that. A gnawing sense of vacancy, of missing heat. When this unit takes its time, when they all creep in their stealthy suits just like the captain taught us to, it starts to feel like I'm possessed. Subtle breaths from their helmet mics. Bodiless sniffs and exhalations. But my extra sense of life is blocked. Blurred. Drowned in the symphony of the cornfield's natural sounds.

Something scurries out of our path ten meters ahead. I feel the aftershocks of its tiny, padded feet on fertile soil. And all the slithering. The writhing worms and even smaller, subterranean things. I feel the sharp tickle of every leaf on every stalk as they brush our shoulders, our sensitive knees, our every scale left uncovered by Zero tactical gear.

"Anything yet, Mr. Hayes?" Uba comms back from his scouted lead twenty meters ahead.

I listen carefully for him. I hear the last gasps of some fat rodent on my left, just before it's squeezed dead by a hissing corn snake. I hear the rat's organs pop individually and all at once.

"Nothing useful," I respond. "But watch your step, Crown."

"What? Ah, fuck!" Connie Clark jumps out of formation, narrowly avoiding a festering crow carcass and the million maggots feasting there. To me, it sounds like tiny, distant fingers probing wet spaghetti. It stinks like a landfill dug in hell.

"What is it?" Aswad holds at the head of her line, B2.

"Nothing. A dead bird. God, it smells like ass."

"You're welcome," I remind her.

"Oh, fuck off. I would've stepped right over it."

She doesn't believe that. I hear the lie behind her voice, behind the quickening heartbeats in her neck. She's just annoyed that I was useful.

"Hey, Daydream, what am I holdin'?" Shankman's fly audibly unzips. One of his hands scrounges down between his legs.

"That's weird, I can't make it out. Something extremely small."

Danny-boy snorts ten paces behind me. "Yo! Hold your fire, Shank!"

Yang catches on late, turning back to holler from the front of our column. "Hey! Enough of that!"

"All units halt." Uba's voice seems to come from every direction. From deep inside us. Everyone freezes, knees to the dirt, rifles raised. Even Shankman holds his line as he awkwardly wrangles himself back into his pants.

"A1, to me. On-line. B2, west perimeter. Ranger file, double time. Go!"

We're all back on our feet, running where the captain wants us. Yang fans out to the left. Danny-boy and I trail his line. Aswad leads Connie and Shank out to our right, vanishing deeper into the tall corn.

She *whispers*, and my eyes snap straight ahead. To something strange. A vast empty silence. Ten meters further. Seven. Four—

The captain's thick forearm catches us before we get there. I almost shriek, but Uba holds a vertical finger to his lips. Yang arrives on the other side of him. Danny runs straight into our back.

"Shit—"

But Uba's eyes quiet him as well.

"Yo—!" I hear Shankman lose his footing ten meters ahead, ten meters west, but he catches himself in the dirt. A small landslide of pebbles commences there, down the strange silent hole's western edge. "Holy fuck . . ." he trails off, at a loss for words.

"Are you in position?" Uba gets no response. "B2—"

"Yes." Aswad comes in a bit breathless. More awestruck than I ever thought I'd hear him. "B2, holding perimeter. Target sighted."

Danny-boy and Yang exchange a nervous look, but I keep my eyes forward. Her *whispers* are pinging like a looping alarm, and I finally notice the low hum of the scout drones circling directly overhead. Directly over this void. This round, deep gap, not just in the Earth but in the stream of life itself. A cacophonous biome in every direction but forward. Four meters directly ahead, there is nothing.

No, she whispers, still frantic, still alarmed. *There is one.*

Uba creeps to the edge of the corn field. Not the natural edge but the one that's been freshly carved, scorched by high impact. He extends his arms like soaring wings, and Yang obeys, filing in on his left. Danny and I follow suit, getting on-line to Uba's right. We're a proper firing line now, all barrels forward, slow-stepping toward the void.

"Mr. Carter, end smoke."

"Copy," Sasha responds over comms. "Switching drones to surveillance."

The miniature recon drones halt their flashing and smoking. They hold position, pointing their small cameras downward to the crater's hot center.

I can hear heartbeats on the B2 line. Thumping, pumping,

like great drums of war, an orchestra completed by their shallow breaths, their restless boots in blackened soil. It's like that old film where the villain moves slow, where the girl's in the closet with the kitchen knife, just waiting for death to find her.

Except we're the ones marching toward it, our modern muzzles leading the way, out from Caitlin Powell's corn and down into her grave. Flat, green land gives way to a deep black decline. An inverted volcano dug out of the field. Uba signals B2, and they begin their trip down as well. Past the scattered wreckage of an unlucky corn harvester. Past the barely visible remnants of its operator, Ms. Powell. She'll be a feast for her worms if they ever wriggle this far down. For now, she remains a splattering of blood and shattered bones. I don't warn Connie about the kneecap, nor Yang about the scattered tract of feces and wet gore. I couldn't if I tried. They wouldn't see it either way. Our eyes are all locked on the great steaming sphere at the crater's bottom, at the alien hatch that still looks closed. It's whistling like a kitchen griddle, like a depressurizing shuttle, sized for one.

"Mr. Hayes," Uba checks.

"Yes." I wince because it hurts at first. Because it's not sound, not stench, not any terrestrial sense I've ever felt. "There's one. But it. I think it's—" A light brightens in my mind. A cobalt shine and silent music. It makes me smile, and I see that face again. That silhouetted woman. But now she's beautiful. She's laughing just like she used to, with brown and golden bouncing curls and matching eyes. Like a human lioness wrapped in that gracious glow the sun would make whenever it shimmered on the untouched glass of Shiloh Lake. She's by our lake again. She's right by our lake, and it all feels right.

"You think it's *what*?" Connie demands.

I turn to her, and she sees my tears. She sees my elation, and it scares her. Without thinking, I shove it back down. I shake my head twice, and it all goes away again. It—what was I just—why's Connie looking at me like that?

"Christ, he's fucking lost it." Connie's glaring at me. They're all staring at me like I've been mumbling nonsense to myself.

"That's a good thing, right?" The group turns to Danny, not catching his meaning. "That means the Spiders are working." He touches the implanted chip at the base of his skull. "It's only reaching for Hayes because it can't feel us. Right?"

Uncertain glances bounce between the unit. Except for Connie. She watches my eyes with heightened alarm. Her muzzle begins to drift subtly in our direction.

But the pod makes a sudden sighing sound, and Zero One's attention snaps back to the enemy. Connie and Aswad drop simultaneously to a knee. Aswad pulls his first round into chamber.

"Hold." Uba shows them his palm, and they freeze in place. I start to wonder if his Spider can control them, too, not just me, but I see the answer in their faces—their reverent fear of this ranking god and his commands. I realize the captain dominates all of us in a way that usually only reachers can.

The pod seems to fear him, too. The sighing, whistling and depressurizing sounds all stop at once. Suddenly, we're all waiting in silence. Just the light hum of Sasha's drones hovering overhead. The soft rustling of corn as the wind shimmies it around us.

Then the nightmare begins.

A thick ooze begins to seep from every edge of the hatch. Black as oil, twice as filthy, spotted with chunks and strands and specks of biomatter. The hideous mechanism behind intergalactic travel.

Flashes of those projected slides from special training creep back behind my eyes. Bodies preserved for thousands of years but made anemic and hairless. Sometimes toothless with missing toenails and paper skin. Always sterilized. The last of their line. It makes me wonder what's even the point. Why travel so far for this sorry status? Without any hope for new generations, without a chance at proliferation, it all seems so uninspired. So self-serving. Scattering mules, clinging desperately to their own limited, hideous lives. I grimace as the odor finally breaks me from that thought. It's eye-watering. An ancient armpit sweating semen.

Yang and Shankman lock and load now, staying high on their feet.

"Hold," Uba repeats. But carefully, quietly, he raises his jet-black rail rifle, a lengthy tank-killer likely designed to be bolted down or mounted on a gunship, a source of pride in Zero One that Shankman has quietly dubbed Black Beauty. Uba doesn't quite level it with the pod, just near enough to be ready. He never aims without intent to annihilate. In that way, it's an honor to be squared in his sights, to be chosen for death by the African falcon. And when the captain pulls his trigger, nothing is more certain. "Stay close to me, Mr. Hayes."

I nod, raising my rifle, copying his readied angle. He mutters his Zambian codeword—one I'm yet to decipher, but it sounds like "Mah-penzay"—and Black Beauty's safety switches from white to red. Crackling strands of scarlet lightning begin to dance around the lengthy barrel. An entrancing static.

But the ooze flows heavier now, especially from the bottom edge, as the hatch begins to recede, arcing up and back, gradually vanishing into the pod's thick hull. The dark goo soft-serves onto the blackened soil like hot molasses. Danny-boy takes a nervous step back, subconsciously scratching at his Spider Byte.

I feel something, too. That painful pinch like white-hot light behind my eye. Then something pops inside the pod. And in one heavy rushing gush, the reacher's gangly body spills down into the ooze. A few thick droplets splatter upward, catching Shankman on the cheek.

"Ah! Shit!" He frantically wipes, but it just smears like engine grease.

"Hold!" Uba seems to sense Aswad's tightening trigger, a hair's breadth from discharging a round. He fidgets reluctantly, caught in Uba's gaze, flirting with insubordination. But he finally curses, straightening his itchy finger again.

Uba looks back to our limp visitor, its spine and limbs bent awkwardly in disagreement beneath the organic travel gear that inspired the G-1s: a photosynthetic body suit, wrapped skintight from feet to shoulders. He examines the failed invader's bleached, hairless skin, stretched taut over its starved cheekbones. Its husky-blue eyes are half open, lulling in different, lifeless directions. Again, I see something unexpected in the captain's expression. Something like disappointment.

"Bhakan." Uba waits, as various known Luminaran languages scroll in his panther falcon's microfont. "Khall."

The reacher's arm moves slightly. But it's just the ooze still settling. Shankman laughs with nervous relief. Danny-boy sighs and smiles, too.

"If you are alive, stand up." Again, Uba's words fall on dead ears. "Anything, Mr. Carter?"

We all hear Sasha's fingers click-clack over his keyboard back on the hovership. "Negative. No pulse, no neural activity. Looks like DOA."

Uba nods, finally letting his rail rifle sag in the crook of his arm. "Alright. Bring the hovership around. Drop crane and body bag for extraction."

"Copy. ETA 30 seconds."

"Arrange transport for the children. Local fire and police. We will brief them when they arrive."

"They're pulling up now, sir. I called when you went in."

"Ah. Very good."

"And some wet wipes if you got 'em!" Shankman spits in his hand and attacks his oozy cheek again.

"Some clean underwear wouldn't hurt. Asking for a friend." Danny-boy shakes his head, and Yang crosses behind us, laughing, thumping the much younger man on his back. The three of them circle up, and Shankman starts patting his pockets, searching for his ceremonial cigar tin.

Connie stares daggers at me again as she pulls Aswad to his feet. He seems just as disappointed as Uba but with an entirely different heat. A bloodlust left unquenched. He watches the limp space man with discontented eyes until Connie bats his shoulder, and they both head over toward the captain.

Uba's human eye studies me uncertainly before it rises to the arriving hovership. Massive cold propulsion engines wash us all in heavy winds, bending the corn and spreading the ooze, exposing the reacher's naked scalp and half-sphered ears. They look like recessed radio dishes. Vestigial leftovers of some previous species that relied more on soundwaves than the fourth dimension. Just one reminder of the long, dim times before the even longer evolution that granted access to the bright highway, the endless network that still seems like magic to our more primitive Earth-person minds. Magic with a dazzling cobalt shine. A shine like . . . wait, what is this? Have I always known that? I—I don't think so. I don't—

That doubt turns like a key, and I'm standing by Shiloh Lake again. I'm just a boy, and that silent music is keeping me warm. I can see her smiling face, hovering closely above mine. But it's not quite right. Her hair. Maybe her eyes. Somehow, I know she isn't right. She's someone else. An imposter guessing well, but not well enough. The imposter sees his mistake in my reaction, and his eyes begin to turn. He reaches for me, but I lunge away. My tiny feet tangle in the knee-high grass, and I am falling. Ass over kettle, straight into the glassy lake where I sank my daddy with all those stones, and—

I land hard on our back in the blackened dirt. And the sound's suddenly all wrong. The corn is quiet, motionless. The hovership's gone, and Sasha is shouting frantically over comms.

"—any of you read me?! Oh, Hayes! Hayes!"

I sit up quickly, wincing at the deep, sharp throbbing in my skull. That painful pinch has compounded into a rolling, burning ache.

"Hayes, answer me!"

"Yeah." I intend to say more, but it's surprisingly painful to hear my own voice. Like the bones in my head have been tenderized. I roll to our right elbow, meaning to stand, but an impossible scene stops me cold.

Connie's still kneeling beside Aswad, rifle raised and ready. Aswad's index finger is still clenched, grazing his trigger. Shankman's cheek is still speckled with ooze, but he doesn't seem to notice. He's just standing there, breathing slow and calm. He blinks twice, lazily, like he's in the audience of a dull performance.

"Hayes, get up!" Sasha's voice is a blend of terror and new hope.

"What's happening?"

"Get the fuck up and grab your weapon!"

"I—yeah."

"On your left!"

"Yeah." I roll left, pawing the soil, finally finding my rifle.

Then I see Uba, towering beside me. Not disappointed at all. Certainly not ordering Aswad to hold fire. He's trembling. Unlike the others, his expression is alive and urgent. Black Beauty is leveled now, ready and crackling against the captain's shoulder. His falcon pupil is honed to a pinprick, gazing with lethal intent down his short-range scope. It's his right hand that's trembling, dragging slowly toward the trigger. Battling for every millimeter. Winning psychic ground against—

"Hayes!"

Sasha's voice sends my eyes forward, and I finally see the truth. The same pod, the same puddle of filthy ooze. But the reacher is tall and handsome. Hairless but muscular. Intimidating. Very much alive. Drenched and dripping, rising to its feet. Its right arm is extended, trembling in concert with Captain Uba's. Reaching across the crater and deep into his conscious mind. The left is also reaching but in a swirling spiral pattern, blanketing the rest of Zero One in some kind of pacifying illusion.

"Stop!" I raise my rifle, and the reacher's cosmic, cobalt eyes latch immediately onto mine—

The wind sounds so nice in the shimmying corn stalks. The hovership's back and our first mission is complete. Shankman's torching a cigar for Danny-boy with that classic silver lighter he loves so much. The one with the old-timey painting of the busty redhead who he says he used to—

"Stop it!" I shake my head so hard I feel sick. So sick I almost keel over. I shove my mind down, all the way down to some special place where the reacher can't touch it. It feels like my heart is on fire. Like the person I love most just died in my arms then gusted away to dust.

The reacher blinks and recoils slightly. Like it's just realized I'm not wearing pants. Its mesmerizing eyes shift from malice to confusion, and I hear a sudden *whisper*. Clearer than my own thoughts. Loud, with deep bass and narrative bravado. A strong male voice to match the sculpted foe that stands before me.

It—no—*he* begs forgiveness.

He says our light is strange and shrouded, but he can see it now. It's a bright one to be proud of. He begs forgiveness. He would see it opened, would help restore what's been forgotten, but his assignment must come first—his sworn vow to the endless others—and he did not choose this place and time. He begs forgiveness.

And his cobalt eyes begin to widen. A thick vein tightens in his hairless skull, and that rolling ache becomes a flaming icicle in my frontal lobe. A pain I'd thought impossible. It's too extreme for me to scream. I feel warm blood in my left ear, oozing around the earpiece, muffling Sasha's desperate shouts. The same warmth trickles from my nose and down the back of my constricting throat. I hear a body thump to the ground on my right. Probably Danny. Hard to tell. He isn't breathing. His heart has stopped.

My rifle slips from my hands, and I follow it into the dirt. It feels soft against my cheek, and the terrible pain begins to fade. I feel numb and high with whatever treats the brain secretes as it transitions toward certain death. I feel much calmer than I expected, like I'm slipping free from everything else—all the unexpected strife of my promotion and the towering prison of my pride.

But, as my eyes fall shut, I see her face again. That beautiful woman, losing her color, desaturating and shriveling to just a husk of her potential. Becoming less than a silhouette. Even less than that bald, agonized version I saw in chow hall two. Just a quiet corpse beneath my heart. Just like the ones I found at Shiloh Lake. Reachers and humans all slain together. All dead and silent except for Logan. I hear my grandmother's screams again. I see my daddy's corpse through his mother's eyes, and I wake up.

My eyes snap open, and the reacher stops. Stops killing me, stops swirling his left arm, stops binding the captain with his right. The reacher freezes just like he froze my friends, and for a split second, I see his dream instead. I see a sky so much like ours and a sun that's just as bright. I see happy people who look like us, with natural smiles and gleaming eyes, all laced with cobalt but some much brighter—some so bright I want to cry.

The second ends. Black Beauty screams, and a flaming hole appears in the reacher's skull. Uba stays firm, ready to fire another slug, as the rest of the unit stumbles clumsily from their illusions.

"Ah! Fuck!" Shankman smears his oozy cheek for real this time.

"What—weren't we just?" Yang spins around, confused, then looks straight up, surprised to see no descending hover-ship above us.

Sasha whoops over the comms with intense relief, "Hoo! Goddammit. Nice fucking shot, sir! Christ almighty, everyone okay?"

As though in reply, Danny-boy gasps, sucking in air and blackened dirt, choking like a drowned sailor, pushing up from his brief death to his wobbly forearms.

"Yes," Uba responds to Sasha. "We are alive, Mr. Carter. Somehow." He studies me curiously—a renewed admiration for his strangest weapon. "Bring the hovership, please. And a litter for Mr. Hayes. I want him brought up first."

"Copy that. Local PD is on their way, too. For Powell's kids."

"Very good."

"I'm fine if anyone's wondering. Just a little alien cum in my mouth, that's all." Shank spits in the dirt and pulls out his sexy lighter.

I'm surprised how much it hurts to laugh. But she *whispers*, and I can already feel her going to work, mending the various ruptures in my assaulted brain and the deeper scars in my unlocked mind. That woman. I've seen her twice at the brink of death—in private places she doesn't belong. It was just the three of us in that house. Me, Logan, and Daddy, I'm sure of that. But I . . . I need a fucking drink.

"Be still." Uba presses gently on our back as he crouches down beside us. "If you could see yourself right now, you would be very still." I watch him for a moment. Then I carefully return my cheek to the charred crater soil. On his way to pick up Danny, Yang glances at me with a similar taut expression. The trained dispassion of veteran soldiers. They're trying not to show it—but they fear I won't survive.

A scene much like the one we all dreamed begins to play out in reality. But quieter. Darkened with death and déjà vu. The hovership arrives, making the sweet corn dance, blowing cold moisture deep into *her* scales. I let my eyes fall shut. I try to see that woman's face again, but she's already fading back down to wherever I've had her tucked away. Down into that dark, sunken place where even the reacher couldn't touch me.

I decide to try something new. I shape my thoughts into a request—an inward feeling like the whispers I've grown used to. A command to cancel a few mental sutures, to keep that mysterious face somewhere accessible. I want that vibrant, lively version but I also need the bleached husk—that bald female thing that looks so much like one of them. I don't want to forget again. Not completely. To my astonishment, the G-1 whispers back.

You will not.

 **2.06**

"Yeah, but you know why they're doin' this shit, right?"

"Who?"

"The territories. You get why it's all half-cocked and quick-like, dontcha?"

"Christ, here we go."

"Shut up, I'm talkin' to the kid."

"You're not talking, you're indoctrinating."

"I'm educatin', you braciole!"

"Ha!"

"In fact, why don't you grab a chair and take some notes. I know how you Chinamen love to read ahead."

Danny-boy snickers guiltily at Shankman's jab. He lightly strides over the kitchen tiles, sounding barefoot but not exactly, probably wearing those leather moccasins his mother sent him when we finished special training. The oven beeps a few times, and I hear the zig-zagging rip of a cardboard pizza box.

Shank waits until Danny has circled back and retaken his seat outside the kitchen. Then he clears his throat and carries on with his special lecture. "Honestly, this ain't all that controversial. Just basic math when you get down to it. That's why they call it Zero *Addition*."

Yang chokes on whatever he's drinking, something thick like melted ice cream. "I'm sorry. I don't know why I tried to stop this, please continue."

"Shudda fuck up." Shank snaps his fingers, hardly missing a beat. "For billions of years, we've been the same. The Earth, I mean. The size of it. We make more people, we build more shit, but it all comes from here an' stays here an' dies here. There's an unchangin' balance, you follow?"

"The conservation of mass."

"Exactly! Whoa. Mr. Diaz has done his homework. Okay. Well, d'ya see where I'm goin', then?"

"Yeah. That's kinda interesting. Never thought about it like that."

"Aha!" Shank snaps his fingers again.

"Humans threw the Earth out of balance."

"Boom. Well, no that's not—I'm sayin' that the *lumies* are the ones who—"

"Right yeah. We threw our total mass out of balance with all our satellites and probes and stuff. And that's why we let the Luminarans land for twenty-five years. To even it up again. But now you're saying we need to stop them because the planet's mass is, what, overflowing?"

"Uh. Well, yeah, but I don't—I don't think the satellites have been um . . ."

Yang starts a slow clap. "Professor Shankman, everybody."

"He's agreein' with me though basically."

"Oh, okay. Danny, do you *agree* that the United Territories' true, secret mission is to prevent the Earth's expanding 'super gravity' from pulling the moon out of its orbit?

"See, you're doin' it again, that is *not* my argument—"

"Do you agree that the Orbital Patrol is quietly wrapping the Earth in a magic, undetectable force field?"

"When have I eva' said magic? When the fuck once have I eva' said—!"

"Do you *agree* that Chicago was an inside job or a hoax or some kind of masterful, secret attack by the Russians to—"

Something thumps loudly on the wooden picnic table at the center of the common space. Everyone falls silent.

The sudden thump is followed by the heavy army boots of Zayd Aswad, echoing angrily down the narrow hallway toward my quarters. With some pain and nervous anticipation, I lift my head from the pillow, but Aswad's shadow stops short, turning into the room he shares with Connie Clark. The door slams loudly behind him, and the blinds rattle excitedly in my open window before settling again.

"See. Even Ass-wad agrees wit' me."

"You're a moron," Yang retorts at a cautious volume before continuing to sip his creamy beverage. I never heard him run the blender. Must be that alkaline veggie powder he drinks to settle his gut.

The oven beeps to signal it's preheated, and Danny-boy's moccasins pad back over into the kitchen. He opens the oven, slides his frozen lunch inside, and flips it shut. Then they all stand in an uncomfortable silence, probably exchanging meaningful glances, but from my blind vantage the scene is done.

As the boredom creeps on me again, I realize it hurt far less than I expected to move my head. I test our arms, lifting the heavy nutrient quilt and pushing it down below our waist. It takes more effort to lift our legs, but I pull them free of the balmy blanket and swing them over the edge of my bunk. Our feet connect with the old wooden floor, and they feel surprisingly strong. A dull throbbing recommences in my skull, but it's nothing compared to yesterday morning. It's been three days since the events on Caitlin Powell's farm, a worryingly slow recovery by our standards. For anyone else, it would be proof of God.

After being brought in for processing, the reacher that Uba decapitated in the crater was officially ranked an X-3, just one degree below the dreaded Y-tier. An unlucky draw for Zero One's first live action. A baptism by fire that either proved our elite status or undermined it completely, depending who you ask. The same uncertainty now hangs over the much-lauded Spider Bytes, which either saved everyone's lives or added no measurable protection whatsoever. As the only man without one, my ruined state is an obvious case for the former. I was also the first to break the illusion, not counting the captain who never quite succumbed. But yeah. I was the only one to truly bake, to be held so directly over the psychic flame.

Most X-tiers can sustain basic mind prisons, though usually on just one or two subjects at a time and only in brief bursts. Long enough to slip past a beat cop or palm your Ret-tag on a busy train. But matter manipulation . . . that's a whole different bag, usually bright enough to earn the classification Y. It's not true telekinesis, of course. None of the known reacher abilities are. But among the various Luminaran Laws enforced by the United Territories, matter moving is the most severely punished.

An X-1 can lock you, probably distort your vision for a few minutes. An X-2 can send you somewhere else, your childhood home, your most carnal wet dream or whatever cerebral prison they can find inside you. But an X-3—or the few scattered and infamous Y-1s—they can change you. Control you. I always wondered what it would feel like to be dismantled. Now, I hope that I'll forget.

The damage was worst in my brain and spinal cord, but it was happening everywhere. Every living cell in my nervous system, central and peripheral, voluntary and involuntary, somatic and metabolic, every facet of my body's vital processes was being issued one command, one forceful whisper from my own hijacked unconscious mind: *Die*.

About half of them obeyed. The other half were on their way until Black Beauty finally screamed. The captain broke free and pulled his trigger when I . . . when I saw that woman in my mind. When I felt Grandma Logan's pain or something like it, a loss so far beyond the stupefied shock I felt back then, beyond the numb fatalism I dwelled in when I watched her pass in that Houston shelter four years later.

I grimace, lifting a discolored hand to massage my eyes. It hurts to think, especially of that day. She *whispers*, and I flinch uneasily. Our legs feel flimsy again. She says *rest*, but some part of me still hears him—his booming, inhuman voice. No. Extremely human. That's the change that disturbs me most. That clinging, festering feeling that despite his bright eyes, despite his powers, despite his oozing alien vessel, he was not so strange at all. He attacked us viciously, but I felt remorse in his unearthly heart. A human empathy I've never spared on his ugly kind, on the countless hundreds whose destruction I've tacitly supervised. Maybe Mr. Prichard has it backward. Maybe the gunners need the sims—to divorce us from our role in this intergalactic genocide.

A reductive sentiment, I hope. Not a term that can be applied to such advanced invaders. Danny-boy said it true enough. We were kind and curious for twenty-five generous years. And decidedly firm these most recent seven. But still they come.

So, now we must do this dirty work. For Caitlin Powell and her orphaned children, for the millions erased in the Chicago Storm, we will hunt these few wherever they land. We will do our best to integrate—to tolerate—the thousands already here, until they expire. Because we are human. Because this is our home. Because the universe is flush with other rocks for our unbeckoned visitors to despoil.

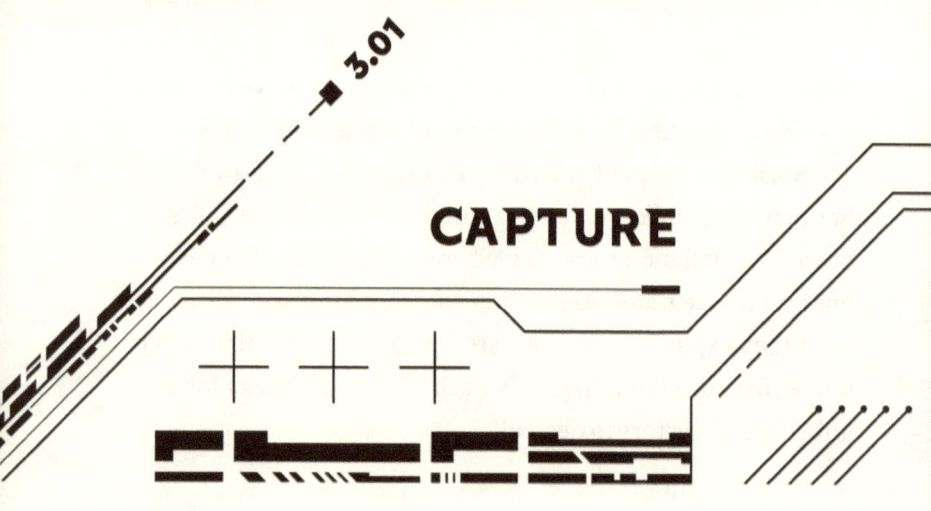

CAPTURE

They should've chosen someone else to throw the switch. Captain Uba would've been perfect. Or Faye Thompson, if the intent is to honor Zero Two. This is her unit's victory, after all, her perfect capture after weeks of deadly hunting.

Instead, our overlords are flexing, not seeming to realize how unsavory this presentation is going to be. If they wanted a show of strength, they got their wish and a few dollars more. A rather sickening deterrent to their detractors, to all the hold-out nations who still deny the United Territories' jurisdiction. A semi-human battle flag in the shape of Taiko Chiba.

I still remember how it tasted. A wash of relief, mixed with mild humiliation. When Faye was elevated to the commanding role of Zero Two, her first and only request was Taiko Chiba. The units needed balancing, she argued, and the captain couldn't disagree. But it was obvious; Uba would've preferred to keep his creature close and send me over to Faye instead.

He simply knew that Faye would never have me. Not with any peace of mind. Prichard's reckless stunt at that first briefing precluded any trust between us. And as Shankman learned the hard way, in the first few hours of special training, little Faye Thompson is rather sensitive about her height. That's how he lost one of his eyebrows and got that jagged scar behind his ear. It was one of those fights where everyone stopped cheering, where the entire yard got quiet before it was over, before Connie Clark finally had the sense and courage to pull the first lieutenant off him. That's how Faye earned her unit call sign, the first one designated among us. That's why, in these twin families, she is better known as *Fangs*.

Maybe she's the one who did this. Maybe the overlords gave loose instructions and Faye decided to have some fun. She seems to have that perverse imp in her as well, that little voice that whispers *burn*. Maybe Lieutenant Fangs wants the entire world to see the creature she commands, her armored beast with swirling eyes and swimming skin. Or maybe Taiko just deserves to throw the deportation switch. Because she lost her human mind. Because she's the real reason we're all gathered here, the main source of Zero Two's skyward fame. Somehow, she captured Kible Thexx AnSorin. The vivid ghost of eastern Asia. The roaming demon of Zhejiang. The first and only Y-tier rogue to be taken alive.

At least they picked the perfect venue. I've never heard a bloodlust like this sea of Russians just gave voice to. Sixty thousand throats raised in exhortation. A patriotic cry, not for their own struggling nation but for our entire planet. They roared as Taiko Chiba climbed the rocket platform, and for a moment I felt corrected. I felt timid and disloyal for ever fearing her strange eyes, for ever cowering at their twisting hues, their nauseating swarming patterns, like endless smoke and colored dye behind wet glass—all anchored by that wide, white pupil in the center, that inverted shimmering hole, like a coon's eye catching moonlight.

But my dishonor faded when the camera sim finally captured its first closeup, when it hovered up to meet Taiko at the launch site and the entire crowd went terribly silent. In sixty meters of high definition, they finally saw her face. Vacant and unsmiling. Not stupid, not disinterested, not proud or disappointed. Just an empty vessel of modern war, with eyes to make dark dreams for kids and hardened men alike.

Much like the Spiders—much better actually—her G-4 suit doesn't play well with my senses. Sometimes, when she moves, she almost seems to be missing frames, like my eyes don't want to see her. And as Prichard just explained, in another one of his overlong product pitches, she is invulnerable to the Reach, even impervious to master matter movers like the infamous Kible Thexx. Or so he claims.

I have other theories about Taiko's famed perfect defense. I wonder if maybe that pain in my skull was so sharp and clear a few weeks ago because that's where they enter. If the reacher's greatest weapon is the human mind itself, then I'd guess not having one at all makes for a pretty damn good shield.

"I am thanking you, Mr. Prichard. You are making your planet proud," President Zhurov finally interrupts him from the other side of the Vostochny Cosmodrome's massive stage. Even from my raised vantage at the back of this rowdy crowd, I see the disagreement between her eyes and her tight smile.

I never learned the names of her slain bodyguards, but I can still see their frozen faces, trapped not in terror but incredulity, too quickly killed to feel anything else. Most of the witnesses still fear us, me and *her*. But Varvara Zhurov knows no such emotion. She is the successor to blatant tyrants, the frigid daughter of famished streets. She sees the difference between dirty bombs and the quiet cowards who pull their triggers. She would defuse me if she could, but for Prichard she seems to have much darker plans. I see cold vengeance in her eyes, chilled even deeper by this home advantage and the wild horde of her compatriots.

"But I am thinking it is time to give this people what they come for." Zhurov turns her intrepid eyes to the hungry crowd, holding the microphone close to her lips "Я прав?"

Another eruption shakes the Earth as their fears of Taiko fade to memory. They stomp the frozen dirt and shake mittened fists above their heads. I feel the cherry picker sway beneath me, and President Guerrero laughs uncomfortably as she takes a nervous step toward backstage. She quickly signals someone there, then turns that false political grin back on the crowd. I hear the chatter of her Secret Servicemen over comms:

"Shield Leader to Cage Leader, send prisoner. Cage, send prisoner."

"Cage copies. Sending now."

"Negative. Hold prisoner." Uba overrides the White House on their own channel with some urgency, as though he's still calculating a threat.

I dig under my helmet, pressing my earlobes closed to muffle the crowd. I look across the cosmodrome to the captain's crow's nest in the high zig-zagging metal stairs behind the launch site. Black Beauty still lies beside him, modded with a bipod for sniper fire. She's dormant, none of that red lightning crackling yet. No target chosen for death. But he is watching carefully, holding steady on something in the crowd, enhancing his panther eye with a tactical monocular.

At last, he says, "Crowd section six. Boxes one and two."

I follow Uba's coordinates, looking down to my right, about twenty meters from the base of my cherry picker.

"Four targets. Black sunglasses," Uba clarifies. "Edge. Sparrow. Colt. Call when covered."

"Edge has cover," Aswad responds immediately, and I see him now, moving carefully through the crowd in his plain-clothes disguise. Blue jeans and a thick winter jacket, concealing the arsenal of blades that would call him master if they had voices.

I try to track his repeating glances and finally spot one of the marks. A man of average height, wearing a fur-lined trapper hat. The chin strap is secured tightly, with both ear flaps covering the sides of his head. A common look in Eastern Russia. Especially on days like these. Days where the wind makes blades of its own, reminding me I'm still an anatomical man beneath this suit.

It's not just the hat. It's the addition of round mountaineering sunglasses that mark this man as suspicious. Darkly tinted lenses with leather side shields. A quirky choice in this context. Or a practical one for any reacher hiding in plain sight. But the sky is clear, the sun is bright, and if not for my visored helmet, I'd likely have sunglasses of my own. I'm missing something.

"Colt has cover. Is it four targets or three?" Danny-boy asks from the roof of the northern maintenance building. He lies there, prone, with his own bipodal rifle, targeting the same patch as Uba and Aswad.

"What? Are we not being ready to—" Zhurov's voice draws my eyes back to the stage. She's just lowered the microphone down to her hip, interrogating President Guerrero, who's interrogating the Secret Service commander about the sudden delay.

"There are *four*," Uba states confidently, with growing impatience. "Sparrow, do you—"

"Sparrow also confirms three hostiles. Box one and two, matching black sunglasses." One of Sasha's stealth drones silently hovers into view above where Aswad is now holding. It turns its cameras to section six, then cloaks itself, vanishing against the woodland backdrop.

Beginning to feel left out, I tap my helmet to dismiss the noisy visor HUD and throw my eyes back down to that fur-lined trapper hat. He's in the top left corner of section six, box one. Nobody near him is wearing sunglasses except another man in a baseball cap, with padded, soft-shell earmuffs. He's at least six meters from the first man, but he's wearing the same black mountaineers. Identical.

"Shield Leader to Zero Leader, are we clear to send prisoner?" The Secret Service commander sounds more nervous and agitated this time.

"We are not." Uba sounds frustrated now as well. Perhaps even embarrassed. "Four possible rogues identified. Three strangers. One native."

"Отправь это домой!" someone shouts from the center of the crowd, clear and loud, either through a bullhorn or some portable speaker system. That bloodlust surges again, thousands of voices roaring back at him. He repeats his call, with a metered cadence this time, "Отправь—это—домой!" The third time, a thousand voices join him: "ОТПРАВЬ—ЭТО—ДОМОЙ!" Then ten thousand, thirty thousand, until the entire plaza is shaking with hungry Russian sounds.

She *whispers* a translation, and I wonder if I needed it. I see all their faces, their spitting lips. They're all just demanding what they came for: *Send—it—home. SEND—IT—HOME.*

But Uba's last detail is still spinning in my head. Three reacher rogues, two of which I've identified, and a third somewhere nearby. There! Another trapper hat with tinted mountaineering glasses, in the top right corner of section six, box two. I've caught up with Aswad, Danny-boy, and Sasha. But Uba insists four. A fourth insurgent in the field. And somehow, he seems convinced that this one is—

"I see her." I raise my rifle scope for a closer look. "A human. A native female in a slate-gray coat. Black mountaineers." She turns slightly this way, ostensibly making eye contact with the other rogue suspect in box two. Her hair is wavy, bouncing freely just above her shoulders. Black, or a silvery blue, depending on the light. If it's a wig, I've never seen one more convincing. More likely, she's had it spliced at one of those genetic parlors in California. And her skin is far too tanned to be one of them—an equatorial beige-brown like warm Irish tea blended with fresh milk. I . . . I am reminded yet again of my anatomy.

But I shake it off. I tap my helmet HUD back on and hold her carefully in those digital crosshairs. An aimed rifle from this range could inspire panic. So, I'll keep my weapon low until the call to action comes. "Daydream has cover on target four."

"Very good," Uba exhales, relieved but equally exhausted. "Maintain visuals. Non-lethals only."

"Copy that."

"Copy."

"Updating bogey count," Sasha confirms.

As I turn my rifle and flip the switch for non-lethal rounds, I hear Zhurov's encroaching shouts in the background of our comms, in the unlucky ear of the Secret Service commander.

"Yes, ma'am, I—just a minute I'm—Shield Leader to Zero Leader, are we *still* holding for—?"

"We are covered." Uba says it like he's already lived this frigid day. Already memorized our flawless execution. And in my peripherals, I see something else. Black Beauty is crackling now, low in its standby white, hugged against his meaty shoulder. Not targeting section six, which he's entrusted to us four. Instead, he's aimed squarely at the launch site, at the raised platform where Taiko still awaits her great convict, a main event that the captain apparently entrusts to no one but himself. He whispers, "Mapenze" to his old partner and its crackling strands flash hotter, that scarlet red. Then he bypasses the poor Secret Service commander again, speaking directly to the holding team with that same cold confidence. "Zero Leader to Cage. Awaiting prisoner."

3.02

And I thought they were loud before. At the first sound of the motor engaging, the cosmodrome rumbles with gratification. Those heavy gears start turning and that classic chain lift begins to climb, *chack chack chacking* its analogue rhythm of pure human engineering.

The prisoner rises into view, but I'm unable to turn us in that direction. Can't do much of anything but spread our feet and pray. This is fucked. I can barely stand upright in this swaying metal frame, let alone hit a mark in a jumping, manic crowd. Even if that inaudible order comes, even if I somehow find a clean shot amidst all this chaos, my hesitation seems more likely every minute.

The other three targets might be reachers—even that I can't confirm—but this woman makes no sense to me at all. I'm tracking all four of them in my visor, finally seeing what Uba must've caught on to before. A conspicuous non-participation. The crowd undulates madly all around them, but those four are nearly motionless, occasionally glancing to each other but no one else. Aswad sticks out in the same way, doing his best not to stare directly at them, intermittently shouting or shaking his raised fists to blend in with the mob—and perhaps not only for that reason. He holds a special hatred for our invaders, I can see that plainly now. A sharpness that transcends the call of duty. In that regard, this woman is his moral opposite. A human who fights for *them*, if fighting is indeed their cause today.

Sasha's scans detected no dark energy leaks. No hot wires or other signs of rudimentary detonation. That's never really been their bag anyway. Suicidal terror remains a starkly human inclination. Besides their deadly minds, no reacher weapons have ever been discovered on this planet. A long-term tactic, I suspect. A preservation of their wartime secrets for when-ever the true invasion does begin. But this woman is human. Brainwashed maybe. Trapped in an elaborate mind prison to make her their pawn, some prolonged illusion that erases her nature. She may have no idea who she is or just how significant this moment will be for her own species. This historic justice. She turns slightly this way again, and I carefully guide my eyes away. Not nearly careful enough. When I see him, a bit of my human nature is erased, too.

Kible Thexx AnSorin. Halfway up the lift now. Twenty meters high. Twenty more to go before he reaches Taiko's plat-form. He's seated in some kind of madhouse electric chair, heav-ily drugged by the look on his face, by the languid way his eyes keep bobbing up and down. His head would be bouncing just the same if he wasn't strapped tightly at the forehead. Similar constraints are choking his throat, binding his biceps, wrists, thighs, and ankles. None of that surprises me. None of that seems out of order, considering the infamy of this threat. It's AnSorin himself that I'm surprised by. I guess I never did the math.

Technically, every reacher that arrives on Earth is thousands of years old, kept alive by that vasectomizing goo, preserved in time despite the various side effects. But AnSorin actually looks it. He'd be tall if he was standing up, but his limbs are gangly and thin. His hands have that pruney, geriatric look, and his skin is saggy, especially beneath his eyes and chin. He might look like a wizard if he wasn't so ghoulishly lacking hair. And the crowd is taking notice. That massive digital screen is cooling their blood back down, greatly reducing the energy of their lusty shouts and chants. It all falls low enough for me to hear the countdown coming through comms.

"Prisoner entering vessel in 3 . . . 2 . . . 1."

The lift reaches the bottom of the platform, inserting Kible Thexx AnSorin and his locked chair directly into the undercarriage of his deportation craft, a bulky, angular replica of a standard reacher pod, with *Dallas Dynamics* etched proudly into the hull. The red, cyberpunk graffiti font seems to pop out in three dimensions over the more subtle matte-black finish. Yet another military operation converted to marketing dollars by M. Calvin Prichard Jr. And this one's going to the stars.

Showy steam bursts from hidden pipes behind the starship, and the crowd begins to find its voice again. Twin mechanical arms ascend the heat cloud in an ominous, choreographed pattern, inserting their nozzled hands into the lower corners of the craft.

AnSorin's anesthetized face, now visible through a triple-pane porthole, starts to twitch in drunk discomfort as fresh and milky preservation gel rises above his shoulders to his chin, above his mouth and nose and eyes until he becomes a thin shadow floating in a liquid whiteout. The crowd roars even louder, unwittingly celebrating the perpetuation of their foe. Or perhaps they're recognizing the imperfect re-creation this all must be. Another reverse-engineered marvel by Dallas Dynamics. A prototype with that inherent and significant chance of human error.

As the mechanical arms retract, sealing both fluid entry holes behind them, M. Calvin stokes the Russians further. "Kible Thexx AnSorin, of the homeworld Luminara."

The crowd hisses and stomps their feet, swaying the cherry picker once again, reminding me in a flash of panic to watch that woman—

Thankfully, she's still there. Just as stoic as before. The four of them are like a motionless constellation now. My HUD locks them all back into their tracking squares as though I never looked away. And I won't be, not again. Whatever disruption they have planned, it's very likely soon to come.

As though on cue, the woman's right elbow subtly bends. It's hard to see from this raised angle, but she seems to pull something from her pocket and ready it by her hip.

"—movement. All four—" Sasha's voice comes in, barely audible beneath the crowd. But I catch his meaning well enough. The other three rogues have slipped their right hands from their pockets, too, all four of them just low enough to be below my line of sight.

"Of the following crimes, you have been found guilty." Prichard's voice booms from the massive speakers. His active translation must be projected on the screen, because every human head now turns in that direction.

Every head except the woman's. Her black-blue-silver shroud stays pointed west and high, where AnSorin's vessel has begun to hum. The same is true of her three captors, or whatever they are to her, all four of them juxtaposed against this wild rabble now. Mountaineer shades aimed west and high.

"Mind confinement. Memory abuse. Memory destruction!" With each worsening crime that Prichard recites, the Russians cry out in deepened disgust. "Matter manipulation with intent to injure. Matter manipulation with intent to kill. And!" Prichard holds all sixty thousand with one word. With one raised finger, he adds their morbid curiosities to his riches. "There is still one charge that these good people have never heard."

His eyes shift subtly to the east, and I see fidgety movements where Zhurov and Guerrero are observing from offstage—too quick and distant for me to make sense of, too quiet for my ears. But there comes a whisper with the answer: *Surprise. Fear.*

And when Prichard turns back to the crowd, to the camera drones, to the entire planet, he is just as pained as all of them, just as tormented by this dark truth he must reveal. "Excuse me, I misspoke." He drops his eyes and shakes his head. "There are precisely two million, four hundred and thirty-six thousand, one hundred and eleven charges yet to be served."

A few clever Russians gasp in the crowd. Some old woman wails in the woods behind me like she just watched her baby drown.

Prichard finds his largest voice. His chest expands. "New evidence confirms what has long been suspected. There is no happenstance in our world, no great effect without causation. Kible Thexx AnSorin, you have been found guilty of two million, four hundred and thirty-six thousand, one hundred and eleven counts of criminal negligence and manslaughter, regarding the white flash incident on the 8th of June, widely known as the Chicago Storm."

Aswad enters my field of view just as I'm totally deafened by the crowd, just as the cherry picker sways so precariously I'm forced to spread our stance and clench the handrails to stay upright. My rifle drops, catching at the end of its strap tied to the rail, metronoming a few inches above our toes, out over the frenzied mob and back again.

Aswad's mouth moves, but no evidence of his voice passes over the comms. He's only a few meters from the reachers in box one, his eyes no longer bothering to maintain cover, hungrily searching their limited expressions and unpocketed hands for violent intentions. His disappointed frown tells me he sees nothing actionable so far. But his own right hand disappears cautiously behind his back, where his favorite knife is likely sheathed. That eight-and-a-half-inch Nepalese kukri. A curved machete built for hacking human branches. All black and stealthy with a double-ground toothy saw on the opposite edge but oddly pretty where he holds it. A polished rosewood grip, with only a few speckled bloody blemishes to prove its tenure. It's the same blade he unsheathed in the chapel. Even then, he was the first to stand and draw in the search of intimate combat.

"And so, the United Territories, in unique partnership with Dallas Dynamics, sentence you to the first permanent deportation," Prichard's voice is amplified just a hair above the sixty thousand. "As detailed in section seven of the External Matter and Beings Embargo, better known as Zero Addition!" Another dizzying roar shakes the cosmodrome, but I swear I can hear a satisfied grin stretching over Calvin Prichard's pretty face.

On cue, that rising, charging hum intensifies in the Dallas Dynamics craft, and the crowd's gaze realigns with that of the rogues. A dim glow feathers my periphery as that hum becomes a satisfying crescendo. A twitchy intuition scampers through me, and I decide I need to be ready. I drop our knee to the grate beneath us, releasing my tight grip on the guard-rail as I guide our belly to the floor. My rifle pendulums within reach, and I take hold of it again. I'm prone and ready to fire on this strange woman if I must. Just non-lethals, she'll survive— assuming I can hit her below the neck before Aswad's blood can boil over.

"Whenever you're ready, Private Chiba!" Prichard shouts over the crowd and his own humming reinvention. "Send him away like he arrived! To whatever unlucky world must endure him next, send him off!"

The cherry picker sways, and I suddenly feel at home. Not way back on Shiloh Lake but in my gun. My old orbiting can-non above it all. I'm floating over the world again, but this time I've got no sims to guide my fire. This might be the first honest shot I've ever sighted. Mine to live with, whatever happens.

I remember the captain's words in special training. I don't feel the wind; I slip inside it. I don't move the rifle; I move our shoulders. Our elbows, hips, and toes. I sway too far left of the woman, then even further to her right. But I remember the captain's words. We commit to the cherry picker's dance. We sway together for a while until my scope discovers stillness. I pick a place between her shoulders, deciding not to hesitate when my planet needs me most.

"Zero Leader to Swarm," the captain comes in clearly, sounding like a patient father to a toddler or some disabled adolescent. "You may pull it now, Taiko. Please pull the red lever near your right hand."

She doesn't seem to hear him. She remains ethereal to my

senses until the satisfying thud of a heavy switch confirms she has obeyed. The crowd erupts a final time, and that cold wind washes over us—that eerie chill of anti-grav propulsion—disrupting our dance, slipping my scope slightly higher, centering on the strange woman's head of hair. The icy wind swims through our scales, sending azure ripples up and down us, reflecting in tiny diamonds off the picker's metal frame. And within her curls. Our same blue wave seems to shimmer in the human woman's wavy mane. I feel us shiver. My finger stiffens outside the trigger guard—just as the woman's right hand shoots up from her hip.

I panic until I see it. Or rather until I don't. Her hand is clearly empty. Even Aswad freezes in rare surprise, his kukri half-unsheathed. The crowd jumps and shakes their fists like vicious beasts in blooded orgy. They stomp and set off fireworks, lifting their Ret-tags to capture the fading exile, now just a speck in the Russian sky. But our four enemies remain still, each with their thumbs pressed to their hearts, their remaining fingers angled directly up. It's a symbol I've seen somewhere, in some thin place beyond my memories. Or maybe I'm just recognizing their posture, their bold and uniform respect. Either way, she *whispers* to me. She clarifies the sign they're miming, and I feel us shiver once again. She says:

Farewell.

 **3.03**

"Oh, you fucking! Жизнь ебёт меня!" Magar splashes the pot with his losing pocket jacks. "Switch with me. California, move your coins, I am sick from this!" He lifts his small stack of poker chips, gesturing for Danny-boy to do the same.

But Danny and Shank are too busy cackling, both bowing in worship to Aila as she flexes her thick biceps in Magar's face. He swats her away, spilling half his chips in an awkward stumble. They all laugh louder, slapping the table, stomping their boots on the cracked and creaking wooden floors of the repurposed Svobodny hostel. Magar's barrage of Slavic slurs only stokes their hysteria further, drawing the eyes of scattered ZA troops from every corner of the hostel's common floor.

A few infantrymen twist on their wooden stools, pausing their volley of flirtations on the thin-waisted bartender at the entrance. Two transport pilots come unglued from whatever trade secrets Sasha's been imparting in the street-lit glow of the southern windows. Even Aswad slowly glances up from his melancholic thoughts by the dwindling fire. Connie's loyal eyes follow his to the large, central table where the card game is being played—a 3:2 blend of Zero One and Zero Two, with Shankman, Yang, and Danny-boy seated on the southeastern curve of the round table. On the opposite side, burly Magar Volkov is made miniature, furiously scooping up his fallen chips beside the towering Aila Hallheim. From my vantage on the couch, with the dusty chandelier above her, she looks like a Viking dream. A Norse statue, blasted into life by deific heat. Familiar somehow. A faded memory from a distant sleep.

"Texas!" Magar jabs his hairy finger in my direction. "You come be here. You watch this cheating сука!" He pats the table between him and Aila, then scoots his chair away from her, closer to Yang.

"Ah ah! No way," Shank interjects, still catching his breath. "No offense, E.H., but we're runnin' a square game here. No squid brain psychic whatevas allowed."

"Octopus," Yang corrects, taking a slow drag on the same cigarette he started this morning.

"Whateva. This is a human table. And that suit makes him half fuckin' reacher. It ain't square."

"Not square for him, you mean. He starts winning, we'll just tell the suit to fold his hand," Danny-boy chuckles, shuffling the second deck. I spot the corners of forty-seven of the cards. Playing out the deal, burns, flop, turn, and river in my mind, I see that Aila will have the best hand again.

"Oh yeah, good idea." Shankman nods and smiles to Danny. "After that, we can go line up outside an' stick our peckerwoods in the snow. Make it nice an' easy for Cuba to rip our Spiders out with his fuckin' teeth. The squid ain't playin'! Or I'm cashin' out—whateva." Shank stands, only to be met with boos and waving hands for him to sit back down.

"I am not saying Texas plays. Just to watch with his reacher powers. And see the cheating!"

"You will be watching the ceiling from your back if you don't start playing nice with me." Aila pays her big blind and smiles threateningly at Magar, but he seems entirely confused.

"I—I would not sex you if all the pigs were occupied!" Magar brightens at the table's resultant laughter, not realizing it's entirely at his expense. A strange win for everyone involved. "Come, Texas." He grabs a nearby stool and plants it between himself and Aila. "Come watch me suck this bitch woman's ass."

Danny-boy collapses against the table, laughing too hard to deal the rest of the cards. Shankman buries his howling face in Yang's shoulder, leaving a few wet teardrops there above the UT's globular, monochrome flag. I think I might escape the moment, but Magar goes on thumping the stool with his heavy hand, summoning me forward. As I abandon the cushy safety of the couch, I feel the eyes of the entire room narrowing on our back. I anticipate discomfort, even fear, but a sheepish smile reveals my teeth as I experience something else. A human heat I've rarely known. The subtle warmth of discovered friends.

That warmth becomes a blaze as Aila's quiet breath tickles my ear. "Glad we're all doing this," she says quickly, surreptitiously. "I was disappointed when we—when the units got split up." She leans away, but her eyes stay on me—almost like she's memorizing my face.

After a few seconds of disbelief, I realize I should respond. "Yeah." My voice sounds awful, unused since yesterday at least. "Same. Same feeling."

If she thinks I'm an idiot, she doesn't show it. Just nods distractedly, studying my nostrils as I inhale, counting the few hairs on my upper lip. "Ever since I saw you, I . . ." She seems to lose herself in the features of my eerie youth. "I can't stop thinking about them. About my sister and—"

"Hey!" Magar interrupts. "Texas, what are the whispers? Already cheating?!"

Aila spins around, pointing her thick finger in his face, but the counter never comes. She keeps swallowing, like there's too much traffic at the back of her throat. That's when I see it. The faded memory she inspired. The last face I saw before I became *us*. She was right beside me just like this. This brawny jawline. These broad, Norwegian shoulders in the solar dome. That Viking giantess with Aila's same bright eyes.

"Anja," I conclude aloud. "You—your sister."

Aila takes her time spinning back to me. Or maybe it's the spinning of time that changes. Stormy flashes strike the gap between our minds.

I see Anja in several places I've never been. Sterile walls. Laminated security glass. She's in a hospital bed. She's in a wheelchair. She's alive in her G-1 suit, but she's shriveled down to half her size. I see Anja by a window, holding handfuls of her own hair. I'm frozen in the doorway of our grandfather's house in northern Norway, seeing Anja spin around, seeing my big sister laughing, seeing her scream in schizophrenic delight as she offers me a bedpan full of teeth with her plucked eyeballs stacked on top.

Aila touches our shoulder, and I land back at the poker table. I look around fitfully, half deranged by the waking nightmare I've just survived—somebody else's nightmare, somebody else's memories—but Aila holds us still. She touches us like Prichard did—like she is no stranger to these scales.

"Hey. You're okay." She summons my panicked eyes back to hers. She studies my face just like she did before—like she knows all the warning signs but isn't seeing them in me, at least not yet. "I don't know how. But you're okay."

As Magar shifts slightly in his seat, I realize Danny-boy's been listening, too. And Yang, somewhat more stealthily. Even Shankman has stopped laughing, taking notice of the silence. The entire common room awaits the answer to a question I've been avoiding, actively repressing ever since that subtle clue from Calvin Prichard in the chapel. A clue that Aila's just resolved. I knew I wasn't the only pilot to clear the G-1 tacs. Probably not the only *skinner* to serve in-cannon for a time. Just the only one to carry on. The only one to remain active all those years, those infinite hours in the exo—to have maintained a relatively, perhaps suspiciously sane state of mind despite it all. Christ, some jokes are just too perfect. My crazy ass made valedictorian by default. I truly am the only survivor of the gunsuits, Generation One.

Another heat rises inside us. Or maybe just in me. A magmatic pride, overflowing to my exposed hands, climbing my neck, pooling behind my eyes. A low rumbling manifests in the air above our heads. The thinnest bits of dust shake loose from the barroom chandelier. Yang looks up at that. Magar looks down at his small stack of chips just as they quake and topple over, spilling from the table to his lap. All the curious eyes and ears stray frightfully away, guiding hands to tremoring cups and falling rifles as the entire hostel trembles at my rarity—or so I fantasize.

Guiding spotlights tilt into view, cutting through the southern windows and pitch-black courtyard just beyond them. A descending hovership shakes the trees and spreads the settled snow like gusted sand. Much lower light beams squint my eyes as they scan the windowed west where several heavy transports now crawl on snow treads in the narrow, empty street. Just as quickly, I'm forgotten.

Attentions shift to unfinished drinks and unbuttoned uniforms as the lounging officers and enlisted fighters prepare for unexpected duty. Only Aila's interest lingers with me, still searching for that answer, for whatever trick I've learned that her older sister never did. Her disappointment cuts my pride back down to size.

The large main entry doors kick open with a gust of winter wind, and Aila's small commander steps into view. "Zero Two. On me!" Faye's sharp call gets her unit moving. Magar lifts his explosives belt from the back of his chair and buckles it from left shoulder to right hip as he abandons his meager winnings. Aila drags her scoped magnum from the poker table as though it were any normal sidearm, holstering its twenty-round drum against the magnetized sleeve that wraps her massive thigh.

Wilson Black, Marco Robina, and the Buggs—Chuck and Derek—all rise from their scattered places to convene at the entryway with Faye. And a premonitory chill crawls up our spine just before Taiko Chiba strides in from the gusting cold, completing the unit Zero Two.

Somehow, her swarming eyes are already on me, convicting me to ugly stillness, until I find the strength and cowardice to look down at the floor. Yang finally finishes his daily cigarette, snuffing it dead behind his cards. Danny-boy's already up and moving, with Shankman hot on his heels shouting, "Hey! I was big stack. After Aila. You owe me two vodkas. No, whiskeys!" They're moving toward the southern doors where the hovership came down, where Captain Uba now stands stoic. Without tracing his eyeline, I already know he's looking at Taiko. Always ready to protect her. Or put her down.

While some second lieutenant marches out in front of Uba and starts directing the lower soldiers, I slide from the wooden stool and collect my rifle from the couch. I sneak one last guilty look at Aila, but she's too busy circling up with Zero Two to pay me any mind. They all gather dutifully around Faye, who seems nearly ready to brief them on the cause of this interruption. But only nearly.

Faye looks up at her elite men and women, then down at the hostel floor, then finally back up to all of them, and I notice something jarringly uncommon. In these uncharacteristic eyes of the great Fangs Thompson, I am sensing fear.

The captain has it, too. Not fear, not the exact same eyes as Faye. Just the same bad news, the same serious posture. I see a man reflecting on his career and contemplating all its costs—all those brave faces left behind and sent to hell for his planet's sake. I see him making those choices a thousand times over, another lifetime of active valor without an atom of regret. I see the most impressive human fighter that the Earth has ever known, now forcibly making peace with his own impending death. No, not just that.

He's making peace with all of ours.

3.04

I've never been this far north. At least not on Earth. Not anywhere low enough to feel the weight of all this added gear, nor this persistent, chilling wind against our back. Too perilous and frigid to risk classic chutes or sky legs, so we must walk. The frozen floor tugs at the heels and toes of our thick boots with every trudging step, as though it means to delay us from the forest. A warning maybe. An adjuring icy plea not to venture any closer—to turn away from this boreal trap. The Russian Taiga. The most beautiful torture I've endured.

"Comms check. Hov—Hovership One."

"Good check, Jester. Reading you fine." Sasha comms back from Zero One's hovership, only thirty meters behind us, landed in the flatland beside Zero Two's identical sister craft. His voice is clear and comfortable unlike Shankman's shivering, congested request.

"Good," Shank continues between heavy pants. "Had to know—you'd hear me—when I said—go fuck yourself."

The Bugg twins snigger in delighted surprise. Yang hums that amused single syllable he does so well, a rare agreement from the old man.

"You, too, Robina! You warm fucks!" Shank shouts again.

That one tickles Magar pretty good. Or maybe he's only just finished translating Shank's first gibe.

"Hover Two copies," Marco Robina chuckles back from Zero Two's cockpit at a more reserved and careful volume.

I glance over to Faye, marching at the head of Zero Two's mirrored wedge formation, fifty meters west of Zero One's. Her face is hidden like the rest of ours, sheltered behind a sealed tundra helmet with an anti-fogging visor and ventilated mask. Almost invisible against the matching white and gray backdrop of this vast Siberian biome. Still, I sense disapproval. I see irritation in her every step for these few words uttered without mission cause. I see a single-minded wolverine, disappointed by her playful pups but only mildly, only sparingly, in that five percent of her conscious mind that is still vulnerable to distraction.

I hardly finish that thought before Faye suddenly drops to a knee, rifle raised, only to be mimicked instantaneously, silently by the rest of Zero Two. All sights to eyes in half a second, maybe less. It's a commander-unit sync speed that freezes me in astonishment. A subtle and beautiful testament to the excellence that she demands. To the doubtless, countless hours she's spent honing this esteemed unit, only arbitrarily designated Two.

"Party hold." Uba's calm, commanding voice drops Zero One to our knees, too. We sink twice as deep as I expected, fresh fallen powder brimming halfway up our thigh. I hear Shankman gasp at that same surprise, but he makes no jokes this time around. Even he knows to turn it off when the call to action comes.

But it doesn't yet. We all just hold on bended knee, rifles raised, light snowfall sprinkling down, threatening to add us to its layers. For several minutes we are white statues beneath the dim, cloud-covered sun. Six hunters to the east. Six to the west. Two seated south in comfy cockpits. Two of our very best hidden invisibly far ahead at the forest's edge: Cyrus Uba and his dark shadow, Taiko Chiba, scouting the approach for our safe advance. They're silent to my ears, shrouded by snow to my keen eyes, but somehow Faye dropped before Uba's call came. An intuition I admire but can't explain.

"Okay, Mr. Carter," Uba finally breaks the silence with a cautious whisper. "Cloak and ping exactly there. No lights, no smoke."

"Hover One copies. Pinging party to drone. Logging coordinates."

A shallow, blinking dot appears in all our visor HUDs. A red waypoint marker, 191 meters straight ahead, ten meters high, where Sasha's stealth drone likely hovers. Not far from where Uba and Taiko are probably prone and hidden, nestled in some sniper's nook.

"Party advance. Speed two, with caution."

At Uba's command, we twelve rise to our feet in silence. Colder and stiffer than before but twice as deadly. With weapons raised and barrels fanning east to west to east, we creep careful now. Just like Fangs, our minds are all locked squarely on the task, this world-class assignment we've received.

Four pods tore through this sector late last night when we were celebrating our first deportation, our first vengeance for The Storm. Four all at once and all together. An anomaly without known precedent. A coordinated arrival that brings everything we understand about Luminaran markers and the pods they summon into question. Is it merely chance that they have found us? Nothing beyond the basic logic of our world being hospitable to their species? I sit with Prichard's words, *no great effect without causation.* I try to remember what that reacher said to me in Kansas. That X-3 that almost smeared us. Before he tore apart my mind, he said something about a promise. Or a vow. A vow that he had sworn to—

"The endless others."

I turn sharply at the sound of his clear voice again. No. A woman's voice. It must have been one of *her* whispers. But eerily lucid. A clarity far beyond my G-1's usual sound. An actual female voice inside my head, not just the imagined sensation of one. But the signature felt wrong in some way. Too abrasive. Too impatient. Too young.

"Hayes, you got something?"

"Negative," I comm back to Danny-boy at Zero One's rear. He'd spun with me as soon as my rifle leveled in his direction. But now he turns back forward and sees me signaling a false alarm. "Sorry, just some . . . interference."

I turn forward, now reading 117 meters to Sasha's pinged drone and whatever the captain has located there. I march on again in silence, secretly hoping for her clear voice another time, and wondering why, after all these years, I only heard it so plainly now. But that loose thread tangles with another— that glowing face that keeps calling me back from death. And the bleached husk that keeps casting me into it.

For now, I hold the sweeter version up like a photo, her dazzling brown-golden curls and eyes. I wonder what her song would be if I could hear it—if she even exists. Maybe these lingering confusions from Caitlin Powell's farm are just the first flashes of total insanity, the first symptoms of the inevitable psychosis that killed Anja Hallheim and the rest.

I shake my head and focus forward. Eighty-nine meters

remaining. And some strange mound coming into view just before the tree line. A rounded lump like a boulder buried in the snow. Another to the west of it, out in front of Faye and Zero Two. I see her eyeline now. She's been watching it all this time. It must be what she spotted when she first dropped to that early knee. I flick my eyes northeast and spot a third lump, then a fourth. A thin crackling of red lightning just beyond them. Black Beauty, aimed and ready, straight down the line of all four snowy bumps. Twenty-two meters and now it's clear. Four reacher pods all lined up together. But no scorched crater this time around. No crater at all, just this strange calm and perfect symmetry. Four smooth landings at one very intentional time and place.

A trap most likely. Maybe that's what gave Uba so much pause—that lengthy party hold. But something truer cancels that fear. A vacant sensation I can't quite understand, until she finally *whispers*. Not with the vocal clarity I'd been hoping for but with useful intel, nonetheless. I focus my attention on all four pods. All my genetic senses ask one question, and she answers affirmatively through the haze. All four pods are already *empty*.

3.05

Shankman keeps his voice low, a panicked whisper meant for Yang and Danny-boy. "We should nuke the forest. Or carpet bomb the whole fuckin' thing!" But I hear him clearly on the other side of the empty pods. I hear them all.

Despite their private channels and muted comms, I hear the units murmuring now, shuffling in this last snowy open air before the tree line, splitting off into their friendly pairs and trusted trios while Faye and Uba decide how we'll all respond to this strange find.

"Anything yet, Mr. Robina?"

"Negative," Marco comms back to Uba. "First two klicks seem clear."

"They *seem* clear?" Faye keeps her skeptical eyes on the dense forest straight ahead, twitching slightly as she blinks, as though even that unwatched millisecond is a risky slackening of her guard.

"Affirmative," Marco transmits back. "There's a small pack of wolves due west. Couple bears to the east in a den. Smaller signatures in the trees and underground. Drone's getting some magnetic interference from the mountain. Nothing human yet."

"We're not looking for humans." Faye shakes her head, tapping her heel restlessly against the snow. "We should scatter all the drones, scan the entire sector." She says that not as an order to Marco but as her counsel to the captain, who towers quietly beside her.

He makes one soft, deliberative sound to let her know that she's been heard, but there's no agreement in it yet. He's still carefully sweeping the terrain with his panther eye, wide east to wider west, so slowly he almost seems animatronic. "And what should I make of your silence, Mr. Hayes?" He finally withdraws his hand from his natural eye, blinking it back to life. It settles on me with eerie patience. "Do your instincts call this a trap?"

Faye side-eyes me briefly, deeply, then her attention darts back to the trees. She's clearly annoyed by my presence here, but she's no fool—certainly no stranger to the superiority that stems and skinners can provide.

My attention drifts to Taiko, relatively naked next to us. Just a thick, white ninja hood and matching mask. Sheathed concussive sticks are crisscrossed on her back. Her G-4 suit is active-camoed a snowy white and gray, each miniature synthetic scale and its million nanos shifting smoothly, subtly to the world around it, keeping her hidden, hot, and deadly. The snow quickly melts around her ankles as she gazes vacantly into the distance. A scrawny sculpture. An unliving weapon.

"We spotted four rogues at the cosmodrome," I finally reply to Uba. "Now we find four repurposed pods without any sign of travel gel." I look back to the Taiga, the endless frozen forest, and a curious peace passes through me, a soothing calm almost like a dream of my younger days. I see myself dipping one little finger, sending a single ripple across our glassy lake, and I speak just like *she* whispers. There's no question in my tone because I already know it's true. "This isn't an ambush. It's their home."

Faye turns my way completely, and I see a flicker of something strange. A knowing twitch between her eyebrows. A concealed shadow behind her eyes.

I shake my head to fix myself. The light reflecting off the snow cuts through my visor, stinging my eyes, and that sweet peace of mind is already gone, faded back down. I begin to feel foolish and out of place. "Either way," I continue a bit over eagerly, "at Taiko's burn rate, she won't last out here too long after the sun sets. I've burned through half my solar myself, so whatever we choose, we should do it quickly. Sir."

Faye tenses sharply at that information, flicking her eyes from me to Taiko like I just told her God might call in sick.

Uba simply nods in confirmation—and disappointment. Like he's known all along what must come next. With those same prophetic eyes he had in Svobodny, he takes a good long look at the endless Taiga, finally exhaling long and slow before he makes the day official:

"Mr. Carter. Please send two of your drones to provide escort."

"Hover One copies. Sending now," Sasha comms back.

I hear Shankman's panicked voice again. "Did he say escort? Did he seriously just—"

Yang shushes him, stepping around the dormant pods to get line of sight on the captain. The other few pow-wows disperse and follow suit until all of Zero One and Two are gathered close, watching the captain, awaiting orders. Even Shankman falls in line after one last grumbling curse.

Uba turns his back to the frigid forest. He looks at all of us with a severe message in his stance. At Faye Thompson. At Miles Yang. At Connie Clark and Zayd Aswad. At Chuck Bugg and his brother Derek. At Danny Diaz, Alec Shankman, Magar Volkov, Wilson Black, and Aila Hallheim. He looks at me, then he looks at Taiko. For once, she seems to look right back. In her own robotic way, she seems to sense his mountainous pride—his paternal culpability for her strange fate and all of ours. Then our hero speaks:

"When Mr. Carter's drones arrive, we will be moving in. Our targets are four suspected rogues of unknown class. My orders are to attempt capture. Your orders are to survive. Rifles free."

The beautiful sound of loading rounds and unlatching safeties fills the air. Our enlisted music heats our blood, and Black Beauty crackles red, vaporizing falling snowflakes into skyward mist.

Hearing the captain mutter his Zambian codeword sends me back to this morning's sunrise, back to when we were latched beside each other on that long ride in Hovership One. As the red and orange light beams glinted above the white horizon, I found an unexpected courage to finally ask him why he chose that word and what it means.

"Mapenze," he told me then, after a lengthy, weighted pause, "is the name my wife gave to our son." He looked out to the horizon for a moment, making no effort to contain his contagious heartache. "She nearly died bringing him into this world," he continued in quiet recollection, finally smiling, filling his human eye with staggering joy. "*Trouble*. She named my first son *trouble*."

Watching the captain now, I realize that same joy and heartache is always there, quarreling between each beat in his massive chest. I decide to find more courage on the hovership home, to seek more replies to my rude questions—not just from him but from all these strangers, all these hardened souls who I should know so much better than I do. But the captain's heat continues:

"For the duration of this assignment, I will be resuming sole command. We will be going in the way we started: the single unit, Zero X."

"Hoo-ah," Wilson echoes that fellowship back to Uba in his low, gravelly voice, pumping his old cop shotgun in hot agreement. His custom stellar shells hiss deep in the barrel, adding a harmony to our rough band.

The Buggs mutter their own eager consensus, bumping gloved knuckles down by their waists. Shankman compulsively pats his pocket where he keeps that sexy lighter and a few cigars. Connie taps her visor against Aswad's, but he doesn't tap back immediately, doesn't find her eyes this time. He's somewhere else, some old memory he can't put down.

Sasha's drones glide in above us, too quiet for the others to detect at first, but as they pass overhead to the forest's edge, all eyes rise in anticipation, all but Uba's human left, remaining faithful to the unit.

In that distracted, anxious moment, he asks us the question we've all been waiting for. He asks it low like the first drum of an ancient war. "What are we doing here today?"

"Defending the Earth," we all whisper back, to ourselves more than to each other, sending our varied silent prayers up to our obsolescent gods.

"What have we been doing, from our first breath and beyond our last?"

"Extending humanity," we all grunt back through gritted teeth and tightening asses.

"Then come with me for your planet's sake," the captain growls, with Black Beauty crackling hungrily in front of his hips. "And see for yourself what that honor tastes like." He turns into the woods, prowling beneath the scanning drones, and we all march in rapture behind him—straight through the gates of a frozen hell.

3.06

Suspense is a useful medicine. It widens your ears. Narrows your sight. Makes you ruthless in all the right ways. Ready to fight with fists and teeth. But it's an addictive fix. Turns on you quick if you don't feed it. Becomes the other thing. Not fear; that's useful, too. The other thing. That anxious dread in a soldier's head that gets his siblings killed.

Shank caught it first. Got jumpy two hours ago and shot

an arctic fox. We all peaked together in that mistake, that false alarm. Now we're six hours into the Taiga, and our tight diamond formation has become a crooked rhombus. Our raised rifles have drooped to our waists, and Marco's scout has scanned twelve square kilometers of Russian snow, finding diddly fucking shit.

"Hover One to Zero Leader."

We all flinch at the broken silence—or blink awake in Magar's case. Derek Bugg sleepwalks a few more steps before realizing his brother is no longer beside him, now hanging back with the rest of us.

"Go ahead, Mr. Carter." Uba's response is quick enough, but I'm surprised to hear fatigue behind his voice—a battered sound like readied surrender. His truest believers hear it, too. Clark, Diaz, and Black all slouch deeper beneath their gear, like their only true mission here was to earn some shred of this man's respect. Instead, he's just lost a bit of theirs. And mine.

"Mr. Carter, do you have something?" Uba turns in a semicircle, scanning the vacant, silent woods, hearing no response. "Mr. Carter?" Only silence. Only dread.

"No, sir," Sasha finally comms back. "But you're reaching the—clear comms."

"Mr. Carter, say again."

"The mountain—netic interference. I've al—optics on drone two," Sasha's voice skips in between heavy static.

Uba looks to the lead drone, hovering high and smooth above the unit, before it suddenly dips spasmodically. It course-corrects but never quite returns to center, spinning drunkenly, losing altitude.

Then the captain looks to all of us, and I feel that cutting wrongness once again. His eyes are as alive as they've ever been, his shoulders just as tall. He isn't beaten, not even close. He simply knows the game is up, not because he's reached his limit but because he knows that we've reached ours.

I'm so wrong it fucking stings. A painful pinch behind my eye.

"Alright, Mr. Carter. That is a mission cancel." Uba's words stir a shameful alleviation in half the unit, the perceptive half who understand him. Shankman isn't one of them. He grumbles over comms in clear disdain—an emotional veil if I've ever heard one, an embarrassed misdirect from his own lingering humiliation. That twitchy misfire didn't just murder an innocent fox; it killed whatever chance we had at a surprise attack. And everyone knows it.

"Recall your drones and prep both hovers for cabin camp," Uba comms to Sasha. "We will get some rest and do another sweep in the daylight. Cover the ground we missed."

"Copy that. Drones—" Sasha's voice is lost in the static, but the drones proceed as commanded, trailing a tight guiding line in our HUDs for the long walk back—just over two klicks. Goddamn, it seemed so much further. Though, with a retreating pace, we just might make it before sunset. Those last strands of natural light will be a godsend after this. But it isn't over. We'll be back again tomorrow, starting earlier, moving quicker, leaving no snowy stone unturned. These cold details embitter the sweetness of our escape.

"All rifles hold." Uba's voice is strong and firm as he marches down Zero X's center, establishing a new point at our former rear. "Take five and resupply. Then we go straight back down the line. Speed three for this first klick. After that—"

"Hover Two to Zero Leader." Marco comes in much clearer than Sasha did. Somehow, that doesn't surprise me;

another gold star for Zero Two. "Sorry, sir. Just wanted to say I have a clear LZ eighty meters northwest. You can probably spot it from your position."

I turn to check his heading, seeing only shadowed whiteness and bits of green, the same snowy maze in every direction. But the captain's panther does its work.

"I see it, Mr. Robina." That trademark acknowledgement without agreement can be heard in Uba's voice. After some thought, he shakes his head. Opens his mouth to—

"Scans show it's clear in all directions, three hundred meters," Marco continues. "My scout's there now. Could land Hover Two on top of it in seven minutes if you prefer an evac."

"Thank fuckin' Christ," Shankman exhales in genuine gratitude, before he clocks the furious eyes of Fangs Thompson. She raises a punitive finger, marching viciously in his direction—

But Uba holds her rage with a touch on the shoulder. "Thank you, Mr. Robina." He looks from Shankman to the other beleaguered faces of his unit. He looks at me, then he examines Taiko Chiba as a hunter might his hound.

"Bring Hover Two to new LZ at maximum altitude, cannons hot," Uba commands. "Mission targets are still unaccounted for. We will confirm clear ground before you touch down."

"Copy that, sir. See you in a few."

Various audible and visible reliefs manifest in Zero X at that confirmation. Our lazy rhombus gets even lazier as we redirect northwest, following the captain's bearing.

Amidst the party movement, Faye slips back a few meters into Uba's blind spot, comm locking Shankman in a private channel. It's a struggle to read her lips from this angle, but I catch the important details. *If you—captain again—put you down myself.*

She never looks at Shankman. Never asks if he understands. Just casually steps back into echelon at the captain's right once she's been heard. I see Shank subconsciously rub his visor—right about where his missing eyebrow would be—and I know he'll die in silence before he ever crosses Fangs again.

I can practically feel it. Not just the sound of his racing heartbeat but the sensation. A quickening thump behind my ribs.

I can feel Aswad out in front of him, beginning to cool at Connie's touch, relaxing down to his typical semi-boil. I'm watching him now and he's . . . I'm looking across the formation into his distant, distracted eyes and . . . it must be torture. It must be agonizing to live with such vivid memories of that day.

He loved Tess like she was a piece of him. It didn't matter that they'd been separated before The Storm. It made no difference that she was already moving on, living with that smug architect in his ridiculous condo along the riverwalk. And that marathon Aswad ran. That mad dash from his flatbed truck to the crumbling highway, from that scorched schoolyard to each panicked, scrambling street. All the way to the twisted rubble of his baby sister's new home in Oak Park. There was no hope for Tess, but Shabnam was far enough west for him to pray. Far enough from the flash that she might be okay. The lines were down, but she might be okay. She and Kareem and little Nargis. *Oh God, Nargis! Please God, spare Nargis, if only her. Spare my niece, God, please!* ‏أرجوك! الله يحميها!

I stop cold at the edge of the clearing. The last few stragglers of Zero X continue around me, all heading toward the sunlit center where Uba already waits with Faye and Taiko. The sun reflects intensely from the piled snow, penetrating deep into our scales. It tastes like hot sugar, and I would smile. I would quicken my pace, excited to bask completely in the heat after this long day. I'd do all of that if she wasn't *shouting*. If I had any understanding of where I just was, of how I was just seeing Aswad, or rather *being* Aswad in that twisted daymare of the Chicago Storm. I don't—he's never told me—I've barely spoken to him. But she's still *shouting* at me in that clear voice I've been waiting half the day to hear again, and—

It isn't *her*. That's painfully obvious now. Too emotive and impatient to match the psyche of my suit, if such a sentiment makes sense.

There's also the fact that *she* is whispering, too. My suit and this clearer voice. They're arguing inside me, and the louder one is winning. The one that seems younger. She's shouting, no, she's *demanding* that I—

"*Stay where you are and live.*"

Something bites me behind the eye. I see a cooling color like silent music, and, oh Christ, it's happening again.

"*Step no further, cousin. Stay!*"

I falter beneath the pain, desperately pressing my hand against a tree. It bursts into kindling between my fingers. The clinging ice becomes hot mist before it splashes my grimaced face. But her young voice is even hotter. A cobalt shine inside my skull. A heat that finally makes me scream into the snow.

The captain's panther finds me first. He sees me writhing, staggering against the shattered birch. Just as quickly, he turns away, looking for Marco's drone but seeing nothing, realizing there's nothing. He spins, scanning the tree line in urgent surveillance, as though that useful medicine never left him. Faye, Aila and Danny-boy see me, too, all with confusion and halted faces.

I fall to my knees, holding the ruined tree like my mama's fingers before she left us. That bony skin she slipped between my cradle bars. *Mama.* Where the hell is that coming from? It was just me, Logan, and Daddy. Just me, Logan and—

I'm suddenly wide-eyed at the sight of her. She's rising from that abyss beneath my heart—her bouncing curls, her bright and flawless gold-brown eyes. I'm desperate not to let her fade again. Can't let my mama lose her color. Can't let my only mama die!

"No!" I shake my head, and I can see the trees again. I see my true family in the clearing. I see what's coming for them.

"No, cousin! Stay and—!"

I push the invading voice into the shadows. Push it all down, shaking my brains halfway to jelly, blinking my eyes a hundred times before I manage to unclench my teeth:

"Rifles free!" I slur and spit and shout. "Rifles fucking fr—!"

A sudden cracking stops me. An echoing pop bounces off the mountains then back down to our quiet clearing, quickly followed by a scrunching snowy sound.

The second sound was Wilson dropping to his knees. As though in prayer, he's now gazing so far up to heaven that he's catching snowfall beneath his cheekbones. He's cranked so deeply in worship that he's practically looking backward—so deeply that Aila, standing behind him, is now looking down at his inverted face, seeing his chin jutting above his nostrils. Her reaction changes me forever.

She seems to scream, but my ears cancel it to silence. My eyes have returned to Wilson Black. Everyone's pulling their weapons and going hot, but I'm still stuck on the impossible way that Wilson's giant spine has been wrenched backward; I'm still catching up to that first sound. It was his skeleton snapping itself like a wooden pencil.

 _ Or any icy branch in the unforgiving Russian Taiga.

3.07 ◼— — — ————◼

"All-around! All-around!" Black Beauty crackles red, and its master stands tall in the center of the clearing, panther eye to short scope, scanning the tree line for Wilson's murderer. "Rifles free! All-around, all-around, all-around!" the captain roars again.

Faye kneels first, burying herself in the snow, powder up to her tits, short rifle aimed due north. The twins get down on the other side of Uba, crouching, aiming south and southwest. Shankman bellyflops prone, aiming east in my direction. Yang and Danny-boy kneel on either side of him, southeast and northeast. Magar hunkers down like a boulder on the other side of Faye. He leaves his rifle on his back but pulls two plasma charges from his bandolier, eyes northwest. Connie and Aswad disrupt the pattern, both aiming west together. But that completes the defensive circle, with Uba towering in the center, pivoting with his rail rifle, urgently searching the dense perimeter.

"Aila!"

The giantess snaps out of her trauma, looking quickly to Faye.

"Get Hayes!" Faye points to the east. "Now!"

Aila's anguished eyes flick in my direction, seeing me tremble against the mutilated birch tree, seeing me lift one quivering knee only to collapse deeper into the snow.

That gets her moving, snatching her heavy magnum from her magnetized thigh, charging heroically toward rescue. She's twice as fast as I expected, churning through the fallen snow like a heated plow.

"Covering!" Yang bursts three shots just south of my tree. Danny-boy echoes his action, spraying a few standard rounds to the northeast. Shankman almost fires straight ahead, before he realizes Aila's between his sights.

"Swarm."

Taiko twitches slightly, hearing her call sign on Faye's lips. Despite the din of violence, she hasn't crouched or covered herself. Hasn't shown any sign of consciousness at all.

Faye continues in that steady, trained articulation. Much like Uba's instructions at the cosmodrome, she speaks to Taiko as carefully as she can, as though any misspoken word could mean the end of her own life. "Emergency One."

Taiko draws her concussive sticks so quickly they seem to teleport to her fists. Two chromium alloy poles—delivered personally by Calvin Prichard—with leather grips and diamond tips, painted totally and purely white for this tundra mission. Her G-4 suit ripples and shifts from its snowy camouflage to a bloody battle-red. Her thin legs seem to engorge with added muscle as her feet spread athletically apart.

"Strangers," Faye enunciates. "Terminate. Terminate. Go!"

Aila arrives at my shattered tree two steps slower than Taiko reaches the further, western edge. Then she's gone—vanished into the tree line before all the loose powder she just blasted up can even trickle back to Earth.

"Returning!" Aila shouts over comms, underestimating the weight of my suit, slipping in the snow before she rights herself, wrenching us away from the shattered tree, dragging us backward into the clearing. My rifle wakeboards at the end of its leash. The barrel of Aila's magnum cockslaps my helmet a dozen times. My retreating view of the forest is a rattling, dizzying image, but I'm as thankful as I've ever been to be held in a woman's arms.

Then I learn firsthand what happened to Wilson.

Our left leg suddenly tightens and curls, digging its scaled heel deep into the earth beneath the snow. Aila trips and falls at that unexpected anchoring. Her ass sticks in the powder, and the back of my head lands in her lap.

I preclude her rage with a panicked denial. "It wasn't me!" I tug with my remaining strength, but the mutinous leg stays locked and unresponsive. I look frantically up and back, re-creating that terrible angle Aila just shared with Wilson Black. "I can't move!"

Her frustration melts to understanding. Then to terror. "Matter mover!" She aims her scoped magnum straight over me into the hazy woods. "It's a matter mov—AGH!" Another crack rings out as her magnum and right wrist snap sharply to the right, exposing a bone in the bend of her elbow, ripping her thick jacket and most of her muscular arm in half. Her spasming trigger finger sprays .50 caliber rounds in rapid succession before the intense recoil sends her weapon spinning off into bloodstained snow.

She starts to scream—but she's wrenched backward just like Wilson, pressed deeply into the snow. Half buried, pinned akimbo, she tries to hold me with her strong thighs, before they're both forcibly thrown open, audibly tearing several muscles in her groin.

Like a haunted fetus ripped from the womb, I begin to crawl away—both scaled legs moving powerfully on their own, stepping and dragging our upper body in a freakish crab walk. I try to dig and brake with my free hands, but they're sucked in tightly, telepathically instant-glued across our chest. That painful pinch becomes a furnace behind my eyes, and I shout louder than I ever have. In pain and protest, I wail until my throat is hoarse and raw.

It seems to help. With horrible effort, I lift my neck and head just high enough to see between our marching legs. Suddenly he's there. That first reacher from the cosmodrome. He's standing in plain sight just beyond my shattered birch, still wearing that fur-lined trapper hat. His legs are spread and grounded like a sumo, both arms trembling, straining, reaching forward, psychically commanding our legs to pull us toward him. Even beneath those darkly tinted mountaineers, his eyes are shining brightly, two awesome cobalt flashlights in his skull. But I see something stranger. His chin dips. His mountaineers slip slightly lower on his nose, and for a moment I see that same desperate look that Aila just had. In his strained brow and wrinkling forehead, I see a selfless fear—not the aggression of a capturing combatant but an authentic panic. An allied distress.

Then his head explodes. My tortured birch is splashed in blood and brains. Chunks of skull ping off my visor. The pain ends instantly, our limbs are freed, and all my strength returns. Physically, I mean. Mentally, I'm defenseless, watching helplessly as Taiko now stands behind the slaughtered reacher, drenched in the backsplash of his natural juices. She catches the rogue's collapsing corpse with her left c-stick and raises the other to strike again, ultimately determining that he is sufficiently terminated.

Then she looks at me, and I feel certain. I know that if I breathe, if any atom of my existence moves even slightly in her direction, she will destroy us next. Not because she's wild or chaotic; she certainly isn't. She just happens to be undecided about which we are, native or strange. Friend or target. Her swirling eyes trace over our chest, our anxious, spasming scales, not too unlike her own free-flowing nanos. She keeps watching, waiting for some small aggression. Any sudden fleeing effort. All I can do is nurse the air inside us, hoping our strength can match her speed if she does come.

But her head turns sharply. Some new detection. Some more obvious foe across the clearing. And she's gone in another burst of spraying snow and rustling leaves. Without her support, the slaughtered reacher falls sideways, catching between two stunted trees like an old-century soldier in barbed wire. His blood seeps and drips through his winter clothes, melting narrow holes in the piled snow.

That's when I remember Aila. I turn, scrambling back to her half-buried body. She's flailing awkwardly, trying to right herself with her remaining arm. I knife one hand deep into the snow and find her armpit. Digging my other hand higher, cradling the back of her helmet, I pull her head and torso up out of the powder.

She paws blindly at her compressor valve, so I crank it for her. A blast of hot nitrogen clears her helmet vents from the inside out. Just as quickly, she's sucking fresh air. She gloves snow away from her visor, revealing a damaged, flickering HUD and her crazed eyes behind it. She stares at her dangling right arm for several seconds, and I see shock and misery combining. But not defeat. She keeps moving, fighting through the fire in her groin to twist and search for her lost weapon.

"Aila. Aila, stop." I restrain her as gently as I can. "Just leave it. Leave it, goddammit—" Her eyes find mine and we freeze together.

She's still hyperventilating, and her comms are damaged, but I receive her loud and clear. Written severely across her features, I see the same unanswered question. *How has Emmett Hayes survived inside the skin of his G-1?* Well, now it seems she has a guess. Maybe Anja Hallheim died in the defense of her own mind, in her unrelenting need to remain human. Maybe Emmett Hayes is only here because he didn't—because he had no loyalty to his humanity at all.

Black Beauty screams, and we both look over to the unit. The captain stands motionless, aiming directly over Faye. A scorched hole cuts deeply into the northern tree line. He holds perfectly still for a few more seconds, then resumes breathing, finally lowering his incredible weapon. "They have retreated further north. We are clear."

Nobody seems ready to lower their weapons, except Faye, who stands quickly, looking around at the perimeter. Into her helmet mic, she enunciates in that careful way, "Swarm. Combat cancel. Cancel. Return."

"Taiko has gone after them," Uba sighs, still looking distantly to the north. "They have likely been jamming us from the beginning. From the mountains." He covers his human eye, letting the panther work alone. "She is out of range. Now so are we." I hear that grim prophecy in his voice. That dark knowledge of what comes next.

"Hover Two, Hover One, please acknowledge." Faye tests his hypothesis, exiting the defensive circle, walking south toward the hoverships. "Hover One, Hover Two, do you copy?" She curses at the silence she receives. "We should find Marco's scout. Try to comm lock him."

"It wasn't Marco." I draw most of their eyes with that claim, especially Faye's. "It was a trick. The drone was never here."

"It was an ambush." She keeps her eyes on mine. Makes sure I pick up the blame she's putting down. "That's all I know."

"Can they do that?" Derek asks Chuck, pulling his brother to his feet. "Reach this many of us at once? Even through the Spiders?"

"No way. I think he's saying we got hacked."

"We're too encrypted for a comm hack," Yang chimes in on the twins, swatting snow from his rifle's barrel. "They could never hold the line with that clarity."

"What if we're still in it?" Danny-boy searches the older men's eyes for some assurance. "How do we know we're not still in it?" He turns those nervous eyes to the tree line, losing confidence in this reality.

"She's too far away for that." All the confused faces return to me. "But she can hear us; she could hear me—back in the forest. I didn't want to do this again tomorrow. That's what I was thinking right before she—"

"She?" Connie steps into view beside the captain, holding her rifle at her hip. "You know who did this?" Her inching trigger finger matches the suspicion in her eyes.

And most of the others. Handling their varied weapons with tightening distrust. Looking from Aila's ruined body to the birch tree that I destroyed—too much like that dinner table and those Russian bodyguards in chow hall two. Even Danny-boy's young eyes begin to change. *Say it isn't so*, they seem to whisper. *Please say you aren't a traitor, Sergeant Hayes.*

But labored breathing draws the mob's attention. The deep huffing of a burly man. We all turn and notice Magar. We see him straddling Wilson's twisted corpse in an awkward crouching hug. Hands clenched firmly behind Wilson's broken back, he takes a deep breath in, then wrenches himself, snapping Wilson's spine nearly back into place. He wrenches again, correcting it completely. But the discs are clearly damaged, no longer able to support his tremendous torso. Struggling to balance them both upright, Magar is forced to kneel with Wilson's head and helmet resting against his shoulder.

That's when I realize he is crying. Lightly trembling beneath the weight of his slain comrade, Magar double-taps his visor to mute his comms.

The twins look at each other, then move in unison to help with the body. All three of them tilt Wilson sideways until he rests against the snow. Chuck and Magar start straightening Wilson's legs while Derek quietly digs in his pack, producing a ring of carabiners and tow cables.

Aila taps our shoulder, then gestures upward with her thumb. I lower my head, and she drapes her left arm around my neck. As I look back up, I catch eyes with Connie Clark again. She's the only one still watching me with distaste. But she finally removes her finger from her trigger and comm locks Aswad. Starts grumbling to him as they return to the captain.

In one smooth motion, I stand up with Aila, a returned strength that surprises us both. After some adjustments, she hops on her better leg, allowing the left one to drag through the powder. We hobble together back to our unit in the clearing's center.

Faye meets us there, watching my eyes before she examines Aila's right arm. She searches thoroughly but finds nothing good to say about it. "Well, our position is blown, we can't trust comms, and speed three is off the table. Time to light 'em up." She nods to Magar.

He replies soundlessly, then remembers to double-tap his comms so he can repeat in a throaty voice, "Yes, ma'am." He pulls a distress flare from his bandolier and fingers the ring of the firing pin.

"Wait," the captain speaks, still watching the distant north, finally uncovering his human eye. "I need thirty minutes." He unlatches the ammo clip from Black Beauty and lets it fall to the snow, sizzling, melting straight down to the permafrost like so much hot butter.

Faye doesn't catch his meaning at first. She tenses in alarm as soon as it finds her. "Sir, you can't. If we just wait for the hoverships—"

"Taiko is still burning at Emergency One. And now she has gone into the mountain's shadow." The captain locks in a fresh clip and latches it shut. Never takes his eyes from that spot in the distant north. "I am ordering a party hold for the next thirty minutes—and a full retreat at minute thirty-one. Is that clear?"

Faye almost retorts. But duty outmuscles her compassion. She swallows her heart back into her chest and shows him the hard face that he has trained. "Very clear, sir."

"Then the unit is yours." The captain sets off at speed four, maybe five, without another breath wasted. Straight into the northern wall of trees, rail rifle pumping out in front of his muscular chest, bounding with the speed and dexterity of a younger man half his size, another fated hunt begins for the Zambian, Cyrus Uba.

"Stop! No, Zayd—" Connie can't restrain Aswad.

He shrugs her off to chase after the captain. That old blood-lust chooses for him—the crushed, irretrievable faces of his older sister and little Nargis.

Faye lets him go without a word, accepting the futility, it seems—not wanting to see her first official orders go ignored. Or maybe living vicariously. Allowing Aswad's bold insubordination as a loophole to her own unwavering vows.

But Connie's eyes find mine again, and I see that accusation still strung between us. *What's it gonna be, skinner? Who the fuck do you choose now?*

Somehow, I'm still hesitating to decide, still scouring my enhanced mind for any source to match that voice, that brash and youthful woman who begged me to stay out of the clearing, that distant telepath who called me *cousin*.

A sudden theory flashes behind my eyes. My recent memory. A quarter profile in a crowd, seen from a high and swaying vantage. A convincingly human rogue with black-blue-silver hair. A woman I would've killed if not for some instinctive hesitation. Seemed lucky in the moment. Damning now—to Wilson Black and any case in my defense.

Even before Connie chases Aswad—as I know she will and must—I decide I'm coming with her. Not to acquit myself. Not to find a better answer to Aila's scary guess. For something just as selfish but not nearly half as sane.

For a sudden need to know if that young woman has a name.

 **3.08**

28:20. We've been running for a hundred seconds, and Connie's just starting to slow down. I was impressed at sixty, but we could still hear Shank, Yang, and Danny-boy arguing then, urgently seeking consensus. To keep Zero One together. To not abandon the captain. But Shank's self-preservation and Yang's quiet wisdom kept the trio in the clearing where they were certainly needed more, where Faye would have kept them by force, I don't doubt. She allowed Aswad's escape and somewhat understood Connie's, but my desertion chafed her raw. I could hear her molars grinding together as she watched the unit's only remaining gunsuit vanish into enemy terrain.

Checking my HUD again, I read *27:51.* All the voices in the clearing have skipped and stuttered out of range, so only Connie's heavy panting fills my comms. She's almost spent. And her signal is thinning, too. The closer we get to these ominous mountains, the denser this haze becomes—this thickening fog of weightless snow that loves to cling and hates to melt, adding more weight to every step, stiffening all the places we need to bend. Blocking out the sun.

It's fifteen degrees colder than it was in the clearing, and my solar is dangerously low. *27:37.* Connie stumbles and catches herself against a tree. Her thick tundra coat snags on a broken branch, gashing open below her left elbow. She finally stops. Hyperventilates there. Wastes no air on words to me.

I respect her silence, working to catch my breath as well. But I do take a few cautious steps toward her, just to make sure she hasn't punctured her inner lining. If she goes hypothermic out here, there's nothing I can do to save her. Nothing that she'd enjoy.

The tear seems non-critical, but something else draws my focus. Another broken branch. Lower. On the northern side of the trunk. Doesn't seem possible for Connie's collision to have caused it. Curious, I step around the tree, leaving the deep foot trail that Taiko, Uba, and Aswad have left behind them. My rifle whips instinctively to my eye. But I hold my fire, beginning to see the scene for what it is.

One-third of a reacher corpse—everything from the right hip to left shoulder, as though an explosion ripped it diagonally in half. I look a bit further north, spotting a left arm and half-buried legs, strewn as though its bottom portion ran a few steps further after the sudden separation. The splatter pattern of blood and ruptured innards tells the same story. Further north, I see the cause.

A pretty hole where the large rail slug continued. Several perforated trees in its ongoing path. That single shot the captain fired from the clearing.

I turn back that way, gazing through the dense haze and endless trees, barely able to believe it. Even with his panther eye's thermals and active tracking, this was a shot beyond world class. It's the sort of precision I might expect from my simmed cannon in zero-g but not from a human being standing in falling snow. I begin to wonder if we can even be useful here, if we aren't just adding to the dead weight that Cyrus Uba will need to carry.

Connie startles me from that image as she scrambles into view. She glares with horror at the exterminated reacher—another one of the rogues from the cosmodrome. Recognizing that, she sighs in relief. She must've thought it was Aswad, killed and mutilated before she could kick his ass herself. She seems to shiver at that possibility, or more likely from the breach in her winter gear.

"We should turn back." I brace for some rude retort, but she doesn't turn around. She's still piecing together the scene, going through the same astonishment I just did. "Connie. Hey." I wave my hand to win her attention. "You're losing heat, we can't—"

Her mouth says "What?" but I only hear ugly static, badly delayed.

"Fuck." I tap my helmet, bringing up my HUD. I swipe down through the menu, clicking through the warning text for the hailing speakers before I engage them: "YOUR SUIT."

She recoils as I bullhorn her from a meter away. Her eyes dart around nervously as she cusses me out in garbled static.

I go back to my helmet, scrolling the volume down to ten percent, then I try again. "You have a tear." I point to her elbow.

My voice projects much more naturally now. "And my solar is dive bombing. We need to—"

She waves for me to shut the hell up. But she checks her elbow and sees the dangling flap of her outer lining. Feels the jagged hole with her gloved finger.

I scroll down to five percent and step in closer, almost visor to visor. "If we go much further, we'll be the ones who need rescuing." She's not ready to believe that, but she doesn't disagree. Her eyes drift beyond the reacher carcass, gazing deep into the hazy woods and the interfering mountains high above. I follow her eyes, dropping my voice to a low whisper, "If the captain can't protect Zayd, neither can we."

I was trying to be judicious. Empathetic. But when Connie shows me her eyes, I see nothing but contempt. She looks us up and down like misallocated funds, like just about anyone could've made better use of a G-1 gunsuit than Emmett fuckin' Hayes.

But rifle fire distracts us both. Our eyes snap north, following the sound, searching for proof of what we just heard. We don't wait long. A second burst rattles off, faintly visible through the mist. It's the rapid flicker of a flashing muzzle— about a hundred meters deeper into the forest. *25:41.* I look from our synchronized countdown back to Connie, both of us breathless once again.

3.09

I put our back to another birch tree, sucking hard through my nose, blowing air from my mouth. The tree isn't wide enough for total cover, so I twist sideways, pressing our left shoulder against the trunk. Connie mirrors us at her own tree, a few paces east, facing west. We only sprinted eighty meters, but the haze is already twice as thick. I can't see anything on the other side of her—an impenetrable wall of fog, getting dimmer by the minute.

She peeks quickly around her tree, rifle raised, searching the immediate area north. Whoever that was, the firing's stopped. But the last burst was close, maybe fifteen meters from this spot. Connie slips back behind cover, glaring at me, urgently tapping her visor.

"Shit—" I double tap my helmet to disable the hailing speakers. My weighted breaths quit bouncing off the trees, and the haze regains its silence.

Connie slowly peeks again, exposing just the edge of her right eye. Her rifle dangles freely on its leash, allowing her arms some needed rest. It's off-putting, watching her breathe so heavily but only hearing my own gasps. It's like that old film— the one where those three kids are tormented in the woods, where the camera's too slow to catch the ghost, but the director's nostrils get an entire scene.

Connie finds my eyes. She nods due north. Then shows me ox horns, spreading her index and pinky fingers, twisting her wrist sharply several times.

I nod, touching my thumb and index finger in a circle, *understood*. Then I twist away, pressing our back against the tree to show I'm ready.

She does the same, closing her eyes, controlling her breathing the way we trained—in through her nose and out her mouth, putting that anti-fogging visor to the test. Her helmet seems to tap forward, as though knocking ritually against Aswad's. Then she finds my eyes again and starts a count on her gloved fingers: Three . . . Two . . . One . . .

On zero, she spins to her left, and I spin to my right around the tree, fanning out northwest to cover this half of the perimeter, rifle raised and tracking, searching for Aswad or whoever he's engaged with. Connie quickly vanishes from my peripheral as she covers her opposite half to the northeast.

Then I'm alone.

My breath sounds even louder, bouncing off my visor to my ears. The snow is much deeper than it was in the sun. It reminds me of that shoreline I abandoned—those knee-deep shallows on Shiloh Lake. It's strange, I can barely see it now. I can see anything, any trivial moment from the past seven years; with *her* help, I'm practically eidetic. But when I search the years before we merged, my human limits fog the way—a thousand shrinking glimpses at my own history, nothing more. My first friends: Rosey, Abbie, Earl. Grandma Logan in the farmhouse kitchen, shucking sorghum, spitting her wise mysteries in my direction. I see Mr. Womack and Ugly Eddy. I see my daddy on that shoreline, making Shiloh red with his own water, dying for some desperate family that was nothing like his own.

I stop right there, suddenly more confused than I began. *Some desperate family.* I can't make sense of that thought at all. The reachers killed my daddy. Shot and drowned him on his own land. I'm the one who found him. Found that whole battlefield played out. But why did I just . . . how come when I think back to that bad summer Sunday, I can't ever seem to—

Fuck. The harder I strain the more my skull begins to throb. My vision blurs and my rifle droops, so I shake my head to stir it up. I try to force that confusion down, but it sticks in my throat again. Goddamn, I'm gonna be sick. I'm about to spray the inside of my helmet when—

A rifle burst rattles my eardrums, dropping us instinctively to the powder. It's the loudest gunfire I've ever heard. Right on top of us or right behind. I spin back south, seeing nothing, feeling all that nausea get cooked away by a lucky eruption of epinephrine. I spin frantically east to check Connie's line. Nothing. Just snow and silence in every direction. Just my hot breath and screaming mind.

Then another burst of standard rounds cuts through the trees where we were standing, sprinkling spruce needles on my helmet like citrusy matches. Shit. We're being fired on. I aim my rifle east, finding the trigger, searching for—

Aswad comes sprinting through the trees with his rifle raised, not aiming quite where we were standing but further north. He doesn't even see us in the snow, eyes locked hungrily on some other target. He fires another burst then curls his lips in a frustrated cuss; garbled static fills my comms a moment later. But he's already chasing, boots stomping right past us, missing my outstretched hand by a finger's length.

"Aswad!" I call after him, clambering back to our feet. "Aswad!"

If he hears me, he doesn't care. Too locked in on a potential kill. Too crazed by that activated thirst, that desperate need to avenge his kin. He fires wildly from his hip, not even slowing to take aim, making a rude waste of all those months of special training.

I double tap my helmet, resetting my hailing speakers to maximum volume. "CONNIE, I FOUND HIM. DUE NORTH! DUE NORTH!" I swipe twice left and engage my fog lights, turning the beam east in her general direction, shaking my head to make it flicker and scatter. Then I look forward, illuminating Aswad's back, terrified to lose him again. He's surprisingly fast, but we're still faster, gaining ground with every step.

She *whispers* to me, warning that our solar has hit reserves. But I have to catch him. *19:59*. If I catch him now, we can still make it back to the clearing with time to spare. Connie will go back if we have Aswad. If I can stop him, then we'll be okay. The captain can handle Taiko without our—

"Shut off the light!"

That young woman's voice shakes my bones from skull to chest. Louder than it's been all mission. Twice as urgent, laced with dread.

"Shut off the light, he's trying to—"

Two things happen simultaneously. Two impossible instants I may never speak of again. The young woman *screams* inside my head, and I feel the reason from a distance. I feel the knife as though I was its victim, all eight and a half inches of that Nepalese kukri plunging through our heart and out our back. Stopping us mid-sprint as that hateful Earthman surprises us, lunges from his hidden place in the tree to our blind left. We look there, directly into Aswad's eyes, narrowly visible between the disguising snow he wears from helmet to boot. A terribly clever and patient trap. She *screams* in sorrow from somewhere further north I can almost see. Somewhere high in an altered tree. She *screams* in anguish as her beloved man violently dies under her command. Then she pushes me out—

—and I'm back in our body, a few meters south, down on our knees, watching Aswad die. But it's not Aswad anymore. It's that third reacher rogue from the cosmodrome. I've been caught in some telepathic lure, chasing him unwittingly, following him north toward those strange mountains. Toward wherever she's been waiting. That young woman. Not a human. Not a prisoner to them at all. Their leader. Somehow, I know that now. I felt it in the one who died, in his remorse as he passed on, in his failure to keep his vow.

Because Aswad, the true Aswad, has just abruptly stopped him in classic fashion. With some effort, he now pulls his custom knife from the reacher's chest and lets him fall, blood spraying, steaming, and freezing into little rubies atop the snow. Regrettably, I look down. I feel the twist of a blade in our heart as well, finally realizing why the reacher was able to move so fast, why even *we* were struggling to keep up. He looks my age, maybe younger, a similar build inside much more tattered winter clothes. All that rifle fire. It was part of the illusion.

This dead rogue is clearly unarmed.

 **3.10**

My rifle glistens in my fog lights. It's wet and reflective from collected powder, dappling white and whiter in the constant downpour. I'm down on folded knees, staring vacantly at all this steel, aluminum, and reinforced plastic in our lap, repeating the same question for the tenth or ten thousandth time. Why are my pockets packed with incendiaries, concussive pellets, armor piercers—why did Mike, Bryce, and Jakey get roasted in solar flames—why did Anja rip out her fuckin' eyes—why did my daddy die outside the crooked shack where he was raised, if I wasn't meant to make it right?

Even when my fists pushed those two Russians into hell, I was a bystander. A spectator to my own friendly fire, just like I always was in that orbiting gun, that cozy womb of surrogate slaughter. Why the fuck is that? Why weren't Grandma Logan's screams enough? Why am I so fixated on Daddy's death but so unsatisfied by this revenge, so immobilized by all the fighting I've seen today?

Aswad's continued plundering finally stirs me. I slowly lift my eyes in his direction, causing my fog lights to cast a humid spotlight on his crimes. He pauses his search of the reacher's corpse to look at me. I expect irritation, but I see refractory eyes instead, a frenzied mind returning to Earth, searching for beauty, seeing none. I see a man who's shot his load and now must live with it. And so he does.

Aswad shifts his stance to make better use of my helmet light. He twists a pair of tinted mountaineers in the foggy glow before he pockets them in his coat. Might as well. The reacher's eyes have lost their shine. And it's almost funny. I've logged a hundred skins, seen dozens of them ragdoll through the vacuum of frozen space, but I've never been this close. Never had so much trouble spotting the difference between this species and my own.

I lift one hand from my glistening rifle to tap my helmet and slide my HUD. The fog lights quit. I mute my comms. *16:12* on the captain's countdown. I close my eyes and search behind them for that golden woman's face. Mama. I'm beginning to find solace in that chance, that orphan's fantasy that I might not be alone. But I see dark flashes in her stead.

A streaking blackness, laced with blue and silver strands. A dashing shape, cutting through the wind. Closer now but more obscured. Blinded by a corrupted rage.

Aswad's kukri hisses free from its rear sheath, and my eyes come open. He's pointing into the northern shadows with sudden alarm. The other hand is finding his rifle, lifting it quietly from the snow, using his crouched hip to align a shot on the shadowed spruce trees—where a second footfall just landed audibly. Or maybe just another unlucky fox. To my ears, it sounded small. More like something tossed or—

Connie completes that thought with stealthy steel. Not arriving from the north but the southeast, pressing her hard muzzle against my helmet, behind the ear.

"Ah-ah," she halts Aswad and me both, her voice projecting lightly through her hailers. Crouching low, she nudges my helmet so Aswad can see her angle. A clear line from me to him. "I've got piercers loaded. Don't make me waste them."

Aswad's lips say something nasty, but I only hear that garbled static.

"Drop the hardware and try again," Connie says flatly, no trust in her voice.

Annoyed, Aswad drops the rifle and his knife. He taps his helmet, adjusting his hailer volume as he speaks. "—HAPPY, YOU CRAzy bitch. Point that shit somewhere else, I already smeared it."

Connie pauses but doesn't shift at all toward the lifeless reacher, refusing his bait, if that's what it was. "Hayes, are your hailers still on?"

I shake my head slowly, grazing my helmet side to side against her muzzle.

She cusses, pausing to think for a moment. "Defending the Earth."

"Extending fucking humanity," Aswad responds with a sardonic laugh.

"Call sign."

"Edge."

"And his."

"What difference does it make?" Aswad gesticulates fearlessly, aggressively in her direction. "If I'm a reacher, if I'm already in your head, then—"

"Where'd your sister die?"

All the energy leaves Aswad's eyes. He stares at her in disbelief.

"How old would her daughter be today?"

Aswad makes a sound I've never heard before, a sort of gasping choke. He looks at me. Then back to Connie with trembling eyes, betrayal contorting grief.

"Daydream, stand up right now."

She steps back, and I hop up to our feet.

"Sit back down—stand up—three jumping jacks, double time."

Her Spider *whispers*, and I comply each time without delay. In my numbed state, I hardly feel the humiliation.

Soon as it's over, she steps around and looks me in the eyes. Still faintly skeptical, she finally nods. Lowers her rifle then approaches Aswad. "Sorry, I had to be—"

He swats her helping hand away. Keeps his eyes low and distant as he slowly collects his weapons from the snow and rises to his feet. He finally scrapes the camouflaging ice from his visor, allowing Connie to see his full, disappointed face. I see the end of something beautiful. A wartime partnership destroyed.

But their moment is interrupted by another encroaching sound—from the north again, which rightly stirs some paranoia. They both turn their weapons in that direction, but their eyes keep darting to other patches of darkness, expecting the same trick.

"Hayes, you got rear?" I hear fear in Connie's voice as she tries to swap out her armor piercers but drops the more ample standard cartridge in the snow. "Shit. Hayes do you—" she throws a glance over her shoulder, and to her horror, my rifle is still dangling low on its leash down by our hip.

But I feel none of her distress.

Another sound from the north, and her eyes snap forward. Aswad drops to a knee and lifts his short scope to his eye—broken heart already forgotten, replaced by the heat of another chance to honor Nargis, Shabnam, Kareem, and his beloved Tess. Another savage compensation for their lost lifetimes.

But my ears are better than theirs.

The approaching footsteps are way too heavy, moving way too fast. No hesitation, no wasted effort to look back. A frightening confidence, to be sure, but I sense a familiar absence there as well. A distorted strangeness above the snow. Just like those last few moments in The Hole, just like when Connie snuck up on us moments ago, I'm detecting an empty gap in the stream of life. A massive gap to match its man.

"WHAT ARE YOU DOING HERE?" the captain hails us at full volume, sounding more winded than I've ever heard him. And for good reason. Taiko's ass and dangling legs swing left to right as Uba jogs up to meet us. Her limp body is strewn over his left shoulder, held in place by his curled left arm. Black Beauty is cradled in his right, still crackling red. "KEEP YOUR RIFLES UP," he says with urgency to Aswad and Connie, canceling their relaxing trigger fingers, spiking their nerves with added confusion.

"Captain, we—I came to—"

"NEVERMIND," he interrupts Aswad then hastily tosses Taiko down.

She lands in the snow like a crash test dummy, head lilting sideways. Her ninja hood is torn, and her mask is gone, allowing her short black hair to cascade over her cheekbones. Her eyes hang open, ostensibly dead, but still swirling with that eerie nanotechnic life. The left corner of her mouth twitches intermittently, robotically. Without moving her head, both of her white pupils flick sharply up to mine.

"SHE IS DEPLETED." Uba spins back north the way he came, unlatching and dropping another sizzling ammo clip into the snow. He pulls a fresh one from his belt and handles it with some ceremony. As though it's his last. Then he pops the clip in and assumes that same stance from the clearing. Tall and breathless. So still he almost vanishes in the snowstorm. His human eye falls shut, and the panther settles in behind its scope. "EDGE AND CROWN. ON LINE."

Aswad hurries eagerly forward. Connie hesitates, then grits her teeth and falls in line. She takes a knee at Uba's right while Aswad does the same on Uba's left, all three of them aiming due north into the deepest shadow of the mountain.

"MR. HAYES."

I twitch free of Taiko's half-dead eyes. I begin to realize how hard I've been breathing, how heavy my rifle now feels as it hangs around our weakening shoulders, our own solar reserves also dangerously low.

"EYES UP IF YOU CAN." Uba nods upward to the dense tangle of northern leaves and branches between us and the mountain's peak—as though expecting some organized horde of monkeys to come raining down upon us.

"Sir?" Connie asks without following his upward gesture, without daring to take her eye from her scope. "How many are coming?"

9:57. And the captain breathes in deeply, like that grim prophecy has finally come, that fated doom he must bravely abide. With that same dark weight and a tightening grip, his amplified breath rolls through the hailers:

"JUST ONE."

 **3.11**

It comes on quick this time. The other thing. The coiled dread beyond suspense. It's between my knuckles. It's slithering angrily down my throat. And I notice something. The source, I guess. The driving force behind this chill. It's nothing solid, just the expanding lack of something else. A vindictive silence closing in.

KRA-KOOM! A bolt of lightning strikes just east of our position, flashing the entire forest in a scorching whiteness. Every snowflake comes alive, an endless wall of hanging powder.

"EYES FORWARD," Uba corrects all three of us, somehow not flinching at all himself, paying no attention to the smoking tree nor the rising smell of a nascent brushfire.

RATTA-TAT-TAT! Someone fires a rifle due south, maybe all the way back at the clearing. A panicked deer dashes from the same direction, then another huge explosion flinches all our shoulders to our ears, heating our necks with its rolling wave.

"EYES FORWARD!" Uba shouts this time, shaking his head slightly, blinking his panther eye.

I mimic his twitchy movements, and the deer seems to flicker in and out of existence like an old computer glitch. A veritable stutter in the simulation. Soon as I realize what that means—what's really happening—it all stops dead.

All the new sounds and stimuli vanish, sucking us back to that chilling quiet. Connie taps her helmet to re-engage her hailers. She taps it again, and again, more agitated each time. The red occipital light flickers as though her voice is being detected, but the hailing speakers seem to be failing; she's not hearing herself. Neither am I—not even her muffled voice inside the helmet. She turns to Uba, then even further to Aswad, and I realize she isn't speaking. She is shouting. Not hearing herself at all.

I try a loud humming sound, not hearing myself either, not even feeling the vibration in my bones. When I inhale, there's no sense of expanding lungs, no sensation of air passing over my tongue. It's as though my mechanosensations have been rewired, a selective brain-change to engineer the perfect silence.

And there's that chill again. Not a shift in temperature but disposition, as though the trees intend us harm. I quickly scan the higher branches, seeing none of the vicious monkeys I expected—only swaying icy fingers, releasing generous handfuls of particulate diamond dust. That beautiful visual has no competing senses to dilute it. I should be terrified, but I can't seem to look away. Can't seem to shake the feeling that something magnificent is there. Right there just out of view. I shake my head slightly. I blink my eyes.

The rogue woman seizes in midair.

She lands hard in the next high perch, looking stunned, staring down at me through those thick mountaineers, her bright eyes negating their deep black tint, her anguished snarl already fading. Her hair is sweaty, tangled, unkempt, as it dances in the last strands of dusky light. The silvery color is illusory; I see that now. Just a reflection from the deepest blacks. But the blue is very real—an otherworldly heat at the cellular level, that same cobalt zeal most reachers keep in their eyes. Her eyes. It's like we're standing nose to nose—like the two of us are tethered across space and time.

That's when the captain starts to move.

His hips, shoulders, arms, hands and panther eye all shift together, guiding his great crackling rifle to the same patch of swaying branches he had asked me to observe. That's when I realize what I've done. The perfect silence is interrupted for half a heartbeat, just one split instant where the rogue woman seems to *gasp* between my ears. Like she's inside me. Like we are one.

Then the perch is gone. Blasted to splinters in a burst of white and red—a gory spray almost identical to the X-3 in that Kansas crater. Black Beauty's heavy slug is chased into the sky by its electric, piercing scream. The psychic deafening has lifted.

But the world seems quieter than I remember, hardly alive outside the passive breath of wind, uneventful besides the distant sound of tumbling lumber: the top half of the shattered tree is crashing down through its brothers' branches, escorted by a falling corpse—one headless rogue who'd seemed so human, who'd called me cousin not long ago. *7:17* on the captain's timer, and Connie's hailers are working now. Her heart is thumping in her neck. Aswad is cussing in crude, delicious joy. But all I hear is the faint and pitiful crunch of snow as my blue mystery hits the Earth.

 **3.12**

The captain watches the woman's body until all the blood has quit completely—one congealing, frozen puddle where her skull is supposed to be. A lower jaw and a few shattered teeth.

The top few discs of an exposed spine, jutting up like barbe-cued ribs.

His panther eye blinks once when he's seen enough.

He says, "Mapenze," and Black Beauty finally rests, pow-ering down to her standby white, crackling low like a fading campfire. Stepping forward, Uba clamps the heavy rail rifle to the sturdy loops on his body holster. He lets it hang there on his chest, barrel angled up over his shoulder. He kneels. Delicately parts the flaps of the woman's slate-gray duster coat, reveal-ing two kunai throwing knives in stacked pockets on her right thigh. A shock baton on her left hip.

Aswad scoffs, disappointed, but he swallows whatever epi-thets he's been brewing, respecting Uba's continued silence. It's a stillness that seemed like caution to me at first. But stand-ing on the captain's left, I see something new in his human eye. It's the same misgiving I've been stirring since the encounter on Caitlin Powell's farm.

He reaches to the rogue's right hand, turning it palm-up. She's wearing a heavy-duty climber's glove, with sharp, angled claws jutting down below each padded finger. Bits of tree bark and ice are still trapped between them. I shiver at the alternate timeline where she caught us in that perfect silence, where those jagged claws found purchase in our throats.

"Sir," Connie's nervous voice intrudes on his forensics. "Five minutes. Until Faye sends up the flare." She clears her throat and averts her eyes, apologizing for stating the obvious.

The captain says nothing. He simply turns the slain wom-an's wrist back over then lifts her heavy sleeve. Just an inch above her glove. Just enough to see some unsullied skin. And he stops sharply. He sees that creamy beige-brown that I remember from the cosmodrome, that sweet complexion like milky tea in the morning sunlight—the living color only humans should possess.

Uba maintains that thoughtful distance, that gap between his training and these unfolding consequences, between his sworn duty and this scary answer to the question: *Which side of history is this?*

Aswad's view of the woman is blocked. And, in the captain's shadow, in this dim light, Connie doesn't seem to believe what her eyes are suggesting.

Uba brings the sleeve back down before she can be convinced. He returns to his feet just as quickly. Wordlessly sets off marching back toward the incapacitated Taiko. Connie watches the corpse a moment longer. Then she searches for Aswad's eyes but finds only their stubborn edges—an unforgiving jawline. She masks her disappointment well. Makes it my fault somehow, scowling derisively before she turns to follow the captain.

Aswad lingers with the corpse. With plundering eyes, he's now studying the thin kunai knives on the woman's leg. But something about my posture stops him. After an awkward beat, he spits derisively instead. Kicks bloody snow onto her chest. Walks right over her sprawled ankles like woodland garbage.

I can't seem to move in any direction just yet.

She *whispers*, and I know that our solar reserves are nearing zero. Not because I can understand her—she's so dim and faded now—but because our joints are terribly stiff. Because for once I'm feeling how heavy she really is, a far thicker skin on top of my own, compounded by the added weight of this ZA snow gear and this heavy thing still hanging around my neck— this UT rifle I never use. Not like that spares me. The captain pulled the trigger, but I'm the one who killed this woman. I killed that X-3 in Caitlin's crater. I killed that incredible matter mover back in the clearing. I stood in meek complicity, watching Kible Thexx AnSorin be launched off into the black beyond. Our greatest enemy. An old man who could barely lift his head.

All for my pride. For this bad marathon that used to make such perfect sense. And why shouldn't it anymore? They killed my daddy, didn't they? I can still see him draining into Shiloh. Draining and drowned down by the shore. I can hear Logan coming up the trail, demanding answers I don't have. I can feel the Marlin in my grip. I . . . I can feel the 336, but it isn't loaded anymore. It's been fired twice already. Was it me? Did I hit Daddy? Did I friendly fire on Mr. Womack, on Rosey Hall or Abbie Ferras? Weren't they just here with me? Didn't Rosey promise me that he was coming back?!

She *whispers*, but I'm too sick to make sense of it. Too busy spinning in my own head. She *fights* for my attention. Flashes little red spots behind my eyes. Pinches me in a few tender places. Soon as I flinch at that discomfort, she starts *whispering* again, forcing one simple concept into center view.

One urgent pointed finger—just like Logan's gospel dance. When grandma thought no one was watching, when I was hidden in the hayloft, looking down through the kitchen window, she'd swim her shoulders side to side and wiggle one finger straight up to Jesus.

Straight up, she interrupts. *Yes*—in urgent repetition. It reminds me of that first warning. That last rumbling moment just before the passenger shuttle cleared lower atmosphere over Old Dallas.

I spin around to look behind us—way too late—just in time to see a figure coming down. A silent specter already midswing. A dark assassin in a heavy duster coat. She cuts with that entire force, her full weight focused along the obsidian edge of her flashing blade—a dao broadsword or something like it—an inky black Chinese sabre with a cobalt-blue leather grip, now painted red.

Her jet-black hair is shimmering brighter than before, lit like an ocean galaxy aflame, the electric zeal of another world. She rolls through her slashing attack, stopping on one knee, heaving in exhaustion and impossible silence, sweat dripping from the thick, cauterized gash carved through her half-balaclava, left cheekbone, and dish-like reacher ear—a horrid wound about the thickness of a passing rail rifle slug. A narrow miss.

And without a sound, without any thud or sudden scrunch of compressing snow, two blood-spraying halves of Zayd Aswad land in the powder.

 **3.13**

I've been impressed by Prichard's tech. Amazed, honestly. His stealthy suits and jamming chips can make an entire unit disappear. Their very souls seem whited out, erased like ghosts. But that erasure leaves a trail. Unnatural gaps in open air. A stifled flow of life. I've been amazed by Prichard's tech, but now I'm seeing how conspicuous it really is. Another amateur impression. A stolen craft that lacks a master's touch.

Aswad is as dead as anyone's ever been. But I'm still hearing his unbroken footsteps in the snow. His steps exactly. That same slow and heavy crunch to match his distant, brooding mind. His rambling muttered cusses, mixing English and Arabic. That subtle, characteristic wiggle of his kukri sheath scratching against the lower back of his tundra suit. I'm half convinced we're being haunted, that his dark spirit is passing on. The other half of me sees the woman—a lethal artist hard at work.

But something's off. She's not camouflaging herself. Not bothering to hide the gory evidence of Aswad. I can see how heavily, noiselessly, she is sucking at the air, not catching her breath but losing it. I glance behind me, noticing that her illusory corpse and puddled blood are already juddering like that deer—in and out of view until the entire mess vanishes completely, leaving only pristine snow.

That's when I finally hear her voice. Just one agonized gasp as her bright eyes flicker black, and she loses consciousness.

Just for an instant.

She catches herself halfway down, one clawed glove digging into the powder, already soundless on impact. She's already resumed Aswad's ghostly footsteps within our human minds. But that instant was enough.

The captain turns, unsuspiciously at first, seeing Connie still walking toward him as expected. Then he sees an empty gap where Aswad should be—where his ears are still reporting Aswad's weighty, knife-wielding approach.

His false eye speeds up, dashing across the entire scene, and Cyrus Uba finally sees something that he cannot comprehend. Not the bisected corpse of his renowned Army Specialist. Not the pigmented reacher with natural hair, rising laboriously to her feet. Certainly not me, standing stupidly at our unprotected rear. The incomprehensible thing the captain sees is the pristine snow behind me, the missing kill that he'd confirmed himself—the first lie his trusted panther eye has ever told him.

I see his perspective shift from that false eye to his human left. I hear our shared ethical dilemma being answered in his heart, the name of his first son jumping out between his lips. And, in one flashing, practiced movement, I see Black Beauty crackling red and falling free from its body holster into the captain's ready arms.

Just as fast, the reacher woman drops her illusions. Her eyes dim as she darts behind Connie in full and sudden volume. I hear a wildness in her breath, a corrupting rage set free again.

"Down!" the captain shouts.

But Connie doesn't move. She's frozen mid-turn, staring at the wild woman who was so clearly decapitated a moment ago, the charging reacher rogue who is now drenched in Aswad's blood, swinging something sharp and shiny directly at her face.

The woman's swinging blade shatters into a hundred pieces, and Black Beauty screams in satisfaction. Connie's visor shatters, too, blasted to bits by the miniature sonic boom that Uba's rail slug dragged behind it, one millimeter away from giving her and the reacher woman a matching scar. Instead, Connie gets many custom ones as her eyes and face catch bulleting shards of broken glass. She goes down shrieking, clutching at her ruined helmet as negative-twenty-degree winds rush in to kiss her shrapnel wounds.

But the captain spared her a certain death. The reacher woman's bladeless hilt swings harmlessly past Connie's throat. She drops it as she rolls through that attack, skidding onto her hip, clenching her tremoring sword hand, badly stunned by the shockwave of Uba's slug. But the sound of sizzling snow draws her eyes back to the enemy. Uba's spent ammo clip burrows into the powder at his feet as he reaches to his belt for a reload—then remembers that was his last.

Time halts between him and the woman.

Connie goes on grunting, lurching in blinded agony behind the rogue, and Taiko still lies behind Uba, robotically blinking now and then to keep her swirling corneas from freezing over, but the remaining combatants are holding still. With ten meters and one human eye between them, they seem to sign a contract. A pact in blood for those they've failed.

Her right hand flashes to the lower kunai on her hip—

Black Beauty falls, burying itself in the snow—

She's on her feet, darting to her right—

Uba reaches behind his back, finding his sidearm—

She leaps for tree cover, and the kunai becomes a speeding blur in Uba's direction.

With one hand, he flips off his safety and fires twice. Bullet one hits her square in the chest. Bullet two hits the flying kunai half a meter in front of his face, diverting it inches wide of his unblinking human eye just as it aligns with his iron sights. He holds there, both hands now holding the pistol perfectly steady at arm's length.

The reacher woman lands in a heap, half obscured by a spruce tree, just her knees and shins still visible from the captain's viewpoint. From my line, I can see her arms sprawled lifelessly behind her—her face and hair buried in the snow.

But that image subtly judders.

Uba spins quickly back to center, fires down his sights, and a second kunai twirls harmlessly into the snow, not even close this time.

But there's no sign of her.

Until she screams, falling on top of him from the trees above, her shock baton already activated, hissing and clicking with electric strands.

Two bullets kill her again, and the baton lands prod-up in

the snow between Uba's feet, clicking and sparking a few more seconds before it vanishes with her third false corpse.

Snow scrunches to his right. Uba aims but doesn't fire.

A tree rustles to his left. He aims again, doesn't fire.

And now everybody knows the game.

Connie has given up her flailing but still moans weakly in the background, both gloved hands desperately covering her wide visor hole. I finally falter to our knees, barely enough solar left to—no, not even—I slip further, landing prone in the snow, one arm pinned beneath our staggering weight, the other outstretched toward the battle.

As my special weapon fails me, I watch the captain forgive his own. He carefully draws his left hand from his sidearm and uses it to cover his human eye. I watch him practice his own preaching, slowing the rhythm of his lungs as he begins backpedaling toward Taiko, his right arm, pistol, and panther eye scanning side to side in perfect unity. I watch the master of death prepare his station, moments from his magnum opus—or perhaps his last hurrah.

A third kunai whistles in from his blind left. He dodges it but is forced to shoot down the fourth kunai on his right.

The woman jumps up, screaming, directly behind him. He ignores her. Backpedals right through the false image, pistol and panther still dancing together.

Then a hopeless barrage of kunai—I count twenty-seven—come from every angle in front of him.

He shoots down four knives that are trajected for his vitals, allowing the others to continue. Then he grimaces, shocked, as the remaining twenty-three all hit home, dropping him to a knee.

Their identical, white-taped grips stick out of his arms, legs, and torso, rising and falling with every breath, every painful twitch of punctured muscle and layered fabric in between. twenty-three thin ropes of blood coil in the snow beneath him, all over Taiko, who he now defensively straddles.

He watches his draining blood land in her mouth and eyes, and his pistol arm begins to droop in demoralized defeat. But Taiko never stirs. She merely goes on blinking rhythmically, staring mindlessly straight up. The captain watches her swirling eyes with his trusted panther, and he seems to understand. He shakes his head sharply, and the kunai all judder away, in and out of his mind. He breathes deeply again, compartmentalizing the illusioned pain.

Without looking back up, he suddenly fires three blind shots—left—right—center. Then his pistol clicks twice—and the slide sticks open. Instead of reloading, he just drops it. Leans over Taiko. Shields her completely with his massive body, both fists and knees entrenched in the snow around her thin arms and legs. He relaxes his human eye open.

He watches her swirling eyes with both of his, and I wonder if my daddy ever knew this moment. I wonder if there's a list in the captain's heart where he keeps a record of his kin. Not just his Zambian son and wife but his extended brothers and sisters—the unnatural siblings that a man must choose for himself. I wonder if I made his list. Maybe all of us did, the entire unit. Or maybe it's just her. Just this demon of his own making, this cold machine who will never reciprocate his regret. Cyrus Uba watches Taiko Chiba's eyes.

And the world falls numb again. The reacher woman's perfect silence blankets our theater—even thicker than before. Connie quits moaning. The wind disappears. Lying as I am, I feel suspended in a timeless void. A universe without consequence.

Then the captain does something strange. A movement

like a lightning strike. Even to my keen sight, his shoulder doesn't turn so much as it teleports, sending his arm and open right hand up behind him, catching the empty air in a sudden choke. A confounding pose. Until the world's ears come unplugged again.

And she appears in his grasp.

The reacher woman, caught tightly around the throat—too stunned to do anything but hang there—one climbing glove digging into the captain's tightening fist, the other holding her second kunai. She meant to finish him as she fell from the sky—for real this time. But by some premonition, he has stopped her—so suddenly that her mountaineers shot forward from the whiplash, finally exposing her full face and shining eyes.

The captain still has his eyes locked on Taiko's. And I am awestruck once again. Not just by this violent miracle but a sudden understanding. Taiko's famed immunity to the Reach. The captain wasn't just defending his favorite weapon, he was using it. He knew only Taiko could see the woman coming. So, he tracked her eyes. He struck wherever she looked.

The reacher woman gasps noiselessly. Not because her powers are still active but because the captain is crushing her windpipe. She stomps her boot hard on the back of his helmet—twice. He reacts as though a butterfly has alighted there. In one smooth movement, he rises to his full height. He holds her high and away from him, her flailing boots just barely scraping the piled powder.

She wildly draws her kunai back to stab him, but his raised arm blurs again in rapid movement, and her nose is shattered against the crown of his helmet. The kunai falls, cutting through the snow between her dangling feet. She chokes, splattering Uba's visor with a red mist of snotty blood.

He doesn't bother wiping it, already frisking her, pulling the shock baton from her left hip. In a moment, it's clicking and popping in his left hand. She kicks at it, but he holds it away from her, deciding where she's most exposed, or if he even needs it, if perhaps he'll just wait for her impending suffocation. But now both of his hands are full, and hers are empty. Almost empty.

Her uncovered eyes suddenly flash like dying suns, and the captain is blinded. He grunts, turning his head away from the piercing beams. And I hear her clear voice again. A desperate final *roar* in my mind's ears. A guttural all-or-nothing battle cry, just before all eight of her climbing claws clap the captain's elbow and drag viciously up toward his wrist.

His fingers die, and she falls free, gasping for air—then dodging as the captain swings blindly with the crackling baton, his human eye fried forever, his panther still sputtering, recalibrating from the harsh overexposure.

He nearly gets her once—twice—singeing the tips of her dancing mane, tracking every retreating sound of her fleeing feet and scrambling hands in the deep snow. His heavy lungs and amplified hailers make a desperate music in the swaying trees, as he backs her further and further, halfway to our useless body now. Biding time for his panther to recover, for his old friend to make him that master of certain death just one last time.

He follows her fearful gasps and weakened scrambles, and he passes right by her true, silent form. Right by her looting hands, now drawing that eight-and-a-half-inch Nepalese kukri from the rear sheath of her first kill.

And just as he remembers his opponent's power, just as Cyrus Uba stops and turns with that rare warrior's instinct, turning just in time to face the wild woman who's made such a mess of his special unit, every inch of Aswad's favorite blade slots a gap in the captain's ribs, lancing through his giant heart.

Even with my hailers muted, I scream so loud three snowbirds scatter, soaring up beyond the higher branches where this battlefield began. Lifting my eyes to track their flight, I see one final perfection he left behind, one last bit of precision to add to the panther falcon's legend. A burning red streak from the south, tailing smoke as it rises high above the tree line. It's directly above the clearing, right on time with his prediction.

0:00. And Captain Uba's fighting days are ended.

3.14

"Hayes?" Connie hears no reply, no sound at all beyond the blizzard's endless breath. "Hayes, what happened?" she asks again, her voice trembling in hidden panic. It sounds like a question and answer together, so, I just keep lying there. Keep sinking, mind and body into the unforgiving Russian Taiga.

"Talk to me, you fucking—!" her last few syllables collapse into knowing despair. She shakes her head like it can't be true. She claws at the snow with her one free hand—the one that isn't busy covering her shattered visor. My silence confirms the captain's defeat, and she hates me for it. She hates that I'm her only ally left in this godforsaken place. *Anyone but the skinner*, her pounding fist shouts. *Any other death would be freer than this!*

In one crazed movement, she pulls her shielding hand away from her helmet and sits upright on folded knees. She sucks the wind's kisses down her throat with drunk abandon. Grunts madly, scrambling, pawing at her leash until she finds her rifle's grip, shrieking hysterically as her lacerated, blinking eyes test the dimming light again. Whatever blurred image they provide, it's enough to mark the reacher woman, still alive, panting exhaustedly amidst her nasty work—kneeling over the captain's huge cadaver, clutching Aswad's custom blade. Connie marks that quiet creature. And she brings the fucking noise.

Her piercer rounds make cannon sounds as they spit wildly from her muzzle—sending sprays of snow high into the air, tearing holes through spruce and shrub and the deepening shadows beneath the mountain. She tugs the semi-auto at her hip as fast as she can, keeps tugging long after it's empty.

She tugs until her adrenaline is spent completely, until frozen waterfalls of tears have solidified on her face. Then she sags forward over her knees, her shoulders already heaving through the final stages of her grief. And there's no illusion this time. No false corpse to tease our senses. No alien tricks.

The reacher woman is still kneeling there unchanged. Connie hit every tree in sight. She hit Aswad and Uba more than once, making a mess of their remains. But the rogue has hardly moved. She was too stunned and breathless to even duck her head.

But now the shock is fading. The strange woman is rising to her feet, sucking quieter air into her lungs, already glaring in Connie's direction with those otherworldly eyes.

Connie shrieks to God, snapping the empty magazine free, reaching to her belt for standard rounds, but the other woman is much quicker.

She takes four lunging steps and front kicks that reload attempt, breaking Connie's wrist against the body of her own rifle.

Connie yelps and snarls like a rabid thing, converting that pain into fresher wrath. As the reacher woman withdraws her kicking leg, Connie catches her by the heel, pulling the woman back in while she pulls herself up. Her shoulder drives into the reacher's womb, executing a clumsy but effective tackle.

Connie lands on top, pinning the woman's upper thigh with her rifle barrel. She throws several left hooks with her good fist, pummeling whatever alien guts the woman has. But between her shooter's glove and the reacher's thick duster coat, the body blows have minimal effect. Scrambling in counter defense, the woman's climbing claws find a home in Connie's right shoulder.

Before Connie can convert that pain into any more violence, the reacher yanks her down and rolls her over, pinning Connie in a full mount. Her hips lock in above Connie's, and her knees anchor deep into the snow. With one ruthless jerk, she pulls her claws free, ripping a chunk of Connie's inner lining and several deep strips of shoulder meat.

Connie screams. Her blood dyes the snow in gushing squirts. She tries to lurch away, but her right arm is tangled in her leash and pinned beneath the woman's knee. The stabbing pain in that trapped fracture spins her eyes into blinking saucers. She lies still. The rogue woman pauses her cocked fist, seeming to know the fight is won.

But Connie's spinning gaze lands on Aswad's frostbitten halves. She sees the captain not much further, ripped to bits by her own piercers. As her shredded eyes begin to focus, I see two paths of moisture cutting through the frozen wall of tears. Two blades of blood, slicing toward her clenching jaw.

She makes a pitiful sound—a convincing dying moan to draw attention to her face, to keep the rogue woman from seeing her free hand on the left, scrambling, finding something in the snow, something sharp enough to cut her fingers as they clench around it.

The rogue woman gasps in unexpected pain. She spins, securing Connie's free arm with a handful of claws, but she's too late to prevent the wound. An obsidian shard of her own shattered blade now juts from her midsection, sending a thin river of blood down to commune with Connie's lake.

Despite the reacher's tightening claws, Connie hisses with satisfaction. She laughs like a maniac as the woman's damaged eyes slowly twist back to meet her own. Damaged eyes, darkening to black revenge.

She squeezes and twists, grinding her claws into Connie's wrist bone, erasing her satisfaction in an instant. The woman's other hand yanks violently—twice—three times—until Connie's entire helmet comes free from her shoulders. I see the embedded shards of visor glass glistening like distant stars in her perforated face. It reminds me of that old film, that one where the terrorist's diamonds explode directly in his—

The woman crushes Connie's right cheekbone with her own helmet, and my mind stops. She swings again, cracking Connie's jaw in half, and my consciousness ghosts away. I forget to be Emmett Hayes.

Connie's unprotected head whips left, sending blood scattering from her lips, and I live a hundred lifetimes in each droplet. A thousand microscopic years transpire before our wet worlds land in the snow.

The woman caves in Connie Clark's eye socket, and that friction incinerates hidden universes. I am their observer and their dying citizens. I am all the false gaps perceived between. As I look back at my own vessel, I begin to see something else.

A brightness alive inside us. A cobalt shine and silent music. A latticework highway between all minds and their starry worlds. It's right there. It's always been just there, just beyond my reach.

She *whispers,* and I finally hear her clearly. Not the young rogue who's killing Connie but the sunken mother inside of me. I hear her last words to a frightened son. A soothing farewell to a boy too young to understand. She says, "There were endless empty eyes," touching her soft fingers to his cheek. Her gold-brown curls would tickle his forehead if she still had them. She lightly kisses him there instead. Her eyes were hot like the rising sun when she continued, "Blinded by the freest worlds. Follow your light, and I will find you. I promise you that, my starshine boy." I live another flashing lifetime in that memory. I hold the moment up like a hologram in my world.

But the reacher—the unique woman who called me cousin—she's holding Connie Clark's helmet up like a boulder. She's filling it with all her rage and stinging pain. She's holding it high enough to kill, to forget her brightness altogether. Her eyes are dimming as she becomes what I have been my entire life. Disconnected. An island adrift from the cosmic highway.

She forgets her vow, but the endless others call me to hand. Her wild hair darkens toward empty shadow as she brings that hateful boulder down—

But I whisper, *sleep.*

My eyes shine, and her terrible violence misses its mark. The young woman goes limp, and Connie's helmet hits the powder a few hairs above her head. The way the rogue collapses across her chest, they almost look like napping lovers.

I imagine that deserves some laughter. But there's not enough solar left to move my face. My eyes droop lifelessly as I remember something else. All those dreams when I was young. Those liminal drifts that seemed so much like distant memories.

If only I could . . . what I wouldn't give for just one more chance to . . .

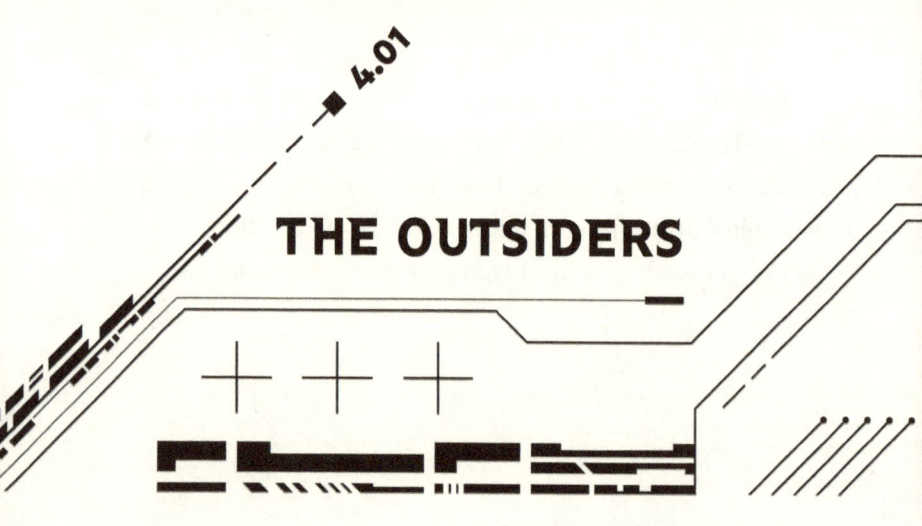

THE OUTSIDERS

The boy watches the outsiders every morning. He takes his full breakfast plate all the way up to the light chamber and then eats with his hands. In his hurry, he almost always leaves a trail—bits of fried egg and forest herbs in the narrow passageway between the commons and the stepwall. But if he drops something obvious like a cowberry, he always stops to pick it up. Just to keep Tysha happy mostly; she hates when Poody is wasteful.

Sometimes he pops the dropped thing in his mouth without checking, and grains of mineral salt will scratch against his teeth. He kinda likes that flavor, though. He used to crawl down to Canna's Cavern and lick the gypsum sculptures one by one. But Tysha caught him last summer, and now he's banned. She'd ban him from watching the outsiders, too, if she knew what he was planning to ask them.

Just like she banned him from The Claw Way, and The Tomb, and Bluewater Lake after total dark. So Poody always scoops up the berries when they fall. And sometimes the smaller things if he sees them. She won't ban him without a reason. She's not like Yono. Nothing like old Mantz who always watches him without speaking. Always frowning and looking ugly, no matter how friendly Poody tries to be. Tysha's much more like Uncle Kible was—probably on purpose, Poody thinks. Kible was scary. But always fair in his own way. Tysha still talks to Kible sometimes when she's alone—or when she thinks Poody's asleep, but really he's just pretending. He can be almost as quiet as her sometimes. Even though he's so dim, sometimes he can still be real quiet.

After she gets home and checks on him, he likes to crawl back out of bed and sit outside Tysha's room for a while. He hears her give Kible updates—how much outsider paper is left, if any newcomers have arrived, if any old ones have passed on to join the light. But her updates sound different since the outsiders came. Sometimes, it sounds more like she's talking to herself. Sometimes, she *tries* to cry, he thinks, but instead she just gets madder. Poody tried to cheer her up after he heard her like that the first time. He waited until morning then went right up to her and said he liked Tysha more as brightstar. He said he hoped his mean old uncle never came back from this year's searching ever again.

It took four days for Poody's eyes to heal after that. But Tysha stayed with him until he was better. She made her announcements from his bedside and spoke to all the others with her light just like she spoke to Kible so far away. Or like she used to before the outsiders came—before she and Cuva brought them in from the forest. She's been so dim since that weird trade. She left the cave for a week with Sila, Jerill, and that man Goroon who always made her smile. He made Poody smile, too, with his funny faces. He could use his light to look like Tysha. Or just like old Mantz with her crooked back and sagging face. Sometimes Tysha would do their voices and make Poody hear all the little cracks and pops in old Mantz's knees. When she and Goroon did the tricks together, there was no way to tell. They could fool anyone, even Kible probably. But Tysha said Goroon and them aren't coming back. They all went to be with Kible wherever he is now. Somewhere better than the cave. She wouldn't tell Poody about her missing ear, but he guessed she gave it to Goroon. They were always arguing about his listening.

Tysha got real angry every night after she hurt Poody's eyes. It was an accident—just one quick blast of her great heat—but she was still upset. Upset that Goroon left without her, too. Even from Poody's bed, he could hear her practicing with her knives. She'd gotten way too dim to make herself quiet. Almost as dim as Poody always is. So, he decided to ban himself on her behalf. In that long darkness before his sight came back, he made a promise to never mention Sila, Jerill, Kible, or Goroon to Tysha ever again. He was specific about that last part. Because as soon as the outsiders woke up, he was going to ask them a lot. He was going to ask every question he'd ever had about the whole wide world outside their cave. He was going to ask them where the cold forest ends and what the ocean tastes like! And how come the outsiders never visited before? How come Poody wasn't allowed to see where they all lived?

And he hoped the man would wake up before the lady. She looked mean, and her face was horrible to look at. But the man seemed nice. A little sad but nice. His eyeballs moved underneath his lids like he was dreaming. His skin moved, too. His skin looked just like omul scales but big and colorful where the sunlight hit them. Poody wondered what that skin would look like outside the cave. The thin trickling beams that reached the light chamber seemed to hardly do it justice.

4.02

The brightstar is losing their confidence. She hears them speaking in the old tongue whenever she passes. Not in hushed voices but defiantly aloud. As though to test if she still understands. To measure just how dim she has become. But she ignores them. She lets there be a question instead of certainty in either direction. She thinks that's what AnSorin would do. Give them nothing they don't demand. So, she shows a brave face. She feigns power even though she is so frightened, even though she is terrified of this ostensible permanence. Her great light is now nearly extinguished. Shining rarely and often outside her control. If they ever saw what she did to Poody, if they knew the darkness the outsiders gave her, then they would find the certainty they'd been craving. She would be ousted without question. That's what has Tysha frightened the most—this new vanity she can't relinquish. This growing ego that feels so much like the Earth people's consumptive pride.

She visits the light chamber every night. Asks Yono and Cuva if there have been any changes. Even though she knows the answer. As dim as she's become, somehow, she still knows that she will know. Maybe not when that damned female passes. She nearly left her to freeze with the other freakish one. But the man. If he dies or somehow awakens, she will know. The way his strange light shined, they may all know when that day comes.

Tysha still wonders if she was fooled. The alternative seems like fiction. But his existence is a fiction, too. The Earth people are all dim. If that were not so, Kible Thexx AnSorin would never have sent up his beacon on this world. There would have been no need. And yet this outsider's light shines so bright and strange. Even at AnSorin's exile, she could hear this man. All his stupid ramblings to himself. She felt the fingers of his psyche. Like a randy tween, she felt his touch run through her hair. The disgusting fool mistook her for one of them—just as he mistakes himself. He cannot be of Earth descent. He must be a man of the light tribe, perhaps born as she was, here on Earth. The son of a pregnant traveler, just as she was the daughter of one, preserved for all that time in her dying mother's womb. How else could he bear no markings of the travel milk, no bleached skin or loss of hair? Just as she was born unmarked, he must be the same. But within that logic, she tastes a tainting pride again.

How can she explain his ears? His dim eyes and his sharp teeth? How can a man of brightworld blood have such Earthly features? And how can he not know? How can his thoughts be so consistently muddled and obtuse—until that moment they were not. Until that last instant when the fiction happened. Tysha was dimmed, rage-blind, bringing down that damned woman's headgear—until suddenly she wasn't. She was awash in a flash of light. Then she was waking up an hour later, bloody and frozen half to death.

Yes, that must have been it. It was simply the blood loss and exertion. Or some paralyzing weapon that she missed. Some grenade or dead-man countermeasure from the huge African or the one who impaled Goroon.

Goroon. Remembering him this way is a heartache. An errant thought already, no longer her fixation. She shakes the strange outsider from her mind. He is clouding her, no doubt the source of her spiraling dimness. She thinks of Goroon. Jerill. Sila. She should have been with them; it was her decision to make. She should have been bolder, should have been their defender. Instead of their avenger.

All her thoughts lead to dimness these days. AnSorin was wrong to appoint her. She shined brightly then, brighter than most of the others combined, but it was a lie. Another fiction she let herself believe. A true leader shines brightest in the darker hours. Not just in moments that self-serve. Perhaps that pride has been festering longer than she realizes. That old yearning. She was an outsider, too, lest she forget. Before AnSorin found her. Before she was tamed, she was the gwáinòu. The street beast of west Shanghai.

She wanted to be human then. She was, in certain places, to dimmer eyes. With the right sunglasses and fresher clothes, she could walk freely south of the river where she wasn't known. Sometimes she was stopped by worried locals, but any easy lie would turn them away. *Her grandmother sent her to buy more ginseng. Her father was trying on work boots in that store there, across the street.* For those with crueler intentions, she had other tactics. With their five senses as her instrument, she plucked many scoundrels into madness—those who sought profit in her rarity. Her unmarked skin. She mistook AnSorin for one of them. One of the liars. Until he shared his light with her. He took her strangeness and made it good. Not for his gain. Not even for hers. For the unbegotten ones—*the endless others, as they all must come.*

He showed her the strength an outsider carries, the honed edge of a lifelong sharpening. Then he brought her here and made her special. Made the liars' manipulative promises something true. All she'd ever wanted was to blend in with this dim world, but she found a new dream in AnSorin's trust. A blinding brightness. An unmatched shine within his tribe. Now all that towering ambition has collided sightlessly with Earth. She has made casualties of her most trusted: Jerill, Sila, and Goroon. Her gentle Goroon.

AnSorin made a few costly mistakes in his final days, but his greatest one was slow and steady, spanning a dozen orbits of this myopic planet around its sun. He was blinded, too; she sees that now—led astray by his hopeless love for one savage girl.

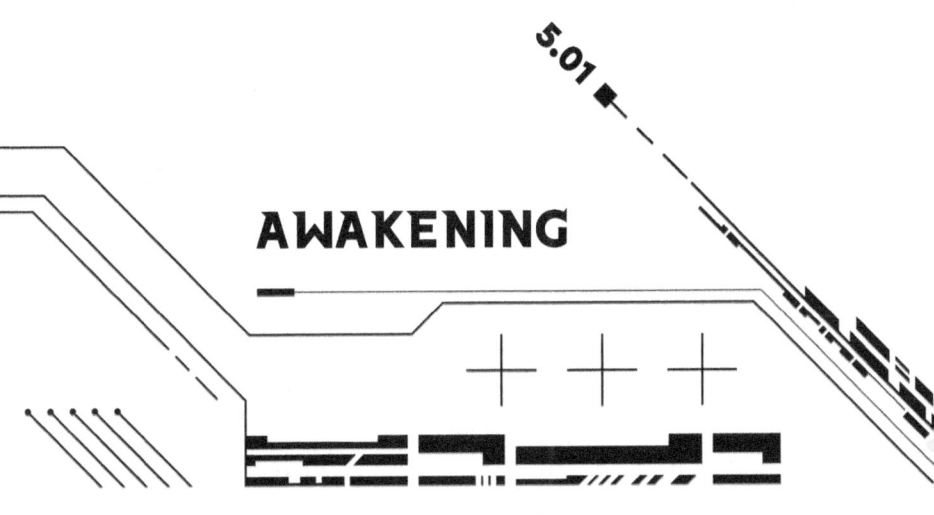

AWAKENING

The ocean is alive above me. Undulating lumps of white-blue light, rippling vibrantly as I shift my head from side to side.

As my vision clears, I see that the ocean is actually frozen. A massive ceiling of ice with thin trickles of morning light seeping through it, giving its lumpy, waved surface the illusion of movement. The few sunbeams are cool and delicious where they scatter over us. An icy medical drip.

I hear a gasp of excitement in my mind. A mix of sudden fear and Christmas joy. A small shuffling of feet from the same direction. I look there and see something strange. A boy. The youngest Luminaran I've ever seen. He's like a pale little elf in stolen clothes. Pants too small, shirt way too large, both terribly ragged from repeated wearing. He looks at me like I'm Jesus risen.

"Khaimall!" A muscular Luminaran wearing my tundra helmet pushes the boy aside. He aims Connie's short rifle at my face. "Khaimall, denzani. Bhokon. Bhokon Tysha futwana!" He shouts over his shoulder at the Luminaran child, who seems reluctant to take his eyes from me, desperate to stay. "Bhokon Tysha mel caska!" he spits at the boy's motionless feet.

"Poody." A third, middle-aged Luminaran nudges the boy with one of Taiko's concussive sticks. The diamond tip is visible, but the rest of its length is now painted over in swirling, webbing designs—a mix of that cobalt blue and a lighter ice-white coloring. "Bhokon Tysha pervare. Pervare."

The boy finally takes his eyes from me. After one more nudge and nod from the older, calmer rogue, the boy sets his half-eaten breakfast plate down on the cave floor and takes off running. His tiny shoes echo back up the passageway, giving me a sense of how large this cavern is. Twisting down and around beneath us, I sense other things as well—scattered flickers like distant candles, each slightly different from the next. As I lift my head from the floor, craning my neck to measure them, to try and guess what those lights could be, some of the brighter ones twist with me. The brightest few seem to measure me right back.

"Khaimall, denzani!" the hotheaded reacher shouts at me with tightening nerves. His itchy finger teases Connie's trigger, ready to unload.

I can't understand a word he's saying. Neither can *she* apparently. This isn't a language we've ever heard. Even the lumie dictionaries we've memorized are coming up blank. Too bad. No way to tell this dipshit he could never disengage the safety without Connie's palmprint, let alone discharge a round.

His face changes—like I just said that out loud, like I just brashly insulted him. Then his eyes dart uncertainly to a deeper corner of the light chamber. The light chamber. Somehow, I know that's where I am. The highest room in the cavern complex.

The floor is black and porous beneath us, carved unnaturally flat. A steep, glistening hill rises behind us toward the inner mountain peak, and a much steeper one falls off in the opposite direction beyond our feet. The ancient precipice of a volcanic waterfall, frozen over. A floating prison with just one narrow walkway to escape it.

The hothead sidesteps to block my view of the exit. He handles Connie's rifle clumsily, no respect for what he's holding. No education. He's lucky it's me who's sitting here. She would've been happy to give him a lesson, a two-part seminar on close-quarters combat and interior decoration. I follow his darting gaze—another fearful glance to that same corner. I roll my head to the right, looking straight along the igneous floor, and I freeze against it. I see a second prisoner on her back who vaguely resembles Connie Clark.

She's two meters away, lying with her feet in the other direction, arms at her sides. The right side of her face is changed forever, crushed into a funhouse reflection of her left. Still, she looks much better than I expected. Clean and mostly healed, resting peacefully on a mix of old blankets and fresh juniper branches. With the right sim surgeon and a little luck, she might even recognize herself someday. Though, that may be the least of her concerns.

Her wounds have received excellent care, no longer riddled with visor glass, already looking more like scars than scabs. Too much like scars. We've clearly been down for quite some time. Even her broken wrist looks mended, almost normal. But she hasn't moved. Not on her own, at least. Her once-impressive physique has atrophied, approaching scrawniness. I can smell a bedsore forming in her lower back. Dried berries on the roof of her mouth. They've been feeding her, helping her swallow, keeping her as clean as they can. She reminds me of Taiko Chiba that first day in the wetroom. Taiko. Another mindless ally I can't detect in this place at all.

I lift our back from the dusty makeshift cot and sit up with some difficulty, stretching the stiffness out of my neck. That gets the hothead going again:

"Khaimall mel—!"

I grab Connie's rifle by the barrel and take it from him. Even at twenty percent solar, it feels like snatching a rattle from a toddler. His eyes go wide and horrified as I point the muzzle at his moth-eaten sweatshirt—some outdated Russian sports logo there, a sea lion cracking a hockey stick between its teeth—then I pull the trigger. He flinches horribly, so I do it twice more. Just to be sure he hears the useless clicking sound it makes. Then I toss it right back to him. He catches the weapon okay, but his confidence falls straight through the Earth.

I stand up on the cool cave floor and stretch our arms back high behind my head. He instinctively points the rifle at me again, but his wiser senior finally steps forward, placing a calming hand on the rifle's sights and pressing it down. Despite the equanimity in his eyes, I hear the flesh of his aged fingers tightening around Taiko's c-stick. Not in fear but readiness. I sense a flickering within him, too. Not distantly, just obscured. An old and heavy wall with wisps of smoke seeping through its cracks. A hardened calm that reminds me of the captain.

My eyes drop at his recollection. Captain Uba. Some radar I turned out to be, some secret weapon. I doomed the unit. Taiko Chiba, Wilson Black, brave Aila Hallheim and Zayd Aswad, who wasn't so different than I should be. At least he channeled his resentment into skills and confirmed kills, just like I pretended that I could. They took his family, just like mine, but he fought back. He defended the Earth, just like I promised that I would. So did Connie. She pushed the captain's killer to the very edge, and even then, I could only—

I look back up to the hotheaded reacher, and he flinches away. But I'm just studying my stolen helmet, realizing something. The battery is dead. The visor has reverted to lifeless glass, but it's undamaged. That must be why he chose mine. Connie's got wrecked by that strange woman. That's right. She was bringing the helmet down on Connie to finish her off, to avenge her fallen friends, and then somehow, I . . . I saw that golden woman again and—

Somebody storms into the light chamber, shoving the hothead out of her way. He almost staggers over the edge into the abyss, but she doesn't care. She halts rigidly, and our eyes connect. The woman. Or maybe some less impressive sister.

Her hair is longer by a couple centimeters, dyed even darker than before. A purer black, no longer glistening that way it was. Those brilliant blue highlights have been removed. Or maybe just faded. Her brightest feature seems to have dimmed beyond recognition.

She twitches as though I've said something cruel—but with far less certainty than the hothead seemed to have. She looks just like I used to feel whenever Logan grumbled her cusses at me in broken Creole.

"Sit down and be silent," the woman commands.

Her voice is tired, revealing a heavier accent than I ever noticed in my mind. An exotic mix just like her skin. And still clearly damaged. A hoarse disappointment to my ears. Uba's last gambit, that incredible flashing choke hold, must have—

"I said be silent!" she rages, and the thin sky beams seem to flicker, as though the sun itself shrinks away. To my surprise and hers, I hardly stir. I'm too enthralled. She hesitates uncomfortably, then speaks again, averting her eyes, "Sit down. Pervare—please."

I mimic her this time, suddenly feeling very exposed. Unsure how exactly to think *quietly*. Unsure how much she and they can hear. I sit back down, folding our legs on the cot, then unfolding them again. I try not to look at her, but she's too much to think about. Even without her shimmering features, she's easily the most . . . I swallow the rest of that thought as best I can.

And the older Luminaran makes one of Daddy's sounds. That clever scoff that matched his smile—that knowing grin just before he laid down his cards and took your lunch. But the younger guard looks mad again. He's about ready to move on me one more time until—

The young boy comes sprinting around the corner. His little lungs are heaving, wheezing asthmatically in between his barking seal coughs. The woman quickly shields him, putting one leg of her duster coat between us. But he swats it away, clinging there, desperate not to miss a moment of whatever is coming next.

I know how he feels. I lock eyes with the deadly woman, expecting to receive her wartime rage, expecting some violent shift to interrogation any second now. Instead, I see doubt. I see the same conflicted curiosity that I've been nursing in myself.

 **5.02**

They go on and on in their alien tongue, but I'm pretty sure I get the gist. The hothead points at me with hateful hands, and the older one keeps calming him down. He offers the woman wise-sounding words and peaceful gestures, which the hothead seems to reject as soft half-measures. He begs her to be bold—to finish us off, by the sound of it—but she says nothing. They hem and haw in her remaining ear, but her attention stays with me. Her eyes glimmer faintly, like an alkaline flashlight clinging to its purpose. I can feel her psychic fingers fumbling clumsily, seeking to undress my unlit mind. A nakedness sneaks in. She prods the skin beneath our scales, and I am forced to look away.

I see the boy down by her hip. If he's blinked once, I haven't caught it. Soon as he realizes I'm looking at him, his hairless eyebrows jump even higher. And there's something uncanny about his face. Or the space behind it. The dimmest candle I've seen yet. A single faded pixel in the endless black beyond.

But it's not like the others. It's recognizable somehow. A misleading perspective I've seen before. It reminds me of the massive stars I charted in my cannon. Not small at all. A colossal burning flame only rendered harmless by its distance.

The woman suddenly slips, losing her balance. My attention shifts back to her and the older rogue, who catches her by the arm, seeming to ask if she's alright, "Hah—Ya ben?"

She keeps staring at me like she didn't hear him.

"Tysha. Ya ben sul?" he says again, with increasing worry.

"I'm fine." She shakes it off, finding her feet and standing upright. "Ah ben. Ah ben." She nods reassuringly to the older rogue until he releases her. He backs away but continues to watch her with troubled eyes.

The kid looks up at her as well, similar concern in his expression. She pets his bald little head, smiling gently. She also seems to search his eyes, holding him steady for a moment. But she frowns when the search is finished, apparently not seeing what she had hoped to.

"Cho," the hothead barks to get her attention. "Mai tenya?" He nods with finality in my direction, clenching Connie's rifle grip and his reckless jawline even tighter. The woman studies me with changing eyes. Her initial intrigue fades, finally making way for that wartime resentment I'd been expecting. She nods affirmatively to the hothead.

"No," the little boy objects in perfect English. "No, wait—"

But the woman firmly tugs him from her leg, turning him toward the middle-aged rogue. "Cuva, can you—balo ken. Balo!"

The kid keeps protesting, apparently in my defense, until the older rogue sets one hand on his shoulder—just the edge of his scarred and wrinkled palm, hardly any weight behind it. But the kid surrenders without another word. As he allows himself to be guided meekly toward the exit, he glances back at me and Connie like two brand-new puppies he couldn't pet. And I feel that strangeness once again. The uncanny gravity of a burning wish.

"Tastes like piss," somebody grumbles right behind me.

The hothead follows the voice. The woman, too. Both of them look confused.

So am I, glancing over my shoulder, seeing nothing but rising cavern ice.

But it makes perfect sense to somebody. There's a small commotion at the exit as two tiny hands suddenly latch onto the passageway corner, catching the older rogue off guard. The skinny little boy thrusts his astonished face back into the chamber, and I see Christmas magic in his eyes. I hear that grumbly voice again:

"Yeah. Like piss and salty ass. You can't drink any of it. The whole ocean's one big—" I bring my hand up to my mouth, finally recognizing the voice, finally noticing everyone in the room is looking at me.

The boy giggles insanely. His eyes are hot with happy wonder when the middle-aged rogue they called Cuva finally pulls him away and out of sight. The hothead starts shouting angrily, pointing Connie's rifle at me again, clearly begging to put me down, but Tysha's mood has shifted completely.

Tysha. That's what he called her, I'm pretty sure. That's her name. I match her glimmering eyes, beginning to find a comfort in the undressing.

5.03

That kid did something to me. Or I did something to him. Felt like I was sleep talking wide awake—like my subconscious took the initiative to answer a couple hanging questions. Only problem is nobody asked. At least not directly. Not in any way I can sanely describe. It was more like a feeling. I wasn't hearing the kid's weird questions; I was asking them myself—answering them like any errant thought. I just happened to skip the thinking part.

"Bhok." The hothead jabs us low in the back with Connie's rifle. "Bhokon, caskan denzani."

I plant our feet in the narrow passageway to take a slow and steady breath. Only been a few minutes since we left the light chamber, but it could take me an hour to find my way back. This place is a maze. No idea where the cavern entrance is or which part of the forest we're beneath. Even if I escaped, I'd freeze to death an hour after sunset. The only thing I know for sure is where I'll be cramming Connie's rifle if this fucker nudges us with it again.

I hear the hothead retreat a step. Sounds like he's ready

to say something stupid, but then he shuts his mouth and swallows it. I twist slowly in his direction, just a few degrees to make sure he got the message, then I continue walking the corridor at my own pace. It's freaky as hell. But I guess all this psychic violation has its perks.

The hothead scoffs derisively at our back, but he doesn't follow us until we've extended our lead a few safe paces. I duck slightly, avoiding a hanging city of stalactites, pausing at the next chamber entrance to test the strength of my restraints— thick leather straps, wrapped several times around my wrists. I might snap them with a few solid tugs, but would it matter? Would I even stand a chance in unarmed combat with this rogue woman who killed—

I lose about thirty seconds. Half a minute of my life goes by without a single conscious thought. It's not an attack. Nothing telepathic happens to me, or because of me, I just get lost in it for a while. This new chamber. It's unlike anything I've ever seen.

The rogue woman, Tysha, has stopped in front of me. She appears annoyed, then uncertain, as she follows my line of sight to the hand-painted murals on the wall, the swirling sculptures of ice and stone, the three-dimensional portrait of a gaseous blue expanse of planets, moons, and stars. A sense of lost nostalgia swims between us as she studies the immaculate cavern art. Lost, she seems to agree, flicking her eyes down to the dusty floor.

"Have a seat." She motions to an ornate stone chair that deserves much better—a king's ass, if this were a human castle. Unworthily, I obey. "Yono, can you . . ." She lifts her eyes to the hothead in the entryway behind me. With some difficulty, she continues in their strange tongue, "Ya Mantz hara. Pervare."

He shifts unconfidently, not seeming to understand.

"I mean—*khem* ya Mantz hara," she corrects.

"Ah. Kai sem." He understands this time but still doesn't move. I feel his mistrusting eyes on the back of my neck.

"I'll be fine, just—khem ya Mantz. Pervare." She motions toward the exit, exhaling some frustration as she takes a lesser seat at the great stone table which runs the length of the room. She adjusts her coat for a moment, then realizes he still hasn't left. "*PERVARE!*"

There's a flash from her eyes and a crashing shout inside my head. For an instant, it feels as though the skin on my cheeks is scorched away.

Yono hurries off without another objection, tripping over himself as he scurries back through the narrow passage. By the sound of his echoes, I can tell he takes a different path this time—not up the spiraling incline but down and deeper into the cavern complex.

I look back to Tysha, who's now wincing, pinching her nose as though abating a sudden migraine. While she's distracted, I run my hands beneath the table, searching for any sharp bump to cut myself free. This woman has clearly diminished since her last fight. Outside of the occasional outburst, the shine in her eyes has all but vanished. If she does intend to torture me, I don't plan on making it easy.

She twitches again, opening her eyes but never looking directly at me. She studies the table's polished surface as though something's missing in the reflection. The entire room seems to dim, drawing my attention to the ceiling.

"Where does your power come from?" I ask.

Her eyes flick quickly to me, suddenly tinted with paranoia.

"Not hearing a generator anywhere," I clarify, looking up

to the strings of bright golden bulbs that encircle the cavern ceiling. God, the ceiling. Dyed in layered hues of cold cyan, sunrise yellow, and a deep forest green. Every angle in this room is a visual feast.

She follows my eyeline again, and I feel that sentimentality seeping through. She doesn't answer my question directly, but I catch something—an itch in the lower corner of my eye. I look down in that direction, beyond a beautiful hand-cut rug, beyond many spiraling cavern floors and dark dead ends, all the way down to some kind of dense and cosmic—

"Why have you come here?" she asks with interruptive haste. The itch subsides, and I look back up, seeing subtle alarm between her features. As an answer to her query, I simply show her my bound wrists. "I meant, why to the forest?" she continues. "What do you want?"

The broadness of that question gives me pause. Especially coming from her. A few intimate images flash through my imagination.

"No—stop that." She waves her hand as though to clear a wisp of smoke, as though my filthiest fantasies are mundane. "Just tell me your name."

"Hayes." I watch her curiously. "Sergeant Emmett Hayes."

"Alright. Good to meet you," she says without much sincerity. "I am called—"

"Tysha."

She halts abruptly, and my goofy confidence melts away. I suddenly feel like a stalker stepping out of the bushes into her backyard.

"I am called the brightstar," she corrects me, seeming slightly more threatened than disgusted. "The people who live here are under my protection."

"People?" I ask uncertainly, thinking she means other human beings.

"Yes." Her feral eyebrows twitch, offended then defiant. "The traveling people of the brighter world."

Another itch crawls up my neck, and I hear inquisitive *whispers* right behind it—not arriving but remaining, as though they've been lingering there unnoticed. Those distant candles. Conscious minds of nearby reachers, listening in from all directions. I turn slightly around, noticing most of them recoil, drifting back to a safer psychic range. All except for one. The brightest one draws nearer, as though my attention makes it easier, as though I grant her old, crooked fingers better purchase within my skull. I feel that painful pinch, and—

I jerk forward, pressing a bound wrist to my throbbing temple. I see Tysha watching me with slightly altered eyes— that same alarm, that paranoia, but now somewhat covetous. A resentful question slips from her lips, "Where exactly do you come fr—?"

But approaching footsteps invade the moment. Two sets. The nearest sounds sure-footed, out in front—the hothead she called Yono. The other is terrible. A human-shaped thing with a sound signature more like matchsticks and dried branches, cracking and popping with each step. And a rhythmic clacking. A tapping of sealed wood against cavern stone. A walking stick, with its own bending imperfections. It sends me back to that old shack behind the lake, gusted alive by the summer winds, groaning and creaking until broken dawn. It's strange the way nature always seems to know the best hours for a haunting. All the best places, just like this, where the harshest echoes can stretch and rattle to their full potential.

As Yono and the other one enter, Tysha stands to receive

them. "Mantz, thank you—" she halts her English, straining, trying again, "Grashalam ya men—"

"Bagh," the old woman grumbles and hisses at once. "Speak our words clearly or not at all." She hobbles into the room behind Yono without looking at anyone—thankfully not at me either; my face makes wretched shapes at her first sighting.

The woman is ancient, if it's fair to call her that. A woman, I mean. To my eyes, she is more like white sand cursed into life. Loose and shifting in every direction. Her skin is a nightmare. Translucent in all the worst places. She might be tall if her back had any straightness to it. Instead, she is a low and hunching thing. A depilated wraith, crackling over the cavern stone.

"By the light, he's a noisy one!" The old woman swats Yono's helping hand away and takes a seat on a long bench adjacent to the large central table where Tysha and I are sitting.

The bench is also stone, cut from the broadest wall. Various colorful tapestries and smaller, carved statues decorate the space above her head.

"Yech! I didn't live all these stars just to be deafened by your chronicles, boy. Be silent or silenced, your choice."

For a moment, I wonder who the old creature is speaking to. The hothead is smirking delightedly at her side, but Tysha seems suddenly nervous, increasingly on-edge the more I—

"Silenced, then. Fine by me," the old woman growls.

"No. Mantz, no!" Tysha turns fearfully from me to the hideous specter. And for one flashing moment, her ancient, foggy eyes shine brighter than anything I've ever—

5.04 ▪— — — ——————————

The jungle shadows are cool this morning. The air is dry. The leaves are beginning to change. Another long summer reaches its end, and the animal has not been quieted.

"You'll never catch me."

We turn slightly, following its frail voice northwest, beyond the river.

"You'll never find me."

Our gaze flicks to the distant south, where the tides have nearly reached the tumbling dunes.

"You'll be crying through winter again, alone."

We resist the urge to look directly behind us. The animal isn't there. It isn't beyond the river either, not after the monsoon rains we had this month. It isn't anywhere near the desert dunes, it never has been. We'd outrun the creature easily if it was ever so exposed. These psychic clues are just more tricks to suss us out.

The animal isn't quick, not in these summer months. Not before it returns to its winged body and soars off above the violet sea. Or swims away in its lengthy serpent form. Or burrows beneath the waters, using that hulking frame with claws like human femurs. We've only caught sight of it once in its island shape. The final day of our first summer here, we saw its fragile, furry summer body just before it slipped back into its eagle skin. Not an eagle like we had on Earth, not even a bird exactly. But feathered like one, with opposable talons more like gorilla paws. It made a mess of us on that first attempt. That's how we lost one of Emmett's hands. Emmett. That's right, we used to call us that. Before the island. Before we learned the summer game.

"Noisy today," the animal taunts us, listening in to our conscious stream. *"Too noisy to ever catch me."*

Its voice comes from the tree canopy above us. Another place we know it would not be. None of its massive winter bodies are nearby. The Eagle is east, the Snake is west, and the Mole is always north. That's where the sea tunnel begins.

"The tunnels, yes. My favorite path. I'll migrate that way this year."

It lies to us. Not always, but this time it lies for sure. It cannot use the same body two years in a row; the mole shape is still hard as stone. The animal will be traveling east today. Or west to its serpent form.

"Noisy and dimwitted. An exhausting combination."

It mocks us, listening carefully. We've practiced all winter and most of this summer to quiet our working thoughts, but the animal is far too skilled. It's a brightworld ghoul designed to creep and crawl and hear, not with its ears but something better. The bright highway between all things. So, this time, we'll let chance decide.

We flip a jungle stone just like we would a coin back home. Home. That's right, we used to call Earth that. The stone lands mossy-side up. We watch it there in the canopy shadows, trying our best to keep the animal out. To keep it from hearing this result as we discuss it amongst ourselves. Better to just move quickly, we decide. So, we scamper off to the eastern side. Off to the mountain roost where the eagle ape disfigured us so long ago. If we reach the eastern shore before the animal crawls back inside the winged beast, it will pose no threat to us. So, we'll beat it there this time. This year, we'll finally take revenge.

"Too bad," the animal whispers secretly to itself. *"Too bad*

for him. I win again." It creeps out from the salty boulders where it's been hiding since last night. It crawls carefully on four legs with its crooked back and sensitive fingers. It disturbs no stones or fallen leaves, making no sound on land or in its mind. The western shore is within sight and so is its immaculate serpent form, glistening like a sleeping dragon halfway between here and the violet sea. Ten or twenty more silent steps and the animal will slither back into that skin. Invincible for another extended winter. An ocean god for another year. It goes on crawling, squinting down at the shoreline pebbles, listening intently with its psychic ears, never seeing us perched above it, crouched in silence atop the boulders.

The animal stops. A mental and physical stillness like invisibility. A trick that's beaten us before. But we rise to our feet and let it listen. We cast our mind north, then to the south, then across the plains to the jungle center. It hears us everywhere. Then nowhere, as our thoughts fall silent once again.

"Practiced all winter," the animal whispers, half impressed, half perturbed. *"I see that part was true. The girl was quicker by two seasons, but she was never quite so fun."* It lifts its eyes to the violet sea. It breathes deeply as though this game will be its last. *"And not quite so stupid!"*

It dashes forward toward the serpent, twice as quick as we've ever seen it move. One last trump card to extend our confinement.

But we're already in the air. The wind is whistling through our scales as we come down upon the animal. A handful of fur twists between the fingers of Emmett Hayes's remaining hand. And the island prison goes up in flashes, the exact same way that it began.

5.05

"—have things to ask him first!" Tysha finishes, still turning to old Mantz.

"I'm not stopping you from that, girl. Only making it easier." The old woman's eyes strobe hypnotically a few more seconds before they dim down to their usual foggy glow.

"I know what you're doing," Tysha says with distaste and a meaningful sneer. "I know well, and I won't have it."

Turning her eyes on the young brightstar, Mantz sees the challenge she expected. But the old woman offers none in return. Just her own imperceptible, silent gaze. "Get on with your questions, then. I'll just be here," she says, laying her twisted walking stick beside her on the long stone bench, "until my brightstar has any further need."

One urge slips from us. One overwhelming impulse to snatch up the old woman's stick and show her brains to the rest of the class.

"Ha!" Mantz spits laughter up at the ceiling. "You see? He was doing rather well until then, you must agree."

"Stop." Tysha waves off Yono as he moves on us again. He's still toting that useless rifle, turning it around to jab us with the stock, but Tysha's eyes pacify him. He grunts disapprovingly as he lowers the rifle and steps back in line beside old Mantz. Tysha watches him a moment longer, then she looks over to us. She wears that same fear that we remember, now laced with pity. "She already sent you?" Tysha asks.

We keep our thoughts quiet, turning our eyes from the young brightstar to the old woman. As a bold test, we hold an array of violent fantasies in our imagination. She sees the edges of them certainly. She sees herself vaguely as the topic of our discussion. But the details remain ours, just beyond her reach, just quiet enough to tease her remarkable senses.

Old Mantz smiles cautiously at us. Somewhere between fear and satisfaction, she mutters, "Rather well, indeed."

"How long?" Tysha asks us again.

We watch her without answering. Her dimness is so obvious to us now, especially stacked against her great potential. Her suppressed starlight is just there, just beyond her grasp. But the longer we watch her, the more her black dread rises to the surface. A cold biting thing. Cold enough to cool us, to turn our eyes away. We look down at Emmett's left hand, no longer seeing the scarred-over stump we lived with on the island. We study Emmett's healthy human hand, and all his old memories begin seeping in. The old woman took so much from us. Months. No, it must have been years.

And yet, no time passed here at all. We see that now. Just a few trifling seconds of her hypnotic light in this higher plane, in this reality where Emmett Hayes was born. All to teach one basic lesson. Taught too well perhaps. Yes. She would have heard all of this before. At least heard it more plainly. We do still feel her searching us. She's a bright one, no doubting that. A Y-2, Emmett would have guessed. But we can see beyond those limited tiers. He was blind, but we . . . we look at Emmett's human hands again. We see where he ends at the wrists and we begin. Our shared scales dance down to our naked toes. Shared. Is that right? Are we sharing, or have we always been . . .

As we trail off, Tysha makes a sorrowful sound across the table. "Damn you." We look back up to her, but she's not speaking to us. She looks almost ready to cry, but instead she clenches her fists in rage. "Do you see now?" She gestures at us while growling at Mantz. "Do you see how much 'easier' you've made it for him with your archaic tricks!"

"I see further than you ever will, girl." The old woman's eyes glow threateningly this time, before she turns them on us again. "But I'll await your permission for the next lesson if it suits you, brightstar."

"My permission? To damage him further?"

"I've only revealed his damage, not caused it. A few stars ago, you might have seen that. Before you squandered the vast light AnSorin found in you."

Tysha is speechless for a moment. Then she speaks in a low and steady tone better meant for enemies. "Mantz. If you isolate my prisoner again before I've had my questions answered, I swear by the light you shall regret it."

"I live for the endless others and regret no choices along that path." Old Mantz turns her dangerous eyes back to Tysha, still indecipherable, still as silent as any mind could be. "But your terms are heard and accepted."

Tysha studies the old woman a moment longer before relaxing slightly, looking back to us. Those pitying eyes are now calcified over. Made even colder than before. For an instant, we see why. We see the source of her dramatic dimming, and it's not a passing cause as she quietly hopes. It's a deep and sinking thing. A compounding suck on her rare light. Perhaps beyond her own power to repair. At least in this lifetime.

Mantz sees it, too, of course. And for all her bold claims of a life without regret, she seems rather pained as the next words pass over her wrinkled lips, "You'll have ample time to ask your questions, aye. And if he's as bright as he seems, you'll be asked as well. Asked and answered, par ya Lum sakar."

Tysha twitches in old Mantz's direction, and we feel the

crippling grip of déjà vu. "What did you—" Tysha starts to ask, apparently not understanding the old tongue at all this time. But as she turns, she sees the ancient woman's intent as well as we do. "Oh god, Mantz, no!" The brightstar reaches desperately for the old woman, but she is too far dimmed to be a match. Even at her brightest, it may have been futile.

And for the second time in seconds time, old Mantz's strobing eyes send us down. Not away but down, we see that now. Down into ourselves, down below the realms of material space. But, by her light, she keeps her word. Not into isolation at all this time. Not into her harsh classroom alone.

The young brightstar is cast down as well.

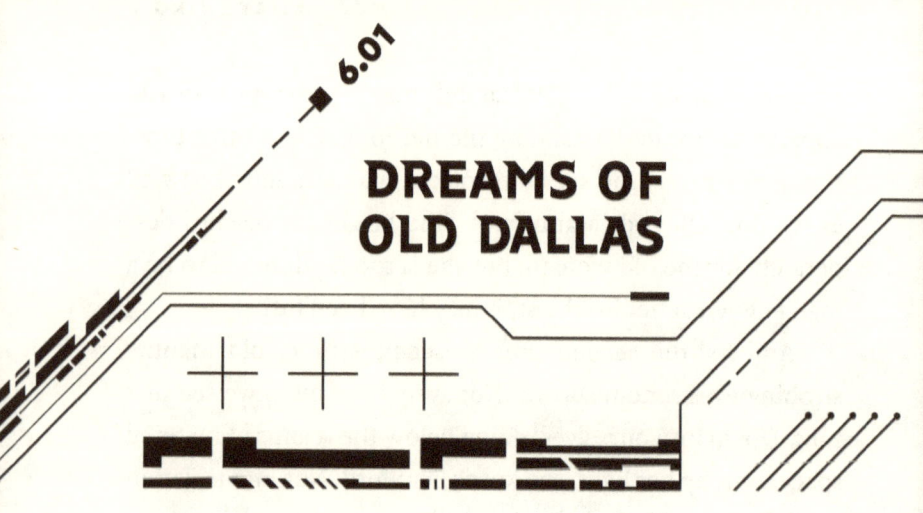

DREAMS OF OLD DALLAS

"Emmy!" Her voice cuts through the wind like a skinny crow just flyin' off. "Emmy boy, goddammit!" I hear Grandma Logan knock over a kitchen chair down in the farmhouse. The screen door thwacks against the porch as she hurries out to come and whoop me.

My eyes pop open as I sit up. My fort is wrecked and droopy all around me like I ain't slept in a peaceful way. Like I been dreamin' about the distant stars and colors in outer space again.

"Shuck stone my time, this fuckin' boy, this useless child," Logan grumbles to our ancestors. By the sound of her moccasins in soil, she's halfway through her garden now. Just a few more steps and she'll be comin' through the big barn door that faces north.

I scamper quick, scramblin' through all the danglin' blankets and old couch cushions until the hayloft's smaller porthole window comes into view. The sun cuts against my eyes, and now I know I'm good and fucked. It's at least eight o'clock, maybe even eight-thirty, and Logan's already got a hand on the ladder down below.

"Wait!" I stop her just before she starts her way up. "Wait, Gramma, I ain't dressed!"

"Jesus mercy, this boy just gave me a command. This child just talked to me like I'm decrepit and told me to wait in my own damn house."

She starts huffin' and almost laughin', and I've never been so scared in my eleven years. I almost lose my privates in my jean zipper, but that don't worry me half as much as Logan down there wringin' her bony hands against the ladder.

"I'm comin'!" I tell her. "I just—the sun didn't wake me, Gramma, but I'm—"

"Someone up there witchu, boy?! Some old wrinkly bitch you callin' names?!"

"No, ma'am. No, Ms. Logan!" I start down the ladder with just my head pulled through my shirt, with two empty sleeves bouncin' on my shoulders like the worst football pads in Texas.

The second my feet land in the dirt, Logan starts switchin' my ass and legs and lower back with a seedless sorghum stalk. It don't hurt too bad, but I yelp and cover my face enough to satisfy her. Soon as I drop my hands, she catches me across the neck a couple times, just to show she's wise to all of that.

"What you lookin' down there fah?" she asks me. "You step in shit?"

I lift my eyes up from the ground before she switches me again. And I ain't cryin' hardly yet, but I can feel it wellin' up—just cuz she surprised me with those high ones, just cuz I bumped my nose when I ducked away. But Logan watches me real quiet, and I see some of the meanness leave her face.

When she ain't scowlin', she almost looks as young as she puts on. But I did the math one time with Roosevelt Hall, and Earl, and Abbie, usin' all their fingers and some of their toes.

We counted forward from the year we found on Logan's old Louisiana license, so now we all know she's pretty ancient. Almost fifty-one.

"That's bettah." She clears her throat and loosens her grip on the sorghum stalk. "Alright, c'mon now. Make y'self decent in front of a lady."

I bring my hands together and push 'em up through my shirt, realizin' right away that I have it on backward. Logan tsks her tongue and shakes her head as I wiggle around to set it straight. I wasn't sure when I grabbed it, but now I'm glad to see which one it is. My old baseball tee with mustard sleeves and plain white cotton everywhere else. Everywhere except the chest where it's got a faded picture from that old film. I ain't seen it yet, but Rosey knows it by heart. It's the one with all them kids who eat too much chew and battle the beast.

"Hey! Where ya shoes at?" Logan snaps her fingers to remind me Earth exists. "Over in the house?"

I have no idea, but I nod yes. I forget to pick my eyes up from the dirt, but she don't chide me for it this time. Just waits right there until I remember. Until I scare myself and look up real quick. And it must just be the sun behind her or my shit eyesight gettin' worse, but for half a second, I almost think she starts to laugh.

Instead, she swats the air and spins away. Walks and talks like I ain't there but best be listenin' anyhow. "Bettah have some good stories fah me, sleepin' half the damn day. Boy bettah have somethin' fah me if I'm gittin' ta fix his hash and eggs the way he likes."

"Oh! Oh yeah, holy smokes, Gram—ma'am—there was like—" I hurry on after her out the barn. "There was like snow and army stuff all over."

She just scoffs without lookin' back at me, except to make sure I don't step on her baby tomatoes that are just about ripe to pick.

"There was this old man with crazy eyes and no hair at all, like no eyebrows at all, and I was up in space for half my life. I was way way up, and the whole Earth was like this, like not even like this!" I try to show her the tiny gap between my pinched fingers, but she just coughs and spits, headin' up the farmhouse stairs to feed me quick and get back to work.

6.02

"Gram, have you seen my Rangers cap? I think it's stoled."

Logan doesn't seem to hear me over her scratchin'. Back and forth, another sorghum seed head rakes against the quarter-inch chicken wire. A million little seeds like popcorn kernels sprinkle down into the second catch bowl.

I take another step into the kitchen from the hallway, tryin' again louder, more polite, "'Scuse me, Ms. Logan, have you seen my—"

She stops scratchin' but doesn't look up. Just sits there, blinkin' down at the kitchen table for a few seconds of dangerous peace.

I get the picture quick enough. I hurry back to my seat across from her and start pickin' out stems from the first catch bowl she filled up while I was sleepin'. Soon as I do, she goes back to scratchin', and the productive silence is returned. One time Logan told me that little boys don't always live to be grown men. Sometimes they just talk themselves to death. I got that picture quickly, too, after she whooped it into focus.

"Hey, Gram," I start real careful, pickin' stems out extra fast so she don't say I'm shuckin' stones. "You think we could get some hogs this summer? Or maybe a milkin' cow or somethin' like that?"

She stops scratchin' to check the stalk. Twists it around in front of her squinted eyes, seein' just a few seeds left over. Then she holds it out for me to take. I stand up to reach across the table, a bit too far for me to get a good grip on it, but she holds the sorghum steady until I can grab it, watchin' me that way she does. Like I should just be thankful she ain't squished me under heel.

That's when I remember the first time I asked her about the hayloft. I wanted to sleep up there and see the stars because it was summer and not too cold. I wanted my own thinkin' space and hideaway, but when I asked her, she just said no. No explanation or nothin' else, just a flat and final no. Couple weeks later, after I quit sulkin', I found the courage to ask again. I showed her some drawin's that I'd done and told her how I'd keep it warm just like the farmhouse. I told her about the owl that lived up there, and so that's why no rats would ever nip me. I'd keep some rocks near the northern window to throw at rabbits and crows or anythin' thievin' from her garden, so I'd be real useful every mornin'. It'd be great for all of us if I was up there keepin' watch on all the dryland.

She was stitchin' wire when I asked her. Makin' the same quarter-inch mesh that she's been scratchin' all this sorghum against today. She stopped her work with similar annoyance, then she asked me why in the hell she had to hear this old plot again? What kind of fool would go out and make all his own careful, clever plans just to return to the exact same woman who already done shook him off? Who asks permission for a private project anyhow? She ain't raised no fools like that, she said. No way a fool like that could exist beneath her roof at all. I built my whole pillow fort that afternoon, and I been sleepin' in the hayloft ever since.

Logan finally lets me have the sorghum stalk, and I sit back down to pick the few seeds still clung around it. I get my words together, then I just tell her plain as day, "I'm gonna talk to Earl Womack tomorrow and see if they got any piglets I can trade for."

"Feed and water, while you're at it," Logan says without lookin' up. "This harvest ain't for pets." She pulls another sorghum stalk from the full basin between her feet. The coarse sound of scratchin' seeds fills the wooden room again.

I try not to show any satisfaction, but my belly jumps in an excited way. A nervous shiver runs down my back like a single ripple across a lake, and somethin' about that feels familiar. Not just the feelin' but this moment. Maybe that's just the anxious itch of farmland repetition. Too many days in here pickin' seeds with Logan, now I got the day job view. I think that's what they call it—when real life feels like a dream that you remember.

An old engine suddenly rumbles somewhere behind me. A suspension squeaks beneath its frame like country music gettin' started. Without thinkin' better, I look up at Logan, and she sees that version of my face she hates the worst.

"Go on then if you're useless!" She snaps me back to my senses. "Go on and see what my son thinks of freeloadin' boys who won't keep up!" She goes on scratchin' twice as quick, already makin' up for my lost time. Goes on cussin' without any words, just nasty grumbles and disgusted nostrils.

I turn back the way she gestured, and that old engine is louder now. I know she'll smack me for it later, but my feet get movin' on their own. I'm already down the hall and out the front door before the grain truck quits its song. The grain truck. Right there, alive for half a second before the engine shakes itself asleep. The driver's door screeches open just as the screen door thwacks shut behind me. I'm up on the porch, but he still looks gigantic—my entire world in six-inch boots and an old USMC jacket. I want to shout but I can't move. Sometimes, I forget to breathe until he sees me, until his quiet eyes catch like a brushfire in our relentless Southern sun.

"Mornin'," he mutters to me just like he would to any stranger, already movin' to drop the tailgate and unload whatever he brought down from Dawson.

"Hey there, Daddy," I say to him like only half of me believes it. Still feelin' that same weird itch like somehow I've lived this day before.

A fifty-pound bag of fertilizer lands in the dirt behind the grain truck. He makes no gestures in my direction, but I know I'm meant to come and grab it. Just as I get movin', a second bag lands right beside it, rippin' open near the seam. He freezes there. We both quickly look at each other, rememberin' what Logan loves to say about stupid hands on hasty men.

Daddy makes no gestures, but I hurry forward, climbin' through the driver door to reach behind the passenger seat. I grab a roll of weather tape, and he hands me his best Milwaukee knife through the truck's back window. As I cut a strip to match the rip in the second bag, he sets a third and fourth down behind the truck with much better patience. The tape keeps stickin' to itself, and I nick my middle finger just enough to summon blood.

If I've ever been happier, hand to God, I can't remember when it was.

6.03

The fourth bag of fertilizer slips through my hands before I can make it to the stockpile. I yank my front foot back to keep it from gettin' crushed, but that just pitches me forward in a wild way. I bang my right knee against one of the stables and lose a shit-ton of skin where my left wrist braces the fall. I shriek like Rosey's little sister, expectin' to see exposed bone when I turn my arm over. But it's just a good, long scrape and a couple splinters. My first instinct is to look up and around at my surroundin's for any witnesses. Thank Christ, the barn's as empty as always.

Not even any cows or goats or hogs like all the other ranches got. Just bins and bins of sorghum seeds, a couple rotten bales of hay from a hundred years ago, a whole arsenal of tools and saws and clamps and engine parts, and this big fat pile of fertilizer. Not sure why Daddy felt the need to add four more bags to the twenty-two we already got. Maybe this is just the backside of some trade he made in town, his repayment for all that labor on old Mike Fortgang's tractor trailer, or another easy win off Ugly Eddy in liar's dice. Shit, I hope not. That man's face could make you wonder if the Lord is good at all.

I try to suck the splinters out but only manage to chew off the tips and bury the main bits even deeper. Givin' up on that extraction, I flex my fingers and shake my hands until the sharp tingles go away, then I hop back up and drag the fourth fertilizer bag over to join its older brothers.

Steppin' back from that finished work, my palms clap together twice in satisfaction. A thick cloud of dust puffs out in front of me, addin' some golden texture to the sunlight streakin' down through the hayloft window. I admire that shape of God a few more seconds before startin' back toward the farmhouse for a bottle of peroxide.

The sounds of an ornery woman slow my feet. Not the distant grumbles that I'm used to or the big boiled-over shouts that would send me scramblin' for a hidin' place. This is a volume of Logan Hayes that I ain't sure I've heard before. A hushed intensity like violent secrets. Like rage and panic makin' love.

I stop at the edge of the wide barn door, listenin' for some clue about how I fucked up this time, but I can't make out a single word. Just more menacin' cussy whispers on the verge of bein' heard. Against my better judgment, I creep closer, through the garden, scarin' off a couple chickadees from Logan's raspberry trellis. I ain't nearly brave or dumb enough to climb up and peek through the kitchen window, so I just hunker down right there beneath it, pressin' my hands against the hot paint, turnin' one ear to listen.

"—make any damn sense at all? Go on and tell me, boy. Go on and try it!" Logan sounds like she's at the thinnest end of her earthly wits with whatever nonsense I musta done. But the way the silence stretches out, I start to think she's finally lost it. Hashin' out some old Louisiana feud with Grandpa Deryl or her dead little brother whose name always escapes me.

"Ain't about bein' sensible," Daddy finally responds, all cool and quiet-like. My heart almost quits itself, realizin' he's less than a step away from the window above me. "Just needs to be done." He says it like a settled fact. "For myself and nobody else."

"Oh, that's a certainty!" Logan stands up quick enough to knock somethin' over—the second bowl of sorghum seeds, by the sound of it. "Done for a witless pride that I'm gettin' used to. For a manly nerve that I've survived alone before!" She spits that last sentence at my daddy, but somehow, I'm the one who catches cold. It's like a snakebite in my belly. Like viper venom chewin' threw my heart and guts.

There's another empty silence, twice as long, before I hear Daddy lean away from the window. His six-inch boots head out the kitchen and down the hall, takin' most of that sick feelin' along with him. To my surprise, the screen door swings open with hardly any force behind it. I know he'd never lose himself to rage like Logan's apt to, but she does have a talent at findin' his limit more days than not.

Lookin' along the side of the house, I see the back of Daddy's head as he trots down the front porch steps, holdin' a big cardboard box of junk. I twitch in fear, expectin' him to turn this way, most likely headed for the mulch pit or the scrap pile in the barn. Instead, he continues north, hoistin' the box up over the side of the grain truck and into its bed. As he does that, my missin' Rangers cap slips free and hits the dirt between his feet. I guess I'm more scared of him than I am of losin' my favorite hat, because I just watch in silence as he picks it up, throws it in the truck, then drives away. Bound northeast toward Shiloh Lake or maybe beyond it to the town of Dawson.

That's when I realize Logan's nasty grumbles haven't started yet. She hasn't started pickin' up the seeds she spilled or scratchin' fresh ones into a new bowl. For a couple minutes or longer now, she hasn't seemed to move at all. Unless I missed somethin', she's still just standin' there at the kitchen table in freaky silence. Like maybe she's the one listenin' to me. Like maybe she's delightin' in my heartbeats, hearin' less and less space between 'em now.

Her fight with Daddy had shit-all to do with me, I can be pretty damn sure of that. But the more intently I listen for

Logan, the more that sickness creeps back in. Not sick like the venom I caught before. This time, it's more like a violence self-inflicted. Like somehow, I've just made the worst mistake in all my years. Like I've just cursed my only begotten kin to go fuck off and die alone.

"The shit you doin'?"

I jolt against the farmhouse like I've been shot. I land in the dirt and crawl my hands backward before I see whose voice just chirped behind me.

"Ba-ha!" Roosevelt Hall laughs in two hot bursts. "Jesus, Em! That ain't no way to sate yourself. No way at all!" Laughin' himself stupid, Rosey falls over the handlebars of his Electricycle, that big, green all-terrain chewer he just got for his birthday. As he bends forward, I see Abbie Ferras sittin' side-saddle right behind him. She's got one of those sly smiles on 'er, like somethin's funny, sure, but it ain't exactly what Rosey thinks.

"Shit, Babs, cover your eyes! Give the boy a chance to tuck himself in." Rosey pretends to block Abbie's view but mostly just tickles her ears and flirts with her pretty face.

"I'm ready now, you spooky bastard." I stand up quick to prove his lewdness incorrect, steppin' out into the garden so we can all see each other better. Rosey's on his tippy toes, straddlin' his big, motorized bike right where Daddy's truck just was, while Abbie hops off the back tire guard to escape his hot advances. I thought she might laugh at my retort, but her dark green eyes stay faithful to Rosey, allowin' mine to roam more shameful places.

She's wearin' her older sister's overalls, greatly modified since I last seen 'em. Sometime between last week and today, all that excess modesty above the knees has been replaced by danglin' strands of severed denim. If she was turned a tad further north, I'd probably be seein' the lowest curve of her big Guatemalan bottom.

"If you can fuck the broadside of a farmhouse, you're more than ready, slick!" Rosey shouts back at me. Abbie laughs at his nasty wit, and I can't hide it, he gets me, too. These days, he gets it all with his broad shoulders and his armpit fuzz already comin' in. He's thirteen last week, so it ain't like I'm diminutive or nothin'. But side by side, I'm startin' to look more like his scrawny little cousin than his best and closest friend. He's even got Abbie on him now, eyes up and down him every time he looks away.

Smack—the farmhouse window hinges open like a gunshot.

"What in the hell. Emmy!" Logan's head and shoulders pop out of the house like a country gargoyle. "Emmy, how long have you been—" her voice breaks off in a mortified suck of wind.

I follow her widenin' eyes down to my naked feet, thinkin' maybe she's disgusted by all the filth I been pickin' up. Then I suck some sick wind, too. I try to sidestep out of the patch, but I'm way too late. Half of her little baby tomatoes are all squished and runny between my toes. I must've walked right over 'em when Rosey spooked me.

I look up at Logan in the window just before her eyes track back to mine, and I see that vein she gets sometimes above her left eyebrow—that one that bulges out about twice a year when the grace of God leaves her completely.

And I get gone for my little life—runnin' right past Ro and Abbie on his motorized bicycle; oh shit, Gram'll hate that, too. That electric sound it's about to make when they come pedalin' after me. That hum like modern man throwin' out his sturdiest traditions.

"Fuckin' boy! Shittin' fucker kids!" Logan gets her licks in without prejudice, bustin' Rosey's taillight with a fryin' pan and clawin' a couple more changes into Abbie's hand-me-downs before they can reach escape velocity. After that, he flies right past me into the woods, with Abbie's arms wrapped tight and desperate around his waist. Not a one of us stops to crack a joke or catch our breath for half a mile.

6.04

"Big wet lips to suck me dry!" Rosey dashes forward three quick steps then throws all his weight into the rope. He doesn't lift his feet at all, and Saber Rock is right there beneath him—until he spreads his knees and slips the jagged stone between his thighs. At the bottom of the swing, his hips buck forward, throwin' his feet straight out ahead for prime momentum, and I won't blame nobody whatsoever for callin' me a liar about what happens next.

Hand to God, the boy soars ten feet higher after he lets go. He screeches like an eagle all the way up and down, and I do hear some fear sneak in behind it, but his perfect cannonball erupts Shiloh Lake in a way I've never seen before. It's the kind of splash you hear about six months later from two other kids who weren't even there. A yearbook moment with fewer witnesses than it deserves. But for Roosevelt Hall, it's just another summer Sunday goin' exactly how he planned.

Abbie and I tread water in astonished silence, blinkin' through the thick rain that he created. Wet strands of hair cling to her cheeks in an oddly perfect pattern, like tattooed whiskers or thin streaks of warpaint slashin' up toward her emerald eyes. She's three months younger than Rosey is, but

I think he still sees her the same way we always have. Like some Mayan queen who returned to Earth after the Man upstairs ran out of tricks. Like we can go ahead and entertain her, maybe even sneak some sweetness if we're real smart, but there ain't a dead dog's chance that these backwoods can keep her forever.

Abbie's clever eyes become big round circles, like maybe I just said all that out loud. I panic for a second. But she panics, too. She thrashes with her hands and looks straight down, first in front of herself then behind. I don't quite know what to make of that, but the answer comes quick enough. She jerks once against her will, then she gets tugged down into the lake. The surface water collapses into her mouth, chokin' off a scream just as she disappears.

"Abb!" I surprise myself by swimmin' toward her, hard and wild, directly into the bubbles roilin' up from below. There shouldn't be any gators left, not after Daddy and Mr. Womack culled 'em all, but *shouldn't and couldn't are bitter rivals of vastly unequal strength.* That's what Logan told me once when I was—

Half a dozen teeth like sharpened stones clamp around my calf and shin. Before I can sip the sweet summer air again, I'm dragged down right behind her.

6.05

Rosey laughs so hard he almost drowns. He comes sloshin' up onto the shoreline where Abbie and I just swam for our lives, and he shows us two handfuls of skippin' stones from Shiloh's bottom. He's got 'em all squeezed in the webs of his fingers like some mad fisherman's brass knuckles. He growls at us and makes claws of his hands before he drops all the false gator teeth in the shallows and hunches over to catch his breath.

My lungs are twice as fried as his, but I scramble up and get after him before I miss my chance. The scrap goes mostly my way at first, a couple quick slaps to his neck and jaw before I tackle him sideways into the switchgrass. Even sprawled beneath me and half underwater, he doesn't quit howlin' with delight. That makes me wild and a little bit stupid. I catch his defendin' forearm between both hands and give him a more authentic lizard bite. I feel his skin shred beneath my teeth, and he squeals just high enough to embarrass himself in front of Abbie. That marks the end of my good luck.

He puts a knee so deep into my ribs I wonder if our friendship will survive it. He boxes my eye with a half-closed fist, and I grab my ears to keep my brains from spillin' out. He shoves me backward into the switchgrass, and every breath I take fills up with sand and mucky water. But Rosey just keeps poundin' on me. He punches my left shoulder eleven times then scrubs mud into my cheeks and eyes and nostrils until I can barely experience the world.

"Leave him!" Abbie comes runnin' up from the shoreline. "Leave him, stop it, stop!" She drags him up and away, but he still stomps on my shin right where his fake gator bite got me. "Will you stop!" she shouts again, both of 'em standin' over me now. "Stop it you mother—" I hear her wrassle him into the shallows. There's a whole lot of splashin' and thrashin' around like a fat catfish gettin' noodled. Then a big gasp from Rosey comin' up for air. Or bein' allowed to come up.

As things settle down, I splash my eyes clean and wipe 'em dry, pushin' up onto one elbow and half a knee. From there, I see Abbie and Rosey twisted up like two spent anacondas. She's behind him, with her legs scissored around his waist and one of his arms wrenched back between both of hers in a crooked Half Nelson. His other arm is pinned beneath his own weight, stuck in the muck. He's cranin' his neck just high enough to keep his nose above the surface, and his eyes are flickerin' in shocked recalibration.

I make an effort to rise to my feet, but the leg he stomped on still smarts a ton. So, I sit back on my butt with two hands behind me, and we all just watch each other soak in the aftermath of our passions.

"Hey, Em." Rosey finally rolls over just enough to slip his pinned arm out from beneath him. Abbie squeezes tighter with her strong thighs, but he muscles himself up to an elbow and glares at me. "I was all talk. Before. But now. You seen it yourself," he pants hard through his mouth and nose, never turnin' his eyes away from mine. "Ain't even one o'clock. And I got this girl. Wrapped around my bigger finger." With each slowin' gust of breath, his angry look becomes more pleased, his exhalations more and more like naughty laughter.

I catch his sickness like the poultry flu. Comin' on slow and mild first, until I'm crackin' up so bad by stomach stitches. We laugh so loud and disrespectful that Abbie releases Rosey and shoves him away, kickin' a splash of water up in his face as she makes for shore. But even as she storms over to our dry pile of clothes beneath the rope swing tree, I can see her fightin' off the devil's efforts to make her smile. And not fightin' half as hard as she was to keep Ro between her legs. Christ almighty. It's all exactly as I remember.

My laughter slows and idles, tryin' to make sense of what I just thought. I look down at the dusty water in my lap then up to all the trees shimmyin' in the wind. Familiar, for sure, this is our favorite swimmin' spot. But from a different distance, somethin' else swims up behind me. I turn around real slow and watch the lake with changin' eyes, squintin' just enough to see more than the usual shines and shapes. I start to see a color in the breeze. Almost like the ripple of a desert heat. Except, if I touched it, I think that I'd go numb. It's the saddest flame I've ever felt. An acetylene ghost all by itself, hauntin' the woods beyond the shore.

"Oh, shit. They musta found 'em!" Rosey shouts.

I turn quietly back to him and Abbie, both lookin' through the western trees to the narrow road on the other side. Rosey's still in his soaked swim shorts, but Abbie's back in her overalls. I can't see what he's talkin' about, but the sound of a loaded pickup is quickly followed by another, headin' north. Without knowin' why exactly, my eyes flick over to Abbie just a hair before she chides him:

"Seriously? You believe Earl Womack?"

"No. I believe Earl Womack, Cady Tucker, and your own fuckin' sister."

"Toni wasn't even in town last night. She was on the phone for two and a half hours making sex sounds with Hayward Marshall. She and Cady were just telling you what Earl heard from Eddy."

"Well, Eddy ain't blind, is he? He ain't a liar, he can't even bluff dice."

"He's a drunk with half an eye turned back to his brain." Abbie squeezes water out of her hair then starts pullin' on her tan ankle socks.

While Rosey searches his wits for a way to come back at her, his eyes drift over to me sittin' in the shallows. "Oh, fuck! Em, I ain't even told ya. Your fuckin' gram scrambled my noodle back there with that goddamn skillet."

"Ain't told me what?" I hear myself respond, already risin' out of the water to get a better view of the trucks on the road. As I join him and Abbie, I hunch slightly forward to keep my ding-a-ling from pokin' through my soggy drawers. Almost like I must. Like that's my next memorized move in some kind of stage show I've performed before.

"Eddy saw three sunspots late last night off the highway to Dawson," Rosey says. "A whole gang of 'em camped out in the woods. Said he pulled over to have a piss and they all scattered just like coyotes."

"Imagine that." Abbie shakes her head as she slips into her sneakers.

"Last I checked, coyotes don't run on two legs. Or make tents outta stolen bedsheets. Will you let me tell it first!"

"Tell him, then. Quit beating around it."

Another truck goes by on the road, but it's headin' south and loaded up with travel bags. I see Mike Fortgang behind the wheel, with his crusty old lady sat beside him lookin' down-right terrified.

"Was there a prison break?" I sound excited when I ask Rosey, even though that itchy part of me already knows how he'll respond.

"You fuckin' wish." He points his finger at my chest and makes sharp slits of his brown eyes. "You better pray that Ugly Eddy is full of shit, for all our sakes. If he's seen what he thinks he has, we'll all have soup for brains before the weekend's done. The lumies don't take no prisoners. They'll grease us all just for a laugh."

"Lumies?" I sincerely ask him, feelin' like I've heard the word a thousand times I can't recall.

"Reachers, you fuckin' bumpkin! Eddy saw three reachers comin' from the northeast. Prowlin' straight down from Dawson."

I take a step back, lookin' from Rosey to Abbie to the woodland road. Lookin' southbound at the stirred-up dirt that Mike Fortgang just left on his way out. Left in a hurry. When my eyes find Rosey's again, he finally sees the panic he expected.

"Holy smokes. What kinda creatures?" I ask 'em both.

For some reason, Abbie laughs real quick and loud at that.

"Oh, my fuckin' god." Rosey pinches his nose like he's got a headache. He pulls his shirt down from a tree branch and starts walkin' toward the Electricycle.

"What kindsa creatures is comin', Ro?" I call after him because that's what happens next. Because I'm still stumblin' along with my best instincts while another part of me comes awake.

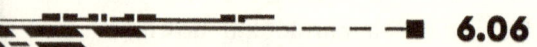 **6.06**

Rosey's motorized bike has special brakes that make it harder to push by hand. But it sounds pretty neat when you trail behind it in this thicker neck of the northern woods. Kinda sounds like a rechargeable flashlight bein' cranked. Except it's never satisfied. The little motor just whines on and on at the same cool volume, like an electric creek beneath the trees.

"But ain't that like sayin' nigger?"

"Jesus, Em, keep your voice down," Rosey hisses back at me over his shoulder. He goes on pushin' the bike, with Abbie walkin' beside him on the other side of its matte-green frame. He quickly scans the trees with nervous eyes before he whispers back to me again. "And no, it ain't nothin' like that. What's the matter with you?"

"But if they don't—" I break off, realizin' I started too loud again. "If Loonymaran is what they call themselves, how come you ain't sayin' that?"

"Luminaran," Abbie corrects me, glancin' sideways at Rosey as she continues. "They don't call themselves that either, we made it up."

"You did not." I keep my voice low. "Ms. Roddy called 'em Loonymarans in second grade, I remember that much. There's a whole bunch of 'em up in Dallas. That's how come they wanna split up the county and make us a proper town."

"Babs ain't talkin' about herself, you fuckin' lump. She means Americans. Human bein's. The reachers won't tell us shit about where they come from, so we can call 'em whatever we want. There's your answer, now shut your hole." Rosey presses on at a quicker pace. His bike hums louder in agreement.

I take a few quick steps to keep up with him, but Abbie makes no such effort. She frowns at the overgrown trail beneath her feet and pinches one of the straps on her overalls. She seems just about ready to lay somethin' heavy on us, but Rosey comes to a sudden stop.

"Oh, shit." He crouches behind his handlebars, lookin' off to his right toward the northern shore of the lake. He lays his bike down in that same direction and scurries forward to peek through the big spreadin' limbs of the old live oak at the edge of the woods. A good forty paces from its trunk, some of the lower branches touch the ground like giant wooden elbows. On more than one occasion, we've shimmied up from there to the higher canopy, with handfuls of stones and capless acorns to slingshot at crows and rabbits and squirrels, or any other young outlaws bold enough to invade our territory—our promised land, assumin' we don't piss Logan off too bad to change her mind.

She bought this swampy northern corner of Shiloh Lake twenty-seven years ago at the Exxon station, back when Dawson was just a few horses better than a ghost town. The shore and shanty here had already been passed on twice at auction, so the old lady widow, Edith Barnes, let Gram have all four acres for six thousand dollars cash. That was the same day she and Daddy arrived on the bus from Mansfield, Louisiana, where Grandpa Deryl had just got himself killed in a pool hall brawl over a busted quarter machine.

Logan whooped and schooled my daddy in this little shack for fourteen years—all the way up until Earl Womack's older brother, Jack, turned seventeen. Daddy was already legal, but he waited for Jack so they could enlist in the Marines together. Two months later, they were in Okinawa, seven thousand miles from all this Southern dryland that ain't even got a name of its own. That's where Jack died. Not sure how exactly, some kinda brain blister or somethin'. The funeral was out this way, but Daddy missed it. When he finally did come home, he was twenty years old, with a newborn son strapped to his chest and just two syllables to describe my missin' mother: *She quit.*

That's when he and Logan combined their money to buy our ranch southwest of here, and far as I know, she ain't returned once in my whole life. She calls this old shack *the quiet house,* because that's how you end up if you live inside it. With nothin' to say, or worse, nobody to say it to. That's why she ain't sold it yet. She'd rather keep the curse than pass it on. In that roundabout way, me and Rosey became the youngest groundskeepers in Texas. Soon as the Lord decides to take her, this whole spread will belong to us.

"Em! Em, git the fuck over here," Rosey whispers harshly, wavin' me closer to the great live oak.

I start to move that way, but I catch eyes with Abbie right beside me—just one sudden second of her full attention as she nears the end of her heavy thoughts. That restless part of me tries to linger this time around, to stay with Abbie and change the course of things.

But Rosey makes another urgent hissy sound, and my legs get movin' just like they're meant to. I slouch down like a soldier in his trenches before I slip in next to Rosey behind a thick tree limb at belly level. A thinner, leafy branch wiggles in the breeze just above our heads.

"What's goin' on?" I whisper.

"We got a trespasser." He points straight ahead to the nearest edge of Shiloh Lake. "See there?" The old shack ain't visible from where we are, but I follow his finger to the muddy path that wraps around to it eventually. Takes me a minute, but I finally spot what he's talkin' about. Fresh tire tracks.

"One of the trucks we saw on the road?"

"Don't think so," Rosey says. "See where they started? Straight outta the trees from the northeast. Ain't nothin' over that way except—"

"The highway to Dawson," I finish for him. Our eyes come together, a little bit excited, a lotta bit scared.

"What's the matter?" Abbie calls out from the trail behind us.

"Fuck—" Rosey almost falls over. "Babs, keep it quiet. Come closer."

She doesn't answer right away. Just holds onto that heavy, thoughtful look a while longer. When she finally responds, her voice sounds twice as tired as it just did. "You know Babs is short for Barbara, right?"

"Say what?"

"I have an aunt named Barbara. It's weird to hear you call me that."

"Well, I don't—" Rosey looks at me like whatever he was about to say would be better in private. "I was just havin' fun, honey. What the hell does it matter?"

"Well, I bet it would matter if I called you Ronnie. Or Rosebud."

He laughs at that and shakes his head. "You can call me Queen of the Night if it'll satisfy you. Git over here now, dammit."

Abbie doesn't respond at all this time. Just watches him with her emerald eyes, speckled in thin shapes of light wherever the sun evades the trees. No humor left in her expression and very little patience.

Rosey sighs, defeated. He turns all the way around to face her proper. Bows like a gentleman. "Abril Damita Ferras, please pardon my simple ignorance. Please cleanse me of my country sins. Please shut the fuck up and git your ass over here before we all git fuckin' murdered."

Abbie twitches then looks at the ground. She shakes her head twice and almost laughs. Her hands are clenched, and her arms are rigid at her sides when she looks back up, not to Rosey but directly to me.

"See you around, Emmett." She turns back south and marches off, stompin' hard on the back tire of the Electricycle as she goes.

"Abbie," Rosey finally calls after her at a normal volume, like maybe that's all she's sore about. He watches her until she's out of sight, then he scoffs and turns to me. "Goddamn. I said please, didn't I?"

"A bunch of times."

That makes him laugh again, but it's nothin' like his usual sound. He looks over at the Electricycle until his smile fades down to somethin' unfamiliar. For the first time since we've been friends, Rosey begins to look uncertain, even afraid. That's when we hear the gunshot.

One thunderclap like a hundred balloons all popped at once. The echo rolls over us from the north, and we both spin around to stare in silence. Straight up the hidden trail through Logan's woods where we was just headed. If we hadn't stopped here when we did, whoever let off that round woulda been right on top of us. A high caliber rifle, by the sound of it. A .308 or a .30-30, fired just up there at the quiet house or somewhere beyond it. Our eyes come together, both seemin' to realize how close we came to an early end, how truly dangerous this alien hunt could turn out to be.

Without a second thought about it, we both get movin' in that direction.

6.07

For six or seven minutes, we creep like Apaches through the woods. Rosey's tobacco-leather high-tops now dangle from an oak branch way back behind us, leavin' him barefoot and natural just like me. We're both ten yards west of the hidden trail, just to be safe. Elbow to elbow, we're slinkin' along, low enough to use our hands as extra feet, sendin' squirrels scamperin' up their trees every time we sneak within arm's reach. We know this land. We got it mapped behind our eyes better than any Texan man alive. Every man except maybe one.

We stop together at the edge of the clearing. Rosey spots the front bumper first, but I'm quicker to recognize whose it is, parked in the shade behind the quiet house at the very end of those fresh tire tracks. It's just obvious enough to make me feel stupid. And relieved.

The grain truck.

I break the silence with easy laughter, and Rosey eyes me like a threat.

"It's alright, it's just my daddy." I stand up to have a better look, but Rosey tugs me back down behind the hedge of sage. "Lay off! I just told you that's my daddy's—"

"Who's he shootin' at?" Rosey hisses back at me, allowin' his eyes to deliver insults. "Or who's shootin' at him?" He points all around us.

"Just once," I remind him but even quieter now, barely chancin' the sound of my own voice as I start to look around at all the best places we've hid before. I look out to the dock for any sign of an invader's ripples, but the water is smooth as glass. The only boat tied there is the little wooden dinghy that me and Rosey finally finished last July.

"What's he doin' here?" Rosey mouths after tappin' my shoulder. His eyes look suspicious and defensive, a combination I can't quite make sense of—until I start to think about how long it's been since Daddy came out this way.

We cut and nailed that little dock together when I was six. I mostly just watched, I guess. But Daddy did let me push the first plank through the miter saw, and I handed him all the nails two-by-two for three days straight. We got started on the dinghy a little while after that, but we only got about halfway done before we left it unfinished in the barn. Come to think of it, that was about the same time that Ms. Roddy got in trouble at the school. She taught grades two and three together, that's how me and Rosey first met Abbie and Earl Womack. Ms. Roddy was teachin' us all about Jim's Crows and the Doctor King and how people used to say words like nigger all the time cuz they didn't know better yet. She said it can be real hard to know things like that when everybody lives mostly separate. Kinda like how some people around here really want the Loonymarans to stay apart from all of us. I went home and asked Daddy about some of that, and he got real quiet. Kinda like the one time I asked him about my mama. I guess some other kids asked their folks about the Loonymarans, too, because Ms. Roddy wasn't allowed to come back to school for a couple weeks. Then she moved all the way out to Atlanta that September.

Rosey nudges me again, and his eyes look real annoyed. I guess he expected some kind of answer to that last question, but I've got no idea what to say. Daddy had that bad fight with Logan, and now he's way out here at the quiet house. He tossed my favorite ball cap into that box of old junk and damaged clothes, and now he's way out here doin' whatever the hell a grown man does with his free time. Maybe grabbin' more knickknacks from his youth to take up to Dawson for a donation.

Another gunshot cuts the air.

Me and Rosey both turn to face the sound. Twice as close this time but not nearly so surprisin'. We've been waitin' ten minutes for it. My best guess would put it another hundred yards northeast from where we are now, just beyond where the tire tracks exit the trees. A pretty solid answer to Rosey's question rushes to me.

"The Marlin." I smile real wide and turn to Rosey. "That's my daddy's 336. He's prolly just out here huntin' game or shootin' targets."

The matter seems perfectly settled to me, but Rosey's distrustful eyes hardly change at all. Not until they drift back over to the quiet house.

"Oh, damn!" He falls back on his ass. "What was that?!" He glares at the shack.

"What?" I try to follow his sight line.

"There—the window!"

I look to the thin pane of glass next to the front door, just in time to see the white curtain settle slightly. Maybe. Too quick to be sure at all.

"There's someone in there," Rosey hisses again. "They was lookin' right at me."

"My daddy was?"

"No. I don't fuckin' know. They was down in the corner. Real low."

I look back to the window, not seein' any signs of life at all. But somethin' else starts to creep up on me. That cold itch I felt by the lake. That bad feelin' I keep pushin' down like an upset stomach. Somethin' about the quiet house is givin' me a panic like I've never felt before. No. I've got that backward. It's a panic way too familiar.

"We should go back." I say it straight ahead without turnin' to Rosey yet.

"I dunno, I just saw some eyes. Just for a second," Rosey responds like I said somethin' else. Like I asked him some kind of question. And that restless half of me almost remembers what it was. Almost knows what's comin' next.

"No." I turn to face him. "We should go home right now. We—"

"Exactly." Rosey keeps his eyes on the shack. "Either your daddy's out there with his Marlin or he's in the house playin' peek-a-boo. He ain't doin' both." His eyes connect with mine, not seemin' to see my dread at all. Instead, he nods in cold agreement to somethin' I didn't say. At least not today. He gets down in the dirt and digs up a stone the size of a baseball. Turns it in his grasp with eager fingers. And when I look down, I see somethin' similar in my right hand. A jagged rock like a recurrin' nightmare.

"No," I beg myself and him at once. "No, we shouldn't."

But Rosey just slinks away around the perimeter. Around toward the side door that leads to the kitchen.

Another gunshot claps in the distance. My daddy's rifle, no doubt about it. My daddy's trademark patience out there in the northeastern woods.

And I stay low as I creep forward. Another twenty paces to reach the window. One twist of my wrist and I'll be inside. One last trip to the quiet house where my young life seems fit to end.

6.08

The air inside the shack stinks like rust and rotten wood. It tickles my nose as I breathe it in, all full of dust and a bad mildew smell. At least it's not too dark. Skinny beams of sunlight are sneakin' in all over the place; the whole ceilin' is like one big wooden disco ball frozen in time.

Leavin' the front door wide open and bright behind me, I take my first full step inside the quiet house since I was eight-and-a-half. The entire room seems to disapprove. The long oak plank beneath me groans in an exhausted, grumpy way. A sprinkle of termite dust traces down one of the sunbeams near my face, and somethin' quick and mousy scurries under the old armchair to my right. Then a long and creaky sound rattles out from the kitchen at the rear of the shack. A slow and spooky disturbance, like a haunted wardrobe pullin' itself open. I squeeze the jagged boulder in my hand just hard enough to break my skin, ready to chuck it and run from whatever demons even Logan couldn't destroy.

But it's just Rosey. He creeps into view back there with his own square of sunlight caped over his shoulders, and our frightened eyes are so goddamn glad to find each other. Until somethin' bumps in his peripheral.

We both look that way. To the furthest corner of the kitchen. To the darkest part of the entire house, just beyond the old wood-burnin' stove. Rosey's only a few steps away from that. His eyes flick uncertainly to me, and I check over my shoulder, half hopin' to see my daddy come stridin' in, all strong and brave and armed with more than these stupid stones. But there ain't nothin' but mud and empty shoreline back behind me, so I turn myself forward once again.

I take my second step inside, and the waterlogged oak threatens to snap beneath me. Promises to drop me eight feet down to the storage cellar underground. Holy smokes. I can't hardly imagine a worse location to survive a broken leg. Crawlin' with spiders and rats and those bad black snakes that match the shadows.

I sidestep to a different plank. Thank God, it's much more solid. I take a fourth and fifth step, then one last nervous hop, which lands me safely next to Rosey in the kitchen. The floor is stone in here, so there's no fear of fallin' through. But that just sends our eyes back to the kitchen corner.

It's real narrow. Not enough space for us to proceed side-by-side. Bein' almost two years older and twenty pounds closer to a full-grown man, Rosey seems the obvious choice to lead the way. His scared eyes say he agrees. He sets his rock down on the countertop and quietly wiggles the nearest drawer until it slides open. Without much deliberation, he withdraws a ten-inch carvin' fork. It's thick and black with a lumpy surface, like some kinda repurposed railroad spike. He blows a cloud of dust away from its prongs then twists it in the smudgy sunlight. Just as we're both startin' to feel courageous, that hidden thing bumps a second time.

One tiny sound from inside the pantry. Almost like shufflin' feet. One undeniable noise just there, behind the tallest, skinniest, darkest door in the entire cabin. Back at the farmhouse, in some of the closets, we have a little chain that hangs down from a forty-watt bulb. But there ain't no electricity in the quiet house, never has been. If it was any later in the afternoon, neither of us would've had the nerve to step inside. But here we are on our promised land, with our first real intruder cornered in the dark.

Get out, that restless part of me tries again. *Grab Ro and get the hell out before it's too late!* But the active half of me just squeezes the jagged rock down by my waist. Just watches quietly as Roosevelt Hall does what he does best.

His broad shoulders block my eyeline as he steps forward with the carvin' fork, as he turns sideways like a Spanish swordfighter, beginning his bold approach. Barefoot on dusty granite, we both inch stealthily into the shadows. The carvin' fork shivers like the black tongue of a petrified cobra, and I've got my ugly rock cocked up by my ear now, ready to strike from medium range. We're both so focused on the pantry, we completely forget the cellar door.

It groans angrily beneath Rosey's foot, and we both halt.

We look down at three planks of wood combined to make a knotted square. Bound all around the edges by rusty iron, with one big steel ring in the center to pull it up. Rosey retreats his foot from it slowly, carefully, but that just makes the oak talk longer. It creaks just like the side door did when he came in, and we both look fearfully up to the pantry.

Nothin' bumps this time. It's deadly quiet, and somehow that's even worse. Like whoever's in there is listenin' careful now. Holdin' perfectly still with their own fork and stone in either hand. Ready to poke us through the eyes as soon as that skinny door opens an inch. I get a headache just thinkin' that. A sharp pinch inside my brain as I imagine my own death.

"Now!" Rosey hastily shouts. Like we had some kind of plan at all. I panic and rush forward straight into his back, but that convinces him to follow through. He takes three lungin' steps past the wood-burnin' stove and kicks the pantry door with his left foot. That doesn't do much but rattle the house and startle the fuck out of us both. Then he quickly grabs the door handle and tugs it open.

A snap of light pops from the darkness like a silent fire-cracker. That scares me back a step, and my boulder hand knocks an old cast-iron pot and lid straight off the stove. They clang and bang against the granite in a sudden violence right behind us. We both whip around to that, then we spin straight back to the open pantry just as our intruder lunges out.

With inhuman quickness, it darts around Rosey and springboards off a cabinet near his waist. It headbutts my chest like a fluffy cannonball, knockin' me flat assed. Soon as I hit the floor, a flurry of claws scamper wildly over my neck, chin, and shoulder until the beast finally digs into my forearm and dashes away, trippin' over the cast-iron pot and tumblin' badly before it gets its feet back beneath itself and bounds out the kitchen door. There's a sudden elegance in its last few grassy hops before it's gone around the corner. The biggest damn jackrabbit I've ever seen.

"Fuck!" Rosey steps over me to chase after it, then he comes right back to check the pantry for anythin' else. Apparently, he dropped the carvin' fork straight away, because now he quickly scoops it from the floor. "Was that a goddamn bunny rabbit?" he laughs, totally relieved, until he takes a good look at me beneath him. "Oh, shit. Oh, damn." He sets the fork on the counter then quickly squats down to pull me up.

He avoids my right forearm where the jackrabbit clawed me, but he ends up grabbin' me by the left wrist that got scraped up in the barn this mornin'. That makes me wince and cuss pretty good, and he almost drops me down again.

"Fuck me," Rosey mutters once he stands me up. He examines the bloody claw marks, already drippin' red toward my elbow. He looks at my mauled chin and neck and some of the dark colors he gave me in our scrap back by the lake. "We might hafta tell folks it was a cougar." He pats my shoulder and coughs up a laugh.

"Yeah. Best let me scratch you with that fork, make it more believable. The heck was that light?" I lean around him to have a look inside the open pantry. It's not quite so dark in there as I remembered, but it's close. The skylight might've been useful a long, long time ago, but now it's covered in fallen leaves and branches, muckified by years of rain. A few trickles of sunlight sprinkle across the higher shelves, but the bottom ones are lost in scary shadow. My vision loiters on the darkest corner in the very back, and that eye strain gives me another pinch between the ears.

"What light?" Rosey follows my glance, peakin' around the pantry door. Couple seconds later, he grimaces just like I did and turns away, massagin' his left temple. "Fuck, I wish we got hands on that damn jackalope. I got a hunger headache like you wouldn't believe."

"Yeah. Me, too." My eyes drift absently, almost like there was somethin' else important, somethin' I can't seem to remember now.

"C'mon." Rosey musses my hair and steps around me. "Let's go see where Crabbie run off to. Bet you a dollar she'll lick your wounds just to see me mad about it." He laughs one big loud note then heads straight for the side kitchen door without even lookin' back to see if I follow.

Before I go, I pick up the cast-iron pot and lid then set 'em both back on top the stove. Not sure why exactly. Logan wouldn't come out here to witness the promised return of Jesus Christ. Then again, I thought I was done with the quiet house, too. Done for good after what happened to my daddy— after all the wickedness soon to come.

Two steps past the cellar door, I stop like death. Not just me, my itchy restless half. I watch myself touch one of the scratches on my arm then wince away with a sudden idea. A spark like that thing I couldn't remember. I watch the back of Rosey's head, almost out the door, almost safely gone. I try to cover my mouth and change it all, to keep it from happenin' all over again, but instead I cup a hand to the edge of my lips just to be sure he hears this part—these last ten words that killed my daddy.

"Hey, how you s'pose it got shut in there anyhow?"

"Say what?" Rosey turns back with a smile, then he stops even deader. His face goes stiff just like it did when we was outside, when he was so certain he'd seen someone's eyes in the front window.

I spin back around to the pantry, and it's all changed. I see the same dark closet but packed with tangled legs and hands and horrified faces. I see two scrawny grownups, man and lady, huddled low in the darkest shadows. They're starin' back at me like they seen the devil, like he might just crawl right out my mouth and crack their bones between his teeth. Their faces are that white already, white as a skeleton left out in the sun. All their clothes are old and worn, like some of my daddy's old chewed up jackets. Just like that exactly.

And I see a boy sat in between 'em. He looks real tired. He's breathin' heavy and his face is drippin' in so much sweat. He's maybe nine years old, and he's got one hand stretched halfway in my direction, almost like he's tryin' to reach out and touch me, almost like he's about to faint from tryin' so hard. He's wrapped in a blanket, wearin' an old ball cap on his naked, little head. It's too dark to see the colors, but there's one big letter front and center, stitched in white. A capital T for the Texas Rangers.

There's a snap of light just like before, and the cellar door falls shut in front of me. I could of swore I was just standin' on my feet, but now I feel cold granite beneath my ass. The pantry is straight ahead, as empty and dark as always. But wasn't it just ... wasn't I just doin' somethin'?

"Reachers!" Rosey screams at the top of his lungs. "Reachers! Help! Fuck—" His strong hands dig under my armpits, dragging me backward to my feet. He pulls me so hard I fall again, but this time, fear and instinct gets me movin' on my own, scramblin' out the kitchen door right after him. "They're here!" Rosey shouts off in the direction where my daddy's

Marlin was poppin' rounds. "Help! Somebody! The reachers are in Ms. Logan's house!"

 **6.09**

A truck comes rattlin' up the shoreline from the south, and I'm reminded how much faster Rosey is. I've never ran with so much fear and confusion at my back, but he still beats me there by fifteen paces. Mr. Womack brakes early, skiddin' in the mud just to keep from runnin' him over.

"What happened? Where you comin' from?" Mr. Womack asks from the driver window. "Girl said she heard gunshots."

I got no idea what girl he's talkin' about until I get close enough to see through the windshield. Abbie's in the middle seat next to Mr. Womack. Her eyes are red like she's been cryin', but she looks relieved and glad to see me and Rosey alive and well.

"Reach—in the—the hou—" Rosey points back to the quiet house, still tryin' to catch his breath.

"He's seen 'em! Charlie, lookit 'im! He's seen 'em back thataway!" Ugly Eddy starts bouncin' in the passenger seat on Abbie's right. He smiles real big with the few loose teeth that he's got left, all crooked and yellow in different directions. His left eye is wide open and animated while the other is stuck lookin' sideways at his sunburnt nose.

Mr. Womack pays Eddy no mind. He raises one finger to the brim of his old bull-hide hat—the one he's still got from his rodeo days—and draws an inch of shade down over his eyes as he gazes out at the quiet house.

"There's three of 'em," Rosey says much clearer now. "Three reachers hidin' in the old shack. They went down in the cellar after we caught 'em." He directs most of this intel in Abbie's direction, maybe tryin' to flex and win her over. Maybe tryin' to apologize in his own roundabout way. Or maybe just because Mr. Womack ain't the easiest man to speak to directly.

"Caught 'em?" Handsome Hayward Marshall laughs as rude as he can. He stands up in the truck bed and sets a double-barreled shotgun on the roof. "Who else you got in there? Mrs. Bigfoot?"

"Nah, she's too busy peggin' yer old man," Rosey hisses back. "Shut the fuck up, Jr."

"You—you're a bullshit liar!" Hayward shouts so hard his perfect hair almost moves a little. Rosey starts to come back at him with another zinger, but Mr. Womack puts a firm hand out the window where everyone can see it. I swear to God, even the nearest jays and crows quit their songs and turn to listen.

"That your daddy's truck? There in the back?" Mr. Womack still hasn't taken his wrinkled eyes off the shack in the distance.

"Yessir." I spit the words up without tastin' 'em first. "But he ain't there. Out with his Marlin, I think." I point northeast where those muddy tire tracks exit the woods. Mr. Womack's eyes don't bother to follow. He watches the house.

"And this boy's tellin' the truth?" he asks me. "'Bout what y'all saw inside?"

Rosey makes a huffy insulted sound, but he turns to me with total confidence. He's grinnin' at first. Then he sees my eyes drift toward the dirt.

"I—I don't know," I answer truthfully. "It was real dark."

Hayward Marshall scoffs at an obnoxious volume. Abbie sighs, relieved again. But an embarrassing glance passes between her and Rosey.

221

"Em, what the fuck." He nudges me with his elbow. "Tell 'em!"

I look uncertainly at Rosey then over to the quiet house. But the sun reflects harshly in that front window, and I grimace away. "I don't know." I massage my left eyeball, wishing I could dig my fingers even deeper. "I can't—I don't remember."

Ugly Eddy gasps, lasering his good eye in my direction. "They gots to him. Oh lawd, they gots in his head, Charlie!"

Mr. Womack doesn't respond, but I hear a subtle click behind the driver door. A sound like three tiny twigs bein' snapped in quick succession. But more metallic. Abbie looks down in that direction, near his lap, and her whole body freezes stiff. She quickly looks up to his hard face, just a mangled ear and muscular jaw from her perspective. Then, very slowly, she looks over to me and Rosey. That's about when I realize I ain't seen Mr. Womack's right hand yet.

On cue, the old rodeo rancher finally looks away from the quiet house. The old Mesquite boogeyman—who was asked to retire because his buckin' bulls were just a little too good at stompin' all those fancy showboys flat—finally glances down from the haunted shack and shows me his eyes. Bright and gray, just like the barrel of his old Peacemaker.

"Mind if we take a look?" he asks me firmly, man to man. And half of me believes he'd honor a refusal. Half of me knows if I just show a little grit and stand my ground, Mr. Womack won't see nothin' left to do but turn this little posse back down the road. He's just that kind of cowboy.

But the dumber half of me quickly nods and steps aside.

Mr. Womack's lips tighten to a narrow line as he looks forward to the shack. His left hand moves to his lap, probably holdin' that big Peacemaker steady, then he uses his right to shift the truck back into drive.

"Oh, lawd. Oh, Jesus keep us," Eddy starts to whimper, retreatin' against his seat like he's in a roller coaster ready to drop.

Quick as he can, Rosey shoulders past me and hops up on the runnin' boards. He puts one elbow inside the driver door to keep himself steady, then he turns back and looks at me. I think he's about to hock a loogie on my forehead, but he just mirrors Mr. Womack, turnin' his eyes straight ahead to the quiet house.

The truck gets goin' without me. Goin' by forever, like one of those huge freight trains rollin' through Dawson. At the very last moment, I feel the urge to call out and bang my fist against the rear fender to halt the wheels. But that courage passes, too.

I watch the empty space the truck left behind: the muddy road, the quiet lake, the northeastern trees on the opposite shore. At the very edge of my bad vision, I see new movement. Somethin' like a man with a rifle in his hands. Somethin' even bigger strapped to his back. I see his human form step out of the trees and watch the truck with a sudden rigidness. He looks from the truck to the quiet house, and the rifle shape seems to tighten in his grip, to go rigid just like him. He's just a blur, and I shouldn't have any certainty from this distance, but I see my daddy look straight at me. He looks at me, and I feel that snakebite all over again, that belly sickness from the farmhouse. It feels like Rosey's eyes a minute ago. The damaged eyes of the betrayed.

That's when my daddy's patient shape becomes somethin' else—somethin' I've fantasized about but never imagined I'd see for real. His gloved hand flashes between his belt and the Marlin's receiver, loadin' three rounds quicker than I've ever loaded one. I see him snap the lever forward, sendin' one glitterin' speck of gold into the air. He catches that spent case without lookin' at it. His eyes are like Mr. Womack's now, straight ahead on the quiet house. His feet are marchin' that direction, straight down the shoreline, a hundred yards between his new shape and these trespassers I've invited. A brand-new shape to me but a resurrected one to him. I see a Private First Class in the United States Marine Corps, ready to die for his witless pride.

6.10

When I finally catch up to Mr. Womack's truck, Hayward Marshall's already around the side of the cabin, peekin' in. His right hand is cupped against the kitchen window, while his left grips the double barrels of that big shotgun. Like a true namby, he's got both muzzles nestled nice and neat beneath his chin, one misfire away from breakin' Toni Ferras's beautiful heart. Still sat in the truck, Abbie and Eddy both look nervous and out of place. They're side-by-side in the split bench seat, avoidin' eye contact for opposite reasons.

But Mr. Womack looks right at home. He's got one of them cigarillos he grows and rolls himself bit between his wide front teeth. The thick smoke floats up from there to the brim of his rancher hat, surroundin' his head in an underworld halo. He's leaned against the right headlight of his huge truck, both arms and legs crossed in a casual way, but his eyes are the most serious pair I've ever seen—lookin' straight down the northeastern trail.

Standin' beside him, about five inches shorter, Rosey fidgets uncertainly. He's doin' his best to keep his cool, to keep his eyes firm and manly in that same direction. The only thing stoppin' him is just how well he knows my daddy.

The ex-Marine is close enough now for all of us to see him clearly. He'd be here already if it weren't for what he's carryin' with him. Not just his Marlin but a full-grown deer, antlers and all. He's got it backpacked. The front legs are broken and cut from the bone. The front hooves are twisted and slotted through cuts in the hind legs, creatin' natural straps for his arms to slip through. The antlered head dangles and bounces over his left shoulder, almost like he's just givin' some tuckered out buck a piggyback ride home.

But twenty paces from Mr. Womack's truck, my daddy comes to a stop. He pulls a serrated knife from his game belt and slices the joints in the deer's right knees. The whole thing slumps off his back and hits the ground just like the dead meat it truly is. He stands there holdin' his knife in one hand and the Marlin in his left, eyes straight ahead at Charlie Womack.

"Y'all look hungry." Daddy sheathes the knife then lets the Marlin rest in the crook of his arm. "Good thing, too. This big boy could feed the county." He nudges the buck with his six-inch boot then stretches his back with a twist to the left. His eyes pass right over me like I ain't there.

"Looks like a good kill," Mr. Womack says without ever lookin' at it. "You expectin' company?" He drags his cigarillo long and slow. They both watch each other through the smoke that he exhales.

"Freezer's gettin' light," my daddy says. "Figured I'd get a head start on winter rations. 'Specially with these young ones always sniffin' around." He smiles softly at Rosey and Abbie, but neither one can keep their eyes up in his direction. "Yours 'round here somewhere?" He looks over to the quiet house; spots Hayward Marshall peekin' around the back corner.

"Earl's mindin' his chores," Mr. Womack answers. He plucks the cigarillo from his lips and drops it in the dirt. His legs uncross, and his pointed cowboy shoe presses the 'rillo into an ashy resemblance of its ingredients. He stands tall and straight, addin' a couple more inches between him and Rosey. "Might be you don't see him around too much more this summer." His right hand comes to rest on his hip, and I catch a glimpse of a single-action revolver holstered just beneath it. His old Peacemaker, still cocked to fire.

That spooks me back a step. I trip over the truck's rear tire, and my elbow bangs hard against the frame. Everybody's shoulders jump to their ears. They look back my way like startled cats.

Everybody but Daddy and Mr. Womack.

A couple flies buzz up from the carcass and swoop around my daddy's ears, but he hardly stirs. The Marlin's still cradled gently in his left elbow, but I realize his right hand is now trigger-ready.

"That's a shame," Daddy says with true disappointment. "His older brother and I were just gettin' started at that age."

Mr. Womack twitches noticeably. Two knuckles pop on his left hand as he squeezes it into a fist. His nostrils flare before he cools himself back down. "I'll thank you for not speakin' his name. I ain't come here for old foolishness."

"None intended, sir. None at all." Daddy's left hand raises slightly in peace. "Maybe you just go on and say your business. I'll oblige however I can."

"Who you got in this house?" Mr. Womack asks impatiently.

Much more careful, Daddy frowns, confused. "Think I asked to hear your business, not my own."

"You best answer him, mister." Hayward Marshall and his shotgun creep forward, startin' to box Daddy in on his right.

"Mm. Why's that?" Daddy turns to face him. The Marlin never moves from his elbow, but Hayward stares at it frightfully. He tries to respond, but his mouth just hangs open. The big country shotty rattles in his soft hands.

"You had a look at your boy?" Mr. Womack interjects. Daddy turns away from Hayward like he doesn't exist. Like his threat is zero. "You got anythin' to say about why he looks so damn chewed up?"

Daddy watches Mr. Womack. Then his eyes flick studiously to Abbie. To Rosey after that. Never over to me. "I'd say that's his business and probably theirs. Somehow, I'm still waitin' to hear yours." His eyes and Mr. Womack's meet again. Neither gives up ground.

"Looky there, Charlie!" Ugly Eddy shouts from the passenger seat. That's the tarp I seent this mornin'. The blue tarp on the truck on the highway!" He points to an old tarp, neatly folded near a pile of ten-year-old firewood. "He was haulin' ass, but I told you I seent it! Lawd, it was him! He was there, Charlie! Charlie—"

"Hush!" Mr. Womack backhands Eddy through the open window. "Put some respect on my name or I'll learn you how! You'll learn it!" He cocks his left hand to strike Eddy again—

"Well, he's right about that." Daddy takes a step forward. The Marlin slips smoothly from his elbow to his second hand. "I came down from Dawson just after daybreak. Bought a few fifty-pounders from the Fortgangs. You can ask 'em about it."

Mr. Womack is still sneerin' at Eddy, one tight fist coiled by his scarred right ear, gored years ago by one of his own bulls. He doesn't cool himself much at all this time, but he does lower his fist and turn back around. As he does so, I see why Daddy uncrooked the Marlin. That old Peacemaker has found its way into Mr. Womack's shootin' hand.

"No, I cannot," Womack enunciates angrily. "I reckon Mike and Sue Ellen are just about halfway to Houston by now." He jabs his Army revolver at the dirt like an extra-long finger. "Scared shitless by all this damn reacher talk! Or maybe by somethin' they seen this mornin'." He nods at my daddy without any politeness anymore. He nods several times like his mind's just about made up. "The boy already told us." He wags the single-action to his right. "So, you can just fess up and step aside, because my business is defendin' this community and its good people. That clear enough for you, son?"

Daddy watches Mr. Womack with unsteady eyes. With thoughtful slowness, he follows his pistol gesture and finally looks at me directly. I try to deny it, but nothin' happens. I try to point at Rosey, but that just makes my belly feel even worse. My stomach squirms like the ancient pit in that old film—that first one Daddy ever showed me, where the world's bravest man comes face to face with his worst fear. A den of snakes.

That's when the explosion comes. A sudden boom like backyard dynamite, like the worst car crash I've ever heard.

We all stagger through our worst instincts. Abbie and Ugly Eddy both shriek at the same high pitch. Rosey spins against the truck then falls to the dirt on his hands and knees. My shoulders jump to my ears, lockin' painfully in that position. Only my eyes turn toward the quiet house, where Daddy and Mr. Womack already have their weapons trained, locked onto the source of the horrible sound. Locked on Hayward Marshall.

Both of his big barrels are smokin', freshly fired. His eyes and mouth are opened wider than one of those cheap sex dolls, not in fake ecstasy but verifiable shock. He's lookin' down at the ground. Down at somethin' small near the back corner of the shack. Somethin' white and red, now ripped to shreds. I can't tell what he's lookin' at until the strange woman screams. It's the sort of unhinged, godless shout that even an animal could understand. A great wailin' sound like the world is ended. For her, I guess it has. It's the same joyless noise I'll hear Logan make when she comes and finds us here. Oh yeah. She's the one who finds us when it's all over. Logan's the one who rushes me away to hide in Houston, I remember now. The pale woman screams, and I remember exactly what it means.

It's the sound a mother makes when her son is killed.

6.11

"It was lookin' at me!" Hayward shouts at the little white corpse halfway between the quiet house and the northern trees. "It—I just—I turned around and it was lookin' at me!" He begs God to buy that history, even though the angle don't seem quite right from where I'm standin', even though it looks more like the little legs were dashin' away.

The pale woman screams again, and Hayward jolts in sickly fear. He takes several clumsy steps backward as she hurls herself into view from behind the quiet house, landin' on her knees and crawlin' forward. She cradles the little white child in her arms, like maybe she can still rouse him with affection, like maybe he'll be alright. But his neck is red ribbons. His poncho blanket is a spreadin' sea of that same color, honeycombed with buckshot from hip to shoulder. His eyes are empty. Blank, blue orbs, centered beneath my favorite cap. A capital T as white as his face. He looks just as tired as I remember. I remember. In the house, in the pantry. It all comes back to me like one bad dream.

"Wait!" Daddy tries to help but only makes it worse. Oh, God. I remember this part, too. He shouts at the other one, the one in the trees, but Hayward Marshall spins around instead. He spins around with his frantic, beautiful eyes, drenched in fear and a boyish need to be forgiven. To be pat on the back while someone says, *Aw shucks, kid, these things just happen.* To be sent home early so Antonia Ferras can stroke his limp ego back to life. Yeah. I remember these scared eyes on Hayward Marshall. I remember seein' him look straight at my daddy just as the pale man rushes up behind him.

He swings it hard. Some kinda modern tomahawk, painted black. The pale man torques it just like a teenager smashin' mailboxes, and Handsome Hayward drops like bricks. A chunk of his scalp bounces into the pile of old firewood. A thin fan of blood sprays from a deep crack behind his ear. He doesn't go unconscious. He spasms. He babbles in the language of mindless men, spittin' in the mud and bitin' his tongue while his eyes work their way back toward his brain.

The pale man wails his own tragic sound, but he doesn't swing his dark weapon again. He just shouts at Hayward's new hideous shape and pounds himself repeatedly on the thigh. He weeps and pushes one of my daddy's old trucker hats back on his bald head, perfectly white and round just like his murdered son. Or his little brother. Or maybe just a young friend he met along the harshest roads of planet Earth.

Then another explosion. A round, red hole appears where his right eyebrow is supposed to be. His skull sneezes its contents at the woods behind him, and the pale man falls dead in the same direction. His weapon lands in the dirt between his feet, and I finally remember what it is. The carvin' fork.

Mr. Womack's peacemaker smokes way out in front of his gray eyes. He's got it gripped firmly in his right hand. His body is turned sideways, one leg in front of the other. His face is twisted in disgust as he finally steps away from his huge truck, revolver kept high and ready for whatever else waits behind the house.

"No more!" Daddy shouts in a tone I ain't heard before. His nostrils are twitchin' and he's breathin' heavy, but the Marlin's stock stays glued to his right cheek. He's lookin' straight down its irons at Mr. Womack. "Not another step past where you are."

Mr. Womack keeps his Peacemaker leveled in the pale woman's direction. He can't see her yet, not with the edge of the house still in between 'em, but he can hear her. He can hear her heinous misery, and he's got no qualms with puttin' her out of it. I remember that revolted scowl he's wearin' now, like even this pain is too profound for the likes of her. This pain exactly.

"You got any idea what you done?" he asks my daddy without lookin' at him. "You gonna be the one to tell this boy's family why he ain't never comin' home?"

After a pause, Daddy's eyes flick down to Hayward. They freeze there, as though time has paused his face. I look down that way, and I stop, too. I realize Abbie is already cryin', stiff and stifled in the truck like she's terrified to make a sound. I want to help her, but I can't seem to look away from Hayward. His spasms have stopped. He's gone to sleep with his eyes half open, payin' no mind to the bloody pillow he's sinkin' into.

"I won't have to," Daddy responds, still not soundin' quite like himself, not lookin' nearly so cool and collected as his eyes rise back to Mr. Womack. "They're gonna remember who brought him here."

"Hm." Mr. Womack wavers slightly. "That's true enough." His eyes glaze over in recollection before his nostrils begin to flare. "Just like I won't forget who took my son away from me." Still aimin' in the direction of the woman's sobs, he thumbs back the hammer on his Peacemaker.

"He was sick, goddammit!" Daddy squeezes the Marlin's body but not its trigger. "Sick in his blood and sick of you."

"You shut your mouth," Mr. Womack growls, almost breakin' his stance. "They turned my boy's brains to scat just like they turnin' yours. You're a fuckin' fool."

Daddy almost sounds evil when he laughs at that. Like he's never heard a sentence that deserves more scorn. "He ain't seen one of them his entire life. Not even close. But he caught a whole sight more than this." He twists his boot toe in the dryland, in all these backwoods where they began. "My little brother was sick and out of time, so I showed him the world."

"You got him killed, you stupid shit! My kin, not yours! Killed!"

"Well, I'm right here!" Daddy roars right back. He bares his teeth like a grizzly king. "Just show me that rod if you're so sure, and I'll punch your ticket to visit Jack!"

"Don't you say his name!" Mr. Womack turns and fires quicker than his age should even allow, with better accuracy than most young people could manage standin' still. The fat .45 round completely removes one of the epaulet loops from my daddy's USMC jacket. A burst of cotton, dirt, and bone ejects from his left shoulder in a dramatic spray.

But he hardly stirs. His cheek never leaves the Marlin's stock. The only change is the heartbreak in his eyes when he finally pulls the trigger.

Mr. Womack's truck is painted red across the hood. The

front, right tire exhales loud and slow where the .30-30 slug is lodged inside it, and the entire truck begins to sag in that direction. There's an exit wound the size of an apple in the center of Mr. Womack's back, but he's still standin' with his single-action army pointed at my daddy. He pulls his trigger again, but it ain't cocked to fire. His thumb tremors in an effort to correct that, then he falls straight to his knees. He still looks disgusted as he lays down carefully on his side and shuts his eyes. He and his giant truck quit breathin' together.

Crack Crack—two little fireworks go off in the truck's front seat, and my daddy gets hit again. Two more dusty puffs jet from his left elbow and the side of his stomach.

"No!" Abbie shrieks before I can. "No, stop it! No!" She tries to grab Ugly Eddy by the wrist, but he stretches out the window like a child hoardin' candy. Only instead of candy, it's a little Walther .22 pistol, silver and shiny in the sunlight.

Another round squeezes off in my daddy's direction, but it misses wide, shatterin' that front window on the quiet house.

"Jesus! Oh, Jesus lawd!" Eddy fights off Abbie like she's on fire, like his one good eye sees nothin' but demons all around him. He fires another round straight down into the dirt beneath him. Rosey's still seated there, petrified, unable to do anythin' but stare at the small bullet hole between his knees.

Daddy sees it, too. He throws the lever forward on his Marlin, gruntin' through the pain in his shot elbow. He tries to butt the rifle to his shoulder, but his arm won't raise the way it needs to. The muzzle lifts about as high as his waist then wavers there like a lazy shotgun. As he strains to lift it, blood dribbles across his boots from his stomach wound. It rains like paint from a punctured bucket, and he looks up from that bad mess to me.

He searches my eyes for better evidence, for any last sign

that it ain't true, that I ain't really the one who gave him up. Time seems to wait for us again, to quit its long count for just a while. And I remember my answer.

"Abb!" I dash down the body of the truck. "Abbie, leave him!" I duck under Eddy's arm and tug the door handle as hard as I can. His shiny pistol catches in the window frame as the entire door swings out and open. Abbie lets him go, and he flails away from her. He spills out of the truck, half in the mud, half suspended in the window.

"Jesus!" he shouts as he spins free. "Jesus keep me!" He aims the Walther straight ahead. But the Marlin explodes at Daddy's hips just a little faster. One last .30-30 cuts through the air, and Ugly Eddy finally gets his wish.

He meets his maker.

6.12

For a little while, nothin' else happens. I'm still sprawled across Rosey's lap the same way I landed on him—kinda like he just caught me at the end of a practiced dance. It's almost peaceful. Huddled together in the shade behind the truck door, it almost feels like any other Sunday—almost like our entire world wasn't just destroyed.

Until somebody moves directly above us. Hasty feet hop down from Mr. Womack's truck. Panicked hands grab hold of the window frame, and I feel Rosey's fingers clench at my chest. I feel his thumpin' heart against my spine and his nervous breath against my neck.

But it's just Abbie. She looks down at us like her dog just got run over. Like somehow, we're all the dog together. She throws the truck door out of her way and latches onto our tight pile. She sobs somewhere between my shoulder and Rosey's chin, but his fingers don't get any looser. He rubs her back and pets her hair in stiff, robotic movements. I'm impressed he can manage that. Without seein' his eyes, I know we're both lookin' at the same thing. No doubt about it. When Abbie shut the door, she opened our view of Ugly Eddy.

He's flat on his back just a few paces from us, shot straight through the heart by the look of it. Legs slightly spread, arms open wide, palms turned to heaven. He's like a snow angel in Southern soil. But his head is twisted to the left. Twisted and arched backward just enough for me and Rosey to see his eyes—both of 'em finally turned in the same direction, wide and frightened, lookin' straight down at the dirt beneath him. Lookin' straight down, like maybe somethin' sinister is rushin' up.

Somebody groans and drops to a knee. I look out that way, seein' yet another manly shape. A man who looks rightly exhausted, deservedly drained. Despite it all, he cycles the action twice on his rifle. A spent cartridge ejects and glitters through the air, followed by a third round he didn't need. He doesn't catch either of them; his eyes are barely open. But he does lay his weapon carefully at his boot. He thumbs the safety into place and lets out a long and deliberate breath. Despite this entire day, he lifts his knee to stand again. He keeps his chin high and proud as he rises to his feet. Then he collapses to the dirt.

"Daddy!" I scramble away from my best friends. I dash through the graveyard of our worst neighbors and slide down beside my father's chest. "Daddy, just—just wait." My hands hover over him without landin' anywhere, without any idea how to get all this red water back inside him.

His air comes out slow and raspy, like an ancient hound that's half asleep. His eyes start to flutter in a rapid, expirin' way.

"Daddy—" I pat his cheeks to keep him awake. "Daddy, don't do that!" my voice pitches higher in unmanly panic.

His eyes come open. He looks up at me like a total stranger, like maybe I'm the one who laid him flat. He raises an unsteady claw halfway to my throat, but the pain stops him there. He stares angrily into my eyes until recognition floats to the surface. He watches me. Then he watches the hole in his belly. He dabs the wet spot on his shoulder, and his expression sags in disappointment. He lays his head back carefully against the dirt and closes his eyes again. "Alright," he softly says. "It's alright."

"No." I look down at the muddy puddle beneath him, thick like chocolate syrup and still spreadin' down to his thighs. "No, Daddy, you're—"

"That was sharp." He keeps his eyes closed. Starts to breathe through his nose as peacefully as he can. "Too bad about Eddy. Too bad about all of it." He presses a hand to his stomach wound then winces hot air between his teeth. "But that was real sharp." He cracks one eye open to look at me, to watch me with unusual care. "I owe you one."

He smiles like dusk at the end of a ruthless day—like we didn't sell an ounce, but at least we earned our beds. I can't see any good reason to smile back. He shuts his eyes forever, and I'm still searchin' for pretty words, for anythin' at all to match his size. Just like I remember, I waste our last moments with stupid silence.

"Don't move him!" Rosey shouts from the driver's seat of Mr. Womack's truck. "Just hang on and we'll be—aw, motherfucker!" He realizes the front right tire's totally flat. "Come on, honey. Come on!" he shouts at Abbie as he runs around the hood.

She doesn't seem to hear him. She's watchin' my daddy with drownin' eyes, with a mouth full of chatterin' teeth. I half expect her to keel over, but she twists her neck like it's made of wood. Her emerald gaze continues to drift over every aspect of the carnage, over Mr. Womack and Ugly Eddy with grave consideration.

"Baby, let's go. We gotta go!" Rosey grabs her by both arms and spins her away to the western trees. Over his shoulder, he shouts, "Em, don't move him, we—we'll be back!"

But I know they won't be. I'm reminded that I'll never see either of them again. The longer I sit here in the mud, the better I remember Logan's screams. Screams like she's burnin' alive in hell. Summoned by gunfire and intuition, she walks all the way out to this haunted shack for the first time in eleven years. Probably already started. Already halfway here by now, which means this is the part where I forget. Thank God for that. A little repression sounds peachy keen compared to this. Half of me is ready to give that wheel another turn. The other half is stuck on Abbie's final look. Just like I remember, all of it. Except for that. That obligation in her eyes to memorize what had been lost.

I don't ever hear a footstep. Just the whisper of unhappy wind against my neck. I spin around like I've been bitten, and there she is. The pale woman from the shack. She's standin' so close to my left shoulder, I almost scream.

"Ha doso," the woman mutters absently. "Ha doso na mer," she says even quieter, keepin' her freaky eyes on Daddy's face. She's almost as bloody as he is now. Neck to knees, her stolen clothes are the same wash of red and brown. Stolen, I always thought. Snatched from the donation box my daddy had in his truck.

My eyes dart to the boy behind the shack. The one who had my favorite hat. He's different now. Posed like a little vampire, legs straight down, arms folded across his chest. The woman must've done it. The pale man is tidied the same way, like he's gone to sleep in an invisible coffin. She's covered his face with a square of fabric, dark blue around the edges, checkered white and black across the middle. It looks just like the pocket square that Grandpa Deryl left behind. The one my daddy loves so much.

"Don't!" I grab the woman by the wrist as she kneels beside me. She was reachin' for Daddy's neck with her filthy, bony fingers—fingers like a demon that ain't never seen the sun. "Get away from him!" I shove her sideways into the muck. I drag the Marlin over to me, palmin' that last round with my other hand.

She doesn't fight me. She just sits there with her strange eyes tilted downward, hardly movin' whatsoever. Her cheeks are smeared in a mixture of muddy tears and human red. Not sure what color I expected, but their blood looks just like ours. Her bald head is wrapped in a floral bandana that I've seen Logan wear in the yard. I remember all of that. But none of this. This bad feelin' in my gut. This nasty snakebite I've been nursin' half the day. Seems like it only happens when someone else is at their worst. Someone like this ugly woman.

"Ha doso na mer," she repeats in that familiar language I've never heard. She lifts her distant, half-dead eyes to mine, and a miniature firework pops between us. One snap of light just like I saw in the pantry when—

I blink a few times and look around slowly. Not sure for what exactly. Not totally certain where I am until I spot the sun behind the trees. I'm sittin' alone just north of Shiloh, with my daddy's Marlin across my lap. How very strange. It ain't even dusk just yet, but I feel like I skipped a meal. Skipped half the day, I guess. I can't even remember how I . . .

My eyes land on Hayward Marshall, lyin' belly down outside the quiet house. Unrecognizable. Totally dead for several hours. But, somehow, I know it's him. Just like I know the corpse beside him, the one arranged beneath my daddy's favorite handkerchief. Somehow, I know there's a pale man under there with hardly any head left at all. Just like I know that rancher hat is Mr. Womack's, and that twisted minion over there is Ugly Eddy shot to hell. I can't remember how they got here, but I ain't surprised to see 'em. That's why I'm suddenly so scared to turn around. I'm horrified to look behind me at the muck beneath my feet, because, somehow, I already know that's where I'll see—

Nothin'. No body to explain the puddled blood. Just a mess of sunken tracks. Tracks like female footprints comin' up from Shiloh Lake. And somethin' heavy goin' down. Somethin' she must've dragged for quite a while, stoppin' here and there to take a break. Somethin' shaped just like a dead man in six-inch rugged boots.

Half of me snatches up the Marlin and scrambles madly to the shore—dashes out to see my daddy with his stiff arms across his chest, with half his body drowned in Shiloh, with Logan's hellish screams comin' up the southern trail.

Half of me flees with her to Houston where she dies slow and quiet from the flu, where the UT Forces scrape me up with nothin' but a guinea pig's chance at killin' reachers, the fairest deal I've ever heard. Yeah. Half of me dashes off to turn that nasty wheel again.

My restless half just watches him go. Just looks down, seeing the ground is finally the distance that it should be. Not seeing white cotton or mustard sleeves but rippling scales. And feeling something. A distant candle like a snakebite, like a mother's dying sound.

Mama. I can't say why, but that's exactly what *she* feels like—the mind inside my suit. The mother I never knew. Just like the father I forgot. Killed by the reachers, I told myself. Shot and drowned beside the dock we built together. I can't even blame the one who wiped me. She tried to tell me, but I couldn't hear the words. *Ha doso na mer.* That same mysterious tongue I've heard somewhere, in a cave beneath the Taiga, in the painted chamber with—

A shadow slithers through me. An acetylene chill I've felt before. With eerie certainty, I turn away from Shiloh Lake, twisting around completely until the quiet house comes into view.

It's rotten now. More haggard than I've ever seen it. A tangle of vines has wrapped through the shattered window like a gangrenous swampy vein. The front door is missing entirely, but no light can be seen inside. Just one thick wall of blackened rage.

I remember that. I remember how to escape this sunken place; I could do it right this second, I'm pretty sure. Instead, I remember the eyes of Abbie Ferras. I remember the muddy tracks that pale mother left behind. Not killing my daddy, just finishing what he started. Because when men like Charlie Womack offer complicity or death, the only choice remaining is where to drop your dying bones.

As I march headlong into the darkness of a brightstar's collapsing dream, I hear those strange words like they're my own, like I've been fluent from the start.

Ha doso na mer, she tried to tell me, looking down at my favorite man.

Ha doso na mer.

He chose the water.

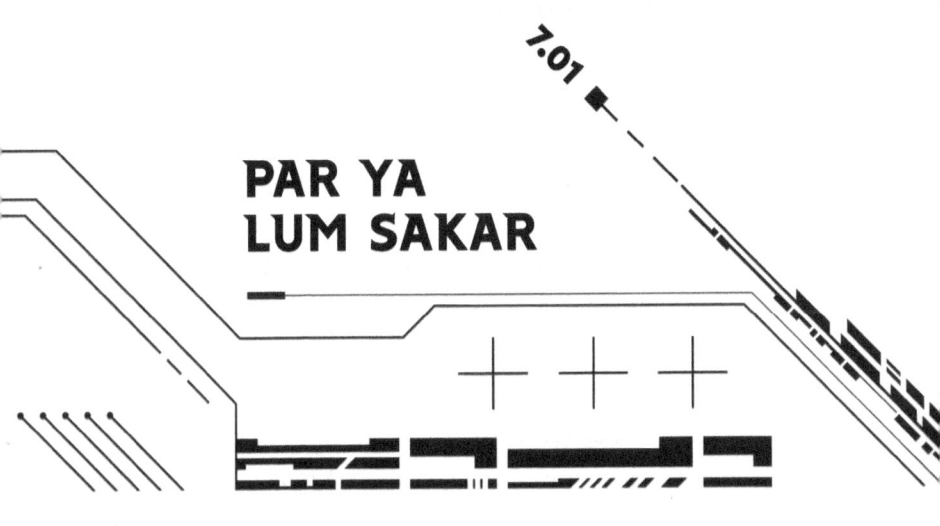

PAR YA LUM SAKAR

The brightstar walks among them, and he reflects their pallid hearts. Whichever shallow expectation they prefer, whichever human form is least disruptive, he presents it to them in kind. Some see a grandmother with two sweet children, laughing happily as they pass. Others see a decorated soldier, tall and strong, firm of back, looking deep into his past. Many more see very little, almost nothing to their eyes. A vagabond. A homeless lunatic, muttering nonsense to himself, pushing his cart of trashy treasures just like he always has. Too many see this man. An alarming majority of Earth's people in West Shanghai have grown accustomed to such low and tenuous life. Life below their threshold for a second glance.

These jaded lights have begun to weigh on Kible Thexx. But he must maintain the disguising illusion at any cost. The aging brightstar knows his own rumors all too well. Earth's people are remarkably adept in that regard. Concocting, spreading, and ingesting their own vile propagandas. Another side effect of living so dim, so negligently individual.

Some honest truths do manage to circulate. None of his accomplishments, of course. None of his greater victories for those that must come next. But a few of the brightstar's hardest choices have indeed become common knowledge. Four to be exact. Four human lights taken for the endless others. Each kept and counted in his mind. And he will keep counting until his own day comes. Until he finds someone worthy enough to inherit his high assignment.

It seems that torch passing may be required soon. The travel milk was not especially cruel to Kible Thexx, but these long walks under the Earth's young sun have taken their toll—these protracted searches for his scattered kind, for those too dim to find him on their own. Never too dim to escape the unique radius of his sight, as is his gift, as is his curse. The Earth people say twenty orbits have transpired since the first brightworld vessel landed on their vapid planet. Just thirty or so daylight rotations after the *first marker*—as they call it—was discovered. Well, that all seems rather unlikely to the brightstar, considering he has been walking on the planet Earth for nearly *twenty-two* of its calendar cycles, but at least their causation is somewhat valid. The first beacon that Kible engineered—using rather vital components from his own travel craft—was indeed meant as a signal to his kin. A hailing net to catch his brother's pod. And he caught it well. But the milk was far less kind to Kendar Shall. As were his captors.

That entire winter, Kible could only watch from a terrible distance. He watched from the icy cave, half a world away, as his older brother's magnificent light faded toward shadow. Dimmer every day, every night, until it was just a flicker, until it was gone. Vanished in cruelty and unturned. Kible Thexx watched for all that time, beginning to pray that Kendar's promised woman and only son would never arrive on this black world. He watched and waited, finding new corruption in himself. Eventually, he, too, would kill for his high assignment, for a progress beyond the confines of time. Just like the men of Earth, he would taste some pleasure in it now and then, some thin and shameful satisfaction when his vow demanded violent tests. Four lights taken, just like his brother's was from him. Each kept and counted against his soul.

But the brightstar counted no regrets.

7.02

Kible Thexx has not been this far from the cave for many stars. Not since he traveled west for Mantz AnCarcem and her young bodyguard, Cuva Khan. The brightstar took his first two lights on his way to them. Two boys of Belarus. Two young men making games of their hatred at the end of a debaucherous night, both too intoxicated to succumb to his illusions, too numbed and sloppy for the brightstar to gauge how much damage he was doing in his own defense. Until it was too late. Until their drunken kicks and curses ceased, and their eyes lulled in their lifeless skulls. One cranium thudded hard against the curb at Kible's back. The other opened like a melon when it struck the cobbled street, bloody streams navigating the gaps between the handmade bricks in northern Minsk.

In that way, a broken and battered Kible Thexx arrived at Mantz's European hideaway dimmer than he'd ever been. Dimmer even than when he left the brightworld as a much younger man. But the rare gifts of his newfound companions reignited him. Especially the discovery of old Mantz. A divemaker would be very useful in the coming times, of that he was sure. As for Cuva, well, Kible prayed a need for such a talent would never come.

But on this present journey, the brightstar has traveled for a very different prize, a brighter light than he ever expected on this planet. In time, perhaps even brighter than his own. Just as vibrant as the high one he thought he sensed two orbits passed. That strange, unsteady shine which seemed to vanish like shattered dreams. So near where Kendar was extinguished in the American country's south. But too long after. And too terrestrial. A unique hue that matched the Earth. It reminded the brightstar of the oldbooks and the ancient tales of the endless others. Those that must come and will shine like stars. The sons of suns and the brightest daughters of destiny's sky. Although, looking back, it's much more likely he was experiencing brain milk decay. Another hallucination in the process of his decline.

But the brightness here today is very real—in this eastern metropolis so adjacent to black hell. In this place where the homeless are stepped over and even the few scattered members of his kin have embraced selfish perversions. Where their high assignments are forgotten or ignored. They corrupt the brightstar's progress here, making the endless others more unlikely every day. A world doomed to darkness, he sometimes thinks. A wasted mission for his tribe. But these thoughts are dimming. Irrelevant to the task at hand. He must reach this girl before her fate can mirror Kendar's. Before another fantastic light is snuffed beneath human designs. The Earth's misguided prodigies could do much damage with one such as her. These M. Calvin Prichards and their similars, spurred on by ego and something else. Boys like him become difficult men. Difficult to lure from the thick shadows of ambition.

Kible thought it might be fear, as it was on his own world in the distant darker eras. A self-imposed terror of violent mystery and secretive minds. A panic that ultimately united them, or so it is recorded. But the Earth people don't seem to be following any known route to a brighter world. They must, he knows, in time. But he also doubts. Perhaps these are the same misgivings that drove his landed kin to common crime and enterprising aims. A creeping suspicion that the Earth is not their dimmer kin at all but something else. A dark divergence from the highway. A second path that must lead to shadow, to its own brand of endless others. A black tribe of infinite creatures who can only die alone.

Kible turns with some alarm at the termination of that thought, eyes darting back down the narrow walkway between the busy market stands. He watches the crowd with a vague sense of distress. A sudden coldness on his neck. The Earth people flow around him none the wiser. Some of them do not even see life when the brightstar stands still, just a light fixture or some pocket of air that they feel strangely compelled to step around. But he sees all of them exactly as they are. All except one. One hiding remarkably quiet within the human herd. But not a human. And not quiet enough.

The brightstar yawns and dons a weary face. He examines a rack of keychains and tourist oddities dangling in his eyeline before turning forward and continuing through the winding market street. But not continuing his search.

It seems that quest has come to an end.

7.03

Kible walks many miles, listening carefully to the girl. He strolls the length of the afternoon, leading her away from the market's noise and the abrasive volume of stacked hotels. He follows her dripping thoughts northwest, guiding them both directly to her home. He knows that place now, among other things. He knows the sheet metal teepee she sleeps beneath each night just north of the river. He knows she is wearing her cleanest jeans and her second favorite sunglasses. He knows her favorites were snatched off and broken by a police officer three weeks ago. And Kible knows how she repaid him.

The brightstar winces, pricking his mind on her remarkably honed gift. They are half a mile from the river, and the air is getting thin. Her suspicions are sharpening, pressing like bladed fingers against his aching back. But Kible offers no defense. He knows she is wild for a reason. He knows the origins of her distrust and the righteous end of that tormentor—that great fat one and his drove. Kible's four lights seem trivial next to hers. All taken at once. He knows the smell of their bloody gallons. The metallic taste in her young mouth. The viscous weight of their dead juices, solidifying in her rare mane. Theirs and their clients. He knows they paid to see her tears, and she will never cry again.

Eleven orbits, all lived on Earth—a fact she barely knows herself. A mother's light sent down the highway the same day the girl was born. Born to Earth. Rare indeed. In her short life, she has been a pet, a product, and a myth—the gwáinòu of West Shanghai, the street beast of the Huangpu River—but the brightstar knows that she has never been a child. Never had the chance.

He also knows she would have demented him by now, twisted psychic screws into his bones, if not for one stark difference between himself and all the others, the handful of their kin who have sought her light before. It is not the safe distance he is allowing, nor the careful way he has kept his eyes straight ahead since they left the market, nor any of the incriminating facts he has gathered on this walk. It is simply the sharing.

While he has been listening, so has she. To all his intentions and tales of travel. To all his great battles and painful losses, and to all his honest thoughts on what he now knows about her. The brightstar knows that he could walk halfway to Beijing, and the girl would follow. Just to keep sipping at that reciprocity, this terrifying exposure she has been craving above all else. But he will stop and rest at her steel teepee at least for now, and she can keep her distance, even sit up on the road if she so desires, because his plans for her lie so much further beyond today.

7.04

One orbit has transpired since the brightstar felt the cosmic flashing—an impossible shine in the American continent's bustling northern lands. Again, he guessed it must've been some sort of hallucination. No single being could generate such light, not even a high one from the endless worlds to come. He was wrong, of course. The Chicago Storm proved very real. And he fears a high one was to blame. The highest mind in this inverted world of shade.

But these are dimming thoughts. More importantly, the girl turns seventeen tomorrow, which means she may finally choose a second name. The brightstar tilts his light in her direction. He hears her speaking to the meditative Cuva Khan, finishing his sealing ritual in the light chamber. Through the girl, Kible hears the aging warrior's reply. Khan is the name of the brightworld capital where he was trained. His cousin and mentor, the infamous light witch Noosha Khan AnShelva took the same name, as did both of their fathers and many ancestors before them. Khan is a light that transcends time, a power passing toward the endless.

Later that evening, Kible Thexx connects with her again. He hears the girl ask Mantz AnCarcem why she carries a wedded name but no second—much like she once asked Kible why he carries the wedded name AnSorin without a wife. The girl knows very little of the brightworld and its customs. Knows nothing of its great kingdoms and the lost lands in between. She presumes old Mantz simply declined to take a second name. Through Kible's unique bond with the girl, he sees the old woman's eyes. He sees them flashing rapidly—too quickly for him to intervene—and then he feels the girl change. A deep and permanent alteration like the passing of many stars. The girl leaves quietly, speaking no further to old Mantz, but Kible Thexx knows that her question has been thoroughly given answer.

In the morning, Kible summons the girl to the great table. Mantz sits on his right. All the others fill the stone benches and honored seats in anticipation, even little Yono, who is still recovering from the milk, finally done travelling all those stars in his handsome father's lap. Their tribe has grown so much in these recent orbits. Kible is joyed and honored to look upon them all at once, to see the girl anointed soon, not yet his successor but well along the path, moving so much swifter than he expected her to—

The girl enters without him sensing. Walks right past his shoulder without an echo as the room falls impossibly quiet. Even the old words and purest light speech become a silence as she makes her way to the end of the long table. She stands there at its head, where the great stone throne has been removed for this occasion. Little Yono tugs fearfully at his father's belt, speaking several unheard questions, but Kono Cora AnAmarka has no eyes for him. The entire tribe watches the girl with horrified anticipation. Her gaze remains lowered, apparently burdened by hidden thoughts.

For the first time since he found her, the brightstar shares himself, listening intently, receiving nothing in return. Even as the girl's dazzling head of hair ignites, even as she raises her shimmering eyes to his and finally moves her calloused lips, even as she speaks her first word as a grown woman of the light tribe, Kible hears only silence. In this way, in the solemn presence of her brightstar, witnessed by her tribe in its entirety, the wild woman known as Tysha remains just that. A first name given by the Slavic captors she laid to rest. And a second taken here. A *silent name*, the first of its kind to Kible's knowledge.

In this way, the brightstar is dimmed again. Enfeebled by his staggering paternal pride.

7.05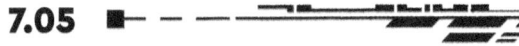

Kible Thexx decides the time has come. Come and gone perhaps. Delayed by his own reluctance to be diminished, to relinquish the title he was awarded when he left the brighter world. This dim planet has affected them all, it seems. More and more, he sees his kin settling here, integrating themselves with this complacent populace. Though, complacency may seem gentle compared to the trajectory of the Earth.

This Zero Addition movement is an isolating shift. The continents are unifying. The scattered lights of Earth are consolidating along a course—but not the right one. They are diving in vicious synchronicity toward the depthless shadows he has feared. The orbital cannons were an atrocity. A crippling tragedy every hour of every day. Now they are noise. Background static in the monotony of war. As his startime passes here, the brightstar numbs. His eyes adjust to the dim conditions of a dying world. Accepting that, he sees no reason to delay.

The brightstar channels Tysha. He stands outside an airfield in Zhejiang, not far from where he found his wild child nearly a dozen orbits prior. He speaks within his mind, and the woman hears him within hers.

Every mind within the cave, even dim Poody's at her side, hears his booming voice as it communes with Tysha's tremendous light. His last instruction as the brightstar is concise: "*It is time to follow the apprentice, my found starchild, as you would have followed Kible Thexx. Her light is tested and unequaled, so it must pass: my high assignment and command. Tysha of the silent second, I give you the brightstar and all its weight, all its duties to the endless and the high ones yet to come. For now, I say to you and all our cousins shining there: farewell.*"

Then Kible falls as silent as he can. He hears the young new brightstar calling back, asking all the questions he expected, but he has no satisfying answers to provide. She is too bonded to his light for him to hide from her completely, but he must try. After all these stars on dimming Earth, his taken lights still equal four; the girl has inspired more change in him than she may ever know. But, today, his peaceful streak comes to an end.

The former brightstar lifts his eyes to the airfield on the horizon. Three landed kin shine like beacons to him there. Two boys and one young female, all captured before he could travel to them. All luckier, at least, than the thousands vaporized before they ever reached the Earth. So many bright lights decimated by the dimmest of this world. Dimmed to madness and now perversion.

Down there, surrounding the lights of his captured kin, Kible can sense another seven. All artificial and corrupted. Without knowing their human shapes, he knows the rumors must be true. The dark soldiers do exist. The infamous *reacher hunters* are hiding there as well, teasing the edges of his sight. Not for long. To this depravity, he must deliver violence.

But something stops his feet. An eighth shape he has just detected. An empty husk that seems to be upright on its own. It reminds him of those drunken boys in Belarus. A body on auto-pilot. An emptiness not unlike death. It gives him pause. But he decides there is no time to falter here. For the future of his tribe, for the endless who must come, he will find a way to—

"*Listen to me, dammit!*"

Kible Thexx spins on his old heels. His eyes flash instinctively with scalding light. But the ridge is empty behind him. Just a few trees shimmying in the wind, the rushing sound of sea stones far below. He turns back around with the same sharpness but sees no attacker there either. Just the airfield in the distance and a string of vehicles navigating the long, narrow road that lies beneath it.

But the old man did hear a voice. An American, he could have sworn. A male shout that sounded personal somehow.

Likely just another symptom of his old prognosis: brain milk decay gradually settling in. Yet another reason to pass on his high assignment before this work is undertaken. Corrupted or not, eight lights is no clean task. If his judgment is askew in this premeditated annihilation, he can imagine no forgiveness that he'd deserve.

With that self-righteousness accepted, the foolish girl starts down the hill, straight into the humans' clever trap, deeper into the skin and dimming hubris of her departed master, Kible Thexx. Peculiar and revealing, all of this. A subconscious introspection, it would seem. A latent perspective shift that might resemble suicide. Always a risk, of course, in these open dives below the conscious veil. A total loss of self. An ego death without return. But Mantz AnCarcem is unimpressed.

She has proctored purgatories, pestilential hellscapes and skyless worlds. She has eaten her own fingers, toes, and teeth more than twice in an afternoon. She has traded curses with a darkmind. In truth, this dreamscape is a kindness compared to the ancient trials of her kingdom. Her divemasters would be disgusted and ashamed that such a narcissistic dreaming could ever pass for an education. But there is discovery in exploration. And Mantz would wager that even her old mulish tutors would be unnerved by the revelations of this day.

Somehow, the outsider has broken through. His catching of the animal was no mere fluke, it seems. The Earthman grows brighter, shouting incessantly already, calling out from his bifurcated dream in some misplaced attempt at a hero's rescue. A fool's errand to be sure; proof that his private lesson was not fully ascertained. And yet, the insolent girl was able to hear him.

For one bright instant, a new tethering occurred—even in this compacted realm, even as dim as silent Tysha has become. That fact alone proves the value of this method. These two youthful lights may be the answer after all—the solution to the query that even Kible Thexx had forgotten. A quilting of the gaps between the endless and ourselves.

But Mantz AnCarcem's high assignment pays no dues to speculation. She has learned that truth, if nothing else, in her great expanding life. So, she will keep watching as she has been, with low expectations and even lower sympathies. She will continue her examination, now admittedly in possession of one nagging, infectious thing that reminds her of young hope.

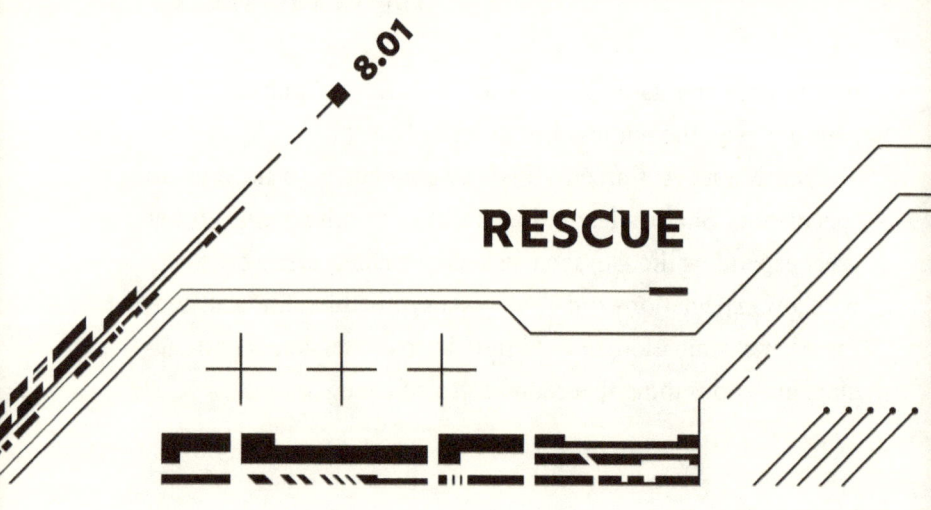

RESCUE

I am a liminal apparition—a spectral spectator to the dream next door to mine. Just a dream, I remind myself. Some nightmarish guess at true events. They couldn't know this. Tysha and that old witch, neither of them could know what happened here. Half of me is sure of that. The other half recalls the accuracy of the dream I just stepped out of.

A shower of blood splashes the runway—a red rainfall coughed between shattered teeth. Kible Thexx AnSorin is paralyzed, lying broken on his back. He's drowning in his own juices on the airfield in Zhejiang, with Taiko Chiba standing over him, entirely untouched.

Only her concussive sticks show any damage, splotched with milky skin, drenched in gore. It was over in seconds. A dozen robotic strikes to make a vegetable of our most infamous invader. Except, I know it isn't him. Just like I know that isn't really the enormous Wilson Black, crawling up from the soil, brandishing his cop shotgun and stellar shells. I wish it was. But all of this is just a dream. Rear projections of the past. The only living minds within this place are mine and Tysha's.

She's the one who's lying there, drowning in remembered blood, beaten more than half to death. That's why the nightmare's flickering now, carrying on in limited detail.

In the fading background, Aila, Magar, and two distant Bugg-y blurs spring up from the grassy edges of the tarmac. I've never seen this day, only heard about it. A full-unit ambush of hidden hunters in spider holes, led and organized by Lieutenant Fangs of Zero Two. And there she is, sprinting down their center line, barking a muffled command to Taiko Chiba, causing her G-4 suit to downshift from battle-red to standby-black. Taiko snaps her c-sticks back onto her magnetized shoulder blades, stepping mechanically aside, just as Faye darts into clearer view with a dripping syringe.

In it goes, pushing sedative fluids into Kible Thexx's twisted, fractured neck. His eyes flash open for one excruciated second, then they dim toward total darkness. Everything does. The whole universe loses power, fading to a depthless black.

I wait a moment, expecting some deeper dream to initiate, some kind of psychic purgatory where maybe I can grab a hold of Tysha and snap her ass awake. But nothing comes. Just a timeless lack of consciousness. An endless void between dimensions. A cold and creeping feeling that I will never wake again.

A high cackling echoes out in rude response. A moist and wretched laughter from everywhere at once, from deep inside me worst of all.

"I thought I taught you silence, Emmett Hayes," the old witch speaks with an easy temper, projecting the sensation of a clever smile. "Well, perhaps now you will learn patience. Aye, I believe you shall." She laughs less convincingly this time, keeping something vivid to herself—some unhappy image from her own distant days.

I see the edges of it. A rattling truth sneaks into view. All these hours. All these days and years she's stolen from us, from anyone else she's used her subliminal powers on. Every time her rare gift is used to teach, destroy, and dement in these endless places inside her hosts, not one of them has gone alone. Not without her.

Old Mantz indeed. As ancient as any mind has ever been.

 **8.02**

A flash of light ignites the universe. So bright and unexpected. A white-hot sun less than a meter above my eyes.

The air is like an ocean now. A swimming haze everywhere I look. A sickening spin. But I can see a shape like Kible Thexx AnSorin, seated near the middle of the room. Just as old and gangly as I first saw him in the cosmodrome. Strapped down just like he was—in that same madhouse electric chair, but now it's bolted to the floor. His neck and forehead restraints are missing, so his head lulls crookedly to the left. Not just from the heavy drugs but his damaged spine. If he is still capable of intentional movement, only his eyelids show proof of it—bouncing sporadically, like he keeps waking up then fading halfway unconscious again. Each time, the world around us dims toward darkness then burns white hot as his dilated pupils are struck by the harsh overhead lighting.

I guess that answers one of my questions. This dream is clearly tied to the perspective of Kible Thexx. Tysha's knowledge of these events must be very limited, generated purely from the scrambled images that passed between their entangled minds. Maybe that's how I got through to her on that hillside before the airfield. She only heard me after Kible shut her out—after the details of this world began to fade. This could be it, my best chance to snap her out of it.

"Tysha! Tysha, wake up!"

Kible's eyelids seem to react. Flickering first, then gradually rising almost high enough to resemble full awareness. High enough to reveal his foggy, tired eyes, looking directly at me. Or directly where I'd be if I had a body. Just as I start to shout again—

A heavy steel door slams directly behind me, and Faye Thompson walks straight through my invisible back. I step around her, surprised to feel the concrete floor beneath our ghostly feet. I also realize I never had Kible's attention at all.

It's Faye who matches his sagging eyes. She wields an electric pacifier near her waist, twin stun rounds already charged and whining within both chambers. She seems ready to put Kible down again, almost eager to do it, but he just goes on drooling and blinking blankly in his terrible chair. Somewhat disappointed, Fangs finally nods to a long interrogation mirror along the side wall.

Kible's eyes slip closed completely—and time seems to skip ahead several seconds like a corrupted video feed. The heavy door shuts again, now on my left. Taiko Chiba has just entered with a third person I can't quite make out. Faye snaps her fingers, pointing to the further wall. Taiko obeys, marching past her, taking a sentry position along the wall just behind Kible's asylum chair. Faye watches their drugged prisoner again for any sign of resistance or illuminating eyes, then she finally steps aside. The third person strides out of the haze behind her, and I see a man whose presence here feels exactly right and terribly wrong.

"Jesus fuckin' Judas." An appalled M. Calvin Prichard Jr. walks a surveying half-circle in front of Kible Thexx. "Your and my definitions of *alive* may have a few discrepancies," he says to Faye without looking at her, without taking his disturbed eyes from the battered former brightstar. After another moment of examination, he finally sighs and clicks his tongue over his right shoulder. His personal sim, that smooth three-centimeter graphene sphere, hovers quietly up and away from its epaulet perch. It starts recording the scene, floating extra close to Kible's wounds, eyes, and dish-like ears.

"Shit, where the hell are my manners." Prichard takes a polite step back and executes an old-timey bow. "Good afternoon your eminence, your grace, your high and shininess. And hail to the first brightstar of Planet Earth."

Kible's eyes just droop again, non-responsive.

"Right." Prichard sags a bit disappointed. "Well, I'm sure you do understand the nature of these rather unsightly precautions—a testament, if anything, to the great power of your reputation. Hell, even *my* technology," Prichard indicates the glowing chip at the top of his spine, already an apparent upgrade to the one he showed off at that chapel briefing, "is no match for what you and some of your tribe's leadership can do. I'm quite sure of that. But, um, actually, I'm sorry, Taiko honey, can you please . . ." Prichard looks up, gesturing for her assistance. To my horrified surprise, she moves instantly, without even a glance toward Faye in the corner.

The nano hive swirls in Taiko's eyes, and with no gentleness, with no human grace at all, she grasps both sides of the old Luminaran's face from behind and cranks his head back against the steel chair's headrest. Kible gurgles horribly, spreading his eyes in shock.

"Hey, no! Taiko, stand down!" My liminal shouts fall on deaf ears. I try to grab her by the wrist, but I ghost right through the scene entirely, lost in a sudden fog as though I've stepped into a dimensional blind spot. A distorted, non-physical corner of the interrogation room. I spin around, feeling with my hands, trying to retrace my steps—before I stumble back into it all, hitting the cold floor with our invisible knees, landing directly in front of Prichard.

The bastard is smiling now. Just peachy delighted to have the former brightstar's full attention. "Thank you, darlin'." He shoots Taiko a wink right over Kible's head. I follow that gesture to her eyes, and for the briefest moment, through a particularly distorted patch of hazy air, I swear I see the tiniest flash of disgusted sorrow in Taiko's braindead face.

Prichard clicks his tongue twice this time, and his personal simulant halts its documentation of the scene. Its miniature cold propulsion engines hum quietly as it returns, levitating millimeters above a small, magnetized disc on Prichard's shoulder. "Strike those last ten seconds and start again. Just audio." The sim chimes twice in acknowledgement, and Prichard's wide smile spreads back above his chin. "Where was I? Oh, yes. Please, I beg you, sir, do not mistake these circumstances for any hostility on my part. I assure you I have fantasized quite excessively about this moment. And I would wager, in fact I would *promise* that you have no fonder admirer on this entire planet than myself."

Kible gurgles again, and his head strains against Taiko's clamped fingers, digging indentations into the loose flesh beneath his eyes. Faye's pacifier is raised and buzzing half a second later, but Prichard is already waving her off, free of any concern.

"I do admit my instructions appear to have been rather harshly elaborated upon." He casts those last few words in Faye's direction. "But I should think you had quite severe intentions of your own comin' here this mornin'. Hm?"

Kible makes no sounds of disputation.

"Hell, without my little opioid cocktail, you'd've probably popped my heart like a homecoming cherry by now!" That big unrepentant laugh of his bounces off the naked walls, followed by an exhilarated rodeo whoop. "Well, technically, you'd've told my brain to tell my adrenal glands to tell my aorta to pop my heart, but—semantics. You catch my meanin', I'm sure. Biology, chemistry, quantum mechanics, these are the true mechanisms of the so-called Reach. Or *the light*, whichever phrasing suits you. That's how y'all got here. Advanced navigation, preservative stasis, cold gravity propulsion." He gestures to the little simulant above his shoulder. "Shit, your whole mission here is scientific—the um, what do they call 'em, Spike?" His simulant chimes twice in reply, and Prichard's upgraded Spider Byte glows slightly brighter. "Yes, thank you. *The endless others*."

Kible's eyes widen in true surprise.

Prichard taps his own nose with fresh excitement. "See, you know! Of course, you know, you're the goddamn brightstar, the elected king of forward progress. You and I," Prichard steps into a more intimate proximity, "we happen to be after the exact same thing here, Kible, if you don't mind me calling you that."

Kible's forehead strains against Taiko's grip again.

Prichard chuckles, raising his hands in surrender but maintaining his proximity. "Fair enough. I ain't exactly wrong though, am I? The distant prophecies, the self-sacrifice. It's all just a glittered up, religious-y outlook on human progress. Humans become something like you folks. You folks eventually become the uh, the *high ones*. And the high ones become, I don't know, fuckin' energy brain mist, but that's what you're really after, right? Evolution on a cosmic scale. I may be seeking somewhat expedited results, but our visions, my good sir, are precisely the same. One universe, made indivisible, under science."

He wraps up his presentation with another old-timey bow, even lower this time, arms spread wide in both directions. And Kible lurches forward, using just the muscles of his upper neck, just far enough to spit bloody phlegm into Prichard's perfectly parted hair.

Faye doesn't wait for permission this time, pulling the first trigger on her pacifier the same second she levels it with her eye. A white flash of compacted lightning fills the room as the stun round connects—but not with Kible Thexx.

Prichard's personal sim has caught the projectile head-on, half a meter from Kible's chest, flattening it in mid-air with an invisible wall of condensed repulsive gravity. Prichard's spinal chip is shimmering even brighter than before as the stun round falls straight to the concrete floor, spinning like a nickel. As it wobbles there toward silence, Prichard rises from his performative bow. He turns his joyless eyes on the woman we call Fangs, and for the first time in her career, she steps nervously in retreat.

"Spike, please note that Mr. AnSorin has willingly offered a tissue sample." Time skips a few seconds again—Prichard is opening a small collection tube. His personal sim vacuums up the bloody droplets from his scalp, holding them in a tight, rapid orbit around itself—time skips again—and Prichard closes the tube's lid, now full of Kible's spat genetics. He places it in his vest pocket. "Well. I am disappointed by the atmosphere of our introduction. But I do look forward to seeing you again, sir. We will do great things together." Prichard looks the former brightstar down and up, connecting their eyes a final time. "I am quite sure of that."

Time skips even further—and Prichard has vanished. Faye and Taiko, too. The room is suddenly as empty, still, and quiet as when I first arrived, but my thoughts are racing so far ahead I keep losing sight of them. Losing my sight entirely, living behind my eyes and the rapid implications unraveling there. Wondering if what I just saw falls under military action or private interest. Did the captain know about this, or have I just witnessed treason? Can such a charge even apply to M. Calvin Prichard Jr., whose corporation is so tightly woven into Zero Addition, into the very implements of the UT Forces? The way he commanded Taiko without any uncertainty or second thought. I was in The Hole when she awoke from tac, and I never got around to asking how. How exactly did Prichard wake her from certain death? And what compensation did he negotiate? Another weapons contract? A team of elite guinea pigs for his mysterious Spiders? Or is there something else? Some backdoor to some master plan that this man has kept concealed.

"Aye, you're seeing far now, child. A terrible distance." Old Mantz's scratchy voice invades my veins again. Drags me back from my descending spiral. "But you're missing your moment, I suspect. Missed it almost entirely now."

Before I can ask what the hell she means, the channel closes. Her witchy presence is gone again. But I begin to hear another voice as I listen closer. A much more devastated sound.

I look to Kible and his dangling head—fallen limp without Taiko Chiba's hands as crude support. The voice is coming from his direction but not from him exactly. It's that same itchy signal that led me here from my own dream. An icy sadness and a blackened rage.

"Tysha," I think aloud.

A salty streak dives down the cheek of the paralyzed Kible Thexx. His thoughts swim through me in vivid detail. He's hearing Tysha's voice back in the cave. His attempts to sever their connection have wholly failed. She has been watching. She is dimming in her grief, succumbing to the same helplessness he felt for his brother, Kendar, long ago.

"It ain't like that!"

Kible twitches slightly at my shout.

"You're not him—you—you don't gotta go through this, you're not responsible!"

Kible's mouth spasms open. He tries to speak, but his broken body refuses the sound. But that's enough. For one flashing instant, I see Tysha's ghost behind his face. All twisted and tortured in the deepest throes of impending loss. I see a rage and humiliation so far beyond my worst of times. And I see my own hubris stacked right on top. I see the bold hero who thought his lesson was finished outside the quiet house. I finally see that this dark chapter's as much for me as it is for her.

"You. You *are* responsible," I start again.

Kible's twitching mouth becomes a gasp. A painful suck.

"Not just for AnSorin. For the three you lost in the forest."

Another tear dashes down the old man's face. Down from Tysha's strobing, spectral eyes.

"They died for you—for you to see what honor looks like. I can't pretend to understand your motives, but I know one thing for sure. AnSorin chose you. This whole goddamn haunted slideshow has been about him deciding you're the best one to get it done—the only one—so you can either go on crying here to prove how wrong he was about that, or you can wake the hell up, right now, and make the old bastard fuckin' correct!"

No twitches or spasms come this time. So much nothing and prolonged silence that I start to feel stupid. I start to wonder if all those convulsions and tears had anything to do with me at all. If any of this does. But then I start to see something else.

I see that cobalt glow coming up from deep inside them both. I see all the anguish leave his face as his head slowly lifts back and presses itself against the steel headrest. Another skip in time—and I see a leather band strapped there to keep it in place. I feel something bump my spectral head as I try to turn around. It's so cramped in here now. In here. Somehow, we're now encased in an angular sphere with smooth white walls. And something cold is crawling up my legs. Preservation gel. Now at my knees, now at my neck.

It passes my ears above my head, and I turn just far enough to see out the small window at eye level. There's a muffled ocean of Russians gyrating below us, and I'm up above them all—the other me. Another Emmett is out there in that swaying cherry picker, lying prone, holding his rifle sights on the other Tysha. She's there in the crowd with her mountaineers shining up in our direction, just like the matching pairs on the other three rogues standing around her. From this vantage, I see that their formation makes a shimmering constellation. A symmetrical diamond. Now their hands are leaving their pockets in perfect simultaneity, and all their thumbs are pressing against their breaking hearts to say *farewell*.

Then we're soaring up with awesome speed, me and this Tysha/Kible combination. We're soaring past the clouds and lower atmosphere, until all the hues of the terrestrial sky fade to black. I'm back. Zooming toward monotony, on my way to a deeper orbit, up toward the exosphere I left behind. Just at the edge of that perspective, I can already see the mesh of metallic stems coming into view. The Orbital Patrol seen from below is a beautiful thing. A glistening grid wrapped around an endless blue horizon.

But I'm pressed forward by a compounding force as our momentum violently slows, nullifying our escape velocity, dangling us between the Earth and its man-made border for a few empty seconds.

Then we're turning, automatically redirecting just beneath the view of the guns and pilots way up there. We're heading east, soaring over Japan and the vast Pacific, picking up speed, flickering strangely, warping and bending the image below as though I'm looking through an asymmetric lens and thickening glass. Or a cloaking pattern.

And down we roar, past the California Republic and Arizona, on a trajectory for New Mexico or central Texas. It's getting hot. The G-forces are becoming a crushing thing, a paralyzing weight even on my bodiless brain. The world is dimming, blackening, fading toward that unconscious abyss. With terrible effort, I turn to see that Kible Thexx's eyes are bulging open, totally ignoring the anesthetic gel.

"Tysh—Tysha stop."

She doesn't hear me. Or chooses not to. Kible's lifeless eyes only widen further, stretching into a mad expression as we spiral down through the lower atmosphere, cloaked by bending light and extreme velocity, a textbook attempt at brute-force stealth. Nobody was ever meant to see this, and I know why. Our new destination is Old Dallas.

"P-p-pl—" I can't find enough air to beg. I see Tysha's gritted ghostly teeth flashing in the reflection of Kible's face.

"L-let—" My liminal lungs collapse. I see Tysha's throbbing veins burying deep into Kible's brain, and the world is almost lightless now—just a thin pinhole of earthly color through the pod's vanishing front window. But I see a sound. A cobalt shine like silent music. A tether of light courses the gap between us, and I snatch it up.

"TYSHA, LET GO!"

The reverse thrusters kick in hard, and I'm launched straight through the pinhole into open air. I'm falconing down to Earth, falling into a valley of buildings I've seen before. It's a compound of some renown, especially to starry-eyed local boys like me, and a way of life to all the union hands and engineers who've been lucky enough to keep their wages in this simulated age.

But I don't have any attention for that place. Not now. I'm way too enthralled by her shining eyes, by her tempestuous mane in this ripping wind. She's falling with me. We're free and visible again, doing our best impression of that old film—that pre-invasion adaptation where the man from space falls in love with the reporter, where his warring identities merge into one. I'm no hero. But I venture a squeeze of her alien hand.

She squeezes back, but there's an urgency behind it. And I can't see her anymore, can't see anything at all. Her eyes are scorching, painfully bright against the backdrop of Dallas Dynamics skyscrapers. I go snow-blind in the reflections, and everything quits.

The longest dream comes to an end.

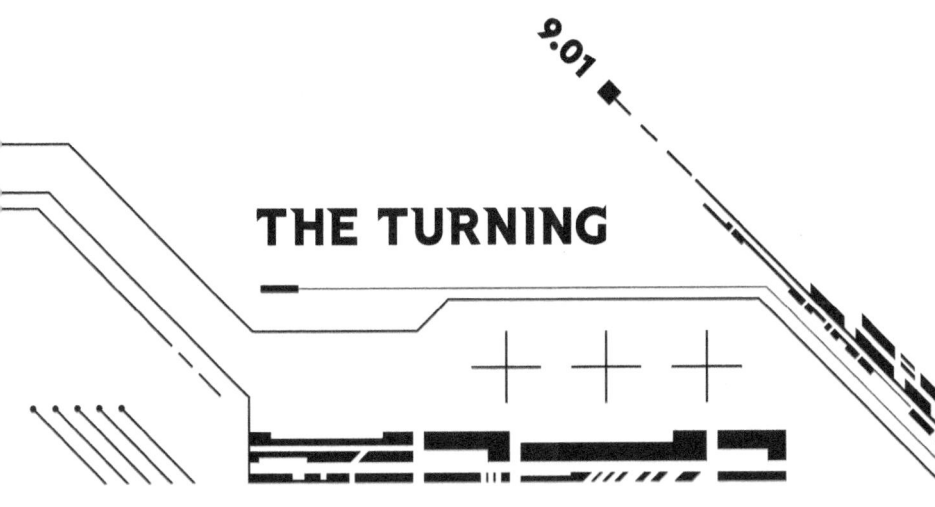

THE TURNING

The world is calm. My hands are pillowed beneath my cheek, and I am folded in a precious, fetal way that might embarrass me in other company.

Tysha looks more like a cat. Her arms are splayed in front of her, a few calloused fingertips lightly grazing my throat. She watches me like she's on morphine—or something better. A dopamine fix like summer love. Like nothing else could match the conversation between our eyes.

But the drowsy bliss begins to fade. Her faculties return, and our sweet connection is replaced by a more pressing disorientation. Tysha sits up in the makeshift bedding, looking around at the great table chamber and all its exotic wonders. She looks up at the ceiling and its gypsum crystals, glinting behind the strings of white and gold lights. She studies her loose sleeping clothes and the back of her hand like there's something not quite right about it. Not wrong, just somehow not what she expected. I stay where I am, ignoring all the same confusions.

"Brightstar."

Tysha and I follow a smiling voice to the western wall. Cuva Khan rises from the great stone bench with some surprise on his face—and a clever twinkle in his eye.

"It is good to see you again." His gaze drifts from her vibrant eyes to the returned shine in her cerulean hair. His own eyes seem to glow brighter for one unrestrained moment, before he lowers them to where old Mantz now also stirs from her deep slumber.

Like us, she has been blanketed and laid atop a thin layer of juniper branches to pad the hard stone floor beneath the bench. Her eyes have opened, but she remains flat on her back with her hands clasped together on her chest. She inhales deeply then exhales soft and slow. I don't hear her speak, but Cuva seems to. His delight fades as he kneels beside her, laying a gentle hand on one of her wrists. He nods intermittently, as though receiving orders, stroking her ancient knuckles with his thumb. With some difficulty, I sit up, realizing my hands are no longer bound. I begin that same disoriented process just as Tysha reaches the end of it.

"What time is it?" she asks Cuva without looking at him, studying her bedclothes even more curiously. "How long did she send us down?"

Cuva's head droops as he continues his mental meeting with old Mantz. He lets out his own heavy breath as he caresses her wrinkly cheek. "It is nearly sunset." He turns, lifting Mantz's walking stick from the stone bench. He carefully parts her folded fingers and places the staff beneath her hands. "You were all in the dream for three rotations."

Tysha is throwing her blankets off, rising to her feet, before she registers what he just said. "What?" Her eyes narrow in disbelief. "Three days?"

I follow her lead again, looking to Cuva for an explanation. He seems to have more urgent concerns, already marching to the chamber entrance.

"Cuva," Tysha quickly asks, "where are you going?"

The proud warrior halts in the doorway. But he makes no effort to turn around. "I make my way to Canna's Cavern. For the oldbooks."

Tysha gleans some dark meaning from those words. Her eyes drift to Mantz, watching her like some lost heirloom in a photograph.

"If you would gather the others at The Throat, I would be most grateful." Cuva's voice is like a fortress on the verge of total collapse.

Tysha understands. Following a moment of introspection, she nods quietly in agreement.

"Thank you, brightstar," Cuva says without looking back. "Your day attire is folded there." Without any nod or visible gesture from him, Tysha looks to the eastern wall, spotting her piled clothes. "Sumella and Lailara were the caretakers. They did their best and deserve high praises."

With that, he sets off down the passageway to his right, the one that seems to spiral much deeper into the cavern complex. Down toward the dozens of curious murmurs I'm hearing again: some just as fearful as before, some with a guarded, rising excitement, and others—a few brighter voices—who have already begun to mourn.

"She's dying," I start the question, looking over at Mantz's resting eyes, "isn't she?"

Tysha halts me with a look—not one of anger but pure surprise, an astonishment verging on jealousy. "You could understand him?"

"What? Why wouldn't I—"

She turns away like her question was rhetorical. A cascade of thoughts rush through her mind, and I can sense their edges, their essential subjects, but none of the finer details—all complex puzzles with missing pieces.

Then she drops her colorful pajama bottoms to the floor, revealing her bare ass and muscular thighs.

"Whoa—" I look away as she discards the loose-fitting top just as easily. She quickly steps into her black pants and other attire, not out of modesty but in a militaristic haste to keep things moving. Then she speaks, and I hear her everywhere. Her mouth moves while she laces her boots, and my skeleton feels warm.

"*Brothers and sisters, hear me well. One of our most radiant lights is in the turning. Our senior mother, to this tribe and so many others, has at last seen her high assignment to its end. The highway calls to—*" Tysha stops there, resting a knuckle against her forehead. And I feel her despair. I feel her heart stretching, threatening to tear itself in different directions.

Then I feel it relaxing back. The brightstar exhales softly through her nose, and her eyes reopen. Her psychic voice gains a mythical volume. "*The highway calls to Mantz AnCarcem, whose second name was Malikah before she renounced it, before she forswore her inherited lands and freed the brightworld's low valley tribes from their long stars in dim damnation. So, please come join me at The Throat to see one of our very brightest complete her passing.*"

Tysha rises quickly to her feet as though stepping away from a microphone. She whips her laundered duster over her shoulders, and I spot something I missed in that harsh battle weeks ago: a stitched column of blue fireballs, each larger and brighter than the one below it, rising from her tailbone to the base of her collar, vanishing beneath the fold.

Movement at the entryway draws my eyes, as two Lumina-rans shuffle into the room—two skinny young girls, carrying a makeshift stretcher of blankets and fresh branches. All three of us watch each other for an extended moment before they continue with their task, setting the litter down beside old Mantz and carefully preparing her for transport.

There's more quick movement at the chamber entrance, and my eyes dash that way again, just in time to catch Tysha striding out without any more wasted glances in my direction.

9.02

"Hey, wait a minute." I round the second corner, heading up the winding passageways. "What are we—" I take a few quick steps, closing the gap between us, shimmying and bending to avoid the narrowing walls and low cave ceiling. "What's the plan now? What's our next move?"

"Are you still pluralizing yourself, or do you presume to have some place in my operations here?" Tysha says without slowing her pace, without showing her face to me.

"I just meant—I mean we saw some pretty fucked up shit in there, pardon my English."

"I pardon you for nothing," she hisses over her shoulder. But I feel a subdued heat against my face. A cold kiss that reminds me of the dryland, of harsh affections found in scarcity.

"Okay, well I just hope you understand that ain't typically how we do things. I mean Calvin Prichard is clearly—"

Tysha whirls with a speed that leaves me lightheaded. The

tip of something sharp flattens Mama's scales against my neth-ers. Mama. That maternal feeling from the dream.

"Speak his name to me again, and I will make a woman of you." Tysha presses her kunai deeper, puncturing the top layer of—

"Don't hurt her. Please."

Tysha stops, seeing the fear behind my eyes. She scoffs, slightly more disappointed than disgusted. "Mantz was right. Your damage runs very deep." She withdraws her knife and re-sheathes it in one deft movement.

"I wasn't talking to you."

Tysha starts with another insult—but her eyes land on the suit. She watches the subsiding ripple of perturbed scales, relaxing back from a near battle-red, all epicentered low on our abdomen where the kunai pricked us. Her eyes linger there, and I catch a flash of that Earthly ego she hides so well.

She buries it in a derisive huff and goes on marching up the corridor toward the surface. "Prisoners will return themselves to the light chamber or face the consequences." She reaches a fork in the cave and points to her right before continuing up the incline to her left. Then she continues in my mind, "*And keep your silence, Emmett Hayes. As she taught you, keep these things quiet, and rest assured: Calvin Prichard will learn it, too. A silence to match his darkness. Par ya Lum sakar, I make this vow.*"

Her meaning finally reaches me—her puzzlement back in the table chamber. With some incredulity, she asked if I could understand the words of Cuva Khan. A strange question. To my ears, his words were English. To hers, it must've sounded like something else, Mandarin Chinese or maybe the Eastern Euro dialect of her first captors—whatever language comes most naturally to her mind. In those last words she telepathed to me just now, I finally heard it for what it was—the same indecipherable language they were spitting back and forth a few days ago. The light speech. That's what Kible called it in the dream.

Par ya Lum sakar. The same words that old Mantz spoke before she sent us down—her final utterance to the living world. It's a promise. Somehow, I understand it now. A pledge to blend your lights together when the hot shit comes. My light—seeming to brighten with every trial that I survive.

"Par ya Lum sakar," I whisper back to Tysha, not sure exactly if she received it. Either way, I won't forget. A silence to match his darkness. Yeah. I'll hold you to it.

9.03

The kid watches Connie from a safe distance—just beyond where her reach would be if she woke up. He's on the balls of his feet with his scrawny knees bent and ready, poised to flee at any sudden movement, any threatening change in her condition.

Her eyes twitch slightly beneath their lids—and he jolts backward. A little quicker than I expected. There's a feral agility in his malnourished frame. Not too aware of his surroundings, though.

"How's she lookin'?"

The pale child they called Poody jumps out of his skin at the sound of my voice. That lands him closer to Connie, which spooks him again, sends him stumbling nearly over the edge of the light chamber's raised floor.

"Whoa. Careful now." I extend a worried hand in his direction, and that scares him, too. He looks up at me with his large eyes, and I hear his wheezy lungs scratching their worst music. "It's okay." I lower my hand and take a sideways step to clear the exit if he wants it. "Just returning to my captivity, as ordered." I sidestep further until I'm along the opposite edge, positioning Connie as a comatose divider between us. Then I ease myself down with folded legs, posing peacefully.

Poody's little heart slows halfway back to its normal rhythm. It's not quite terror, I realize, but a mix of eagerness and panic. His itchy questions start again, seeming to germinate beneath my skin, coming much clearer this time. I can almost hear a tiny neighbor rehearsing his words behind thin walls.

"You're starting to remind me of somebody." I offer an amused smile, but his eyes still seem too gobsmacked to receive it—like my voice itself is magic. I chuckle at that, then take a good long look at the translucent icy ceiling above. "I've never seen anything like this. Not even close." The trickling dusky sunlight blends with the aquatic cavern ice. "But the way you been living here, so detached from everything else, it makes me think that you and I—"

"You speak the old tongue!" Poody points his skinny finger at my mouth like it shouldn't be there—like he's finally caught the universe in one of its lies.

I drop my eyes from the ceiling, taken aback by his intensity. "Oh. Uh. Yeah, I guess I can understand it now, but I'm not sure how to—"

"You are speaking it!" He points another index finger at me, so ecstatic he looks insane. But he quickly drops both arms as though he was chastised this morning for similar rudeness.

"I am?"

He points again out of reflex, then drops it just as quickly, fidgeting his entire body, keeping his wide eyes locked on me.

"How can you tell?" I look down at my hands, half expecting to see different colored skin or something.

"I—I am dim!"

"You are dim!" I project the words up and away, trying to hear some clue in the chamber echoes. "What the hell does that mean?"

"Dim—dim is—dim is like—!"

"Jesus, kid. Take a breather."

He sucks in a gust of air like he's about to dive underwater. That makes me laugh pretty good, and he smiles back at me, revealing an adorable array of missing teeth. But he quickly shuts his mouth and starts looking around the room for some way to prove his point.

"Dim is—dim is like her!" He points at Connie. "All the Earth people are—" He starts to point at me again but stops himself, not observing good manners this time but seeming to lose confidence in which species I belong to. "They are like me. No power. And to them, and to me, the light speech sounds like—like—"

"Gobbledygook."

"Yes! Like that!" He points at my mouth again, and I laugh harder. It's an infectious sound that gets him going, too, and I feel warmed. Not just by his delightful giggles but something else. A distant fire. That far-off star that lives inside him. I see it again. A deeply familiar flame. A remote inferno, bright as any other, burning just beyond his grasp.

"Wait a minute." I raise a pensive finger, and he goes stiff like I was giving an order. "I'm doing the light speech right now. The old tongue. You're sure?"

"Yes, sir."

"Right *now*?"

"Yes!"

"Then what are you doin'?"

"I am—" He stops, and his eyes look confused, trapped in a derailing paradox. He looks at the floor with a furrowed brow, subconsciously rubbing at his bald scalp.

Then he looks back up, and his eyes are alive with a thrill that few adults ever feel at all. "I am speaking the old tongue!" He claps both of his small hands to his mouth in shock.

"Sorry, what?" I try not to smile, failing completely.

"I am speaking the old tongue!" The first few words come out muffled before he uncovers his mouth.

"We both are?"

"Yes!" He gasps at the sound of his own voice. "Yes! Yes! Yes!" He does the weirdest little dance I've ever seen, turning every syllable into a finger jab around the cave until he finally points right at—

The young hothead, Yono. He's staring at us both from the entryway like our heads are twisted backward. Poody flinches again and forgets his footing. His right foot slips over the edge this time, and he tumbles from the flattened platform to the natural decline a few feet below, rolling end-over-end half a dozen times before finally catching himself further down the icy slide. He's terrified, already panting in a suffocated asthmatic loop.

I move to help him, but the hothead steps between us, showing me a knife—a crooked little homemade shiv with a five-inch obsidian blade. She *whispers*, and I see three different ways to take it from him without making too much of a mess. But a fourth sight stops me. He's not wearing my helmet today. I take my first good look at him—feisty and muscular, to be sure, but not yet a man. I see a fifteen-year-old who hit his growth spurt early, a boy who's overcompensating in preparation of true grit. And I see no reason to stunt all that hope with humiliation.

As I sit back down on the cave floor, he loosens his death grip on the knife, lowering it a few degrees. He keeps his eyes on me as he makes his way over to the edge where Poody fell. "You alive, Poopy?" After no immediate response, he snaps his fingers. "Hey! Get your ass up."

To my relief, I hear the boy begin to move, carefully rolling to his belly so he can push back up to his feet without slipping on the ice. He does slip, but his tiny toes spread, and he catches himself again. I hear him crawling now, a sideways gorilla-like shuffle, one hand and foot at a time.

Yono glances down to check on him, laughing at the sight. He shakes his head with vicarious embarrassment, but he crouches, extending a hand, allowing Poody to climb up his arm back to the safety of the flattened floor. "You would be dead if I didn't come." Yono watches the scrawny boy, lying exaggeratedly prone, catching his breath. A large purple bruise already stands out on one of his knees where it collided with the platform—and some blood on the palm of his scuffed little hand. "Still tumbling down into the mountain's belly." Yono makes a chomping sound and claps his hands.

"You made me fall!" Poody shouts at Yono's ankles before he drops his head again, sacrificing vital air to get off that retort. And Yono almost gives himself whiplash, looking back down at the child with disbelieving eyes.

"He's got you there, kid."

The hothead swivels back in my direction with the same dramatic surprise—that silly knife held out between us both again. I begin to hear his bewildered thoughts and frightful plans at self-defense if I make any more sudden movements.

"Relax," I tell him. He jolts again at the sound of the light speech on my tongue. "We're all friends here." I nod to the knife. He follows my eyes but doesn't lower the blade an inch—not until Poody suddenly hops up and kicks him in the shin.

"Agh! The fuck?!" He shouts after Poody, who is already running past him and out the entryway.

The kid stops there and points at Yono's mouth. "I'm telling! I can hear you! I'm telling!" He takes two steps down the corridor then comes right back and stares at me with those wondrous, terrified eyes, before he waves a rapid goodbye and takes off again. I can sense his travel now—a warm dot descending the steep wall before he branches off and ventures up the higher path. An impassioned heat that was always there, just woefully neglected.

I don't understand it. Seems like Tysha cares about him. Apparently not enough to let him in on the conversation. No way she could've missed that dormant fire in his guts; I saw it straight away. Felt it like a candle under my chin. Like my own heat in someone else. Just like—

My eyes snap to Yono, and he shuffles backward—like a grizzly just caught sight of him in the woods. Or something worse. Some deadly mystery of Earth. I start to itch. Start to feel jealous, then afraid, then exposed. I see memories I never lived. Distant flashes of naked skin. A bright blue lake deep underground. A dozen mirrors zigzagging up the mountain shaft. A goddess glistens in the spotlight. Her caramel curves exceed my dreams of the other world. She doesn't see me. Tysha doesn't hear me touch myself in the craggy rafters high above.

Yono's shiv clatters across the floor. He staggers to a knee, one hand clutching the stone, the other holding his face. There's a hard lump in his throat to match the one in his faded jeans. He stares at me. Quintessential eyes of dread. Then he scrambles for the exit like a child half his age. I hear him going, trailing Poody up the rising path, but I see no dot. No dim candle whatsoever. The only fire I feel now is the one that's right behind me.

I spin around, but nothing's there. Just a feeling. A sinking sense of nothingness, of passive floating in the dark. Feels like I'm lost. Like I can't remember who I am. That makes me angry. That draws my eyes to Connie Clark.

Something's changed. A candle I couldn't see before. Not even that. Just a wisp of latent smoke. It's coming closer. No. I'm walking toward it. I'm kneeling beside Connie, studying the left half of her face. The side without the scars. I'm stroking her temple in tiny spirals with the edge of my right hand. Remembering. Putting my baby boy to bed. *My starshine.* I'm noodling the effects of galactic travel from his mind. Singing our family song. Our lullaby of endless eyes on freer worlds. My beloved son is sleeping now. When he wakes, I will be gone.

I float my hand away. Slowly. Like I'm rising from a dream. The further I get from Connie's face, the colder my fingers feel. But our wrist is warm. Our chest is burning up. I look down at Mama's scales and see her dancing. Mama. The dusk light is barely trickling through the ceiling, but her solar cells are charging at a violent, reckless pace.

I spring away. I retreat from Connie Clark, afraid to look at her again. I don't know whose memories those were, but I need to sift them from my own.

I shake my head. I abandon the chamber just as hastily as Yono, climbing down the steep stone face to take the rising corridor toward The Throat, whatever that is. I just know I can't stay here. She's *whispering* for me to turn back, *begging* me to finish that spooky ceremony, but I'm too scared to listen. Not of *her*, not exactly. I'm terrified of the satisfaction, of how damn sweet the idea tastes, of how much mind and body I would trade just to know a mother's love.

 **9.04**

Their grieving voices are a symphony. A psychedelic opera like hot honey in my skull. A deeper loss than I can humanly withstand.

Old Mantz is in the turning. Sixty-one psychic minds are singing the ancient words that Cuva Khan just read aloud, and it is breaking me to listen. It's not the light speech. Might not even be a language any of them can understand. It sounds more like conjuration than information. A chant to channel the living light—to guide the spirit of Mantz AnCarcem to a brighter, higher place.

An afterlife, I thought at first. Just more of my Baptist inclinations leaking out. They are mourning outside the cave, and I feel some of it. The hottest edges of their grief. Their profound acceptance of this loved one's total end. They haven't noticed me yet. Haven't sensed me creeping up the long and narrow cavern entrance, the tunnel mouth they call The Throat. The sun is setting in the distance, cutting color through the trees, and I'm reminded of the captain. I realize how cold and lonely human death is compared to this.

Our specificities are lost forever; the tribe agrees. But, if we will it, our borrowed light can carry on. Mantz speaks to each of them. She gifts sixty-one separate bits of her fading internal sun. One by one, I see their eyes flare in response. I feel their hearts shatter individually as they rest their hands upon her own.

But I look away. I retreat my eyes to Yono, still somewhat diminished by our encounter. I see the others waiting their turn, some recognizable from the dream. Yono's aging father, Kono, looks up to the skies with a particular longing, something lost so long ago. I see those two skinny girls who carried Mantz here—Sumella and Lailara. They're both watching Yono with eerily similar desires—desires I begin to feel—so I flee elsewhere. My eyes dash for desperate shelter, and I see Tysha.

She's standing at the back of the line, squeezing Poody's scrawny shoulders. He looks up at her with one of his questions, but she's too busy mulling her own. *Where did this light in his eyes come from? How has she missed it all these years?* Even from this distance, I can feel her sinking shame.

She looks at me directly—like I haven't been hiding in The Throat but shouting her name from the cavern's lip. I see her face just like I dreamed it—that brief connection as we plummeted toward Texan soil. She looks down at Poody then back to me, and I see wonder—a mesmerized hope that makes it hard for me to breathe.

"*Don't you look away!*" an ancient voice hisses between my ears. I feel a shine like holy hell as Mantz chastises me again, "*Don't you dare look away from her, Emmett Hayes. Not now.*" I cry without blinking. I sob like I never have or will again as the old witch speaks to me one final time. "*Par ya Lum sakar. I give this piece of mine to you.*"

My eyes shine so brightly the cavern entrance becomes a spotlight. A tight beam of heat shoots over the gathering, lasering toward the sinking sun. Sixty-one faces turn to watch me.

They see the outsider, escaped from his cell, shooting off some kind of fiery weapon.

But Poody claps immediately. He does his little dance, pointing up at the sky with naive excitement. And they see the brightness I found inside him—the flickering candle they all assumed he couldn't have. Then they stand aside. They part as Cuva Khan marches his way forward. The divemaker's disciple. The ruthless warrior even AnSorin quietly feared. That man steps out from the ranks of his frightened people. He puts his broad chest between them and the outsider, his own eyes still hot and brilliant from his master's final gift. He stands witness to her demise, certainly hastened by my failure to promptly rise from her last dream.

That man extends his hand to me. He smiles despite his pain, and my extended family expands in real time. One by one, they offer their open hands, even proud Yono and little Poody, even the nervous skinny girls, even Tysha, still searching for an answer in my gaze. And I honor Mantz's dying wish. As I step from The Throat into the turning, I keep my eyes on the brightstar.

And I feel it all.

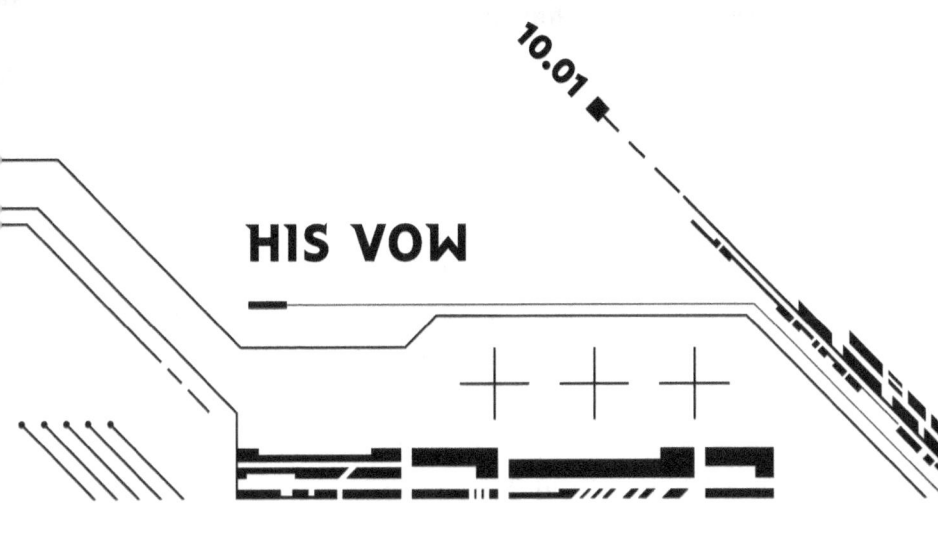

HIS VOW

"I don't understand." Tysha studies me like an elusive magic trick, like she must be missing something. "He has the scattering."

"Yes," Cuva agrees, leaning against the cavern wall, watching the distant flames of Mantz's raging funeral pyre. "She told me while you slept."

"Told you?" Tysha follows his eyes, climbing the fire to the starry skies above. "Mantz could see it in the dream?"

"She could see it in your shadow. Out there." He nods to the sprawling Taiga, to that bloody brawl with Cyrus Uba and Connie Clark. "This is no simple gift." He swings his gaze to meet with hers. "A scatterer leaves echoes of his work."

Tysha grimaces at that phrasing. The great funeral blaze breathes a manic life into her cavern shadow—into both of theirs—and I begin to itch in conflicting directions. I feel suspicious, somehow envious of myself, then stringently loyal to the memory of old Mantz. I feel wise and well-prepared, then I feel impatient and annoyed. I see Tysha and Cuva Khan turn simultaneously in my direction.

283

"Jesus." I take a nervous step into the cavern depths.

"What?" Tysha looks at me, then quickly over her shoulder at some potential threat. Cuva does not. He watches me calmly, penetratingly unshaken.

"Nothing." I look away from him, finding Tysha's eyes much easier to endure. "Just wondering if maybe this isn't the best idea." I gesture toward the huge fire and billowing smoke.

"The barrier is raised. Your dim people will see nothing." She waves a hand at the scarcely visible dome of disrupted air, a massive cloaking arc bridging the gap between the tree line and the mountain peak.

"Uh huh." I watch the refracted sky, admittedly impressed by the size of it—the casual use of advanced tech, still without any obvious power source. "And what makes you think I won't run off and tell 'em myself?"

Tysha scoffs. "I make no guesses at your intentions. Only the consequences." Her eyes shimmer threateningly, harshening her features in the dim light, but something else jumps out at me. An unmotivated color on the icy wall. A bloody hue like aged merlot. The rising sound of grinding teeth in Cuva's cavern shadow.

"Do you understand me?" Tysha asks.

"Yeah." I shake my head, and Cuva's shadow returns to normal, dancing to the rhythm of Mantz's pyre. "Just clarifying that I am still a prisoner, not a defector. I appreciate the hospitality, but if it comes down to my people against yours—" A twinge of pain draws my eyes to Tysha's. But I see no evidence of hurt feelings. Just a tight jaw and steely gaze. "I won't fight my friends," I clarify. "I'm not even sure what you people are fighting for."

A cloud of bats suddenly detaches from the cavern ceiling,

flapping chaotically, darting off through the cadaverous smoke, ripping through the cloaking arc into the night.

Cuva Khan chuckles, as though a sad joke arrives on the wind. "The high ones taunt us." He twitches sharply, almost hungrily, then drags the cave with his sturdy fingers as he strides off to join the others around the roaring funeral flame.

"All jokes aside." I twist my gaze from the melting glade, checking Tysha's eyes again. "That guy scares the fuck out of me."

She laughs. Just one breathy, involuntary sound before she aggressively pretends that she did not. "Tell me," she starts abruptly, clearing her throat, "if you can remember, tell me how did this occur." She tilts her head and draws back the hair concealing her left cheek. In the flickering pyre light, I see her rail slug scar and mutilated alien ear.

"The captain spotted you." I find it difficult to look away— to ignore the richness of her scent. "You got off lucky."

"How did he spot me?" She pulls away, studying my eyes again.

"He was watching me. I saw you first, and—"

"Your eyes were barely open. *How* did you see?"

"I don't know. I just—" Another itch runs up my neck. More impatience like angry hands. Like hot annoyance seeping out.

"What?" she almost shouts. "What did you see? Why can't you—"

"I saw your pain." My answer stops her. That impatience falls away. Becomes a stinging, sinking feeling, and now I'm sure it isn't mine. "I felt everything. In here." I tap the scales above my heart. "Like we were connected."

She drifts away, dropping her hair back over her scar. Some of the strands are already fading, losing their cobalt shine. And

I see their faces—each lingering longer than the next. I hear their names. *Jerill, Sila, and Goroon. My sweet Goroon.*

"I'm sorry." I shake my head to clear the heartache—Tysha's heartache, leaking into mine. "I don't—I'm not doing it on purpose."

"It's fine." She steadies herself. "This power you describe. This connection." She exhales carefully, breathing some of the color back into her hair. "This feeling that other lights are blending with your own." She watches Poody in the glade. An irregular calm shows in his shoulders. He gazes thoughtfully at the drifting swirls of ash. "We call this gift the scattering. It is not common. I have known only one other who could wield it."

"Kible Thexx," I quickly answer. "In that dream, you and he were—"

"No." She shakes her head. "We were light bound. Entangled by years of meditation. The old words and some images can pass freely in this way. You are different."

"Bullshit." I smile stupidly, waiting for the joke to land. "You mean you can't . . ." I gesture at the air between us, feeling too embarrassed to finish the sentiment.

"It is *you* that we have been fighting for, Emmett Hayes." She sighs as though accepting it for herself, straightening her posture, looking back out to her gathered tribe. "A nexus to unite the Earth world to our own. And to the endless others, as—"

"They all must come." We finish the mantra together, and she turns to me with fresh surprise. She looks ready to cut me in half. But another tiny laugh sneaks through her teeth. I expect her to take it from me, to scowl defensively and walk away. But a silence spreads between us. An eye contact I've never known.

That's when the explosion comes.

An electric pop like a giant bug just got zapped above us. The starlight on her face seems to brighten incrementally. Then someone shouts out by the fire. It's Yono, pointing up to the tree line—or higher, it's hard to tell from here. Tysha checks my eyes suspiciously. Then dashes off to investigate.

She's covering her mouth when I catch up to her. Others are gasping, looking up at different sections of the sky. I step into the glade, following their eyes upward but not under-standing, seeing nothing there. I'm forced aside as some of them begin fleeing toward the cave. And something strange is happening in The Throat. The dangling string lights are flicker-ing erratically, clinging to life on limited power.

"I told you not to trust him! I told you!" Yono points a fin-ger at me, aggressing closer until Cuva stops him with a patient hand. "He's sabotaged us!"

I locate Tysha in the crowd, wrangling Poody, directing him toward the cave with all the others. To my relief, she sees the confusion on my face. I feel her lingering suspicions dimin-ish—but only slightly. Her nervous eyes flick back up, not to the empty sky but to some random section of the mountain. Random, until I look closer, seeing something out of place. A travel pod, heavily modified. An entire ring of them, maybe twenty vessels in total, bolted into the stone with heavy cables rigged between them. Just like the string lights, the few visible systems in the pods are fluttering weakly, losing power.

I look back up to the starlit sky, and I finally see it. Or rather I don't. They're all terrified because there is nothing; the cloak-ing barrier has vanished entirely.

She *whispers*, and I hate myself. I allow her maternal voice to leak back in, and I feel sick. Sick like maybe Yono is right about me—right to fear us. Mama. She started something in the light room, and I didn't let her finish. Something like a lullaby, except to wake somebody up. I look back down the flickering Throat, and I hear the name again. She whispers:

Connie Clark.

10.02

The string lights flick off again, and all three of us hold our breath. But we keep our pace, heading down and down, passing the great table chamber now. Down the labyrinthian spiraling cavern with nothing but a torch and Tysha's glowing eyes to light the way. Down toward that mysterious heat I sensed back before old Mantz sent us down into ourselves. I asked about their power source, and Tysha did her best to think of something else, to hide it from my nascent senses. But now she's guiding us right to it—me and Yono and his stupid knife. I would've swapped him for Cuva Khan in a heartbeat, but the boy wouldn't have it—wouldn't abide me and Tysha going down here without his valiant supervision. If he had human skin and hair, he would've fit in nicely where I was born. All hot and dumb, thinkin' his fists'll match whoever they need to. He better hope I'm wrong. Better hope Khan finds Gunnery Sergeant Connie Clark still fast asleep up there. Better pray her bio-locked rifle is still tucked away wherever he left it, or he's about to grow up fuckin' quick. Rapid aging onset by Semper Fi.

The lights flick back on, and we all resume our breathing, pausing at a trident in the road. Three possible paths. Down the largest, widest passage, I hear a sound that seems familiar. A rhythmic dripping like drops of melted ice landing in a more massive wet collection. Too wide and placid to be an underground river. It must be an aquifer or some kind of lake.

My eyes find Yono, already watching me—not hiding his misgivings quite so well this time. His shameful memories, those peeping images I witnessed. He looks at Tysha, then down the wide passage, then everywhere else, as though to mask his psychological trail. He clears his throat, and I clear mine, checking the torch to confirm that there is indeed still fire there. Luckily, the lights go out again just as Tysha turns to face us.

She watches our awkward silhouettes for one suspicious moment, then decides she doesn't care. "The Tomb is just a bit furth—" At the sound of her voice, a dozen bats dash out to greet us from the narrowest passage on the right. The entire area strobes darker between her rapid, startled blinks.

"Ahh!" Yono burns a few calories swinging his five-inch blade at the screeching cloud. When he's finished, I feel his hot embarrassment like a rash on the inside of my stomach.

"Maybe I should go first." I move to Tysha's side, paying more mind to the torch in my right hand, incidentally grazing her hip with my left fingertips.

"Maybe you should give me the flame." She snatches the torch from me and carries on ahead with all our light. The ceiling is so low she's forced to crouch, practically doubling over. I start to follow her, but Yono shoulders past me with those jealous eyes. He waits there protectively until her buttocks fade from view, then he slouches after her, leaving me in severe blackness with nothing but the sounds of fleshy wings, dripping water, and my own spectacular imagination.

"Hey, let's keep it tight here, huh. Ranger file." I hurry after them, and— "Fuck!" I thump my scalp against some craggy nipple in the cavern ceiling. My head swims for a few nauseating seconds as I take a knee to assess the damage. I feel new moisture that might be sweat but is probably blood. The passage gets darker and smaller as my jailers leave me behind.

"Hey, Yono!" No voice echoes back except my own. I close my eyes and nothing changes. Perfect blackness everywhere. But I manage to take a sobering breath. I imagine the shard of flame that old Mantz gave me—her dying command to keep my eyes on the brightstar. And I can see her. Tysha's light is straight ahead, tethered to mine beyond the limits of space and time.

I open my eyes, and the passage becomes visible, lit brightly the whole way down. I laugh at the beauty of it, at the magnificence of my new power—

"*Hurry, you fool, before the lights go out again!*" Tysha shouts within my head.

I flinch obtusely, looking higher, seeing the string of overhead lights have flicked back on, running the length of the narrow passage. I wave a hand in front of my face, confirming that my eyes are not shining whatsoever.

"*The hell are you doing?*" she shouts again.

"Yeah sorry, I—" bump my head on the exact same nipple in the exact same part of my idiotic skull. But I swallow the curses along with whatever's left of my human pride.

10.03

"No. I don't like this." I slide back behind cover, turning my ear from the cave's final passageway.

"She's in there? You can sense her?" Tysha moves to peek around the corner, but I block her path with a cautious arm.

"The problem is I don't sense *anything*. We should wait for Cuva."

"Are you kidding?" Yono kicks away from the wall he was leaning against. "There are three of us. Let's fuck her up." He steps around the corner, clenching his knife down by his hip.

I yank him back behind cover, putting a finger in his face. "Don't do that again."

"Don't *touch* me again." He knocks my finger away, mimicking my admonishment with his crooked blade.

But I look him in the eyes, and I know he believes me. He scoffs and walks away from us, a few steps further from the long, wide passageway—the last thing between us and our mysterious destination. That persistent heat. It feels stranger the nearer we get to it. Not unlike the sensation I felt in Poody, that incredible distant flame. But this one is right there. Just there in the darkened chamber at the end of the hall.

"You ready to tell me?" I turn away from that mystery, finding Tysha's eyes. She seems to know my question before I finish it, "What exactly we're doing down here?"

"It's none of your business." Yono points his knife, this time from a safer distance. But Tysha quiets him with a look. Sends him sulking away and mumbling curses. Then she watches me for a few vetting seconds, finally giving in.

"It is a star tomb," she admits.

Yono tsks in disappointment.

"It powers everything here. Keeps the cavern warm. Sustainable." She touches a hand to the cave wall, smiling at some sentiment I don't understand.

I look around at the flickering lights, all strung together but not plugged into any source that I can see—male and female inputs dangling at either end. "It's a wave reactor," I realize aloud. "You're keeping a *nuke* down here?"

"No. It is different. This is . . ." she looks at the ground, formulating an explanation. "Mantz. She gave you a piece of her power before she passed on?"

Yono makes another disgusted disbelieving sound. I ignore him, moving a hand to the scales above my heart, remembering the ancient bit of light the old woman gave me.

"This is the same." Tysha nods toward the passageway that leads to The Tomb. "But much older. Many, many more lights given—in their entireties." She falls quiet as though there's something else. She averts her eyes a bit resistantly, seeming to hope I'll leave it there.

But a part of me refuses. "Whose lights?"

"Don't." Yono begs and threatens her at once. "You dishonor them!"

"You are not one to decide that," she spits right back in his young face. His eyes reveal damage, watching her turn resolutely in my direction. She explains, "This tomb holds the total lights of every brightstar in our tribe. Those before myself and Kible Thexx. Their final gift."

At the end of that confession, I see an expression I know well. A determined jawline betraying doubt. A quivering brow repressing fear. In Tysha's beautiful, shining eyes, I see the natural conflicts of a soldier.

And something starker stirs in me—one last human thread I need to pull. "Is it dangerous?" Her fleeing eyes tell me it is. "Could this thing *go off*?" I demand more loudly than I mean to.

"Mel caska! Show some respect!" Yono gesticulates with his knife, pacing in furious circles, gripping the handmade hilt so tightly I hear the wooden handle creak.

"The highest mind, the reddest hands," Tysha mutters

distantly, a blend of guilt and uncertainty. "His final spoken words to me."

"Whose words? Kible Thexx?" I wait for Tysha's eyes to find me, but they remain fixated on her past. "Tysha. Has one of these tombs ever exploded? On Earth?"

"Fuck you!" Yono slashes the air between me and him.

"Relax. I'm just asking—"

"You're asking because you already know. Your mind's made up. Your minds are always made up!"

"Kid. Quit pointing that at me."

"So, I'll just tell you—I'll tell you so you can be fucking satisfied!"

"Tell me without the knife."

"We blew it up! Alright?! We cracked a tomb and blew your fucking city to the fucking highway! Fuck Chicago! Fuck all of you! Kharre mel caska!"

"Yono, stop it!" Tysha's shout diverts his eyes, and I make my move.

Kissing our right shoulder against his chest, I flick his wrist and snatch the knife with embarrassing ease. He makes it worse, swinging an elbow with stupid slowness. I duck beneath it, spinning away without ever touching him again. His momentum trips him up, sending him staggering against the wall and into the passageway, finally landing on his ass. Uninjured physically, but terribly hurt, he stares at me. Then he stares twice as long at Tysha.

"You're no brightstar." His voice is wet with fresh despair. I feel that humiliated itch in my stomach again. A tear dashes down my cheek before I ever see one arrive on his. "You're a betrayer. You're a fucking—!"

The left side of Yono's neck explodes where a standard

round cuts through it. A spray of blood paints the wall and cavern floor with a stunning suddenness. The echo of a rifle shot catches up to us, bouncing off the stone like a wailing bobcat.

Tysha shrieks and lunges toward him, but I yank her back behind cover just as a second round divides the air her head was just occupying. Another wailing echo mixes with the piercing sounds of the ricochet before it finally quits, spinning hot and flattened a few meters behind us. She tries to get out there again, forcing me to hug her tight, gathering up her flailing arms, holding her as close to our chest as I can without snapping her in half.

"He's gone," I tell her.

"He's not!" She lunges again at Yono's tremoring body, now splayed on the cavern floor. His eyes are wide in horror. His hands are clutching desperately at the gushing entry and exit wounds where his throat and jaw connect.

"He's as gone as she wants him to be." I squeeze her tight, trying to control my own violent shaking, trying to shut out all the mortal panic that's racing through Yono and flooding my empathic brain.

Mama *whispers* a plan of action, and I couldn't agree more. It's the least terrible option, the only chance that we have left.

"But he's not gonna die," I promise Tysha.

She finally hears me. Quits fighting back. I lax my hold, and she looks up over her shoulder, searching my moist eyes for honest hope. I give her more than that.

"He's not gonna die," I vow to us both, adopting the language of her clan. "Par ya Lum sakar. None of us die today."

10.04

"Hold fire!" I shout around the corner, receiving an eerie silence in return. "Connie, it's Hayes, hold fire!" Not a single breath or twitching muscle echoes back to me, but I do notice something useful—that same familiar empty air where Connie's Spider must be jamming my expanded senses. A low patch almost completely flat against the floor. "She's lying prone near the back of the room," I speak quietly, turning to Tysha. "She'll be very accurate but slow to adjust." I eyeball the small section of the passageway I can see from cover; Mama whispers its shape: *2.4 meters wide. 3.1 meters tall.*

"Yes. She's there." Tysha looks like she's sleeping standing up. Down by her waist, her fingers twitch individually as though trying five different locks. "Too close to The Tomb," she sighs in frustration, allowing her eyes to blink back open. "Her light is too thin, I cannot—"

Yono chokes on his blood again, and I lose Tysha's attention. He gurgles, looking up at his brightstar with deathbed remorse, and I quickly look elsewhere. Not because I can't take it; I've seen worse. Not because it's my fault; I've already made peace with that. I quickly step back from the passageway corner to the opposite wall beyond Connie's view, because I just figured it out. In that sick instant, it all clicked together.

I now understand why Connie dug herself in down here instead of creeping up and out. I understand why she worshipped the captain and loved Aswad and hated my guts, because I can finally see her mission. Her entire career comes into focus. Her entire life. This isn't an ambush; it's self-defense—of the planet Earth and her own tribe. Her back's to the wall and her barrel's forward, just like it's always been. This is her last stand.

"It was me." I say it while I still can. "I didn't mean to. I lose control sometimes. But it was me. I woke her up right before I went outside."

Tysha keeps her eyes on Yono, but I still feel something in response. Something like confirmation—and disappointment.

"I just want you to know that I—"

"Save your confessions," she mutters over her shoulder. Her cheek is dryer than I expected, no tears at all for dying Yono. "I have no energy to hear them now." She turns away from me. Cold as stone. But a warmer itch endures. "You must survive and tell me after."

That stops me. Lost for words, I simply nod to her turned back. I know she sees it. We're seeing so much of each other now. I lift one foot to the cavern wall, testing the craggy grip like a sprinter's block. "Don't come out until the shooting stops."

She acknowledges me without sound. Takes a deep breath and shuts her eyes. "*Whenever you're ready,*" she says in my mind—in that bright, clear voice that lured me through the trees. She's sounded even clearer since the dream. A lucidity like cloudless rain.

I breathe deeply, too. I look down at my best version of a mother. One last look at her beautiful scales before the action comes. Before we go battle-red and redder still. She stops me there. She *whispers* like the wind of a different world. I can't quite make it out, but I feel a peace between us. A conspiring heat.

So, I set our feet. I lift my eyes back to the battleground. No time for a countdown, not if I'm going to keep my vow. I link with the brightstar, mind to mind, and I shout, "*Now!*"

Our scales go hot. The cave wall fissures as we push away.

We move so fast my eyes dry out. I clench them shut to block the wind; I don't need them now. In that split second, Mama charted the dimensions of the entire passage—all the way to The Tomb.

As my eyes squeeze closed, Tysha's snap open, lit with a brightness to rival the sun. Every light bulb bursts on the wall behind me, and I go numb. From the ankles up, the brightstar kills my sense of touch, leaving only feet and fists with any sensation for this mad-dog sprint. But as I hit the first wall, as we run up the side of it, a brand-new sensation almost stops me. Mama *screams*. We corkscrew up to the ceiling, then back down on the opposite wall, and she *wails* in disembodied agony. We hit the floor again, and a third bullet skins my knuckles—we *growl* together inside my skull.

As we ascend the first wall for a second time, everything slows. Only six more spiraling steps and we'll be there. Just five more steps. Four more. Another bullet tears through her scales somewhere. She clenches tighter, gritting through it. We hit the floor again, then start back up the wall, up to the cave ceiling. And a bullet rips through our plant foot. My eyes snap open. We're upside down. Our trajectory shifts. The final step now requires three. Failure is certain.

Then I see Connie.

I see her lying prone near the back of the chamber, tracking me with my own helmet visor, now fully charged, coursing with the same transmitted energy as the great glass sphere behind her. A sphere packed with pure cobalt light, floating above a carved stone altar. Hovering with that same anti-grav propulsion that carries them all here. Brimming with that heat but clearly damaged. A large spider-webbed crack on one face of it, as though someone laid into it with a hammer. Or the butt of a short rifle. I see the muzzle of that same rifle, aimed just out in front of me like the captain taught us. I see Connie ready to shoot where I'm going to be instead of where I am. And I feel her disgust. I feel her distrust for me confirmed. I feel her blaming me all over again for Aswad's death. For the captain's. For her own capture.

As I twist helplessly through the air, I see all of her animosities like any unattended darkness. I see her own abyss just there, just within my reach, just as her steady trigger finger begins applying its deadly pressure.

I whisper, *"Peace."* I shine a light, not from my eyes, but along the gap between us. That infinite space becomes a trivial divide. For one flashing instant, she forgets her hatred. Her killing finger stalls. I take all three of those staggering, necessary steps, feeling hot blood squish between our toes, then I'm in the air again, soaring like a spear in Connie's direction.

She finally fires that shot—now a hair too late. The bullet sails past my ear, taking just a few skin flakes for a ride.

I collide with Connie at a terrible speed. Her trigger arm doesn't break but rather disintegrates. I hear every bone, tendon, and nerve snap, crackle, and fry in an ensemble of subcutaneous devastation. Her rifle scatters across the cave floor in shattered pieces. A second tundra helmet splinters while she's inside it. But I fight to keep my vow.

I twist all that deadly momentum into me and Mama. Connie comes with us, but I hold her tight. We roll too many times for me to count, but every craggy knot and stone, every rough contact we make with the cavern floor, is absorbed by our G-1 elbows, our scaled knees, hips, and shoulders. We pulpify, careening off the back wall, sliding along our alien back until we drag to a well-deserved stop. Connie's on top, with only a cracked visor keeping the two of us from trading spit. Pressing my broken nose flatter, she hangs for a moment between a concussion and battlefield shock, staring into my eyes with distant perplexity before her brain decides that's enough for now. She falls limp in our clutching arms.

I lax our hold, letting her slide free to the cavern floor. I feel a sting of panic, seeing she's covered in blood, painted neck to ankles in a muddy red. I sit up to find her wounds, to administer aid, but my vision fills with floating spots, and I slump back down. My neck feels rubbery and useless. My head lulls sideways, and I see Tysha at the end of the corridor, already bandaging Yono, wrapping her removed shirt tightly around his neck to stanch the blood. As her focus fades from me to him, so does her power. The imposed numbness lifts, and a tight gasp escapes me.

I see all the exit splatters, spiraling the passageway floor to ceiling. All of Mama's shattered scales, glistening beneath the remaining string lights. An expiring organic trail leading straight to us. I finally feel all the gruesome holes that Connie gave us in our mad dash, and my brief panic lifts. Thank God. We didn't kill her.

She just killed us.

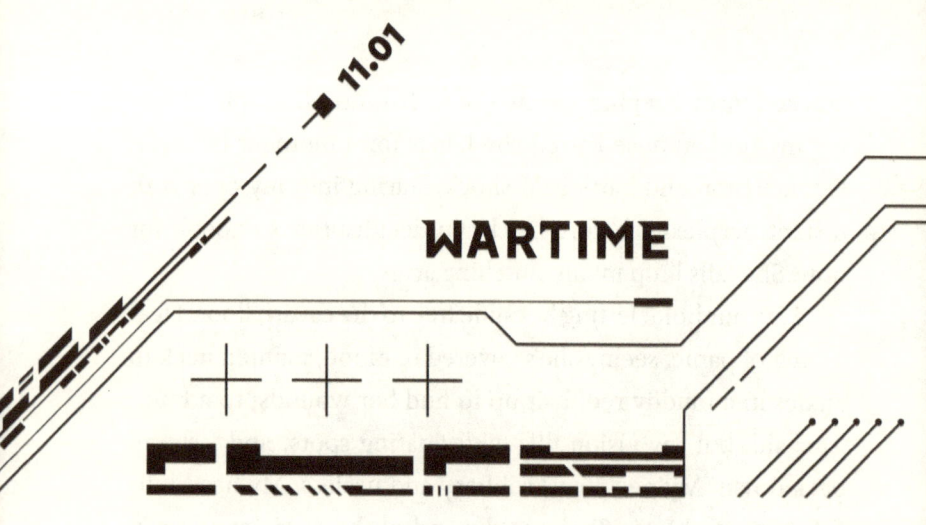

WARTIME

+ + +

It breaks his spirit to see her ritual tarnished. Cuva's hardened heart feels soft again as each shovelful of snow extinguishes his master's pyre. The old divemaker deserved so much more. The entire planet should be mourning the passing of Mantz AnCarcem. Every light in this sunsector should be lifted in one direction, paying witness and tribute to one of their greatest. Not just in their history but spanning the endless yet to come. And yet, he knows she would have had it no other way.

All the others have fled down The Throat. All except that impossible child who never obeys. They fled because their safety is no longer likely. Without the barrier, the great flame they ignited to send Mantz up has become a beacon to those nearby—to those relentless enemies searching, combing the forest and skies for the captured outsiders. He had decided not to trouble the young brightstar, not while she was so dim and dimming further, but for weeks, Cuva Khan could feel them. Their shrouded, lackluster lights, circling mulishly above that dusky battlefield. Sometimes nearer. Sometimes so closely overhead, he feared the barrier would not be enough.

Thank the high ones, he does not feel them now. That provides him some limited comfort. He has not felt the humans for several days, and that is a strangeness, too. Strange that they should quit so suddenly and completely. Perhaps they cannot grasp the value of this hybrid Emmett Hayes. To them, he may merely be another pawn of annihilation. Hands to hold a weapon, much like that previously comatose female he now faintly senses far below. Too close to The Tomb for him to destroy her. Much too close to their ancestral light for Cuva Khan to be at ease.

But he trusts the brightstar and her new pet more than he expected. As with so many things, his departed master is proved correct. Combined, those young ones shine with a rare potential. A synergized radiance that could very well change this fading world. But there is a vast chasm between what could be and what truly comes. This fact, above all others, he knows too well.

"Mr. Cuva!" the young boy shouts again from the mouth of The Throat. "Mr. Cuva! Mr. Cuva!" Poody goes on with his energized prattling and conspicuous noises, gesturing wildly with his bony fingers. Just like he did about the bear cub, the nest of rabbits, and the few warblers that scattered into the air just a bit too quickly for the child to hold his piss.

All wasted breath and pointless movement. Cuva Khan, the master of beasts and much lesser life, needs no such frantic alarms. He feels the creatures as they approach and long before. He sees beyond the limits of his kin, not just the light within conscious shells but the dimmer hues. He sees a ubiquitous network that once numbed him, an omnipresence that only devalued the light itself. Made it disposable.

But the boy is young and raised on Earth. He knows nothing of the devils the brightworld kept. The toothy creatures, the clawed incarnations of slaughter that evolved on their much older globe. Grizzly bears are a plush toy, a quiet meal to the demons that Cuva once conquered—that he bent to his will. The boy is young and knows nothing of Cuva Khan, who sullied his second name. He'll never hear the red bed stories or darker myths. Certainly none of the vile truths. None of the butcheries and vast killing fields, known only to him for lack of survivors. For that, at least, Cuva is glad. For that alone, he keeps his patience, silences his own youthful echoes, his incessant calls to make war again.

"Mr. Cuva, please!"

The blood pirate finally lifts his eyes from the improper burying of his beloved master. He sees the boy, no longer in the cave but hurrying out, skipping clumsily sideways so as not to lose sight of the growing blemish in the western night sky, pointing and pointing that way he does at the enlarging thing. The human ship that is almost upon them.

"Mr. Cuva, Mr. Cuva, Mr.—!"

"Quiet." Cuva watches the blemish, estimating two minutes or less before its arrival. "They may be listening." He turns back to the nearly doused flame. Watches it a few more seconds before setting his shovel down. A tarnished turning, now proven unnecessary. A haunting shame. He turns back to the frantic child and merely nods to the cave. "Go. Tell Tysha they've come. No more questions."

"But what are you going to—?"

"Poody!" *His past mind screams a war cry, demanding hot blood and splintered bones. His younger self rips the boy's arm from its socket and points it up at the intruders, vowing carnage and certain havoc—*

But the aging beastmaster sees the fear in the eight-year-old's eyes. He finds his patience again. "You have done very well. Thank you." He sets a hand not atop the boy's head but firmly against his shoulder. He carves a soldier from his youth. "Now go tell the brightstar the battle begins."

Without another word, the boy sets off toward the cave, stumbling twice but never falling completely, moving with more speed and focus than Cuva Khan thought the child was capable of. But the human shadow in the starry sky is larger now, large enough for Cuva to see all the guns and glass and stolen science that propels it closer—near enough for Cuva's limited comfort to fade completely. He should feel their lights at this small distance. Meager as they are, he should have felt them before the boy ever spotted them. Even shrouded as they were by those abominations in their spines, he felt them all when they came last. All except for one. The one he and Tysha abandoned in the snow. The mindless thing, not quite human, not quite machine.

Sixty seconds more before this stealthy vessel is upon them—this enemy craft that so far seems devoid of life. But the boy is gone now, out of earshot, and for that Cuva Khan is glad again. He breathes deeply, closing his eyes, diving down inside himself like his master taught him. He follows those incessant twisted shouts until he finds the prison forged by Mantz AnCarcem, the bolted cage where they trapped his former self so long ago. He breathes deeply one last time, finally breaking his first promise to the pacifist, Kible Thexx.

And his eyes come open. He appears gentle for a moment, taking in the frigid air and scent of flame, the stench of flesh put to the torch. But that stirs a hunger overdue. A thin smile creeps across his features. He shudders privately, fantasizing at the delights so soon to come. The twisted faces. He allows himself some laughter, a low belly sound like scheming shadows tasting life. Then he is away. Not moving like a man, not anymore.

At last, Cuva Khan The Darkmind returns to war.

11.02

The forest is quiet as they approach. A stillness that seems unnatural. Like the trees are listening. Like the snow itself is tracking their footsteps.

"Party hal—" Before Faye can finish, all sixteen Russians kneel with rifles raised. Before she even opens her mouth, her Spider-2 *speaks* to all of theirs, those bulging upgrades protruding from each of their spines. Larger but less unsightly than the originals, all glowing just below their tundra helmets. Mercurial marbles, glistening with an entrancing smoke between light and gas.

"What's wrong?" Prichard micromanages from the plush safety of his hovership. "You see somethin'?"

"No, sir." It makes Faye mildly ill to call him that, to march to his sick drum after all she's seen. But there's no way around it now. His schemes are tight, she can't deny him that. So far, it seems nobody can.

Not even Zhurov, who actually fought for this, who stubbornly insisted her own SOF bloodhounds must lead the mountain raid. She demanded a contract that guaranteed Russian exclusivity to the Spider-2s, and oh, how convincingly Prichard stood his ground. How slyly he fiddled President Guerrero to counteroffer on his behalf, to work the great Faye Thompson into that fine print. Of course, the new commander of Zero X should be at the helm of Operation One, this overdue revenge assault. This total destruction of all alleged rogues in their alleged headquarters in this abominable forest zone. And should the esteemed first lieutenant perish with all those Russian lab rats, with all her inconvenient knowledge of his schemes, oh, how convincingly he will mourn. Oh, how regrettably he'll gather up that combat data for the inevitable production of his Spider-3s, 4s, and fucking 5s.

"Do ya *hear* somethin'?" Prichard guesses again in that obnoxious twang he somehow makes pompous.

"No, sir. But I am *trying* to." A delicious silence follows Faye's retort. The Russians remain stiff and humorless, as a proper unit should. Still, Faye catches herself imagining how the Buggs would have reacted—one harmonious snicker back through comms, sometimes a whistle or hissing tongues like pressing steam—the sound of a burn. Childish, she always thought. Unnecessary. But their behavior was stately compared to trash like Alec Shankman. Always piling on with another jibe, distracting the unit even further. How the captain ever tolerated such infancy, she'll never know; why he would risk so much to save one weapon, she will never understand. Uba was wrong about Taiko Chiba; Faye sees that now. Faye sees her standing there between the wedge of Russians just like she always does. No remorse in her swirling eyes, no sense at all of what was traded to keep her alive—if it's even reasonable to call her that. To call *it* anything other than what it is. A machine in human form. Another ghoulish step toward M. Calvin Prichard Jr.'s vision of a unified world. Thank god, she thinks. Thank god they canceled that hanging order for an entire fleet of G-4 pilots. One abomination is plenty. One mindless husk is reminder enough of what the human world still has to lose.

"Understood." Prichard finally breaks his thoughtful silence. "Stay safe out there, Fangs."

He ends his comm lock and leaves her be, but her satisfaction fades too quickly. Something about his intonation in those last few words, that sinister cuteness she so often reads between his lines. She looks at Taiko again, wrapped in her brand-new high tensile hood, with her brand-new concussive sticks criss-crossed between her shoulders. They're more impressive than the lost ones and a few millimeters longer—that old Dallas Dynamics guarantee. Innovation stacked on growth, or the other way around. Faye wonders if those Yakutsk medics had to peel away Taiko's frostbitten cheeks and forehead meat or if that ruined flesh just healed itself. Faye watches Prichard's inhuman weapon, and as this new silence stretches out, she begins to feel something more unsettling. Something like claustrophobia's naked ghost crawling up behind her. That's when Taiko's dreadful eyes suddenly shift, staring right back at Faye with that chilling lack of life. No. She's staring right through her.

Faye spins fast, rifle raised, just in time to spot a flapping woodpecker, at first seeming to dive-bomb straight for her throat, but suddenly darting off to a nearby hemlock. Landing there harmlessly. Hopping along a thin leafy branch until it settles against the trunk. Clutching there with its Jurassic talons spread in four directions, pecking firmly at a fresh hole in the clinging snow. That tightness in Faye's gut resolves itself. The first welcome sign of natural life since they arrived. She almost laughs. Until a more threatening wildness turns more heads than hers.

It's the too-human grunting of a bull moose, if she's ever seen one. Two meters tall at its broad shoulders and twice her height at the tip of each antler. She watches with no subtle awe as it approaches from the north, grunting and moaning the entire way, but with no obvious aggression. If anything, it seems sick. Or so unfamiliar with human beings that it perceives no threat at all. Still, Faye nods to the Russian in position seven. Her Spider *clarifies* the command. He rises from the left wing of their wedge formation, rifle readied, nestled against his shoulder. He waves forcefully at the great beast with his other hand, attempting to turn it away.

It keeps coming—sounding more and more human as it draws nearer. More and more peaceful, even slowing its gait to a more passive stride. Number Seven waves at it again, grunting right back at it this time, doing everything he can to shoo it off without giving away their position. Faye watches that scene, increasingly puzzled. She double checks their heading, due east. Still another one hundred ninety meters to the dropped ping signifying the cave. She'd planned to harrier down right on top of the smoke pile, skipping any navigation of the forest entirely. But Prichard wouldn't risk it. Or rather, he wouldn't risk himself.

In his defense, the scene was more than fishy. A sophisticated cloaking field, suddenly dropped. Jamming frequencies, all disabled. An active tower of flame in a forest clearing, not unlike the one they wandered into a month ago. She couldn't disagree with Prichard's rationale. She also couldn't unsee that shine behind his eyes. That constant gleam that everybody seemed to miss or misinterpret. That penetrating commitment to his own distant aims—and nothing else.

Number Seven finally quits his waving. He flips off his safety, going rifle hot. He turns slightly in Faye's direction, and his Spider *purrs* a violent request.

"No." Faye holds his eyes when he turns to her completely. She taps her chest, meaning for him to check his own, where he has two SOF hand axes strapped. Both meant for throwing.

He nods and quickly pulls one free. Spins it deftly in his hand once, twice. But as soon as Seven turns back to the moose, now just ten meters away, it stops cold. It quits its howling, looking lazily off to the east, yawning broadly, as though suddenly losing interest in the human patrol altogether.

Seven looks back to Faye, not sure whether the quiet kill order still stands, but she's just as uncertain. Another fluttering of wings draws her eyes back over to the wedge of Russians, where a second woodpecker has just landed, barely visible in the limited light, directly atop the stoic helmet of Twelve. He doesn't seem to notice, but Fourteen does. A third has just landed on the barrel of his raised rifle. Hopping curiously there, just like the first one that alighted in the hemlock branches. He shakes his weapon, and the bird takes flight, only to land on the shoulder of Fifteen directly in front of him. Only now does Faye notice Taiko and her swirling eyes.

Not prioritizing the birds among the unit nor the bizarrely nocturnal moose now rubbing its antlers between two birch trees, somewhat like a blade against a whetstone. Instead, Taiko is looking straight up. Up at all the highest branches and interlocking piney needles. Taiko Chiba watches with emotionless eyes as dozens, no, hundreds of woodpeckers, hawks, and stealthy owls now darken the moonlit sky at the forest ceiling. And something's falling. Fast. A boulder or—

Faye hops backward just in time to dodge it. She has her rifle free and cocked, with her trigger half-squeezed before she stops herself, seeing the intermittent sparks and shattered ocular glass. Before she realizes it's—

"Drone two just dropped." Prichard comes back in over comms. "And you got a beetle or somethin' coverin' your helmet cam. Hell's goin' on down there?"

But a panicked shout sends Faye's eyes back up to Fifteen. He breaks formation, standing, trying to swat something off his back, letting his rifle swing wildly on his leash as he spins around, scratching and flailing ineffectively with his brawny arms. Fourteen seems trapped between discipline and rescue. Moving to help, then halting, then moving again and—he's too late. Fifteen screams like no grown man ever should. He shrieks at a pitch he shouldn't even be capable of, again and again, until the entire unit is in disarray. Something finally darts away from Fifteen. Too quick for Faye to track it.

"Taiko!" Faye shouts—her Spider *commands.*

In a flash, Taiko is airborne, snatching the shadowy projectile out of the sky. Something flutters, flapping wildly in her grip before she squeezes it dead. A woodpecker with something still clutched in its lifeless beak. Something glowing. A glass marble and connective diodes, still swimming with cobalt light and gas. It's Fifteen's Spider-2.

"Rifles free!" Faye shouts at the top of her lungs.

The confused but glorious racketing of readied weapons fills the air as Fifteen starts vomiting blood, shrieking like a possessed child, clawing at his gear, scratching bloody, squirting rows in his own exposed throat.

"Faye! Answer me, dammit! What are you—"

Faye smacks the dial on her helmet, blocking Prichard's transmissions for good. Then she puts two bullets in Fifteen's face just as he turns his rifle with crazed, treacherous intentions on Fourteen. The blood that splatters Fourteen's visor seems to suspend him in instant trauma. But Seven is shouting now, too, not in madness but self-defense, as the bull moose comes charging directly for him. The man finally lets his hand axe fly, but the moose deftly blocks it with one broad, flat antler as a shield. It lets out a wet and thunderous wail, freezing Seven in his tracks, but Faye puts two more rounds in the moose's chest. It becomes dead momentum. Its heavy body sweeps the legs of Seven, and by the sound of it, cracks several bones below his knees.

A snarling wolverine lunges at the blind spot of Nine, but Eight shoots it out of the air. Ten starts panicking about his own landed woodpecker, but Eleven bashes it flat for him with the butt of his rifle. Number Two wastes eleven rounds on scampering deer and smaller creatures, and Twelve sharpshoots the snout from a grizzly bear fifteen meters south. But the beast doesn't seem to register any pain, doesn't behave even remotely similar to how a grizzly bear fucking should. And Twelve sees something else he can't explain. In the too-clever gaze of the grizzly, now carefully maintaining cover behind a snowy tree, he swears he sees a glow. A slight shine of deep red light behind its eyes, its manlike eyes. Through his Spider, Faye sees it, too. She sees it all in each direction, but to her this scene makes perfect sense. For a month and more, she's had no doubt this day would come. Soon as she saw the great Cyrus Uba's frozen corpse, she knew one thing with absolute certainty. Spider-2s, 3s, 4s, or fucking 5s, Fangs Thompson knew, if she ever returned here, she would not survive.

As though summoned by her own fatalistic inner thoughts, the hundreds of birds start falling, raining their screeching beaks and shredding talons on SOF-AB, Operation One.

11.03 ▪ ▬ ▬ ▬ ═══════════

Poody has never felt so alive. Never felt so required. He's never stubbed his toe so bad without crying out. Never ran so fast through the total dark or crawled under the bats without being scared at all. He can't be scared because Cuva Khan's watching. Even down here, he can feel his eyes. His terrible eyes. He's doing bad things up there, Poody can tell. Bad things like what made Tysha so sad when the outsiders came. He didn't know it then, but now he does. He knows the light speech, and he knows some stuff old lady Mantz knew, too. He feels warm ever since she went away. He remembers what she told him right before she died. He could never forget, not for a million stars. She was always cranky in the cave and smelled weird like wet towels. But Poody thinks maybe she was good. He misses her now. Even though sometimes it feels like she's still with him.

The lights go out again, but Poody goes on dashing through the dark, one hand dragging along the wall while the other waves out in front of him just in case. In case of what, he doesn't know, but it makes him feel better. As far as he knows, caves stay the same for always always. And he used to come down here all the time when he was allowed. Or maybe he was never allowed, but he wasn't always *not* allowed. Poody guesses Tysha must have un-banned him from The Tomb. She must have told Cuva that while he was putting out the fire. But Poody didn't hear anything, and he's been hearing all sorts of things today. He definitely definitely heard old lady Mantz when he put his hands on her before the fire. She looked dead already, with her mouth half open, but Tysha made him touch her. She didn't say for how long, so he just tapped her wrinkly knuckle one time. But that was enough.

Poody felt like he was flying when she talked to him. Like he was in outside space above the Earth. And all the stars he saw were people. And all the people were his family. He saw his papa who he knew about from all the stories Tysha told him. She never met him, but she knew the stories. Everyone knew the stories of Kendar Shall. He was real famous on the brightworld. Much more special even than Kible, who was his little brother. Much brighter, the old ones would say, but never more details than that when Poody asked. Even old Mantz would shoo him off when he got too curious. Always with that face. The sad face that brightstar Kible always seemed to have when he looked at Poody.

But when Poody touched old Mantz this morning, she was happy. And sorry. Sorry for not being more useful while he was dim. Sorry for not seeing why he was so dim to begin with. Or not wanting to see. But as Poody soared through that out-side space dream with old lady Mantz, through the last dive she would ever make, she showed him all that she had witnessed. She showed him the argument his mother had with Kible Thexx when she arrived. She showed Poody his mother for the very first time.

He was just a few months old when he and his mother landed together, many orbits later than they had planned, more than two extra Earth decades in ageless space, spiraling off course in the travel milk while the world went on without them. And Poody's mother refused. Refused to believe the great Kendar Shall could perish in such a way, in the possession of cruel and curious Earthmen. Refused to believe his beloved baby brother, Kible, could have ever grown into such a bitter coward. She was honored by Kible's symbolic claiming of her and Kendar's wedded name, AnSorin, but it was yet another act of resignation, a touching sentiment of defeat. Nazara Thume would rather die than do any such thing. Not while she could still feel her promised man. Not while she could still see the scattering of so many lights that Kible Thexx had long named dead. The brightstar tried to reason with her. Tried to pacify what he perceived as madness, but she was unmoved. With her rare gift, she knew that he would stay stubborn, too. He would never go, would never let her leave, not after all those stars spent mourning Kendar. Not after all that time spent wishing he'd been stronger, just as she said. Nazara felt his pain. She cried her first tears on Earth as she whispered in his ear. And the infamous Kible Thexx, who was barely a man the last time she'd seen him, fell limply into her arms.

Quickly, she met the eyes of the wild teenaged girl, a girl Poody could recognize as a younger Tysha, and Nazara *whispered* to her, too. Not to make her rest but to calm her with a great request. To beg that she look after Kendar's child, her starshine boy. To give him a good name when he starts speaking, something fitting. Nazara smiled, seeming to admire Tysha's untarnished skin and natural hair, but old Mantz could hear the truth. Thoughts of envy. Thoughts of loss. Thoughts of ruthless violent rage. If Mantz was younger, in her prime, she may have forced Nazara to dream, may have unlocked her true potential. Instead, she could only sit quietly in the corner, watching the desperate woman leave.

But she did a good thing, Poody thinks. He's glad she told him, and not too mad she kept it secret for so long. Not too mad at Tysha either. More mad, but still, he understands. Somehow, this new warmness makes him understand things better. And be less scared. Old Mantz is dead and burnt, but he still feels her. Pushing him forward just like the scary eyes of Cuva Khan. And there's a tugging, too. A feeling like he can't fall no matter how bad he trips. Because someone strong will catch him. He's almost to The Tomb now, and he's feeling that feeling more and more. A different warmness that reminds him of his mama.

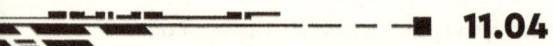 **11.04**

As she masks his pain, his heart rate slows. So does the gushing from his ruptured neck. Yono becomes less frantic as she cradles his head in her perfect lap, just like he always dreamed she would. But her bloodied hands aren't free to pet him with any affection here. Neither is her heart. He senses that now, even more than he usually can.

His gift has been a poison ever since the outsider opened his eyes. He smells the urges of the Earthman at every passing. Yono sees his cravings, repressed and inexperienced beneath that disgusting skin he calls a uniform. Yono has been with more females in the cave than that man-child has laid in his entire life! Back on the brightworld, Yono knows he'd be unstoppable. If he still had his dark skin and crimson hair, he'd be a king. A roguish lover, making hot and hotter myths. He'd sniff the lights of every woman he desired, turn their hidden dreams into wet realities. He'd try a few men, too, just to complete the legend, to make no promised pair ever feel safe from his seductive power. His father married young and squandered their identical gift, but Yono would take no wedded name for as long as he survived. No one woman could ever be enough, not while he could taste their lusts at every passing, not while their carnal fantasies flashed so vividly behind his eyes. No woman could ever satiate that calling. None except the one who's holding him right now. And she yearns for another.

Even as Tysha ties her shirt around Yono's throat to save his life, he smells her desire. Her soft breasts brush against his forehead, barely concealed behind a nylon combat bra, but she couldn't feel further from him. Unlike Lailara's fleeting lusts or Sumella's more constant, cloying crush, Tysha's smitten scent keeps growing stronger, creeping up on her as well, he thinks. A slow and confusing thing, more pungent than he's used to. A vibrant aroma not unlike the one his father emits when he speaks about Yono's mother. All these years and the old man still hopes. Still prays to the light that her lost pod will soon arrive. Lost, he says. Simply astray out there somewhere between the stars. But Yono sees a different constellation when he looks up. On the darkest nights outside the cave, he sees those man-made satellites of certain death, and he knows exactly where his mother's pod has ended. They all know. That's what makes Tysha's misguided infatuation so much harder to swallow.

Yono smells her desire and so much more. He sees her love-shine travel. Unlike his father's shine—always aimed hopefully to the hanging stars—the brightstar's yearnings are beginning to point just like a beam. A highway tether, brighter every hour since they suffered Mantz's dream. Especially now. Yono can see her treacherous passion blazing straight down the corridor. He drowns in the surplus heat of her noxious love stink, all aimed at the floor of the bloody Tomb. Aimed at the Earthman who would so readily have her if he only knew—if he wasn't so busy being dead.

11.05

Tysha turns her power on herself, and she remembers. She sees that old cage in her mind's eyes—that repurposed kennel where all her first memories are staged. She numbs her own stomach with her light, and she's reminded how that gift was first acquired. She remembers training herself not to feel, not to hear what they were doing, not even to see. She remembers their groping hands becoming distant sensations, their sweaty faces becoming dim shadows until they faded down to blackened nothings. She learned to make her whole world black and silent when they would come. She even learned to fill that space with better things. Anywhere she could imagine, she could take herself. She envisioned her mother's face and a blue-haired man who could be her father. She imagined a bustling West Shanghai, even though she'd never seen that either, not yet. She populated her private place with kinder people, people who smiled when they saw her, but not like *them*. Never with those uneasy, unsettling grins the kennel men and their customers always came with.

Tysha dulls her own twisting nausea and does the same to Yono's pain. She remembers how practiced she became without even knowing. She manipulated her own senses a hundred times before she realized it was a power, a gift she could control. When she learned that truth, her captors learned quickly, too. She can still hear the great fat man begging. The Slavic underlord, Korol Shulga, pleaded just like she had so many times—backed into the corner of his smoky office, one hand raised, the other crawling, while his panicked tears cut cleaner smears down his greasy face. She'd cried just like that a dozen different nights, a dozen sobbing attempts to make him stop—before she realized it was the tears that delighted him most.

As the kennel boss fled from her new power, from the shimmering eyes that she'd awakened, Tysha remembers feeling ill. She was smiling just like them, wearing the gore of twenty men, dismembered and dead in the halls behind her. She felt a delayed disgust at how much horror she'd painted on the other girls' faces—the human pets she'd just freed and scarred in simultaneity. Even the older woman—the wrinkled, dead-eyed slave the kennel men had kept for years and years before they'd ever smuggled themselves from the wreckage of Ukraine, before Tysha was even born—even Oksana, whose skin was freshly marked and burned and bruised every day she'd ever seen her, even numb Oksana, who was barely alive and conscious to begin with, even that old wraith had shown a sudden, gut-wrenching terror. Even she had fled and recoiled from Tysha as though she was no better than the kennel men at all. As though she was worse.

So, she let it go. Tysha had been clenching that crooked glassy shard so tightly that it stuck to her palm when she forced her fingers open. But she shook hard, and it fell to the ground. Landed with a slap in the thick streak of blood the fat man had dragged across the concrete floor. Then she was walking. She was leaving his office and his infectious evils behind for good, when she heard him shout one final time. Not across the airwaves but in his mind. She heard his hot intentions like any actual battle cry.

She turned just in time to receive his hands, his filthy, hairy hands on her again. His clammy, pudgy, disgusting fingers around her throat. And she'd wanted to be better, she'd really wanted and hoped she could be better than the kennel men, but in that last long hour of Korol Shulga's ugly life, she was worse than they had ever been.

Tysha didn't smile, cry, or feel much of anything when the kennel boss was finally gone. Not for years. She turned her power on herself and saw no reason to turn it off. Until AnSorin found her. Until she was given Poody and Goroon— her sweet Goroon, who smiled like the happy people in her protective fantasies.

She won't endure that pain again. She numbs her twisting stomach to suppress another loss. She hides the sound of her throbbing heart, and she blinds herself to the strange and fading shine of Emmett Hayes. He is vanishing in her periphery, unattended and unturned just like her allies in the forest, just like Kible, Kendar, and the great Nazara Th—

"Muhr-nerf!" Yono gurgles some indecipherable shout, suddenly lunging away from her lap, snatching at, and missing a shifty figure in the dim passageway. The tiny interloper startles Tysha, too, until she recognizes his round face and naked head, drenched in sweat and determination.

"Poody!" She resists the urge to lunge at him, instead maintaining pressure on Yono's wound. "Hey! *Get back here!*" Her eyes flash threateningly, broadcasting her booming voice to his young mind. She is stifled just as quickly by his defiance.

Poody goes on dashing down the corridor, right past all the red and glistening colors Emmett Hayes's shredded uniform left behind. The wheezing boy sprints boldly into the chamber she banned him from, seeming to barely register the dying Earthman on the floor. As though he expected to see him there. As though his current mission demands a much greater urgency. But he does pause at the base of the altar. He gapes helplessly at the great gypsum column that old Canna Dhoz

AnFannan carved before his turning—back when only Canna, Kible, and the few other founding members of the tribe lived in the cave. Poody gapes at all the stories brought to life, at the beautiful stone dish that seems to cradle the hovering star tomb that glows above it—a shine so bright and pure it almost damages him to look at it.

Then Tysha finally sees what's in his hand. She sees it trembling down at Poody's waist, and Yono's clogged shout finally arranges itself in her mind. She thought maybe she'd lost the light speech again, dimmed by her dark memories, but now she understands. Yono was trying to say *my knife.*

And Poody is climbing the gypsum altar now, slipping twice but carrying on, badly scraping his bruised knee but barely grimacing. Tysha watches with horror and blinding pride as AnSorin's heir becomes a man. A man clearly demented.

"*What are you doing?!*" she shouts in his head. "*Poody, get away from there!*"

"*I can hear my mama.*" His telepathic response leaves Tysha dumbfounded, silenced again. "*She needs the light to help Sergeant Emmett.*" His voice is calm despite how frantically he's climbing the salty altar, now carefully rising to his feet in front of the great sphere itself—directly in front of the weblike crack the Earthwoman gave it, a crack where some of the ancient light is already leaking out in thin celestial beams.

"*Poody, what are you doing?*"

"*I can hear her, Tysha.*" He turns Yono's knife in his hands; the black blade is now jutting down from his tiny fist.

"*Poody, stop it. You're scaring me, I—*"

"*My mama needs the light!*" He draws back the blade with that same determination.

"*Poody, no!*" Her eyes flash in fear and protective instinct.

She tries to send him somewhere else, tries to numb his hand so he can't bring it down, but his proximity to The Tomb makes that impossible. Yono's homemade blade finally finds a target.

The spindling crack in the intergalactic glass becomes a shattering, exploding, deafening burst of cobalt light and older heat, a blinding flash of life itself, of ancient brightstars' total gifts. For one moment in history, the entire planet shines like the brightworld did, a brightness that makes the infamous Chicago Storm seem like a harmless spark. An impossible shine that no person of Earth has ever seen or should ever expect to see again.

But nobody is killed. Nobody is harmed in any way. The star tomb is gone, shattered completely, now just chunks of glass in the great stone dish. It's all contained in a tidy pile, as though the orb simply dropped straight down without any outward momentum whatsoever. Poody still stands atop the altar. His pale skin appears to have been pinkened by the extreme light burst, but it's unlike any sunburn Tysha's seen. Deeper. Spread equally, even on the back of his neck and his skinny calves, neither of which were facing the explosion, none of which seems to be causing him any distress or pain as he looks down, studying his own arms and hands.

The previously flickering string lights are lit brightly again. Brighter than before. Tysha looks around, realizing the entire passageway is glistening here and there where the gypsum catches the gifted light, and—

She's the first one to notice the other thing. It stops her breath. She watches in frozen astonishment as a dead man gingerly sits back up, as he winces, still drenched in his own blood, still wearing a skinsuit full of entry and exit holes but no longer perforated himself—only badly scarred where the wounds should be, where she can see them rapidly closing. Emmett Hayes sits up, alive in his radiant uniform, in his blinding outfit, more fully charged than it's ever been, dappled in the hue of The Tomb's old power.

Disoriented and confused, the sergeant's eyes finally find hers. He's uncertain until he sees her—until a sense of victory finally comes alive on his stupid, human face. He smiles at Tysha of the silent second. And for the first time that she can remember . . .

The brightstar smiles back.

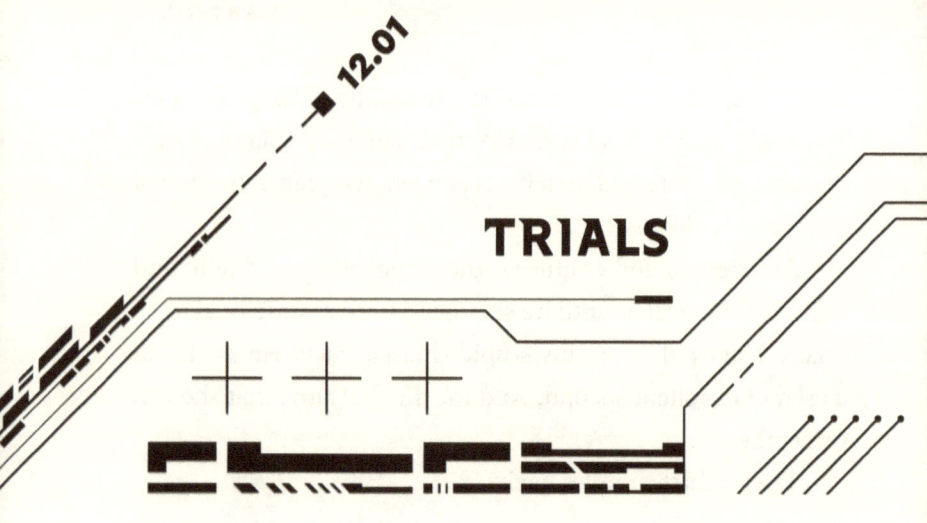

TRIALS

We caravan our wounded back through the narrowest passage. Tysha crawls on her hands and feet, tangled up with an exhausted Yono. He staggers several times, gurgling and grunting his continued pleas to be left behind.

But she keeps her patience with him. We both keep an eye on the knotted shirt around his neck, half-soaked with blood. Still only half. No change in its redness since we were all washed in the light of The Tomb.

My suit was designed to patch me up, to repurpose starlight to that end. With our solar cells still bursting and overloaded as they are, I'm not especially surprised that my life was spared. I just expected it to take weeks. I expected Yono to be comatose, at best. Annihilated, at worst. Blasted to ash in a blinding storm just like Chicago. Instead, we all seem improved. Touched by some interstellar grace, as though humanity's coldest day is just some old collective memory we all got wrong.

For that and more, I'm thankful. Resting here at the rear of our crawling group, a couple meters behind Poody, who hardly needs to crouch at all, I rest my chin on *her* warm scales. It hurts a little, some lingering tingles in my fusing forearm bone, but I'm much more distracted by the sight of the exit wound. For the first time in seven years, I can see my natural arm. I see thin hairs and sunless skin, mostly healed but badly scarred where one of Connie's rounds burst through us both—me and Mama. To my alarm, her damaged scales haven't healed at all.

For over seven years, the line between us has been dissolving. Just a few more months in orbit might've done it. The end of symbiosis. A total merge into something new, into simply one. The opposite is happening now. Ever since we desynced on the tarmac, I've seen the separation growing. I've felt the shifting weight of a second mind clawing its way toward independence.

Poody sees it, too. Sees something more than human science coursing through these shimmering scales. He hasn't spoken a word since he cracked The Tomb. Hasn't seemed himself at all, but the look in his eyes tells me enough. He no longer sees me and my strange uniform; he sees *us*. His sweet naivete may have been the only casualty of the explosion.

Connie mutters something dreamily, stirring slightly on our back. I turn my chin in her direction; I request the power of my second mind. We *shush* her gently back to rest, back totally limp on top of us. I feel a thin dribble of drool, puddling between our shoulder blades. Good thing I left the helmet behind. Connie might have drowned herself awake if she was still wearing it—awake enough to throttle me with her one good arm. I wonder if a woman like her can ever let the battle die, ever allow defeat to be the end. If we manage to escape this place alive, I guess we'll all find out together.

Poody starts moving again, seeing that Tysha has gotten

Yono several steps further. We're nearing the end of the narrow tunnel, nearly back to the trident paths and whatever hidden passageway she plans to sneak these people through—an evacuation that may do little good if Poody's intel is correct. If Zero X has found the cave, if they've bolstered their ranks with reinforcements, handpicked by Calvin Prichard or Lieutenant Fangs, something tells me collecting prisoners won't be at the forefront of their agenda. And I haven't forgotten that long dream. The interrogation of Kible Thexx. His fraudulent deportation. If Prichard finds out I'm hip to that, he and Fangs may find it tidier to list me among the martyred dead.

Connie stirs more sharply than before. I allow her nightmarish fit to pass naturally this time, then I go on army-crawling, turtling her beneath the hanging bats, hoping to find old allies where new enemies seem likely.

12.02

"The lake is actually four separate caverns." Tysha gestures to the widest passageway straight down the middle of the trident. "All connected beneath the surface. We can swim from one to the next without too much trouble."

"And that leads to an exit?"

"It does." Tysha's eyes drift subtly from me to my unconscious backpack, Connie Clark. Her destroyed shooting arm dangles crookedly beneath my chin; her scarred right cheek feels leathery against my neck.

"And this way," I ask, twisting toward the long, rising corridor opposite the three other paths, "takes me back up the way we came down?" Tysha doesn't answer. When I turn to look at her, I see more disappointment than I expected. More injury. But little surprise.

"She'll tell them you helped us. They'll see for themselves." She indicates all the dried blood and bullet holes, almost laughing at the absurdity.

"I'll tell them, too. I'll make them understand."

"You will be killed, you naive—!" She steps forward, forgetting Yono, catching him just before he falls. She retakes his arm, attempting to loop it over her shoulder, but he resists. Standing on his own weight with trembly effort, he lifts his chin, finally rising to his full height. And I see that he has changed as well. His anemic eyes show me something slightly fairer than their usual contempt. He gently swats her hands away, then slowly walks over to join Poody, resting quietly against the passage wall.

Somehow, Tysha seems less sturdy without him. She keeps her eyes from me, feigning toughness with crossed arms and a tightened jaw. But I see a self-soothing hidden there—an exposed nerve she can't seem to tamp back into place.

"I won't make Connie a deserter. And I'm not leaving her behind," I cut Tysha off before she can suggest it. She scowls, shaking her head at my stupidity. "We're going back up," I tell the brightstar. "That's it. I'm sorry." She looks ready to let me have it, raising an argumentative finger toward my face, but Poody's shuffling feet draw our attention.

His eyes are low and contemplative as he approaches. He looks like he has an unfortunate speech prepared, like my favorite hamster just died and nobody's told me yet. He watches me carefully with his big round eyes, then all that grown-up gravity falls away.

He takes many rapid little steps, and he throws his arms

around me, almost knocking Connie clean off our back. I don't have any free hands to return the gesture, and that just about wrecks me. My heart scatters across the floor. I stare ineptly at the top of his pinkened head as he digs his face into the warm scales above my belly.

"Take care of him, Mama," he whispers directly into her scales.

"What?" I ask him quickly.

He looks up at me as he backs away—like I've just eavesdropped on a private conversation. He opens his mouth to try that big speech he had prepared, then he drops it again, like I couldn't possibly believe him.

"No. Wait a minute," I call after him.

But he seems set on staying silent, retreating shyly behind Tysha's leg just like the first day I saw him. And the brightstar's eyes rise to mine—looking nothing like they did at our first meeting, nothing like anything I ever hoped to see in such a stunning face.

"I haven't released you," she finally croaks, clearing her throat and posturing up with straightened shoulders. "You're still my prisoner." She bites back an urge, but I still feel it—was already squashing it in my own gut. A throbbing need to set Connie down, to drop the whole world and hold the brightstar up against me.

Yono stirs, abruptly leaning away from the wall behind Tysha. His neck doesn't seem to be bothering him anymore, but he grimaces painfully, trudging off down the wide passageway to Bluewater Lake. Tysha doesn't notice his exit at all, not until Poody starts moving, too, following Yono toward the escape plan. She turns to watch them go, and our vivid tethering comes undone.

"The light is already thinning," she says to me as she watches after them. The string lights above us flicker and dim a bit further, crediting her claim. "You should take The Claw Way." She nods to the third passageway of the trident, a jagged corridor on the far left. "It's rough. But much more direct."

"Thanks." I get lost in her eyes again. I regret these next moments before they come. "What about the others? Shouldn't they—"

"I've already called them," she interrupts. "The entire tribe will be here soon."

"But can they fight? Where will you—"

"We will do what we *must*," her last syllable comes out in a snarl, bouncing off the cavern walls and within my mind.

I take a cautious step backward, more out of reflex than self-defense, but the effect is the same. A space is made between us, a dividing line. And I begin to hear the first footsteps coming down the main corridor. Heavy feet. Entire lives strapped to beleaguered backs. Dozens of refugees starting all over again. I start to say something, I don't even know what, just any last words to soothe the moment, to make the parting feel correct—

But the brightstar spins away in a whip of heavy fabric, marching after her young and younger man. I stamp a final image of her into memory. Her slate-gray duster coat, alive at the backs of her calves. That procession of cobalt fireballs, larger and brighter, dancing up her spine, vanishing beneath that black-blue-silver mane I fear and love.

Love. The only thing easier done than said.

 **12.03**

About halfway up The Claw Way, the string lights finally die, leaving just the thin glow of Mama's scales to beat back the darkness. She's not nearly as radiant as she was when the star tomb burst an hour ago, but the energy gain is undeniable. Connie Clark feels like an empty pillowcase in our arms. I'm half afraid that I might drop her without noticing, but it's safer to carry her out in front while we ascend. Easier to keep her mind sedated without devoting too much attention to the task. I have no wits to spare after that bitter farewell. Tysha. I will see you again. I'll deliver all these sly lines I'm coming up with now that we've gone our separate ways—now that I'm traversing this constricted, quiet dark.

Mama *whispers* a warning, and I stop to take another knee. I cradle Connie close to our chest and bow my head as the cauldron of bats swarms all around us yet again. A few of their stray claws and piggy noses graze my ears as they go by, but otherwise they cut a perfect detour right around us—always darting at the final moment before total impact, as though the colony has placed some bold daredevil's bet.

One of them finally loses, swooping straight up into my nostrils like a rising fastball, flapping and spasming wildly between our chest and Connie's hair. I snatch it up with the hand that was supporting Connie's legs, and it starts biting, fighting savagely for its little life, doing its best to make me the next patient zero. I toss it away with much more force than I intended, and I hear it splat against the cavern wall like a much squishier thing—a soapy sponge or a plastic bag packed with old grapes. The thick, winged cloud passes just as suddenly as it arrived, leaving only their screeching echoes and nervous droppings. Despite it all, Connie never flinches.

Mama *whispers* again. Three more minutes before they swoop back up from the other direction. So, I carefully scoop up Connie's limp legs, and we go on hiking. It's a straight shot, just like Tysha said. No choices to make at all except perseverance. And perhaps some stealth or apex toughness once we reach the surface. I smell something like wet fur and decaying bones in that direction. A wolf den, I'd bet. But her whispers have stirred another nagging question. He called her Mama. Poody threw his skinny arms around us, but he spoke specifically to her: *Take care of him, Mama.*

If I ever called her that in front of him, I can't remember. If I've ever spoken about her like that in front of *anyone*, I don't know when it could have been. So why did he say it? And what possessed him to smash the star tomb? Tysha and Yono seemed to expect a very different result, even a catastrophic one. But maybe I'm overthinking it. I wasn't exactly clear-eyed when it all went down. Maybe the kid just got confused. Saw the cracked, glowing orb and finished the job. But if he was mixed up, he sure as hell didn't show it. Hardly even seemed himself. Ever since Mantz's turning, he's had that stoic look in his eye. Like he was tossed into one of her dreams. Like some painful truth had aged him up and stripped the innocence away.

I look down at Mama's scales and all the ugly scars that Connie gave her—the crusty bits of fallen guano trapped in her fleshy chinks. A far cry from the beautiful thing she was when we first met. When she was just a uniform. A hanging space suit I stepped into before I could even buy a drink. I remember the shiver that ran up my spine when I first felt the inside of her. All wet and slick, like a soaked chamois cloth left in the cold. She was just an item when they sealed her up around me. Just a skintight costume until I crawled into that dome. That cramped, round room I shared with Anja Hallheim. It was almost pitch black when we strapped in. Just like this cave. One big shadow with our nervous laughs and anxious jokes bouncing off the glass and steel. Anja was twice my size, and even I could tell that she liked girls, but that didn't keep me from fantasizing—imagining her great big knockers beneath all that alien science. Goddamn I was a stupid boy. Flimsy and cocksure in the same breath. We all were in different ways. Invincibly unrefined.

Then the dome began to turn—twisting on its gyroscopic motors until the triple-paned glass beneath our feet was aligned directly with the sun. A gravity-free delirium for just a few seconds. Human baked goods strung upside down. I remember laughing at least one more time before everything changed. Before the suits started waking up. Before those two cocky kids inside them started sinking down, down, down.

Thought I was a lunatic for most of this life. Just another lonely spaceman having words with himself. Then I landed back on Earth and started seeing the separation. The distance between intuition and transference. Between imagination and true memory. My mother ran off the same week that I was born. That's what I've gathered from the few bits and pieces Logan gave me—and all the hanging chunks that my daddy left unsaid.

Maybe this is why he never talked about her. Maybe my mother was someone just like Tysha, a woman from the brightworld, never blighted by the milk, never sterilized. Maybe there's some truth to these strange memories, to those maternal words I heard when my eyes shined in the Taiga. *Follow your light. My starshine boy.* What other way can I explain this rising power, this growing glow that no other human has possessed? How can

I have lived and thrived these many years when Anja Hallheim died in madness, when one in ten still fades in tac? How can all of that be true, unless the brightstar is correct? Unless I am the great uniter they have hoped for. The hybrid man on a shadowed planet, destined to bind divided worlds.

A thin moonbeam crosses my eyes. A crack appears in the cavern darkness as The Claw Way's exit comes into view. She *whispers*, but I'm too emboldened to lend an ear. I carry on striding toward the night sky just as the batty storm cloud crashes around us, swooping up through all our gaps, shoulder to neck, ankle to ankle, right under our elbows and Connie's spine. They become our winged cavalcade, swirling forth into the wolf den, out into the trees and frigid air of the Taiga twilight, shrieking an announcement for the spaceman, trumpeting the arrival of the last skinner pilot, the first Earthborn son of the brighter world.

12.04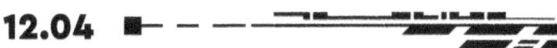

I look down at the glade beyond The Throat. We're much higher than I expected to emerge, at least twenty meters up the face of the mountain. A short rope ladder is folded and bolted at the edge of the cliff, providing easy access to all those jury-rigged travel pods, now totally powerless and cold on the carved ledge beneath our feet. But my eyes stay on the glade. As I inch our toes closer to the edge—heavy winds howling through the deserted wolf den at our back—I see a disrupted pile of ash where Mantz's pyre was just ablaze. I look down at that happy space, where all the others were dancing and chanting a few hours ago, where I was unexpectedly added to the ancient ranks of their alien tribe, and I begin my silent count of the fallen dead.

Four human bodies at the tree line. Torn to shreds at their throats, stomachs, groins. Spec ops troopers, all dressed in tactical grays, hued off-white to match the midnight snow. Geared up for a night raid by the look of it—heat sensors on all their visors. But their positioning doesn't make sense. The way they're splayed down there on this side of the tree line, it almost looks like they had their backs to the cave. A final stand, facing the wrong direction. As I look closer, the picture begins to paint itself.

I spot the wolves I'd expected to find in the den. Nine of them, all shot to hell on the other side of the tree line. Two more spec ops bodies there. Facedown and staggered like they fell one after the other. Like something caught up to them as they fled from more concentrated forest. Something big enough to tear through Kevlar and padded coats, to remove a leg from the further trooper and half a skull from the other. I see a warzone in the trees. A hundred bullet holes and shattered branches. Scorched earth and demolition craters. I see a seventh trooper who looks like he was burned alive. I see a trail of panicked footsteps stretching out of view behind the foliage. I smell a much thicker death riding the wind from there. A corpse pile to make these few visible combatants seem like a snack. A patch of land that reeks like flesh and matted fur. Splintered beaks and broken claws. Mounds of bloodied feathers and exposed organs making wraiths of their former hosts. I smell a haunting.

Then something finally moves, drawing my eyes back to the glade. A single figure is standing in front of The Throat. So motionless I must have missed them. Right there, directly beneath me, draped in a compounding camouflage of fallen snow. One stolid survivor, not just of this fresh carnage but so much more. More torment than one lifetime should allow. Without those powdered shoulders even turning, without those bedeviled eyes ever twisting up in my direction, I know exactly who it is. And I realize the fighting isn't done, not even close.

Not while Taiko Chiba still holds her chromium rods down by her hips. Ready to add to the pulverized circle of carcasses piled around her. Two wolverines, half a dozen birds of varying sizes, and one massive goddamn grizzly bear that looks to have almost got her. Gashed Taiko's right thigh from waist to knee before she caved in its hungry face, now frozen in a snarl. I see her nano hive already working, sewing up her wounded leg, repairing their own shredded stitching where her pale flesh has been exposed.

Then I see Faye. Dead in the same creature pile. Crushed beneath the gargantuan bear, still clutching her spent sidearm, which matches the tight pattern of exit wounds near the center of the grizzly's back. Just as I realize none of this adds up, that the very forest itself seems to have waged war with Zero X or whatever this slaughtered unit is, I feel a cold tongue lick the inside of my spine. An otherworldly chill invades every synapse of my unguarded mind.

"So, that's what happened to The Tomb," a voice inside me hisses like cursed smoke. It rumbles like the devil's own night terrors.

I try to—

"Do not fight me, boy! Do not even try, or I will make a supper of your belly! Do not resist, or I will make mutiny with the smallest life inside you. I will gnaw at your viscera with your own microbes, and you will die screaming. You will suffer and I will smile, so do not tempt me any further if you cherish life!"

I don't move. I don't even breathe. I comply completely, automatically, totally dominated by self-preserving fear, an instinctive hindbrain terror unlike any I've ever felt.

"*Very good,*" the dark voice grins, this time sounding almost familiar, sounding somewhat like a sinister version of Cuva Khan. "*Very good, indeed. Now set the Earthwoman down carefully, quietly.*"

I do as he says, backing up a few paces before setting Connie down in the den, away from the falling snow. One of her boots clips a bat skeleton, and it crunches lightly.

"*Quiet, you fool! Be as silent as you never have. The aberration has not noticed you yet, and time runs short.*"

"How—"

"*SHUT YOURSELF!*" His psychic shout is deafeningly loud. I stagger to a knee, hunching over Connie in a rush of crippling nausea. "*And listen only,*" the voice continues. "*You did well to draw out the leather wings, I can make use of them. But nothing else remains. Nothing but you and me to keep the mindless minion here, away from The Throat.*"

I see Tysha behind my eyes. I see Poody and Yono and all the rest. The old, the young, the innocent dozens still alive in my abandoned tribe. I see their ongoing scramble through the cavern depths, their fearful faces and huddled shadows making their way to Bluewater Lake with desperate haste.

"*Yes,*" the voice hisses with something like sympathy— some reluctant pity it feels today but perhaps never has before. "*Now let me speak to the other one inside you. To the mother. Let me in completely, and we shall stage a combat like this world has never seen.*"

12.05

She stands alone. Battle-red and smoldering but more effi-ciently than before. Conserving her heat somehow. Circulat-ing her solar reserves without losing much at all. Her G-4 suit has clearly been upgraded or improved by some other means. Adaptation maybe. A biomechanical evolution in rapid order. Yeah. It was the cold that got her last time—a crucial flaw that they've corrected. The hive mind. The nanoscopic galaxy alive on Taiko Chiba's flesh. She can't be captured. Can't be inca-pacitated and left. Not without consequences. Any conflict she survives will only amplify her threat.

Taiko twitches, finally detecting something. Distant echoes. We can hear them, too. Voices. She wheels around to face the cave, stopping there, seeing no obvious enemy. Seeing only The Throat and whatever hidden life it shelters. With her head cocked slightly, curiously, she starts toward it, listening, stalking the foreign prey that her programming demands.

We land in the glade with a crashing suddenness—one knee to the permafrost, two palms in the snow to brace our fall. A splash of powdery snow shoots up around us, raining back down, sizzling wherever it meets our scales, draping us in a cloud of hanging, heroic mist, just like that old film. That series of animations where the Earth's champion arrives too late to defend his friends but just in time to save the world.

With our back to the cave, we rise to our feet. We fill our chest with vital breath and level our eyes with the forest. We track the remnants of vicious massacre and putrid death to the heaping pile where it began. About two hundred meters west of the cave, beneath the tallest trees, we see the mass grave and festering remains of Zero X. As we quietly bow our head, hoping to the human god it isn't true, the lone survivor, just behind us, slowly turns in our direction.

We are still confusing to Taiko Chiba—still an imperfect match to either category, native or stranger. But we've also changed since our last encounter, charged by The Tomb beneath the cave, fused by The Darkmind up on the cliff. There are three of us now. Three lights combined within the skin of Emmett Hayes. Mindless Taiko has no idea what we've done. But she can measure the alteration. A telemetric shift in our dataset. A weighted scale, cranking unmistakably in the non-human direction. We hear her beginning to clench the leather grips down by her waist. A rising hiss of evaporating snow starts at her shoulders, boiling hotter between her toes as she digs them into the frozen earth, and we have no doubt that our great contest has begun.

In a blast of powder, our head start extends to twenty meters. We streak right through the tree line, moving faster than I thought we could, catching snowfall in our scales, pumping lubricating tears into our eyes to keep them from drying out.

Taiko's twice as fast. A living bullet at our back. I start to look over our shoulder, but the dark voice *overrides* the urge. Keeps us focused forward, searching, scanning, finding—

We drop to our knees, sliding fast, cutting a heavy wake through the powder, snatching up a sidearm as we go. An old locked-breech semi-automatic with a few shots left in the magazine by the weight of it. We drag our other hand like a rudder, then kick ourselves backward into the air, spinning and sighting Taiko ten meters behind us. I hesitate.

Taiko darts out of view behind the trees just as we fire. Two rounds wasted, not even close. Cuva Khan *curses* foul damnations as we complete our acrobatic rotation, landing back on our feet, still sprinting west, away from the cave as fast as we can. Glancing backward, we see that Taiko's pattern has already changed, no longer chasing directly in our wake but blurring herself into the background, zigzagging between the trees and snow like another species entirely. The pistol seems useless now. But at least it bought us time.

"Eyes forward, damn you!" The Darkmind corrects us again, just in time to avoid the trunk of a massive spruce tree. That evasive leap sends us soaring through its outer branches, receiving half a dozen heavy lashes and a thousand jabbing needles. At this speed, it feels like forest shrapnel, a Taiga grenade exploding in our face.

We lose all body control, tumbling wildly through cascading snow before coming to a sudden stop against a strangely naked log, blackened by some prior explosion, needles and branches blown away. We take two heavy, choking sucks of air before she's on us, striking with both concussive sticks at once.

Cuva takes the reins, dodge-rolling us away just before the scorched tree becomes an explosion of shattered timber. *"Focus!"* he roars in our mind. Taiko chases, striking again without hesitation, without any human pause at all, and Mama *whispers* a split-second calculation. We put a bullet there, hitting Taiko's swinging concussive stick directly. The chromium alloy reverberates, sending a shockwave through her arm that would make any strongman scream in horror, but her face doesn't change. Her altered momentum becomes a tornado kick, cracking two ribs beneath our right armpit. We're sent airborne, losing the gun in our forced takeoff. Taiko pursues us into the sky with both c-sticks spread like raptor wings.

The Darkmind *screeches* some psychic call beyond human

comprehension—some beast-like tongue I wouldn't believe if it didn't pass through my own head. The cloud intercepts her just in time. Seventy bats swoop down from the higher trees like one fat, leathery fist, punching Taiko out of the air, biting and clawing with everything they have, chewing chunks of nanos off her back like fat mosquitoes.

She's already killing them one at a time. Her entire focus shifts from one target to the next as she strikes them down, head swiveling with a birdlike rapidity just before she brains the next one and the next one with one of her sticks—left, right, left—three dead every second and speeding up. Already learning their flight patterns.

"Attack! While she is diverted!"

Cuva forces us forward two quick steps, but Taiko's eyes instantly lock onto us—those swirling, lifeless orbs, discriminating only between the current victim and the next, prioritizing each threat as it arrives. I resist The Darkmind's efforts. I retreat a step, and Taiko goes right back to butchering our dark defenders. One by one by one. Within that meticulous violence, I find a plan.

"No!" Cuva protests as I dash us off into the forest—deeper, even further from The Throat. *"Fool! Coward!"*

But I let him see. I share my vision of what must come next, and the awakened warrior falls silent. With stubborn reluctance, he allows our tactical flight to carry on. *"Further north."* He points a mental finger. *"That one fled before I could tear our light from him."*

Before I can ask what he means by that, we are consumed. A wave of death dominates our senses as we dash right though the slaughterhouse curtain, no longer ankle-deep in powdery snow but petrified remains. Owls, hawks, and a few more colorful birds. Wolverines, foxes, four catlike creatures. Another seven troopers, all mangled and chewed into chunks and shreds of their former selves, all perished in an impressively tight arrangement. A gruesome testament to the unwavering discipline Lieutenant Fangs inspired. But the man I need is missing.

"Further north, I said. Quickly!" He tugs us away from the transfixing scene, leaping carefully between the corpses, human and beast. I stop us at a fifteenth trooper, half crushed beneath an incredible moose, but The Darkmind *snarls* again. *"Further, you tripe! Faster!"*

We see it now. A tiny light, barely visible in the lower branches of a fir tree. It's just beyond another impact crater and more scorched earth, decorated by some unlucky trooper's lower pieces: a combat boot with most of a leg still attached. A red tangle of nether regions exploded away. We continue past that mess, approaching the small glowing thing in the tree. An orb. A shimmering sphere almost exactly like the star tomb Poody destroyed, shrunk down to one hundredth scale, embedded in the upper spine of the demolitions trooper whose upper half is draped in the fir like some morbid ornament. Another iteration of the Spiders, I assume. An impressive one.

Gripped by a truly memorable revulsion, we flip the trooper over, immediately spotting the bandolier that I expected. Just like the one Magar always carried, it has six pockets of varying sizes, fitted for an array of breaching explosives, frags, and signal smokes. It even has Cyrillic script on all the latches and pocket labels—just like Magar's. I feel the twisting sting of another lost friend, of my entire unit. The ghosts of Zero X, all around us, all gone. Thankfully, as we swipe the snow from the trooper's damaged visor, I do not recognize the eyes.

It's a woman. Fair-skinned with Eastern Euro features. Two bushy eyebrows more like mustaches and one tiny, subtle tattoo on her left cheek. A hunting bow with a winged arrow. Oh, thank God. It's the fucking Russians.

"I was careless with that one," Cuva adds.

I start to respond in our shared mind, then I realize he sounded different this time. Sounded physical. We spin around, but there's nobody there, just empty forest.

"Or maybe just too slow," Cuva groans from somewhere above.

We follow the voice but still don't see him. Just vacant trees and falling snow, nothing alive in any direction. Until he moves.

He shifts his weight, cradled five meters up in a white paper birch tree, hidden in the shadow of its thick branches. He draws back a handcrafted ghillie hood, revealing his bleached alien features. His eyes are tired, drooping heavily. His skin is clammy despite the cutting cold. Somehow, his head appears to be floating in empty space, leaned against the tree trunk with nothing beneath it but frigid air. Until he exhales, long and slow.

Now his thick torso ripples into view, followed by his muscular thighs, straddling one of the sturdier branches. That kaleidoscopic shimmer continues down around his toes, and I finally recognize the effect. Luminaran travel gear. Just like that downed traveler wore back at Caitlin Powell's farm. Just like us. Our ancestral apparel. But there's one damaged patch of his suit that doesn't change, was never cloaked at all, I realize. A bloody section beneath Cuva Khan's right nipple. A deep wound still plugged with jagged shrapnel. He inhales, and I hear a smothering liquid sound. His lungs are filled with blood.

"*She is coming, you fools!*" Cuva spasms schizophrenically in the tree, and I hear his raspy darkmind between our ears. "*Grab it, you cull! Now!*" The voice compels us back to the bandolier, reaching to snatch a grenade, to continue the plan, but I freeze us there, noticing that only one device remains.

A plasma charge. Not exactly what I had in mind. Was kind of hoping we might survive this next maneuver. But I can feel The Darkmind seething again, so I let it happen. We carefully unlatch the pocket warhead, pulling it free from the dead woman's weapon sleeve as we prepare to run.

"Boy," Cuva wheezes distantly. "Hear me first." He labors his eyes back open, squinting down at us from his perch.

"*No time for sermons!*" The Darkmind interjects. "*The wings are dead, you mawkish drip. She is already—aaaarrrhhhhh!*" The black voice drowns in a spiraling death cry, as though being banished back down into the unconscious depths of Cuva Khan.

My mind begins to clear. The feverish urgency, the alien bloodlust—it all melts away like defrosting glass. My vision narrows as I resume complete control. And the fear returns. A sense of exposure and imminent death. A certainty that I can't win this fight alone.

"Alone?" Cuva gurgles, drowning slowly in himself. "Can you not see her?"

An entire tree crashes in the distance, back where we left Taiko with the bats. I hear her making rapid progress in this direction, one thunderous footstep at a time, but Cuva's cadence hardly changes. He seems entirely unafraid.

"A scatterer is with you," he asserts momentously, eyes awash with veneration. "The boundless light of Nazara Thume."

"Nazara." It's not a name I've heard before—zero results in

our eidetic memory—but it has the ring of a forgotten song. An itchy intuition drops my eyes to our solar scales, rippling hotter than I expected, a rising fire with a maternal voice. Mama.

Cuva chokes painfully, nearly slipping from his perch. When he opens his mouth, a thick line of blood paints down his chin. "My corruption ends today. Unturned." He shivers frigidly, lifting his eyes to the starry sky. "Perhaps my beam will reach the end. Perhaps the highway . . ."

The final words of Cuva Khan are taken with him. His bright eyes don't fade to darkness; they flick off instantly. I spin around, thinking I saw something shoot away, something like a narrow laser across the sky, but if it went, it's already gone. The stars appear unchanged.

That's when Taiko Chiba lands directly in the pile.

Her left heel crunches through the ribcage of one of the fallen troopers there, but she makes no effort to pull it free. She twitches like a bird, searching up, searching right, searching down, then spotting us. She almost disappears, standing motionless behind a wall of falling snow. Her chromium rods are drenched in the battered bits of six dozen bats. Her teenaged face is nearly undamaged except for two deep claw marks, soon to be scars, cutting straight across her nose, connecting one swirling eye to the next. She looks at us with no resentment. No aggression, no anticipation, no sign whatsoever of human thought.

Then she becomes an undead missile, launching straight in our direction.

12.06 ▪- — — ——

The fallen trooper scatters backward in a spray of anatomy, painting the trees behind Taiko Chiba in defrosted bloody chunks. She soars ten meters before returning to the ground, and her second lunge is more dramatic, blasting snow into steam, closing half the gap between us before I can decide which way to run.

No, the whisper comes, slightly clearer than I'm used to. *Plan*, she reminds me, directing my eyes to Taiko's chest. It's all one swirl of inky red, a nanoscopic galaxy operating as one mind, one interconnected hive designed to thrive and kill, with Taiko's unliving body as its host. *Yes*, the suit agrees. *One*. Taiko takes a third titanic step, and I see it all.

An overlay of cosmic math, of every particle of light, of every living world in every drop of melting snow. A cobalt latticework between us, connecting our bodies like puppet strings, connecting every single nanosimulant in the inky red G-4. For one rapid endless instant, I see every object of the universe converging into one. I see like *she* does. Then I see Taiko Chiba, soaring into range, spreading her rods to crush my brains.

I flick the firing pin free from the plasma charge, and hot ignition steam spits from its crown in a halo of scorching moisture. I toss the warhead high and due southwest, hitting the angle perfectly but overshooting the velocity we had in mind. Mama *whispers* an updated calculation just as Taiko closes in.

Taiko claps both rods together like a homicidal percussionist, but I'm already dodging swiftly backward through the trees. She misses my nose by about six centimeters, and a strange silence is created—a sudden vacuum like higher orbit—before a delayed sonic boom crashes forward. The sound is like heavy artillery in a belltower. The change in pressure sucks the air from my lungs. My right eardrum bursts in a splash of blood, and my left eye threatens to escape its socket as the mach wave sends us tumbling helplessly through the forest. So far, so good.

Our back collides with the sturdy trunk of another white paper birch, and a heavy downpour of loosened snow rains around us from its higher branches. For one precious moment Taiko loses sight of us. She certainly can't hear us moving beneath the thundering powder shower as we rise patiently to our feet. I look up to the nearest canopy, imagining the resting shape of Cuva Khan. I cock our right leg back in preparation, holding it there, holding the name he left us with. Nazara. Nazara Thume. Mama seems to recognize it, seems to smile behind my eyes as her calculations realign: 5, 4, 3, 2, *NOW.*

I kick with everything we have, and a blast of snowy permafrost cannons out at Taiko, shredding her suit with earthy bullets. She shuts her eyes, shielding her face with crisscrossed chromium rods just long enough for us to hop up and kick off the tree like an Olympic starting block. We torpedo past her, cutting through the air in a nauseating spiral, but I nail it perfectly this time. I extend both arms, cancelling our barrel roll as we soar over a slaughtered moose and the crushed SOF trooper beneath its corpse. A spare hand axe glints between them, strapped to the trooper's chest.

I snatch the weapon by its handle, digging its sharpened edge into the snow. It anchors in the femur of another trooper, dislocating my shoulder in a sickening, stinging pop. I remind myself to scream when this is done. For now, I yank the axe free with my better hand, kiss it to my opposite ear, and let it fly.

Taiko spots us. Her eyes lock vividly with mine, and she becomes a missile again, soaring with that same inhuman speed and disregard for her own wounds. A predictable haste, no pause at all, already halfway to us before I can formulate a prayer.

My heart skips a dying beat as she swats the hand axe from the air, eyes locked onto it as it arrives, no problem at all for her perfect focus, assessing each target as it comes. I threw it slightly wide, a few degrees to Taiko's left, exactly as we planned. Her swirling eyes track the deflected axe, ensuring its threat is totally canceled, never seeing the plasma charge finally descending on her right. She never sees it. I feel a sharp pinch of twisted remorse in that protracted millisecond, that last endless moment before the fuse quits spitting heat.

Then Taiko Chiba's teenaged face becomes a shadow.

12.07

I don't lose consciousness exactly. Just time. Some stretch of seconds or minutes where I can't seem to remember who I am. Why is it so cold? What is that smell, that fleshy stink like burning hair? Then I blink twice. I twitch sharply, and my identity comes rushing into view.

I sit up with urgency, wincing, looking down, seeing something sticking out of our hip. Something long and smooth, splattered with fresh blood. Too symmetrical to be shattered bone. It doesn't belong there. I grab hold of it and tug—

Then I'm on my back again, blinking up at the trees, remembering who I am. I sit up quickly, wincing worse, looking down at our stinging hip. That bloody thing got longer. And bloodier. I only pulled it halfway out.

Gently, I take hold of the foreign object one more time. My head swims and somersaults, but I fight to keep my eyes open, struggling to maintain a steady grip as a river of blood oozes between my fingers. I half expect to see my liver on the other end of this thing, but I know we can't heal until it's removed. Here goes nothing.

I gasp like icy water just jetted directly up our ass. Screaming would be appropriate, but a wave of nauseated relief stuns me to silence. The thing was deeper than I thought, eight centimeters at least, scraping fully against my pelvis bone as I yanked it out. It's some kind of pole with a leather grip and a sharpened tip that looks like diamond—not just dripping with our fresh guts but also caked with the brighter colors of dried blood, fur, and bone.

In a sudden panic, I scramble to a defensive knee, brandishing the concussive stick out in front of our chest. Taiko, she—

—is nowhere to be seen. I spin around, clearly still missing some information, some memory of how I got here. And now I'm draining blood like an uncorked keg.

Relax, she finally whispers. *Be still*, she purrs inside us. I don't understand what the hell is happening, but I shake my head. I blink a few dozen times, and the full picture finally starts to develop. I look northeast. I keep looking there until it all sinks in.

There's a hole in the forest. A scorched sphere where so much matter used to be. A blasted gap in God's design. One long claw of the moose's antlers is stabbed in the trunk of a birch tree, as though it was fired from a cannon. No sign of the animal it belonged to. No identifiable remains of the axe-wielding trooper that was crushed beneath it. Most of the other carcasses are burning—impromptu burial pyres in every direction with little moisture left to negate them. Everything within fifteen meters of the blast site looks like a different climate entirely. A volcanic jungle around a crater—slightly too deep to see its bottom from this vantage. But I do hear something. Or *feel* something. A strange sensation I can't nail down.

Keeping pressure on the wound, I rise to our feet. "Agh—fuck!"

One of our feet. The left is okay, but the right leg is numb from the kneecap down. Our left shoulder is still out of its socket, so we quickly become a high-tech zombie, dragging one dead leg toward the crater we created. As we approach, that odd sensation thickens. It's almost visible. A distant star in a faraway galaxy, suddenly bursting into life.

I drag us faster, remembering that guilty pinch that I was feeling, that rising dread just as the battle came to an end. I move too quickly for my bad leg, tripping suddenly in the ash, bracing the fall with my better hand. As I faceplant at the edge of the crater, the chromium rod bounces down into it, slipping and sliding toward the bottom, until it collides with Taiko Chiba's naked armpit.

That sends her eye in my direction. Just one eye, no longer swirling with nanoscopic life. I don't see nanos anywhere. Just torched spandex and roasted Kevlar. And broiled skin. Oozing, cauterized wounds wherever skin remains.

The right half of her face is stripped away, totally dead. Her short black hair is disintegrating strand by strand. Her right arm and leg have vanished, not blown off but completely melted to the torso. Her left foot is on fire, and her left hand is spasming wildly, flapping in a seizure. But her left eye is clearer than I've ever seen it. It's alive with every human emotion all at once.

"H—H—H—Hayes," Taiko finally gasps through facial tics, a hyperventilating panic to match my stupefied face. "H—Hayes," she heaves again, clearer, with some rising excitement, like she can't believe her mouth is making sound. I just stare from the edge of the crater, totally idiotic, unable to reply. But she sees the recognition in my eyes. I feel her compounding joy throbbing in my chest, the ecstatic rapture of an emancipated mind.

She shudders violently, painfully, but the tears welling in her remaining eye are lit with triumph. After the tremor passes, she looks up at me again, and something changes. Her bliss quickly shrinks away, becoming a choking panic.

"H—H—H—"

"Stop. Don't move—" I start back up to a knee before collapsing face first again. "Taiko, don't move, I'm coming down!" I try to drag myself over the edge while maintaining eye contact, but she's still shrinking back and drifting away. She isn't looking at me anymore. She's looking over my shoulder, almost like she's tracking rising movement, almost like she's—

"HAYES!" Taiko screams a piercing warning just as I turn around, just as the stealth drone crackles off an electric blast in my upturned face.

12.08

My eyes blink lazily awake. Unexpected details assemble into view. A long stretch of reflective wood straight out in front of me. A dim room flipped on its side.

I lift my cheek up from the table, and the room straightens itself out. Dim as it is, my eyes don't like the light. They drift back down to the stretch of wood, squinting weakly at its smooth surface. One natural cut of red mahogany, impeccably tidy besides my puddle of drool. It's also not a table. Too shallow straight ahead and way too wide in my peripheral. It's a bar if I've ever seen one. Wiping my face, I find more spittle. White and crusty, smeared across my trigger knuckle. That's when it all comes rushing back.

I spin around in search of Taiko Chiba, but she's not in here. I'm not out there, not anymore. I'm sitting in a swiveling bar chair with leather lumbar support. Our left arm is slinged, and the shoulder's been popped back into place. Similar aid has been rendered to our impaled hip, now wrapped tightly in clean gauze. Clean like it's been changed once already.

I swivel the chair around further, counting enough empty seats and tables for about twenty people to sit comfortably. A modern saloon with swinging wooden doors at the entrance. A brand-new deer rifle displayed above that—bolt action with a hunting scope. All so pristine. Western themed but immaculately overlaid with contemporary finishes, even futuristic. Untouched surfaces, spotless glasses racked and hanging. An impressive array of shelved liquors and mixers, all still sealed. Like it's opening day and I'm the first customer. The only customer. The sound of pouring booze finally makes his presence known.

Malcolm Calvin Prichard Jr. Before I even turn to look, some cutting instinct says it's him. I hesitate, not wanting to see his satisfaction, not wanting to give it up so easy. But as his gravity pulls me in, sending my gaze behind the bar, I see someone unfamiliar.

It's not the greasy medic from the tarmac. Not the stylish billionaire nor the eccentric showman that I suffered at Camp Cooks. Certainly not the psychopath I uncovered in that long dream. This time, there's just a man. Dressed rather unintentionally in drawstring pants and a long sleeve thermal shirt. A dirty rag is tucked into his frayed waistband, and his hair is hanging loosely, like he brushed it quickly six hours ago and hasn't fussed with it since then.

His personal simulant chimes twice in his right ear, and Prichard quietly turns, looking over his shoulder in my direction. The delight in his eyes is disarmingly genuine. He holds up a finger, signaling that he'll be over in just a moment. Then he goes right back to fixing his drink, pouring something oaky and smooth over a chilled whiskey stone. The bottle is the only one uncorked in the entire room, and I can just make out the label beneath his thumb:

Gray & Turner
Since 1919

Something naggingly familiar pricks me there. But Prichard finishes pouring from the round bottle, setting it down next to an empty sink. Carefully, he strides in my direction with a bourbon double in both hands. One tumbler has the frozen stone sunk at the bottom of it. The other is fixed up neat.

Poison comes to mind. I decide to refuse whichever drink he gives me—wholly deny him whatever game he thinks he's playing at. I prepare opening lines and countering questions. I stack everything I have in the path of his advance.

But he halts uncommittedly. Offers me both glasses, either one. And I see nothing but peace in his blue-green eyes. An exposed presumption of good faith.

Without pausing much at all, I accept the glass with the whiskey stone. Calvin Prichard beams with warm relief. He raises his neater pour in my direction, offering a silent toast. I don't return the sentiment exactly, but I allow myself a receptive nod. I sense no psychic compulsions of any kind, no forceful whispers from his upper spine or anywhere else, and yet I feel impelled to drink along. Something much more profound lifts the gifted bourbon to my lips. That little orphan inside me, maybe. That scared boy in a lonely world.

Of course, I cough like an idiot at the taste of it. Even chilled, it burns my throat all the way to my guts. I set the glass down way too quick, splashing the polished bar with its first wasted alcohol, and Prichard laughs—not with any of his usual discourtesy, just a gracious titter to soothe the mood. That gets him coughing, too, choking and chuckling as he pulls the rag from his waistband to quickly wipe up the spilled Gray & Turner.

"My Uncle Gage woulda kicked your teeth in for wastin' his medicine like that." Prichard's nostalgic smile slides to sadness, to the rawest edges of contempt. "Luckily, I take after my daddy." He winks at me and sips his drink like we're the oldest, closest friends.

"What happened to her?" I change the subject, defensively, doing what I can to deflect his charms. "Taiko. Is she—?"

"Alive?" He smiles curiously. No trace of insincerity. "I reckon so. Thanks to you."

He seems to search me for a response, but I'm too busy turning that one over for myself. *Thanks to me?* Pretty sure I tried my best to vaporize her, to make it quick, and I couldn't even manage that. Left her dismembered and mutilated, G-4 suit destroyed. Without all those nanos to sustain her, I'm surprised she's even . . .

My eyes drift back to Prichard's, finally giving him the response that he was after. Without her nanos, Taiko was conscious. She knew my name. It was like hearing a hammer cry out for mercy right after you bashed it against a nail. And they've been bashing her for a while now. Bashing and crashing her against much worse than bats and birds. Could it be true?

All this time, somewhere behind those lifeless, swirling eyes, has Taiko Chiba been watching back?

"Connie Clark can thank you, too." Prichard grins, taking another sip of that thick bourbon. "Those sons o' bitches did a number on y'all, but don't you worry." He leans forward, checking my bandages as he speaks. "They're gonna get it worse than they gave, I promise that."

"Who?"

He starts to laugh. Then sees I'm really not getting it. "The rogues, son. The fuckers who did this to ya." He nods to Mama's scales, to my and Nazara's accumulated wounds.

Nazara. That's right, she has a name—revealed by Cuva Khan as he expired. And somehow known to me as well. Known like the taste of my own teeth. A maternal beauty with golden hair and matching eyes. A mother lost in scattered light.

"I underestimated them," Prichard continues, resisting the urge to run his fingers over the bullet holes in his design. Instead, he pulls something small from his pocket. Handles it thoughtfully before tossing it on the bar. "We all did." The small thing rattles in a rapid spin before it stops. Faye Thompson's first lieutenant pin. Tarnished with blood and so much more.

"No." I blink away from the silver token. I remember Tysha, Yono, and little Poody. I hear the dying words of Mantz AnCarcem, of Cuva Khan. "They ain't like that. Not all of 'em. Those people down there are just tryin' to—"

Calvin Prichard rests a hand on our mended shoulder. I surprise myself by allowing it to remain, by doing nothing but gazing deeply into his deep blue-greens—deep and clear, rinsing away my muddled thoughts, pressing my lips closed before they can utter treason.

"They had a Z-1 in the trees. First we've ever detected. And you survived him. You defeated him on your own."

"No. He helped me stop Taiko. His name was—"

"You saved Taiko from *him*. You saved the mission." He squeezes us with those wrestler's hands, that same riveting grip we felt back on the tarmac. "You're a hero, cowboy."

I remember the captain's mission parameters, and I know that Prichard's wrong. I remember Aila dragging my limp weakness through the snow without a second thought for her own safety, but I don't argue with him. I don't do anything at all.

"Atta boy." Prichard squeezes our shoulder in approval. He knocks on the bar, grunting just like my daddy used to—like I ain't half bad when I apply myself.

As he slips away to pour us a second round, I watch the empty space he left behind. As he returns with two full glasses, handing me the one with the whiskey stone, I feel no compulsion whatsoever. Nothing beyond his beguiling care. As Nazara *whispers* something to me, something small and far away, I touch my glass to Calvin Prichard's, managing to meet him eye to eye. He nods with admiration, just like my daddy never did.

Gray & Turner, since 1919. It cooks my guts again, but this time I keep it down. This time, I remember where I've seen it. An empty bottle in the pantry. A dusty memory in the quiet house behind the lake. An Old Dallas staple, I'm pretty sure. An oaky river, connecting my past and present self.

Prichard's simulant chimes twice, and he turns away to listen closely, as though their psychic link might travel better through a slightly wider ear. And I finally spot the trick. That familiar muffling of my senses has been iterated on again. He has a brand-new Spider beneath his collar—something even better than the copies those Russian troopers had implanted. Copies. Yes, exactly. Digital recreations of this new piece he kept for himself. It's purer somehow, slipping in behind my eyes like only the brightest of them can. The brightest rogues.

"Thanks, that's perfect." Prichard responds to whatever his simulant just whispered. "Let's go with, uh, window two." He points to the saloon wall directly opposite the bar. And something impossible occurs. Some engineering feat beyond anything I've ever seen in the public world. Where there was just flat, reinforced steel, there is suddenly a window. No accompanying sound, no motorized gears, just solid metal instantly becoming crystal-clear observation glass. And open air behind it.

It makes me jump, quickly wincing at the pain in my bad leg. It's better now, not totally dead weight, just the prickliest sleeping leg I've ever had. Prichard is already halfway to the window, so I grit my teeth and shamble after him.

"Alright, now keep your eyes peeled. It'll be coming down in the northern sky." Prichard gestures up toward the remaining stars.

I'm too busy gaping at the vast horizon. By the look of it, we're about half an hour from sunrise, treading air in a uniquely massive hovership. The light hum of the cold propulsion engines is audible now, but none of the vibration can be felt. In fact, I don't feel much at all. No sounds of any crew, no distant sense of nearby life—not even Connie and Taiko, which triggers a few fresh alarms.

"It's that one, right?" Prichard points down to the forest beneath us, the sprawling Russian Taiga now three thousand meters below. Picturesque from this soaring vantage, a breathtaking space in the dawning light.

"What?" I don't understand his question.

"Their headquarters. It's that mountain cluster there?" He

points again, not just broadly at the Taiga, I realize, but directly at the pyramidic mountaintop above The Throat. Above the entire cavern complex.

I lean away from the window and watch him for a moment. He's smiling again in that casual way. That effortless, friendly expression, almost curious, looking down at the forest like any tourist would. And I begin to feel my senses laxing, my tongue preparing to share its secrets with my closest, oldest friend.

Nazara *whispers*, and I finally hear the warning. I feel him gently pressing her down inside me while he strokes my bones with his other hand. I realize I *have* seen this man before. This man exactly. Smiling while he traps you. Kissing your cheek just before he bites your throat and laughs.

"What's coming down?" I ask him quickly.

"Hm?"

"In the northern sky, what's coming down?"

One nigh imperceptible twitch tugs the corner of Prichard's mouth. Then a chasm of silence spreads between us. Just the smooth sound of his slow breathing, always through his narrow nostrils—and a pinprick of fire in my peripheral, beginning to brighten the night sky.

"I was at your funeral three weeks ago," Prichard says at last. He looks up at the comet or something like one, something resilient against the darkness, and getting brighter. "A special ceremony for all five of you, dead and lost. There was a political jism in the air," he chuckles in a frustrated way, shaking his head. "Truly suffocating."

His shoulders finally droop, revealing all the tension he was holding. All the background calculus seems to fall away as his vanity dissolves, exposing something like a human man beneath it all. "But the captain's wife was there. Miyoba Uba." Prichard pronounces it the way she must have said it, smiling lightly. "She was breathtaking—even more forceful than he was. And his son was there. Proud. Upright. A little Cuba clone. All the kids there, all the parents and lifelong friends and fuckin' third grade teachers tellin' Bible stories were just so goddamn—"

He cuts off sharply, reining himself back in. I see a private sorrow in his eyes. I see something so devastatingly familiar it takes everything I have not to choke on my own tongue.

"But nobody showed up for you, Sergeant. Not a fuckin' soul. And I just cannot possibly tell you how relieved I was to see that." Prichard laughs again, almost cries. He blinks back the moisture, revealing extensive practice at just that. He looks out at the horizon, at the planet itself and all the endless stars beyond it. He stands in the starshine of the visible universe but seems entirely alone.

And I see it all. Everything I was not long ago. Everything I would have been with a bit more time, with a far greater mind and more ambition but the exact same isolation. I see an Old Dallas boy in an empty world, stacking pride however he can. And I see how much they've already changed me. This suit. The captain and Zero One. Yono, Poody, Cuva. Tysha.

"I asked you what's coming down." My voice is steady this time.

But Prichard doesn't twitch. He remains eerily still, watching the falling thing, as that protective glaze returns to his eyes. "I already told you, cowboy. Twice now. The world don't quit when you stand still."

That cryptic callback sends my eyes up to the object, and I decide to do our own calculations. Nazara *whispers*, revealing an unmistakable trajectory, a flaming meteor, moving more like an intercontinental ballistic. A targeted thing, cutting intelligently through the lower atmosphere. Heading directly for the stretch of forest right beneath us.

"Today, it's been eight years. Since The Storm. Since you..." Prichard trails off, glancing at her battle-worn scales again, her cautionary ripples firing. His sharp blue-greens flick back up to the flaming thing, and he inhales one long and ravenous breath.

His mouth doesn't move, but I still hear him. Both of us do in our shared mind, deep inside our hybrid skin. *"Happy birthday,"* Prichard whispers, just like they do, just as the blazing satellite comes streaking down into clearer view, too fast for me to do anything but watch the impact.

I watch the mountain, and The Claw Way, and The Throat, and Bluewater Lake become one flashing fire cloud, one colossal mushroom of devastation and compacted dark energy flashing free. I watch Tysha get vaporized. Poody and Yono vanish, too. My entire tribe goes up in smoke, and I stand by, complicit in annihilation one final time. It wasn't a satellite, I realize. It was my old ordnance. Decommissioned.

EX-129. The orbital cannon we'd called home.

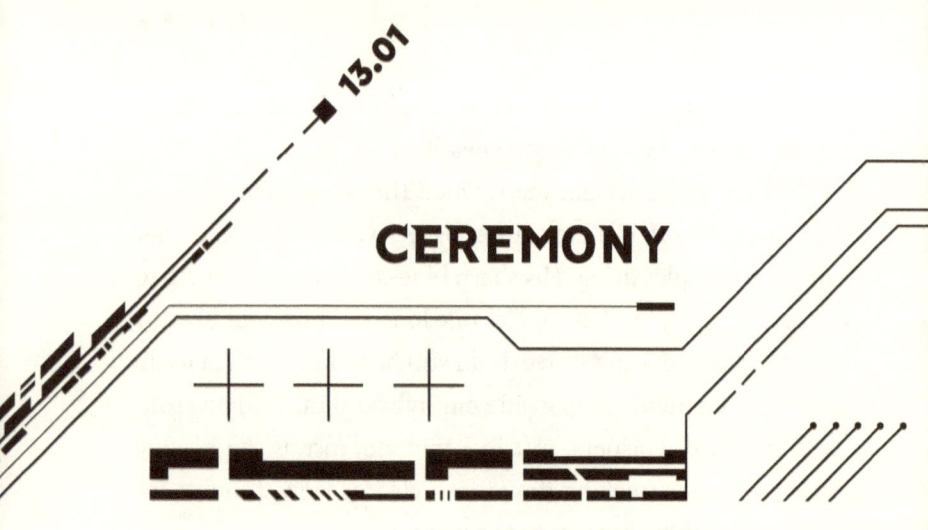

CEREMONY

Varvara is shaking the American's hand again. Her most elite unit has been atomized along with all the Spider tech she was promised, and the northern fires are still raging, virtually unchecked for eleven days, but she is smiling for another photo, eagerly shaking the recreant's hand.

Six months ago, he broke her little finger with a handshake. Then he proceeded to slaughter her best men, Lev and Alik, like they were dogs. But today Varvara is grinning, reaching up around his skinny neck to bestow him with the hallowed Order of Saint George. He is not bowing even slightly to receive it, not showing any semblance of respect, but Varvara Zhurov is all smiles. All best wishes and humble gratitude for the man who "prevented" the Second Storm.

Emmett Hayes was behind enemy lines for thirty-four days, conveniently escaping just before the actual impact, but Calvin Prichard's trusted words assuaged all doubts. The Earth's favorite engineer/entrepreneur/warlord detailed every daring moment of the orbital pilot's double rescue and cunning sabotage, including a stunning digital reenactment, generated by

Prichard's new production company, Artificial Mind. The first of its kind, nearly indistinguishable from live-action sound and video, the entire thrilling mini-series was generated and distributed by simulant filmmakers just a few days after the Taiga impact, pinged directly to the private feeds of every Ret-tag on the planet, free of charge.

Eyewitnesses in Yakutsk, Brask, and a few liars as far south as Ulaanbaatar, corroborated the trajectory of the dawnlight fireball. The last orbital gun of Generation One was visible in the northern sky just before Emmett Hayes diverted its flight path via remote hack. He brought his own exocannon straight down onto the rogue headquarters, thwarting the reachers' plans to bring the space vessel down on Tokyo, the Earth's most populated city and the birthplace of Taiko Chiba. The rogues hated her, of course, for ending the reign of Kible Thexx AnSorin.

So, President Zhurov is wearing her finest suit. She's graciously stepping aside for Aksel Knudsen, who will add whatever fruity token the Swedes brought with them to the heavy pile around the sergeant's neck. And lo, Mia Guerrero will come forward next, undoubtedly pausing to pinch off one of those tears she always times so well, before she ties her big blue American bow on all the cocksucking.

The Medal of Honor. What a laughable prize to present this man, this abomination who mutilates more allies than he protects, this thankless cretin, pouting through an entire ceremony designed for him. Sulking like some disaffected child while Varvara makes every effort to be courteous. Why won't the bastard speak! How can he maintain such insipid silence in the presence of his commanders! It's as though he swapped capacities with that Japanese monstrosity. Chiba was sent to rescue him, and she returned with even less humanity than before. Far too hideous now for the public eye, too disturbingly incoherent. Varvara would rather flatline than live as a vegetable or whatever challenged creature that failed experiment has become.

She wastes no pity on her. Though, she does vaguely remember what it feels like. Remembers when she was just a girl, making all those wintry choices. Remembers deciding which order to let her baby brothers starve and die. She can at least recall that bitter taste, those low times for her great fatherland. These days, a different flavor comes to her with greater ease. A cold dish that she will serve on her own terms. Yes. Once the deceivers have been whetted, they will be fed what they have sown. Another fine dinner with Calvin Prichard and whatever stooges stand between them. Emmett Hayes may have dessert.

But, for now, Varvara smiles.

13.02

Calvin imagines his perfect world. He drops the opacity of his ambitions and lays it atop this actuality. Every trivial detail. Every audience member becomes ghostly duplicates, what they are and what they could be. What they should be. He sees all the errors here.

All the wasted movement delaying the inevitable, preventing progress, not just desired but required. Calvin Prichard envisions a planet and all its pieces. Nine billion minds, sharpened by perfect communication. Not just words but transferred essences. Core concepts and intellectual power synergized in one direction. If only AnSorin had listened to him. With his cooperation, this would have all been so much simpler. The puritanical fool. Unwilling to acknowledge the basic science that drives his organic gifts. Unable to see the parity between evolutionary biology and evolutionary invention. What is the difference exactly between a brain and a computer if the functionality is replicable? Why waste time quibbling over shape and texture when the same fundamental elements comprise all things? The same stardust, merely reconfigured. Christ, he is sick of all this squeamishness. And so vastly disappointed to see it propagating in other corners of the universe, in more advanced minds than humans can possess.

Spike chimes twice in Calvin's ear—two encrypted strings of high-pitched binary. His new implant burns as the translated message reaches his mind, twisting his neck slightly, involuntarily in pain. An embarrassing side-effect. He makes a mental note to tweak down the density in the consumer models. They'll all be watered down anyway, diffused and duplicated to reach scale. This 1:1 heat transfer was just for him. For the deeds that must come next.

Spike chimes again, more impatiently, and Calvin finally steps forward. He lifts the microphone to his tidy beard, and he smiles big and wide that way he practiced. "Alright, Chicago. Y'all ready for this?" A few thousand people shout and clap. Twice as many Ret-tags lift into view, recording video. "Goddammit, I said are you ready?!" Ten thousand civilians roar in Gaia Plaza, where just eight years ago there was rubble and raining ash. They blow air horns and slap their patriotic hands together, not just for this city, not even for the nation, but for their home planet and its invasion, now nearly ended. "Alright, well let's just see if she heard you. Your own native gal, born just two miles from where I'm standin'. The baby mama of Zero Addition. President. Mia. Guerrero!"

Twenty thousand survivors, visitors, and members of the press make their appreciation known as the United Territories anthem blasts from every speaker on the stage. Out strides Guerrero, both cheeks already soaked with grateful tears. She waves with one hand, cradling two decorative cases in the other. The bottom one holds that relic they wanted to end the day with, the Medal of Who the Hell Fuckin' Cares.

But Calvin Prichard whispered in Mia's ear, real delicate just how she likes it. A couple publicized scholarships here, a few hovercruisers there. He gently laid his perfect world on top of hers, creating one big surprise for Emmett Hayes, one metaphysical leap toward the united spacetime that they will pave together. And very soon—

"You are wrong."

Calvin flinches sharply, nearly knocking Spike from his shoulder dock. He spins around, not sure what he's searching for or what the hell he just heard. But Spike chimes twice, reminding him he's still on stage. He quickly turns back to the crowd. Tries to fix his face. Erases most of the panic.

Rogues? He searches the audience discreetly. No, a wasted effort. His hunter drones would've sussed them out. They've been circling, scanning the grounds since late last night. But he did hear a voice, he's certain. A booming, feminine sound. But what living rogue could ever penetrate his new implant? Not even that Z-1, that incredible beastmaster, was able to reach him aboard the hovership. But that hull was heavily layered with signal jammers to hide the cargo he was anticipating—all that extra heat he rounded up. It's possible he miscalculated. Or underestimated. Theoretically, if someone even more elevated than a Z-1 is somewhere nearby, they might still be able to—

His eyes halt with a strange immediacy, a snapping magnetism of attention to one figure on the stage. No. That's not possible. If that were true, he'd have seen some proof of it by now. But there have been signs. That outburst in the chow hall almost had him convinced of it straight away. But it couldn't be true. This is paranoia speaking. Flimsy conjecture without evidence. So, who then? Whose voice did he just hear that reminded him so much of *hers*.

These gaps begin to gnaw at M. Calvin Prichard. Confounding variables to say the least. But for now, he simply decides not to underestimate any parties. He begins diagramming a few longshot contingencies in the back of his expanding mind. Anything to safeguard the more essential operation yet to come, his great global masterpiece.

In the meantime, he keeps a watchful eye on Emmett Hayes.

13.03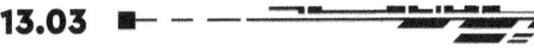

"Jesus, look at 'im. Look at 'im!"

"Wait, is that real?"

"He looks like fuckin' shit!"

"Did they torture him? Do we know if they—"

"He looks like the most popular gimp in hell!"

"Will you quiet down!" Yang finally turns on Shankman. "I can't hear shit over the two of you."

"My bad." Diaz puts up his hands, not wanting the fight, always backing down first like he owes them something. "My bad, Miles."

"The fuck is there to hear? He's just standin' there!"

"You've been shouting in my ear for twenty goddamn minutes, Shank."

"He's just standin' there, collectin' fuckin' ribbons, lookin' ready to shit himself—look at 'im!" Shankman gestures at the immaculate two-meter wall panel with both his hands.

But Yang seems determined to never look at the screen again. He stares Shankman down while he scrolls a thumb over his brand-new Ret-tag, hiking up the broadcast volume until the UT anthem is blaring from every Dallas Dynamics speaker in the barracks, until the entire building is flooded with jingoistic horns and strings. Shankman quickly hops to his feet and mimes the perfect soldier, saluting with crossed eyes, sticking out his lips, letting a little drool run down his chin. That gets Diaz giggling again, cackling himself to tears while Yang tries to play the drill sergeant in Shankman's face. Asking him *what's so funny* and *who he thinks he is*, all out of some misguided hope that he can elevate that low-city trash above his breed. Connie Clark makes no attempt to interfere.

She wouldn't waste the energy even if she had it. Even if she had two good hands to throttle them with, she'd keep her silence. At least she can't hear that nauseating scratching now, that incessant nibbling like hungry mice are in her marrow. She's managed not to vomit yet today, and the blaring speakers are actually helping, distracting her mind from the tissue printer strapped and bolted to her entire arm like some portable iron lung, pumping collagen and synthetic calcium into the nanoscopic construction site beneath her skin. A billion bionic silkworms, chomping and shitting 24/7 until all three shattered bones will have been regrown. Another fine gift from Calvin Prichard. For her heroic service, for her dramatic sacrifice. For her silence.

Fine. Better than fine. Easiest deal she ever made. On top of that, she'll be commanding Zero X if the unit carries on, if the invasion even lasts that long. Invasion. What a perfect designation that has been. She can hardly imagine a more compelling spur. A conflict with vengeance baked right into it. A violation made personal for every citizen of the planet. For every survivor of The Storm.

Connie sits up straighter at the thought of him—at the burned-in image of Zayd's corpse, always right behind her eyes. She sucks air in through her nose, refusing to let herself cry again, forcing the rising bile back down, staring even harder at the wall. He doesn't deserve it. Wherever he is now, she'll never let him see these sympathies. He'd just despise her for it anyway, for being taken alive after all that action, for being so fucking weak!

All three of the idiots turn their heads in her direction. Morons maybe, but never oblivious. Too hardened by death and their captain's training to ever totally drop their guards. Still, she wonders what the hell they're looking at. Who the fuck do they think they—

She winces, looking down at her good hand. A shard of porcelain juts from her palm along with a thin stream of seeping blood. Her black coffee is dribbling over the kitchen counter, no longer contained by its shattered mug. She looks back up to the boys and sees something even more unnerving, something like pity in Miles Yang's eyes before he holsters his sidearm and clears his throat. All three of them sit back down awkwardly on the couch, no longer interested in their own argument. One of them carefully lowers the volume to a normal level.

Low enough for her to hear the scratching again, the incessant chafing like sandpaper on the inside of her skeleton. She barely makes it to the sink. Splashes somebody's dirty dishes in all that bile she thought she'd tamed this time around. Another wasted government breakfast. She retches again but has nothing left to give. Just more thick phlegm from a tortured throat. She spits, then runs the faucet, hot and cold together. Anything to drown out her internal noises and the speculative mutterings from the couch. Their misplaced concern just makes it worse. Their conflicting theories. If Shankman asks her if she's pregnant, she swears she'll put him through the fucking wall. She retches again, dryer than before, so dry it burns. She finally yanks the coffee cup shard from her hand just to feel some semblance of control.

The thin, red stream becomes a river, a hypnotic flow dashing down her wrist, halfway to her elbow before she comes back to herself. Holds her forearm under the warm water until it's clean. Then she runs it directly over the wound, a gushing slice, draining in pumping bursts just like her man, just like that rippling red lake he made in the snow before his heart realized the game was up.

Shankman shouts again, and Connie lifts her head. He's gesticulating wildly at Calvin Prichard's two-meter bribe, but it takes her a moment to come back this time, to return from the place where her partner ended his campaign. She feels that urge all over again, that stomach-churning need to spew and sob herself into a miserable sleep, until she realizes what Shankman's pointing at.

Sigil of Freedom Recipient: Emmett Hayes

The traitor. Standing there in center screen. Now holding a polished wooden case. A beautiful hand-crafted thing, lined with velvet or something finer. Some pillowy fabric, perfectly shaped to cradle the prize he's just been presented. A platinum sphere. A miniature replica of the planet Earth, except all the continents are transparent diamond glass, thin and clear enough to reveal the hollow center where some otherworldly light is swirling independently—as though it carries life.

That recognized phenomenon only distracts her for a second, only sends her back to that lowest cavern chamber for an instant. Instead, she lingers on something even more familiar, on the eyes of a man that she knew better than herself. She feels a tightening in her chest like a phantom's clenching fingers. The world sees the sergeant's scars, his tattered war suit, scorched and perforated with battle damage. But Connie sees his gaping wounds. She sees the withering eyes of Zayd Aswad looking back at her from the skull of Emmett Hayes. That same thickening darkness and flattened grief. She sees a man who thinks he has nobody left in the entire world. Nothing at all worth living for.

Nothing but the nightmare that some fools have called revenge.

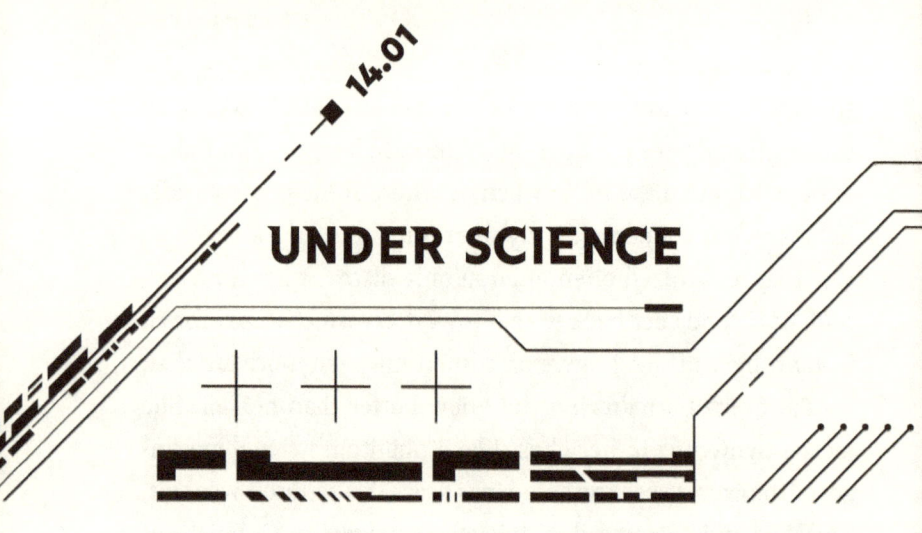

UNDER SCIENCE

It's amazing how quick it happens. The many sharp turns between imagination and actuality, all the hopes and dreams of your former self suddenly popping into fruition. That's all we are, really. An expiring formula in an aging container. Whatever chemistry adds up to an identity, it's always changing. It matures like barreled whiskey, or it decays like everything else.

It doesn't matter who you are right now. Matters even less who you were, who you wanted to be. Nothing is willed, not actually. It all just happens. The entire universe is on algorithmic rails, and that's exactly how I dreamed it. That's the same monotony I used to see every time I closed my eyes. The tedious math behind all things. But I get it now. For the first time in my natural life, I feel totally free. Liberated from the pain I might have felt in a world with different rules. The agony of loss, of disappointment—no longer necessary. Eleven days ago, I would have had second thoughts, even been deterred. But now I see what must come next, and I feel nothing. I imagine his throat between my hands. I picture his empire burning all around him, around us both, and I am blank. I don't even feel the satisfaction. Because when it happens, it won't be me but one of my many versions down the line. He'll see the truth the same as I do. We are merely cogs in the cosmic clockwork, and no man can whim his own design.

"Hey, Daydream."

My eyes come open. The world returns. A familiar horizon and midday sun. Symmetrical patches of farmland down below, beyond the hovercopter's wide viewing window. Highway trucks like worker ants. Electric drones in parallel lines. The industrial march.

"Over here, cowboy," Prichard calls again, waving from the front row of seats on the other side of the aisle. His voice scratches the insides of my ears at a grating volume, but I just frown and tap my headset like nothing's coming through. He laughs at that, wagging his finger like I'm a naughty boy just having fun. He waves me over with added urgency, already turning to look out his eastern window, expecting no more resistance from me at all.

I consider putting a fist through the fuselage and ending it here. I imagine a spinning, fiery blaze, with the two of us on opposite ends. Not quite so complete as what I've been planning, but much more certain. Mutual destruction ahead of schedule.

But something flickers in my peripheral. A single, distracting twinkle across the hovercopter. A light blue spark almost like a voice whispering, *wait*. I swivel quickly, desperately in that direction—

And I see nothing. Two empty seats and an open window. A bright blue sky, twinkling in indifference to my pain.

Suddenly, it's easier to stand—to shuffle from my empty row and walk the aisle toward my captor, my warden and

benefactor for the past eleven days. He killed them all and resurrected me from the flames. Wholly erased my new beginning
and painted a masterpiece in its place. He smiles as I get nearer,
a little too old to be a brother, too alive to be a dad. Instead, I
see a man who's only just begun to massage my pride, who may
never stop unless I make him.

But I feel no shame. Until this formula decays, I'll just go
on lapping up his milk. Because none of it matters. These are
all just causes toward one inevitable effect. The final footfalls
of my ignoble marathon. I will be the end of Malcolm Calvin
Prichard Jr. and his schemes aboard the Earth. A beginning,
too. Another chance for a fading world to twist away from its
own shadow.

"You alright?" Prichard's eager smile shifts toward something like concern—something like it but a little too smart.

"I'm fine." I remove the headset as I say it, sick of hearing
his voice so close to my brain. "What are we looking at?" I lean
over the aisle seat, boxing him in between me and the large
viewing glass, envisioning his fluttering corpse on the way to
the ground.

If he's threatened, it doesn't show. He just watches me with
those clever eyes before turning back to the eastern window.
"Spike, maintain course, negative-thirty-degree roll."

His simulant chimes twice, and the view of the horizon rapidly becomes a view of the terrain below. The flight maneuver
presses me closer, practically chin-to-shoulder with him now.
And I finally see it. Not for the first time but certainly my last.

The world's largest factory. Two hundred and fifty acres of
glass, steel, and concrete, making use of vertical and negative
space. A man-made valley, so vast and deep it almost looks like
another world. Like that old film on metallic life—that futuristic

corner of an inevitable galaxy, where the planet itself is a living machine. I've seen this Old Dallas compound on the net a hundred times. On city billboards and smaller ads through barroom windows. And once from even higher than we are now. It's the same stretch of land we were spiraling toward in that fading dream, that dwindling vision I shared with Tysha when she briefly let me in, when she held my hand and matched my eyes and made me believe her world could come.

Nazara *shouts*. Not a whisper but a panicked *gasp*—like she's been drowning, floundering beneath some psychic surface tension. I flinch at the sound of her sudden warning, a horrified call to escape before it's too late, to rip and slash, and take our chances in the sky. I feel her scales going battle-red, but I keep control. I push her back down into the abyss, and Prichard doesn't catch the slightest whiff of his near death.

He's got that lonely genius look in his eyes as he gazes down at his great creation. "This is where we'll do it, Emmett. This is where it all changes, I swear to god."

And I swear, too. A vow to avenge the woman who I dared to turn away from, to seek fiery restitution for our tribe. I will kill the devil in his palace. I'll bring it all down on his clever head. Par ya Lum sakar, Dallas Dynamics will become Calvin Prichard's tomb.

Mine as well, if the cosmic clockwork values justice.

14.02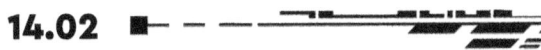

It takes some effort to keep him silent. The wide-eyed farm boy I used to be. The displaced teenager down in Houston, trading rumors of this place. He couldn't count past ten without his toes, but he was convinced he'd make it here. He'd get Logan in one of those rockets, so she could see it for herself. Up where the world was just a shadow, they'd be free to live again.

I wasn't wrong. Just got my manifest mixed up. It wasn't Logan up there with me, but we lived as freely as we could, me and *her*. Free and unaccountable until the rest of it came true. Until the farm boy made it here and looked around at what he wished for, all this cutting techno glamour, somehow in excess of his fantasies, this living temple and its creator, both of which he must destroy.

"Well, shit! I know your ass ain't hungry, but I'm half-starved, so here's my plan." The instant Prichard hops from the hovercopter, it lifts back into the sky, gusting us both with frigid winds as it soars off. "I say we take a pit stop at the commissary. I'll grab some takeout, then you and I can crash a couple kiddy tours on our way down to the inner rim. Sound about good?"

"Sure." There's still something strange about that hovercopter. I find it hard to look away until it vanishes into a massive charging tower. "What's a kitty tour?"

"Ha! Oh hell, you're serious. Children, boy. Humans at a kickable height."

"There are kids here?"

"Fuckin' better be, what a pay to ship 'em in. In fact, let's get some of them ribbons back on you. They'll go nuts for all of that." Prichard waves absently to the box of national treasures in my grip. "No better marketing than nostalgia, and you only get one chance to plant that seed." He winks much too slyly for my liking as an automated SUV pulls up directly in his path—all gunmetal gray with *Dallas Dynamics* etched across the body in that same red, cyberpunk graffiti font. One of the rear passenger doors pops open for us to enter. "You readin' me, cowboy?"

"Yeah." I pause my scan of the massive compound, not sensing as many lives as I expected. But still too many. A couple thousand human heats. Likely more down in the valley center, down beyond that inner rim where something strange is blocking my attempts. A jamming signal like the Spiders. Like a hundred of them, overclocked and fused together, just about exactly where an egomaniac might keep the biggest bomb on the entire planet. "Loud and clear."

If Prichard notices my forced smile, it doesn't show. He just grins that way he does, like the whole world is a game and he's player one. "Then move your ass, cowlick. I got shit to show you." He hops into the SUV with one of his rodeo whoops, and I start a countdown just like the captain's. An internal deadline. Before the next sunrise, it's all coming down. Or it's going up in flames, I don't care which. A couple thousand Texans will be evacuated if I can help it. Sacrificed if I cannot.

14.03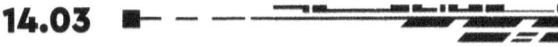

"Alright, troops. One last time for Sergeant Hayes, good and loud. I want all his old buddies in the exosphere to hear ya!" Prichard raises his arms like an orchestra conductor, waiting for the kids to return to formation. He pump-fakes once, drawing a few giggles, but none of them cry out early this time, already too well trained, too enthralled by his infectious energy. "Okay, X-Y-Z—" he brings his right arm down, and all the boys shout:

"Defending the Earth!"

He drops his left, and all the girls reply:

"Extending Humanity!"

Prichard stumbles backward into my arms like their tiny voices bowled him over. "Whoa! How did you—that was the best salute I've ever heard!" Their delighted giggles ricochet off the hyperloop station walls, creating an eerie echo all around us, a poltergeist contrived from innocence. I'm quick to push Prichard back to his feet, but none of my irritation seems to reach him. He just goes on miming shock and satisfaction for his junior militants as their magnetic vactrain arrives silently behind them. "I mean that was just—I'm speechless." Prichard starts dealing out high fives to each of them, one by one. "I bet even the sergeant's never heard anything like that." After a pause, he turns expectantly in my direction, a look that I could snub without too much difficulty, but all the second graders follow suit—twenty adulating faces that never knew the prior world.

"He's right." I avoid individual eye contact, taking them all in as a unit. "Best I've ever heard."

The smallest one gasps—the shrimpy little thing who hasn't quit gawking at me since we surprised them back in the museum. Her clothes look handed down, and her hair sticks out in odd directions, as though her entire look was thrown together by single-father hands. She stares at me just like Poody used to, just like that first time I saw him in the cave. And I sense something—not a distant blaze like he possessed, not even a sizzling candle, but there is something in her unlit mind, something like a single spark inside a vault beneath the ocean. In all of them. The isolated glints of human potential.

"*Yes,*" the wind agrees. A weightless voice against my neck.

I spin around to look behind me. Nobody nearby. Nobody but humans between me and the northern canyon walls. The sun is setting there already. A galloping shadow storms the valley, meeting no resistance in its streets, reminding me that my borrowed life will end in darkness. But something twinkles in its path. High on the museum roof, I see a quick flicker in the shade. Blue again. Two shooting stars like surveilling eyes. As I step forward, daring to dream, the cobalt eyes flash even clearer. Much higher up. Too high up. Now passing overhead. Aviation lights. The distant wingtips of a cargo shuttle, blinking off into the eastern sky.

"Whoaaaa."

"Let me see it—"

"Move over."

"Stop!"

I flinch aggressively toward the children, feeling my fists tighten at our hips. Thankfully, they've forgotten me. They're swarming elsewhere, vying for a better angle on a kneeling Calvin Prichard, all trying to see what he's holding between two fingers. A tiny glass marble, glowing brighter in the shade of sunset.

"You know what this is?" he asks the smallest one. The light inside it dances across her face. Gleams in her giant eyes.

"A flashlight!" shouts one of the kids.

"A firefly!" guesses another.

But Prichard never shifts his attention from the smallest girl. "Any ideas?" He twists the shimmering pebble between his fingers, showing her all its sides, waiting patiently for her trembly nerves to dissipate.

"The sun?" she finally guesses.

The kid who said firefly laughs the hardest. The rest of the class adds to his noise. None of them are old enough to be truly cruel, but it embarrasses the little one just the same. She bows her head, and—

"That's exactly right." Prichard silences them all without raising his voice, with nothing but their own amazement. "We all carry a sun in here." He taps her forehead with his little finger. Then he leans in much closer, delivering a message only she and I can hear. "Some much brighter than others." He stands without ever looking at her again, but he leaves the marble in her palm.

The kids start crowding her to see it, but a depressurizing sound signals the opening of the vactrain's broad side door. Their teacher quickly steps forward to usher them aboard. "Hey—stop. Stop that. Everyone say goodbye to—" she halts, realizing Prichard is already striding off.

I'm right there with her, still a bit struck by the tender moment, not to mention the swirling fragment of light the penniless girl now has to herself.

But Prichard waves a corralling hand as he reaches me. "Let's get the fuck out of here." He quickens his pace toward another automated SUV, already pulling up in his path. That's when I realize his personal sim, the floating orb he calls Spike, is lagging behind, still hovering around the excited children, stealthily documenting the entire scene, capturing every precious smile for whatever propaganda he has planned.

"Hey, Prich." I catch him stepping into the SUV. He stops cold, looking back at me with some surprise. "Thanks, but I think I've had it for today." I tug wearily at the various honors around my neck." Mind if I take a rain check on the rest of the tour?"

He watches me for a few seconds with the blankest face I've ever seen, no detectable emotion in any direction. Then he suddenly grins and tosses me a salute with two casual fingers. "No problem at all." Spike chimes twice as it hovers past my ear, and a section of pavement twenty meters behind me opens, revealing a subterranean ramp. My own automated vehicle comes driving up it. A sleek, sporty thing with panoramic glass shaped like a teardrop. "I've got a bunk all set up for ya down in the inner rim." Prichard nods the opposite direction of the museum, toward the center of the compound. "At midnight, we do a total blackout. View from your balcony should be somethin' else." He looks up at the dimming sky with great affection, a few brighter stars already visible. "Take it easy, friend." He shuts the SUV door exactly as Spike reaches his shoulder, and they both head off, driving up the spiraling highway toward his tower of operations on the valley's edge— his isolated office and private residence. I turn from there, looking back down to the inner rim.

It's a five-kilometer loop, denoting the exact center of the mechanical city. A flattened circle of concrete, clay, and saltwater reservoirs layered one on top of the other, likely to neutralize ground-penetrating radar from above. A giant shield to keep outside eyes from looking in—and to keep whatever's in from leaking out.

Yeah. I'm close enough to feel it now. When I close my eyes and spread her scales, we can just about taste it in the air—that old space salt swimming through us, that galactic gasoline with an outdated placeholder for a name. Dark energy. Of course, he'd have a reactor here. His private sim is a subtle tease of whatever cutting edges he keeps below. He's probably just vain enough to power this entire compound on one singularity. One massive cold propulsion tunnel, tucked right down there in the securest storm cellar known to man. Not a bomb. A supernova battery. One dark collider to rule them all.

And someone else.

My eyes lift open, not focusing on anything in particular, hovering vacantly in the direction of Dallas Dynamics' inner rim. Something else? I ask Nazara, struggling to trace the origin of that thought. It felt different somehow. Not so much like one of her whispers but—

No, the thought presses through again. *Not something*, it insists. I insist. I formulate thoughts without meaning to.

"Someone else," I correct myself aloud, unable to look away from the central concrete, unable to want to look away— feeling the corrupted gap those jammers make, those buried, overclocked Spiders somewhere beneath the saltwater and clay. They're meant to keep us out. Us. The scattering few. And they are meant to keep him in.

"Kendar." The name slips from my lips like I'm asleep, like I'm just rising from a dream. My eyes flood with baffling moisture as my mouth moves on its own. "Kendar, my love." The suit feels cold as Nazara walks us forward. Her scales flicker indecisively battle-red as we shamble toward the sunken core.

The teardrop sports car adjusts its trajectory, slowly looping around to cut us off. I cling against it, sliding along the polished surface, looking like a man whose stubborn legs intend to drown his upper half. But the passenger door swings open, and I'm able to catch hold of the ceiling handle.

"Kible?" I manage to stammer, struggling to regain my sense of self, remembering those final plummeting moments of Tysha's dream with Mantz. "Do you mean Kible Thexx? Alive?"

She gives no answer. Maybe she can't while I'm fighting her off. Our temperature drops as our solar cells continue to purge their converted light, not using it just discharging rapidly, almost like she is leaking out, trying to send her essence down to the dark collider.

"I—I'm sorry." I shake my head, lurching us headlong into the sports car. I clench my fists and stiffen our back, shutting down the purge attempt. "We're almost there," I mutter unconvincingly, pressing her back down into our abyss. "Almost finished."

The teardrop shuts itself and speeds away from the war museum. Speeds us down the final ramp into the zone of the inner rim.

As we go, it occurs to me. This suit. This surviving proto-type. This second mind in my G-1. It must've been here. This must be the place where *she* was born.

14.04

As Prichard promised, it all goes black at exactly midnight. Every bulb in the entire compound quits its luster. Down in the valley's shadow, none of the distant lights from Dallas, Fort Worth, or Waco can reach us, which makes the stars a stagger-ing sight, bright and clear enough to reveal the curvature of the Earth. It's too grand to turn away from, so I sit and cherish it for a while on the penthouse roof.

I count the few dozen human lights remaining. Prichard's eerie Spider shines the brightest, way up there in his secluded office space. A few overachievers and graveyard shifters are scattered in the middle perimeter, but I detect nothing this far down. There's no one alive between me and the world's largest dark collider. No one between me and that caged singularity, buried just there, waiting to be set free.

I'd planned to wait another hour, but all the unknowns are piling behind my eyes. Security measures. Point of entry. Point of exit, should I find Kible Thexx down there in need of saving.

Or Kendar, whoever that is. Another familiar name like a faded dream. I couldn't risk scouting the inner rim while the lights were up, while Prichard was still moving around up there. But his Spider's unusual glow has been totally still for thirty minutes, and my night sight is about as good as it's gonna get.

So, I kick our legs out over the edge, sending us into the endgame, falling for a couple gut-lifting seconds before we land hard on the blacktopped street. I hear it crunch and crack beneath our weight, but that damage hardly matters. Nobody to hear it tonight and nothing left of it tomorrow. Just an ash cloud and cable news. A new pockmark on the Earth to divide its people even further.

I move quickly, staying low, listening to the wind for hunter drones, but everything I detect is high above us near the valley's edge, surveilling the skies and surrounding farmlands for any reckless hippies who might dare to infiltrate. This place is far less prepared for the inside job, for a kamikaze saboteur who's strong enough to dig himself deeper.

I set a new land speed record for being wrong, making way too much noise, jerking to a sudden stop behind a warehouse wall. There's something around the corner, something heavy enough for me to feel it in the soles of our feet. A subtle disturbance in the pavement, a near-silent drumming like leather shoes creeping over stone. I peek around the corner of the massive warehouse—the last standing structure before the wide-open valley center—and I almost snap my neck, ducking back behind cover. Christ in hell. It was looking right at me. Twice as close as I expected. Close enough to see the Milky Way's reflection in the oily black tungsten between its eyes. On a more overcast night, it might've been invisible, standing still, or crouching, rather. It was slouching forward just like I've seen it in those viral demonstrations, those haunting robotics shows that resulted in nothing but bad press. But those infamous prototypes were riddled with loose wires, exposed batteries, and noisy pistons, totally lacking the polished zeal of all future Dallas Dynamics products. Nothing like the creature that I just saw. An ape-like machine, made in the image of its creator.

M. Calvin Prichard's Modern Man.

And it clocked me, sure as shit. When I peeked out, its two lenses even seemed to twitch, drawing me into focus. If it has thermal sensors or image receptors beyond ultraviolet, it may even be watching me right now, looking straight through this concrete cover while it calculates my level of threat. It may be seconds away from sounding an alarm if I do nothing. Seconds from stirring its master in his quarters, sending the entire compound into lockdown. But if I attack it, that result seems guaranteed.

I peek again, turning half a pupil around the corner, even less. It reacts instantly, lowering its chin like a metallic cave-man, preparing to rush an encroaching threat. Its mouth comes open without any of those pressurized piston sounds from the prior models, without any sound at all that I can hear, and I see its bottom row of teeth—all sharpened black diamonds in perfect symmetry. My plan to destroy it becomes a plan to survive.

But something pings in my periphery—the fuzziest corner of an intuition. Looking up that way, I see the warehouse's title etched into its concrete wall. Thin, sunken letters, painted black:

Advanced Research In Defense

There's something in there I could use. Without knowing how, I know there's all sorts of treats in there. Rail rifles and concussive sticks. Patented alloys and molecular edges that make steel seem soft and silly.

Thirty-five meters between me and the Modern Man. Maybe four seconds to get up this wall and through a window before I learn how quick this new model is.

But it closes its mouth. Its posture changes. Those motorized facial features that horrified America shift closer to human confusion. Or some new detection. It turns its head sharply, listening elsewhere, then it throws itself in that direction with animalistic athleticism. Not a single step wasted, galloping off on its leather-padded feet like the perfect hybrid between primate and machine. Once it's out of sight, Nazara *whispers* a bitter correction to my four-second guess. It would've reached us in *two*.

I have no patience for her sour mood. I'm too relieved, if not puzzled, about the source of this quick luck. What threat could there possibly be down here that deserved the machine's attention more than us? I put our back against the wall, looking up to Prichard's office in the distance. His Spider still hasn't moved. Still feels inactive just like Connie's did when she was deep asleep. Somehow, it seems our stealth has been preserved.

The core's entire surface now looks clear, totally open for us to crawl around and find a service hatch or ventilation duct. But I can't say I like this. Maybe all those old films have warped my sense of spycraft, but this mission suddenly feels too easy. Any moment now, I'll trip some wire and fall through the floor into a shark pit—or some more modern snare to match the master of this arena, some desynchronizing signal like back on that tarmac where we first met. Nazara's light is mightier than ever, despite the anxious dread this compound gives her, but it's no coincidence that I've chosen sabotage over a street fight, not simply pride that's stayed my hand these eleven days. Prichard's new Spider is unlike the others. Sharper somehow.

Much more powerful, I'd guess. Either way, it's my move first. And I haven't seen enough action yet to break my vow.

I push away from the factory wall and make many quick leaps out into the open space, using the height of each jump to survey the vast surface area for any point of entry. I find a rectangle—four cuts in the pristine concrete, directly centered at the canyon's basin. I scurry over to that bullseye for a closer look, but I don't see much. No latches or handles to turn the rectangle into a door. But it does feel different beneath our feet. Not quite hollow but somehow less dense. I press my ear against it, knocking with my knuckles to test a theory. It's confirmed.

I crawl us backward to the edge of the rectangle, knowing this next move could be the game. No retreating after this. No more medals or accolades. Just down and deeper until the end. I pause for some final protest from Nazara, but she stays quiet. She makes me nervous like only she can. So, I cast a vote on her behalf.

I draw our elbow back then bring it down hard at the rectangle's perimeter. The concrete cracks, but it isn't pulverized. I draw back higher, tighter, and strike again. That does the trick. The edge of the rectangle now has a lip for me to get leverage. I dig my hands in underneath it, losing a trigger fingernail in the process, but I'm able to force the hidden hatch upward, standing to our full height until a pair of hydraulic hinges lock it into place. And the way is opened.

It's another large, subterranean ramp, just like the one that teardrop sports car emerged from this afternoon. One long, shadowy tunnel, spiraling down, totally black until a thin trail of guiding emergency lights begins flicking on. A service road to the dark collider. And something else. A voice like thousands sewn together.

"*Oh, Kendar!*" Nazara comes alive with renewed intensity. "*Kendar Shall!*" she screams inside us with that red rage I've felt before, that blinding heat I can't control.

In synchronicity, that same shooting star flashes behind me. That recurring twinkle sends my eyes back to the ARID warehouse, back to where I left the Modern Man. A medieval clashing echoes there. A clanging, cutting, ripping interruption, way off in the distance and inside my mind. I see white light like muzzle fire, white at the edges but tinted blue. A cobalt explosion, then suddenly nothing. No unusual sights or sounds at all. Silence.

Nazara couldn't care less. Before I can even think to suppress her urges, we're rippling red and heading down, chasing the guiding, spiraling lights, overtaking them, sprinting past the flickering trail into total blackness. She doesn't need to see; she *knows* this place. Worse than that, she knows this mission.

This infiltration, this hidden core. She already knows the cost of failure. I can feel the jammers now. A white signal wall, and we're passing through it. A chaotic wave. A thousand tangled lights like endless screams. Like the dead are here, alive.

Nazara stops at the end of the road—some massive obstruction I can barely make out, some great dead end. She stops and waits there while I whimper, while I feel them all through her rare gift. Not mine but distinctly hers. The scattering. Maybe it's been hers all along. I've never felt it at this level. Never heard so many voices trapped in time.

She is unperturbed. She waits patiently for the emergency lights to catch up, trickling forward along the floor, between our feet, culminating at the obstruction. Still dim but visible now. A steel door like a nuclear bunker. Wide and tall with several matching hinges on either side. A five-spoke vault handle for manual entry. Covered in dust and rust, but I remember. I can see it clean in our shared mind.

"Wait," I beg her.

She ignores me, and we step forward. She grips two of the spokes like a nautical wheel. Grabs hold of it just like she did when she had hands of her own. I can feel them like ghostly limbs tracing over mine.

"Mama, wait!"

"I am not your mother, Emmett Hayes," Nazara speaks aloud, using a more resolute version of my voice. "Nor am I Nazara Thume. Not anymore." She sets our feet wide as she cranks the handle. There is a screeching, scraping sound as the old locks begin to turn. "But I will show you where she ended." The iron wheel spins freer, faster. The giant doors crack open, revealing a dazzling light on the other side. "And you shall see where we began."

14.05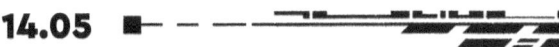

There are hidden signatures in private places. Instrument tags, family photos, lucky dice. If you listen carefully, a cockpit can speak its pilot's name—or, in my case, everyone else's.

First time I docked at the orbital station, I found a leather-bound journal in the OP lounge. It was decades old with natural paper, but it must've been sealed for most of its life. Looked factory-fresh. Just one narrow crease on the front cover where a zero-grav pen was clipped in place. I was the only recruit on deck that week, so whoever left it was long gone. Left it for me; I remember thinking that.

But it wasn't empty. First three pages were full of doodles.

Sharp geometric angles and perfect circles. Illusory logos that seemed to sink into my lap or leap two inches off the page. I'd never seen such casual mastery, such electric skill on ancient parchment. Destined or forgotten, I felt compelled to take it with me.

Then I got scared. Soon as I left the station, that journal felt like contraband. They'd find it on me. Know I stole it. Kick me out of the patrol. Assign my gunsuit to someone else before I ever tried it on. I had no way to dispose of it in orbit, and I didn't want to, not really. It was too rare and clean and lucky. So, I decided to camouflage it. Make it my own.

Couldn't draw for shit. Could barely string a few words together without feeling humiliated; I was pretty much illiterate at the time. So, I just started writing names. Every name of every person I ever met. No order to it, no chronology. No spelling accuracy. Just whoever popped into my head, I wrote 'em down. Sometimes, I could only think of somebody's last name, or their middle, or their first, so their identity would end up divided across several different lines. After each session, I'd check the list and cross out anything I'd just duplicated, so pretty much every page became one big scratchy mess. It was hideous. And beautiful. A total social history of Emmett Hayes. Not even six pages long, including the geometric introduction.

I didn't know it at the time, but that would end up being my last project as a natural man. Soon after that, *she* changed me forever, leaving that hideous treasure as the only evidence of my former life.

"We must continue," Nazara urges with my lips. "Time is short."

I resist her for another few seconds, still transfixed by the charred remains. Our flight recorder. Our black box and its only contents. My old journal. Salvaged from the Taiga. Sealed behind fiberglass like some alien artifact. Propped up against the remnants of our exocannon. Just a scorched and crooked ID plate, recovered from the wreckage.

EX-129-OP

I feel a tightening at our wrist as Nazara tugs me away from that morbid display. I stagger onward, through the broad, sterilized hallway—concrete, glass, and steel in all directions, lit entirely by one uninterrupted floor panel. A wide, seemingly endless LED, embedded beneath our feet. It runs like a river, underlighting the entire space like a modern ghost story. A white light tinged slightly blue.

This place is a museum. And a laboratory. Some alcoves have tables with active projects, robotic arms soldering motherboards, connecting wires. Others are reserved for exhibits like my fallen cannon. Or like this next one here, this family of human skeletons. Two males, adult and child. Two females of the same. If they're not real, I've never seen a more graphic recreation. A few teeth are missing from the mother. The son has lost his entire left leg. Nothing is bleached for presentation. All four of them have that natural grime from an actual lifetime. And unless my anatomy is confused, they're also all deformed. Not an inch of tailbone between the lot of them. Strange. They all seem smoother than they should—like the spinous processes have been sanded down. We're also clearly lingering again, but Nazara hasn't tried to move us.

"Par ya Lum sakar." She breaks the silence with a whisper. She uses my hand to touch the glass, and I feel an old prayer pass through our heart. Looking more closely at the skeletons, I don't see a family anymore. I see a complete collection. Disfigured and dissected here and there but not naturally deformed.

Not natural to our world at all. This time, I notice I'm a fool.

"Hayes?" a soft voice asks from somewhere else.

The voice is so faint, I hardly register it. But we're already turning. Gently, without surprise, Nazara guides my eyes in that direction, as though she's been waiting for the call. And dreading my response.

"Hayes?" Taiko Chiba repeats, muffled behind thin plexiglass, suspended in a harness above a wide, steel operating table.

"Yeah. Oh Jesus, yeah! Taiko—"

"Look first." Nazara halts me on the bottom step of the alcove. It's a large, elevated operating theater with pearl white walls and floors, seamless like a photographer's infinity background. Taiko is floating there, slightly off-center, with industrial surgical arms working on the ruined right side of her body. Her left half is scarred but mostly intact, except for her left foot, which is already amputated at the ankle, replaced with a sophisticated prosthetic—matte-black, designed for power. She is also starkly, clinically nude, stripped of every layer of her incinerated G-4 suit.

"Hayes?" Taiko breathes again, as though I didn't just respond.

"I'm here! Taiko, I—let me get to her," I beg Nazara, but she keeps me restrained, tightening the suit at our knees and hips. "Stop it! Why won't you let me—"

"You look but do not see," she patiently reprimands.

I don't catch her meaning, but I look again. I lock eyes with Taiko and see that her right eye socket is patched over and gauzed, likely still healing from some procedure. Her left eye is even clearer than I last saw it, no longer swirling with that nanoscopic infection, that domineering hive mind. But I see nothing returned. No semblance at all of recognition. One of the robotic surgeons starts drilling screws into her right hip, a gut-wrenching, gnashing sound, but she doesn't register that event either. Doesn't flinch.

"Hayes," Taiko checks again, not even making a question of it this time, as though each effort becomes more futile. A mayday routine on autopilot. Another robot lifts a brand-new bionic leg from the steel operating table, and Nazara relaxes her hold on us.

"This way." She pulls us back down the theater stairs. She walks us further down the hall, and I make no effort to defy her. My mind is elsewhere, revisiting those final moments in the Russian Taiga.

The plasma charge. That eye contact I shared with Taiko. I did everything I could to end her life, and she thanked me for it. She made my name sound like a gift, and I knew why. Even without these empathic powers, that look made total sense to me. She thought I'd freed her—not just desynced but liberated—from those fucking nanos, from Calvin Prichard, from her usefulness in this bad war. I saw her eyes, and I knew all that. Because I wanted the same thing. I wanted to believe my prior self was still an option, but I should've known better. We're not so different, after all. Both walking corpses. Useful skeletons. Calcium racks on life support until someone like Prichard pulls the plug.

Neither agreeing nor dissuading, Nazara walks us onward. The laboratory narrows, starting to resemble a hospital hallway. That single LED strip narrows as well, still unbroken from the entrance, running straight ahead like a milky river. Milk with blueberries blended in, brightening steadily as we go along, almost painful to look at now. But it's not the brightness that disturbs me. It's the voices.

A waterfall of torment closes in—a thousand screams falling together, tumbling through unbroken chaos. It reminds me of The Darkmind. A league of shrieking cousins to that shadowed persona in Cuva Khan.

"Yes," Nazara answers. "Now move between them, if you can."

The tighter walkway ends abruptly, releasing us into a new area. It's a second museum that makes the first look like a gift shop, a tiny mudroom to a great cathedral, wide and tall. Craning my neck, I half expect to see falcons nesting in its higher rafters. But the grandeur of the space becomes an afterthought once I bring my eyes back down, wincing at first, recoiling from the compounding harshness of the bright floor.

"Between them," Nazara reminds, bringing my hands together like a wedge. "The gaps between." She spreads them slowly in front of my eyes, parting the violence like hanging coats, cutting through the vibrant noise until I can clearly see the floor. Or rather, until I can't. There is no LED panel beneath us. There's not even solid ground. Just columns and columns of sunken glass. A honeycomb basement, two meters deep in all directions. And I'm in the gap, alright. The gap between humanity and everything else.

The columns are cages. Solitary prisms of reinforced glass, with steel-wire mesh between the panes. And monochrome prisoners. An acre of bleached bodies, huddled in corners, buried alive. The only colors are bloody smears—dragged fingerprints and bony scratches left behind by desperate captives.

I'm standing right on top of one, covering her airholes with our feet. I quickly step away, but there's no escape. No place to stand except the roofs of other slaves. And one is awake. A hairless man in homemade clothes. He's looking straight up.

Straight into my eyes. I don't recognize him, but he *knows* me. His subdued light scatters into mine, and I feel his loss. I feel the agony of a presumed betrayal, now confirmed.

He lunges at me, hands reaching up, eyes flashing with vicious intent, but the glass seems to catch his heat. It reverberates and pops with electricity, then he's blasted back down to the hard glass floor, convulsing in constrictive spasms. The cobalt glow drains from his eyes.

"Me paka!" an adjacent prisoner shouts, pressing his dark hands against the glass between them. "Dad, get up!" the young human calls again, bashing his fist against the reinforced pane before he sinks against it, demoralized.

He's using the light speech. A human teenager, almost as dark-skinned as Captain Uba but with fiery red hair, a deep crimson buzz cut that shouldn't be possible with his complexion. But the color matches his thin eyebrows and stubby lashes. Stubby, as though they've been plucked in recent weeks. A bilingual human with plucked and colored eyelashes; that's my best idiotic guess, until the young man lifts his shining, cobalt eyes in my direction.

He has Luminaran ears, and entry and exit scars on opposite sides of his throat. He's thinner than I last saw him, undernourished and fatigued, but his eyes are just as angry and unrequited as before. An unmistakable contempt. Somehow, I'm looking down at Yono. Not vaporized in the Taiga. Not crushed in a collapsing cave. But cured. All-natural and saturated. Glistening like only one other of his kind I've seen before.

Something pings in my periphery—an icy spark like invisible fingers at my chin, lifting my attention up from Yono, guiding my gaze along the course of the milky river that led me here. I ride that lightning across the floor, across the hundreds of converging cells, all wired into the waterfall I've been expecting. But, instead of cascading, it rises.

It swirls at the furthest end of this holocaust, mesmerizing and obscene, a great sphere of tempered glass, propped up on towering, metallic legs, jutting out in eight directions like a fat black widow spider.

I see between them—between all their lights, not given freely, not turned in ceremony but taken alive. It's like a star tomb, industrialized. A massive ball of raging, corrupted, crackling, stolen alien power. Not the dark energy I expected, but the outcome will be the same. I fucking swear it.

I see Malcolm Calvin Prichard Jr.'s last invention.

14.06

Yono shouts his curses at my back, but I'm too busy running, searching the occupied prisms beneath the floor. So many pale, familiar faces. Hundreds of diffused and damaged lights, scattering into mine like desperate hands. I can't stop to help them. Not yet. Not until I find a certain complexion, one specific head of hair. Tysha must be here. That blue shooting star that I keep seeing must have been some kind of message.

"You are wasting time," Nazara spits through my tight lips. "You must destroy it at once!" She turns our shoulders forcibly in the direction of the dark collider or giant spider, whatever it is.

I resist. As I scamper over the prison cubes, each bald head confirms my other theory: that star tomb changed us. It healed Yono's throat and supercharged this suit, sparing me a certain death. Ever since that day, Nazara's power has been ramping up, even surpassing Taiko's G-4 in the forest. More and more, she's speaking through me, unsealing her memories of this terrible place. Somehow, by basking in the direct heat of all those ancient brightstars, my strange friends have been restored. Yono, Tysha, Nazara, and—

A thought like lightning strikes us both. My search for Tysha is forgotten. Our heart explodes with hot emotion, and Nazara turns our burning eyes due west. She coils our legs then launches us in that direction, soaring ten meters before we land on hand and foot like a feral cat. Like an electric lioness, eyes wide open, looking down, we're burning so hot the glass beneath us clouds with steam.

There he is. Just as beautiful as the day we fled the brightworld. His hair is short and prickly, but it's just as golden as we remember. Golden like ours was at the time. His skin is tanned like treated leather, more like his father's. He looks so much like Kendar. Our miniature luminescence. He's grown so much while we have slept. *Our starshine boy.*

"No." Nazara shakes my head. Or maybe I do. Maybe I'm the one confused. "Not ours. That woman is dead." I sink dizzily against the glass, pumping the brakes on our hot burn, regaining control. As the steam begins to fade, I see his weakened, delighted eyes down in the prism cage.

"Mama." Poody smiles sweetly. His soft gaze drifts up from her rippling scales to my stupid face. "I knew you'd come." The words scratch his throat on their way out, doubling him over in a fit of pitiful coughs.

We watch him through the same tortured eyes. With every thump of our shared heart, my boldest fantasy slips away. Back in the cave—that big speech the kid couldn't muster up. These nagging images. These memories of a golden goddess, of a loving mother I never had, of Nazara Thume. That much is true. Somehow, a mother's spirit has carried on inside this suit. The only mistake I made was hoping she was mine.

"Stand back, kid." With some difficulty, I rise to a knee. "And cover up."

Poody sees my intentions. His dim light scatters into mine, electrified with an enraptured terror. He scrambles to the opposite corner of his cell, shielding his face, but peeking one eye between his scrawny elbows. That'll have to do. I make a fist and raise it high, giving Nazara one last chance to protest the action, to tug us back to our original mission and torch this kingdom at any cost.

No spoken answer comes. Only a loosening of her control—a rippling of scales from battle-red to their default hue, an implicit shift in heat from our bent knees to my readied fist. So, I bring it down. Down like a hammer to their chains, like crashing rage and reckless love against the shackles of this world.

"*STOP!*" A dark voice ricochets inside my skull.

My liberating strike halts centimeters from the prison glass, halts so fast I feel something pop inside our forearm. A ligament thunder crashes up our shoulder, and I expect to cry—I expect to scream—but I don't even wince. I can hardly breathe or blink my eyes. We are frozen in time.

"Jesus Mary," a more human voice sighs from somewhere above. A male voice, emanating through loudspeakers, echoing up and down the warehouse museum, seeming to originate in the long western wall directly in front of us. "Honestly," he starts again, "I knew you weren't the sharpest cut of cheddar," he pauses to yawn and scratch himself somewhere, "but I never did take you for a meatball, boy. Not half this thick." He clicks his tongue in an admonishing way, and I know it's over. This revolution never even began.

Just like on that stealthy warship, a large section of steel on the western wall suddenly becomes transparent glass, revealing a wide control room. The steel-glass is thin and clear, totally flush with the control room's ceiling and floor, creating a dollhouse studio effect ten meters off the ground. I might think the wall had vanished entirely, if not for the gooseneck microphone mounted dead center, with a very irritated Calvin Prichard standing behind it. His hair is uncharacteristically matted. He's draped in some cross between a kimono and a jiu-jitsu gi, with Dallas Dynamics branding across the chest. His feet are bare, tapping noiselessly against a brown rug, possibly cowhide.

"That is barbed, chromium wiring in metallic glass," Prichard continues, jabbing a finger down at the honeycomb prisons, pressing an intercom button with his other fist. "Now, I'm not sure which anatomy lesson you took a sick day on, but typically ya wanna keep all the blood and bones *inside* your arm—and how many was it?" He turns to his right, waiting for Spike to chime twice in quick response. "Seventeen alarms!" Prichard furrows in amazement. "You give Special Operations a whole new meanin', boy." He slacks his eyes and thumps a limp wrist against his chest before smacking the gooseneck mic aside and turning away, side-eying me like a disappointed parole officer.

He seems to be muttering to himself, clearly all alone up there behind the glass, but he nods his head and gestures in frustration, as though reluctantly agreeing with someone else, someone off to his left in the opposite direction of his personal sim.

With a capitulating huff, he finally reorients the microphone and presses the intercom. "Alright. Well, if you ask me, we've had a pretty severe breach of trust here, sergeant. But I guess I'd best hear your side of things before crackin' the whip, so go on ahead."

His strange Spider's psychic constriction vanishes as instantly as it came. I collapse against the prison glass, desperately sucking air, grimacing at the searing pain from elbow to shoulder, realizing this injury is nothing compared to what the cavern tribe has suffered the past eleven days.

"You—" I can barely move enough air to make a sound. "You made me think they—"

"And you made me think we had somethin'!" Prichard responds as though he heard the rest of my intent. Heard it clearly. "I was snug as a bug twenty minutes ago. Happy as a clam. Cool as a catfish, right up until you started your little larceny tour. You got any idea how long it takes to manufacture—!" He spins away, cussing at himself, like he'd rather be whooping my ass than wasting words. But his cooler half prevails again. "Alright, cowboy, I understand. I do." He shows me the peaceful side of his right hand. "Especially with *her* tuggin' at your noodle all the damn time." He gestures toward the center of our back. "Can't hardly blame ya for gettin' mixed up, so let's just—let's just call it square and try again."

At first, I'm sure I misunderstood him. Must've misheard one word, one subtle pronoun he shouldn't know. Then I feel an old instinct start to turn.

My own rising heat, I might've thought. My own dryland country rage. But it's too unmotivated. Too much like the scattering, only nearer, trailing down inside myself, back to that old jeep, to chow hall two, to the wooden chapel on Camp Cooks—to every time we've lost control in this man's presence. No, not we. This time, it's distinctly *her*.

"Try again?" As Nazara speaks, violent images strike me like ghostly screams. As she labors my hands together, pushing us to all fours, shifting us back to a more stable knee, I see nightmarish flashes everywhere. Vivid memories of what this warehouse contained before. "Yes," she says. "Come down here and let us try." I feel my jaw tighten behind a hungry scowl.

As Prichard reaches for the intercom, his head flinches slightly to the left. His hand withdraws, clutching the back of his neck in apparent pain. He holds that pose, listening to whoever's up there with him—a strange voice I can almost hear, almost recognize. When he turns back to the microphone, his eyes are narrowed in new caution.

"Us?" Prichard finally asks, holding his fist to the intercom button. "Would that be you and me, sergeant? Or you and somebody else?"

A snicker escapes my lips. The tiniest laugh. I shudder from hips to shoulders, feeling my body heat begin to bleed into the suit.

"Sergeant?" Prichard asks again. "Are you—"

"You know who speaks." Nazara lifts my eyes, revealing a sizzling tear down my left cheek. Our expression feels tragic and unforgiving. "Just as I know who speaks to you."

Prichard takes a step back. He touches the nape of his neck, not in pain but disbelief. He keeps his hand there, massaging his strange Spider like threatened treasure.

With new urgency, he turns slightly to his right, muttering a command to his simulant, Spike. That quickly, his custom Rettag illuminates on his wrist. He raises it, aiming the tag's microprojector at his eyes. Blinking impatiently, scrolling through some private feed, he nods in a sing-song rhythm, mouthing silently to himself. With his eyes still on that projection, he steps forward, hastily pressing the intercom, speaking as clearly as he can:

"Ah-kem nay nain-yuh cass co-shoom."

A dark jolt shoots through us. Cold and electric like a dozen funny bones flicked at once.

Prichard seems confused by our reaction. But inspired. "Say guard-uh core loo poodin orbiss," he continues with mounting confidence, despite the wretchedness of his sound.

It's sickening somehow—like chocolate cookies with dogs-hit substituted. Recognizable but totally wrong. In that way, it's emblematic. Another twisted imitation, reverse engineered. He's trying the light speech. Forcing it forward without any of its cosmic logic coming through.

"Bendarno!" Prichard clenches his fist like an orating dictator. "Bendarno core taz naysh." He loses his place in the microfont. "Core taz—"

"Kor tahz nais cambo lu Lum," Nazara corrects him with finality and some reluctance. But there's no taking it back now. The true light speech carries across the room. Very old words, spoken in a particular way.

Poody shudders in the cell beneath us. A few of the sleeping prisoners stir awake. One of the elders asks us, disbelieving, and many others repeat the name:

Thume?

Na Thume?

Thume ha Lum!

Their psychic calls are like tight drums, tuned to the sound of vengeance. With that cavalcade as answer, with taut shoulders and clenching fists, Nazara Thume lifts her eyes to Calvin Prichard's once again.

And he is lit with awe. Amazed and mesmerized, he can

only tremble in response. But I see no fear. Rather, his eyes are wet with met ambition, as though some lifelong dream has been achieved.

The old words touch me, too. Another flashing of prior life, images and understanding bleeding in. Scripture pages from the oldbooks that Kendar entrusted to Canna Dhoz. A warning of dark and darker worlds, of endless shadow and entropic doom. I realize I've heard those words before. In paraphrased English, simplified and filtered just like Prichard tried today. That's right. Back in that old jeep, he was the one who said—

"*And there were endless empty eyes, blinded by the freest worlds.*" Prichard looks down at us from the control room. Seeing the recognition on my face, he nods gravely, pointing to the suit again: "*Betrayed by those who knew the light.* I tried to warn ya, cowboy."

"Ha!" Nazara laughs without any humor, with vitriol and kept contempt. "Sightless cowards make false alarms." I feel her attention drift inside us, rushing high-pressured blood to our ruptured elbow, twisting sinews back together at a reckless pace. "You have heard the words but not their meaning."

"*And whose fault is that?!*" Prichard's voice doubles in that darkened way, rolling though my ears and mind together. He fumes, wheeling away to compose himself, then he storms right back to the intercom. "If you knew *half* of what it cost me to grow the skin you're livin' in, ya wouldn't say such hurtful things!"

"Cost?" Nazara gasps. The surgical throbbing in our elbow slows and cools, not finished just forgotten. Our chest feels vacuum tight. Our eyes begin to boil. "Cost is a capricious token in your world. An arbitrary guess at true misfortune."

"Jesus fuck me doggy. Do ya hear yourself, woman? Are ya even tryin' to communicate or just rile me up all over again?

Maybe I shoulda let ya bust that glass open—use your little rugrat as a translator."

"Kharre mel caska!" Nazara shrieks in a piercing octave I didn't think my lungs could make. And we're rippling red. We're back on our feet, coiling to leap in Prichard's direction.

But his hand is already reaching, freezing us in place with that black blasphemy he used before. I'm caught in a telepathic war between his strange Spider and Nazara's rage. She's salivating. Growling and thrashing like haunted flesh, she steps us forward. The second step has more force behind it. A third, and now she's smiling, making my face do wild things—hungry, drunken, sinister taunts to intimidate and destroy. Her ambitions are converging just like Prichard's—just one bloody shower from fruition, after all these years.

To Prichard's abject terror, she raises our right arm to reach right back at him, to show him what true dominion is, to show him the shape of choking fingers, eager to plunge into his throat. That's when our ligament snaps completely. Her focus vanishes in the pain. Our elbow cranks like a rattle ratchet as Prichard uses every enhanced muscle in our body to slam us straight through the warehouse floor.

 **14.07**

Not sure why he called it metallic glass. Shattered just fine. Fine as sand, from what I can tell, tinkling down into the cell beneath us like it's keeping time. Prichard was spot on about the wiring though. Barbed: check. Chromium: check. Makes for a solid hammock. The kind you just can't seem to get up out of.

"Stop it!" Poody's little voice shouts from the adjacent cell. Adjacent. That's good. Thought maybe we came down right on top of him.

"Don't worry, kid." I twist in the net of wiring, slow and steady, navigating the razorblade quicksand. "It don't hurt so bad as it looks."

"Your back bones are showing!"

He stumps me with that one. That and the nausea. An utter revulsion, climbing up his guts and scattering into mine. I feel his disgust like it's my own.

"Alright. Don't look at the blood, buddy. Look up. Tell me what the man in the room is doing."

Poody retches once. One ugly gag at the back of his throat. I can't see him from this angle, but the sounds and scattered sensations are more than enough. When he speaks, he sounds relieved. "He is gone. The big window went away."

I tilt my head backward, looking straight up past my eyebrows. He's right. The dollhouse glass has reverted to solid steel. And we're not as deep in this cell as I thought, suspended just a few centimeters beneath the warehouse floor.

I try wiggling in place. Everything moves alright. Hips and shoulders are still in their sockets. I can sure feel our ruined elbow, no loss of sensation there. "I think my back's okay, kid. I'm gonna roll out."

"No! Your—"

"I'll go slow, don't worry." I grab the wiring between its barbs. "Nice and slow." I pull the chromium, slicing myself anyway, one long piano-wire papercut, but it's worth it to roll us a few more centimeters toward the edge. "Easy peasy, lemon—"

"Please stop." My lips speak for Nazara. Tightly. Like screaming would be so much easier. "He is correct. I am snagged."

My fingers eagerly trace the edge of the shattered prison cell, just one last stretch and tug from pulling us up to safety. But there's something a little too spooky about her tone. "Snagged where?" I glance down the length of us, not seeing anything obvious. Just a dozen or so rips and scratches from the chromium barbs.

"As the boy says," Nazara's intonation comes again, short and pained. She carefully draws our good arm away from the ledge. Slides my fingers over our hips until my thumb can reach our lower back. "Here." She taps lightly, wincing each time.

I feel the chromium wire straight away. One long strand, caught like floss in giant teeth. Snagged in her scales, I guess. Easy enough to reach. But soon as I grab hold of it, our entire body constricts. It's like we just cramped everywhere at once, like we're being electrocuted. It takes an unnerving, focused effort just for me to release the wire.

"What—what happened?" Nazara gasps, blinking my eyes in a confused flurry.

"Don't!" Poody shouts even more fearfully than before. "Your back bones!"

"Kid, quit looking over here, you're making me sick!" I feel him turn away, eyes darting somewhere less disturbing. Not for long. After just a few seconds, he's peeking over this way again, filling my heart with his fear and panic. I open my mouth to chide him more, but Nazara's voice arrives instead:

"You must use him."

"I don't even understand what the hell he's—"

"Use him to see." Trembling, she guides my hand. Taps our back in that tender place beneath the wiring. "Here," she gasps, as though she's just touched the coldest place on Earth.

I feel something new this time—something totally unlike

photosynthetic scales or chromium wire, something firm and slick stuck in her scales. And I feel him watching. I feel Poody's disgusted full attention boring into that same spot. So much raw focus, I can almost see it. I can . . .

"Yes," Nazara shudders. "Now be quick. Go."

Her last word is a gust of wind, knocking me from the spotlight of my world. I'm falling, dropping like a rock through time and space, spinning through the gaps, the vast and overwhelming emptiness between life—lives rushing by me like other spotlights:

Calloused feet in prison prisms.

Shriveled hands, rubbing at the glass, trying to see where the Prichard man has disappeared to.

A flowing kimono caught in a giant freezer door. Prichard pulls it free with one hand, clutching something heavy in the other, cussing to himself and someone else.

And someone else. In the medical hall. Someone is looking up at Taiko Chiba, seeing more than I ever have. Seeing her sensory system like mechanical thunderstorms. Flashing neural sputters, disconnected everywhere. Seeing how to fix her. But doing nothing. Turning away. Walking along the milky river in perfect silence.

"Go!" a woman shouts—a twisted shadow falling with me, nose-to-nose. "The boy!" she shouts again, summoning a distant spotlight nearer. Or sending me toward it—out of the gaps and into a much lower point of view, looking up from the adjacent cell, seeing my own hand scratch blindly at that firm thing stuck to our back. No, not stuck to it. Jutting from it. Two exposed, bloody discs of a spinal cord. Inhumanly smooth.

The kid's eyes are better than a mirror; nothing's reversed. And I can still feel it. Snagged chromium wiring, grazing my fingertips. I can watch myself floss it up, not between giant teeth but streamlined vertebrae. It barely tickles. But the twisted woman screams and disappears as soon as I try. The many spotlights shiver in her absence, flickering in all directions, threatening to collapse the entire space.

With one last tug, the chromium wiring falls free, but the flickering only intensifies. I begin to feel a tingling in my fingers, and I can see our body slackening, starting to roll back toward the center of the chromium hammock. I see my eyes still open, going senseless. All the furthest spotlights are shutting off at exponential speed, except for this one. This low point of view becomes one pointing finger, two skinny pointing fingers, gesticulating madly at my rolling corpse. A frantic panic fills my belly. A distant heat comes rushing forward. "Your back bones!" a little voice shouts.

The hand at the end of my ruined arm moves by itself, clutching the ledge with sudden strength, halting my dead man's roll. That reunites my elbow bones in a sickening crunch, and I'm thrust back into my own world.

I try to let go, but my fingers dig in, cracking the glass ceiling of the adjacent cell. My good arm is still wrapped behind me, fingers squeezing tightly, pushing those exposed vertebrae back into the suit with a slurping pop. I don't realize how bright Poody's eyes have been shining until he blinks and stumbles backward in his cell. His bony fingers cross each other drunkenly as his little knees knock together and he collapses to the floor.

"Kid!" My arms are mine to control again, just strong enough to pull me up out of the hammock and sprawl across the warehouse floor. "Kid, can you hear me?" I peek down into his cell, tapping on the glass, leaving bloody fingerprints.

"Oh Christ. Again with this?" a tired voice exhales behind me.

I spin around a bit too quick, and that bad elbow screams in self-defense. Breathing hard through my teeth, T-Rexing the busted joint against our ribs, I watch as Calvin Prichard descends weightlessly from above.

He's standing aboard the circular center of what used to be the control room floor, now levitated by a complete ring of cold propulsion jets along the bottom edge. Despite its size, the platform glides down elegantly, landing near the western wall. An identically sized landing pad sinks beneath its weight, leaving no visible lip around the edges. He's still barefoot, and I finally get a good look at that brown rug beneath his feet. It's cowhide, alright. And orangutan fur. And leopard spots. And dolphin skin. Taxidermied panda heads are sewn to either end.

"Every two seconds, he's crawlin' on the damn floor," Prichard grumbles to that ghost on his left again. With both hands and forearms, he cradles that heavy thing I just previewed in his conscious spotlight. It's some kind of frosted hexagonal cylinder with a faded, yellowed label on the side. Oxidized lead binds the top and bottom. He looks defenseless for a moment—just one tempting instant—before I realize he's not alone.

Soon as he steps away from the hoverlift rug, two Modern Men fan out from behind his robe in eerie synchronicity, exposing their sharp rows of black diamond teeth as they scamper hastily in my direction.

"Ah ah!" He stops them with his voice. "Protocol two, please. Self-defense. Until I say so." The metallic missing links both shut their mouths and take a step back. Their brows relax and their postures settle into uncanny impatience. "Sorry 'bout that." Prichard steps forward, nestling in between them. "They're low-brain simulants but not without some sense of fellowship. The one you wrecked up on the service was their little brother."

I don't know what he's talking about. I'm too distracted anyhow, increasingly bewitched by the frosted cylinder in his hands. Its clouded contents spark irretrievable recognitions, misplaced associations on the tip of someone else's tongue. I try to ask Nazara, but the words dribble out dreamily instead.

"Who is that?"

Prichard's congeniality dissolves. His eyebrow cocks. "I'm sorry?"

"I—I said, what is that."

"*No*." His voice rumbles in that darkened way. The entire room seems to tilt a few degrees south before he collects himself, nodding frustratedly to his ghost. He steps forward to get a better look at us, finally clocking the dark puddle beneath our bent knee—a bloody pond to match the crimson stream running down our backside.

I watch the cylinder, circling around us, moving with Prichard as he sidesteps in a wide, surveilling arc. When he spots the jagged gash in our lower back, he hisses in irritation. "Goddammit. You saw it, didn't you?"

I swivel in place a few degrees to get a better look at the hexagonal cylinder. It balances precariously on his hip, ribbed with melting condensation.

"I hiked all the way to cold storage in my damn pajamas, and you already fuckin' saw it, didn't you?"

I can almost read the faded label. *Creator Styles. Mineral Tissue.* That's wrong, but Nazara's waking up. We're watching the cylinder together, and I can almost remember what's inside.

"Boy, I'm talkin' to you!" Prichard drops the cylinder like spoiled potatoes, dumping it carelessly over his thigh.

I gasp, practically jumping out of our skin to lunge and save it. The Modern Men react to me in parity, dashing forward with bared teeth and scowling, tungsten faces. I'm way too late.

The frosted cylinder falls like iron to a magnet, like it was shot from a cannon aimed at hell. On contact with its lead casing, the warehouse floor reverberates, cracking in a wide spider web pattern, nearly shattering the cell beneath Prichard's feet.

But the cylinder doesn't bounce. It doesn't slide or skip or wobble. It just sits there, perfectly cold and still, like it hasn't been disturbed for years.

I land a full meter shy, one good arm outstretched to the faded label. An avalanche of frost breaks away when the cylinder hits the floor, revealing the words that I misread, unleashing flashes from the end of a forgotten life: *Just like this. Eyes to a cylinder. Bleeding out on a warehouse floor. Concrete back then. Boxes then. Stacked around a lonely desk.*

"Stop!" Prichard halts the apes before they bite. Black diamond fangs hover at my neck. They break the skin at the crown of my skull. *More rudimentary defenses back then. A laser trip- wire and steel balls. One explosion after so much distance, after crossing the oceans of Earth to find my man. I am a fool. I am in the turning. My last thought is blinding rage.*

"Kendar," we speak together, seeing him clearly at long last. A floating eyeball, threaded to a bisected brain. Half a jaw- bone, partially obscured by that faded, defrosting label:

CRATER SAMPLES 00. LUMINARAN TISSUE, MARKER-1

14.08

"No." Nazara levels my chin for a closer look at the frozen cyl- inder. "This is false. This . . ." She stares into the floating eye, and I see flashes of a man. Tanned, leathery skin and violet hair.

Bright pupils that shine whenever he laughs, as though the highway originates within him. "He lived," she swears aloud. "His light scattered across the Earth."

"I believe you," Prichard interjects, as though he's been waiting years for the opportunity. "I bet my entire world on our experience that day." He snaps his fingers, and the Modern Men retreat their teeth from my neck and skull. Within their optics, I see simulated disappointment.

"Ours?" Nazara sounds truly mystified as she crawls us backward to a knee. "You are a slaver. A swindling coward. We share nothing in this world."

"You shared something with me." He points his finger at us, and it takes some effort to remain upright. Our front foot skips an inch in his direction, tugged by psychic gravitation. "You pushed that black bible talk into my head like a broken goddamn record. Louder every day. Closer every hour. I thought I was losin' my fuckin'—" He breaks off, dropping his eyes to the floor. When he looks back up, his blue-greens have begun to glisten. "I didn't know you were real until your voice stopped in my mind. Until I finally saw you, ripped to pieces, clawin' your way to this." He sets his foot firmly on the frosted cylinder.

"You blew her up. You killed Nazara Thume." I hear sounds of grief from the cavern tribe, from all who knew the name. "You lured her here. Used Kendar's remains as bait."

"I sure as shit did not!" Prichard shouts indignantly. "I thought the queen of hell was comin' for me, and I ain't the religious type. The trip mines were old Retcon ARID leftovers that I knew nobody would miss. I wired a dozen of 'em, all up and down here while I worked. Shat in a bucket for a week, too scared to leave. Eight years ago, Dallas Dynamics was just one stockroom in just one basement, you understand? I didn't know Kendar from calamari."

"That is not Kendar Shall!" Nazara leaps to our feet.

The Modern Men dash forward, but Prichard grabs them by their metallic scruffs. Quicker than he should be. Inhumanly strong. His left shoulder slips free from his kimono, revealing some kind of skin rash or ugly burn.

"You would've killed me." He holds the machines at bay like snarling brass knuckles. "Would've destroyed anyone in your way because you *could* see Kendar Shall, I'm sure of that now. *Look closer.*"

His other voice rumbles, and my neck cranks itself down. My vision narrows on the contents of the cylinder.

"He ain't meltin' because that ain't water—not behind the glass. It's an ionizing chamber. Radiation for preservation, the way they used to do it. I was twelve years old when this boy came down. This ain't my work. It's a goddamned Hail Mary, chucked from the old world to the new. I ain't even the one who caught the game-winner. Not really."

He allows our gaze to drift back upward, meeting his own.

"Don't you see?" Prichard squeezes the Modern Men a bit too tightly. Their snarling faces droop as they shrink submissively to his ankles. "It was you who showed me." He searches my eyes for Nazara's recognition. "The soul is imaginary in human beings. Religious fluff to distract from our impermanence. But in your species, it is material." He points a firm finger at his dark collider, which seems to groan and darken at its mentioning. "Your identities can travel. On radiation scatter. On photonic emission. I have seen the code of your subconscious, and it is beautiful."

I watch the swirling dark collider, reflecting brightly in his eyes—all the prison prisms, all the chromium wires, feeding directly into his largest Spider. "You're digitizing them," I realize aloud, studying that sickly discoloration on his neck—that strange burn, spreading down to his left shoulder. "The implants. They were alive."

"They were life stuff." He rubs his fingers together. "Consciousness extracted, decoded, purified." He produces a marble of light just like the one he gifted to the quiet girl. No traces of cobalt in its swirl, a totally white sphere of dancing smoke. "I may have broken a few eggs—every creator is guilty of that—but my eyes are open now, and it's contagious. The people of Earth will not be blinded by the whims of evolution. *We* will be the freest world, united by this." He squeezes the marble. "An entire planet, synchronized in mind, body, and purpose. No quarter given to invaders, no opportunity for betrayal. In the galactic tomes of history, it will be said that innovation was the only soul which Homo sapiens required." Prichard raises his arms in dramatic finality, as though at any moment, the entire room of prisoners might erupt in rapturous applause.

But only one answers the call. A single voice back near the entrance. Hard to make out at first. A sound like choking or painful sneezes, muffled by the glass above Yono's cell. Then an unrestrained cackle. A contemptuous laugh, perfected by teenaged bullies across millennia. He shouts, "Yam cereba nis dereta!"

A skinny voice giggles from the north. I feel her heart turn over with new hope. I see her face and know her name. Sumella. She presses slender hands against the glass between them all.

Near Yono, I see Kono, watching his unbridled son, pride and fear excited together, as other voices chuckle, too. Dim chortles here and there. Their best cynical participation.

And there is Poody at my feet, eyes wide at Yono's obscenity, as though it nudged him from his dreams. Guilty joy on his sweet face. But he must *sleep*. He must not see what follows this collision of incompatible designs.

"The hell was that?" Prichard demands. "What'd he say?"

"Doesn't really translate." I keep my eyes down, watching the kid just like Nazara Thume used to. Near or far, it made no difference to her eyes. "Kinda like that old poem you're so hung up on." I laugh almost as derisively as Yono.

Prichard clenches his fists, and I know I have him, hooked and sunk this time.

"It rhymes if you sing it right, if you know how to hear it. That's your biggest problem, isn't it? Listening." I look up slowly, realizing what an embarrassment he is.

Prichard winces, clearly fighting the urge to grab his discolored shoulder. He grits his teeth and twists his head, turning the room in my mind again. "*Tell me,*" the dark words come, two voices heard together, one much older than his own. I can't tell if I hit the ground or it rushes to meet me, but I'm on our ass again. "*Tell me this great message that she refuses to speak clearly,*" Prichard spits as he steps closer, standing over us. "*Tell me the truth!*"

"It wasn't for you!" I watch the uncertainty take his face. I drink it up. "All this shit. Your whole manifest destiny," I laugh again, looking around at the vast and sterilized room, "it's based on a lullaby you overheard. Not meant for you. For him." I tap the glass above the kid. "And him." I nod to the remains of Kendar Shall. "Congrats on doing your homework—one shiny gold star for that—but it's a goddamn bedtime story. And you missed the moral by a fuckin' lightyear."

No snickers come this time. Not even from Yono. An unnerving silence sweeps the room from east to west, leaving me with the itchiest instinct to glance behind me—to check the exit. But Prichard's eyes have taken on their rarest shape. I see damage. I see that galactic loneliness, spilling out quicker than he can catch it.

He spins away. Staggers back between the apes. Musses his hair with a psychotic, grieving energy. I feel short of breath just watching him. I feel an emptiness like the coldest distant void.

"Goddamn you, Emmett!" His voice is wet with slobber. His eyes are dumping water like his family was just destroyed. "You still think this is all just happenin', don'tcha?" He paces back and forth, side to side, touching his face with manic hands. "You think I just bumped into you on that tarmac, after you just happened to get promoted, after you just happened to be the only survivor of Generation One? You think this sweet fuckin' fairy tale you've been livin' is just one big happy sunshine coincidence? Really? *You think I don't know where the fuck you're from?!*"

That dark voice commands our legs to spasm, kicking me and Nazara backward with jarring force, sending us tumbling end over end across the floor. As we tumble, I swear I see something. A single spark of blue starlight about ten meters back, above Yono's cell.

"Alright," Prichard huffs exhaustedly. "My fault again." He grips the fold of his kimono. Shrugs it all the way down to his left elbow, revealing more discolored skin. "Here I am expectin' a sixth-grade dropout to read between the lines." He unveils an unusually vascular bicep. One firm pectoral. Bulging, leathery abdominals all along his left side. "Well, here's a lesson you can't miss." He turns his back to us, shrugging his right shoulder naked, too.

And I finally see it. His new implant. So much more powerful than the others. So much more authentic. Because there is no Spider. Nothing mechanical whatsoever. Just one long line of surgical stitches from the base of his skull down to the ass of his kimono. On reflex, I touch our back. That slice the chromium wiring gave us. That streamlined alien spine, embedded in the suit.

"*Yes,*" his dark voice growls, seeing the direction of our thoughts. "*That's why they all went mad. The other thirty-one.*" An irradiating ripple passes through us, from my scalp down to our heels, as though our anatomy has just been catalogued for later use. "*They all got soulless copies of that she-devil's final state. Her blinding rage.*"

I see flashes of Anja Hallheim, cackling like she's possessed, eyeless sockets sobbing blood.

"*All but you.*" Prichard turns to face me. His pupils are dilated for a moment. His teeth are clenched in horrid strain—until he blinks. He manages to exhale, relaxing his humanity back into view.

"You got the real deal, cowboy. The original nerves and spine of Nazara Thume are just beneath those scales. Because I know you." He approaches me with pleading palms and streaming cheeks. "I know what it's like to be born in the fuckin' dirt. To have nothin' gifted. Have nobody but yourself, your own goddamn grit." He squeezes his fists so tightly he draws blood, oozing between his sickly fingers. "Back in that old jeep, on the way to Cooks, you said any man who could count his sins would never be a match for you. Well, alright then. No men at all." He extends a veiny hand, wet and red enough for an oath. "Just two Old Dallas boys, finally going the same direction."

His offer hangs there for me. No compulsion. No psychic gravity pulling me to my feet. Just this sincerest version of Calvin Prichard, pleading for the kinship he's designed.

"It's loneliest," I mutter back.

"What?" He cocks his head closer, eager to hear my answer.

"That old poem. The part you missed." I watch his writhing, discolored hand. I hear his nascent second voice, *whispering* harshly from the gaps. "It isn't *freest* worlds, not literally. It means loneliest. Their eyes are empty because—"

Our eyes connect. His bright blue-greens write a petition, begging me to stop it there, to just take his fuckin' hand and—

"Because without the highway, you can only see yourself."

His eyebrows twitch with understanding, with unanticipated regret. He's still looking at me, but his focus is slowly fading, slipping away. I feel weightless watching him, falling at an eerie speed while his offered hand slackens to his hip.

Quietly, discreetly, I pull one knee toward our chest, preparing to—

"He didn't die in the pod." Prichard's chin stays low, his eyes now hard to see. "He was right here. Awake." He points at the warehouse floor in slow repetition, splattering his blood like modern art. "I tried. To explain. To make him see." Somehow, I miss Prichard's face as he turns to the dark collider. His entire head passes through an errant shadow as he strides to the center of the room. "But he wouldn't join me. Not by choice."

"Thought that wasn't your work." I slide a second foot beneath us. Get my good hand ready to spring us up. "Thought you were just a kid when Kendar came down."

Prichard chuckles absently. Then pauses. "Are you serious?" He turns to face me, but the giant Spider collider churns even brighter, masking his features in silhouette. "Son of a bitch!" He laughs louder, sighing, shaking his head. "I was wrong about you, cowboy. You really are just another meatball, *after all.*"

As the dark voice rumbles, Prichard steps forward, exiting his shadow like parting smoke. His left eye has lost its human green, painted over with an electric zeal, that intergalactic husky blue. The skin around it has darkened rapidly, leathering outward with wisdom wrinkles. The hair above it is going silver at the root, and a bald face flashes. Just one flicker of an elderly man in a contorted scream. A tortured face I've seen before.

"Protocol one." As Prichard walks back to his chimeric rug, both Modern Men rise to their feet, already snarling, staring hungrily in my direction.

"Oh, Jesus." My eyes track Prichard's transplanted spine, finally realizing which pod he's talking about, flashing me back to that plummeting dream with Tysha and old Mantz. "Oh, you sick fuck."

A few stricken *gasps* bounce around inside my head. The eldest voices beneath the floor. The brightest few who can hear my thoughts, who can parse Nazara's knowing silence. She knew all along who Prichard was speaking to. That mysterious ghost over his left shoulder.

And here comes another. One bright blue spark only I can see. One cobalt inferno, finally rushing up behind me in total silence and deafening rage.

"Engage at will." Before Prichard finishes the command, his simulant apes are at top speed. Their black diamond fangs are flared for shredding. Their fingernails have popped, revealing serrated tungsten claws. And their heads are spinning—one off to my left, the other to my right, clunking and rolling across the warehouse floor. Sparks are spitting from their necks as their decapitated bodies drag deep scratches in the prism glass, crossing each other before they come to a stop on either side of my shielding hands, never making a sound.

A silent sword tip puckers into view as though cutting itself free from a pocket universe. A pristine blade of white palladium casts mirrored twinkles across the room, forcing my eyes to blink and squint. But I don't dare to look away. Never again.

A parade of blue fireballs ripples up the spine of her severely damaged duster coat, still swaying from the speed of her approach. Her black-blue-silver hair seems to swim in a gentler gravity of its own. I see a galactic mermaid, brighter than she's ever been, enhanced by that bursting star tomb or something else, something causing her hand to tremble as she levels her new blade on Calvin Prichard's spinal scars—on the stolen bones of her late master, Kible Thexx.

"*Par ya Lum sakar.*" Her telepathic voice is strangled with regret. Her teeth are gritted against each other when she whispers her vow to me alone: "*A silence to match his darkness.*"

Prichard turns just a little too slow, just a couple heartbeats too nonchalant, only further exposing his gruesome neck.

And the brightstar soars—dashing, leaping, spinning, a pulsar ballerina, before she brings her hatred down. A diagonal slash to behead the coward and freeze that fear on his face forever.

14.09

Hot air ejects from Prichard's mouth. One sharp gust like evacuating life. His eyes are stretched in unplanned pain, stupefied by this violence so far outside of his designs.

But he isn't killed. He isn't even nicked by the brightstar's blade, which is already clattering across the warehouse floor, followed by Tysha, staggering backward, holding her wrist, grimacing as though she's just slashed an invisible wall, some sort of repulsive field or—

"Spike?" Prichard asks, in disbelief, looking down at something on the floor. He kneels, as though in a trance, lifting a small graphene sphere between his fingers. He turns it, revealing a deep anti-gravity dent and exit rupture, studying the damage with heterochromatic eyes, one Luminaran and electric, the other human, blue and green. He doesn't react to Tysha as she scampers away to collect her sword.

He merely reaches down, fishing through his undone kimono, finding that metallic epaulette that's sewn into the right shoulder of all his shirts—his personal sim's landing station. He rips that matching graphene disc from the kimono's silk, sets it on the floor, carefully sets Spike directly in the center, and is rewarded with that familiar high chime.

Tysha halts her next advance, uncertain of the sound, calculating what manner of trap this could be, while Prichard leans closer, his human eye now optimistic, now—

The simulant chimes again, slow, fading away, deepening to a low and powerless hum. Then a pop of static. A string of smoke drifts up from its tiny corpse into Prichard's quiet face.

He kneels there for a while, eyes down and shoulders hunched. I feel nothing. Even Kible Thexx's stolen power seems to vanish from detection, to darken completely, to become something else. Tysha senses it, too. She takes a cautious step forward—

"A stowaway?" Prichard asks without looking up. "On the hovercruiser?"

Tysha stays where she is, holding her glittering blade between them. She opens her mouth to—

"No!" Prichard twitches sharply. "She woulda freed 'em weeks ago, woulda been caught on the cargo cameras. That's stupid—stupid—stupid!" He shakes his head violently, smacking the floor with an open palm, rubbing his left shoulder like a shelter addict.

"She wasn't with them at all," he decides excitedly, looking down and around at the upturned faces in the floor. "Abandoned them. Saved herself? No. No! She wouldn't—couldn't—she must've been waiting. For *him*." Prichard turns slowly, showing me one human eye and something else—a sunken ruby hole now on the left, a cobalt blue iris, diffused through a tunnel of blood, sucking me in, stealing everything I am.

Robotically smooth, he turns that eye on Tysha. Studies her duster, noticing the scorched edges and blackened gashes—its new ghoulish, reaper aesthetic. "She was in the blast." He laughs in sick astonishment, dragging two hands through his sweaty hair.

Tysha twitches, and so does he, in haunting unison. His expression changes.

"No. Beneath it," he says with more confidence. He tilts his head, gazing directly into her bright eyes, no longer guessing at all. "Bluewater Lake. That's very clever." He grins. The Thexxian infection spreads more rapidly, devouring a few more centimeters of his face and neck, his bare chest. The ruby deepens, spreading to his human eye like invasive roots. "This morning, in Chicago, it was *you*." He takes a step forward, and Tysha retreats a step back, flicking her blade defensively. "Not in the crowd. Already aboard the hovercopter." He smiles proudly this time. "Oh, my child. Look how bright you have become."

"Stay back." She slashes the air between them. Her image flickers. The sound of her footsteps fades in and out. "You—you are a corruption!" She shakes her head, trying to push him from her mind, trying to vanish from his eyes.

But he keeps coming. One foot in front of the other, that sick skin change spreading past his nipples now. His new pigment is only a shade darker than her own, but it throbs with steroidal veins and clenching muscles, likely accelerated by intravenous nanos. A biohybrid of his boldest gunsuits, G-1 and G-4.

"If you found that sword in an ARID warehouse, it was designed to kill your kin," he hisses through gritted teeth. "Put it down, my child. Put it *down.*" That ruby glow shines harsher. The corrupted voice of Kible Thexx blends with Prichard's in monstrous harmony.

Tysha's eyes go dim. Her fingers throw themselves open, releasing the sword. She drops to a knee, catching the hilt in her opposite hand. But she freezes there, forcibly halted in genuflection.

Prichard strides fearlessly into her range, leveling the belt of his kimono to her quivering cheek. He runs his hand through her dimming hair, watching the twinkling dots of cobalt vanish like dying stars. The strands go depthless and black between his fingers, even losing their reflective silver streaks. The only thing glistening on her face is a stream of tears, touching the corner of her mouth.

"Get away from her, you—!"

Prichard points his finger at me like a pistol, and my teeth clap sharply together. He turns one of his bloodshot eyes in my direction, and I see that loneliness I diagnosed.

"You know why I made that suit, cowboy? You know why I tried so fuckin' hard to bring Nazara's voice back from the dead?" His neck twitches like a mechanical owl, listening closely, waiting tauntingly for my reply while he grinds my jaws together. "Yeah. Me neither."

He drops the hammer on his finger gun, and we collapse, flat on our back, head lulling limply to the side. I stare at the dark collider, and our symbiotic body tingles like bloodless limbs. I feel Nazara's rippling scales harden to stillness, rapidly draining of their many colors as the entire suit obeys Prichard's suicide command.

"*You have struggled against your own end,*" he says to our connected minds, to all the travelers in the room and a few distant others I hadn't noticed. Harnessing the corrupted gifts of Kible Thexx, he broadcasts, "*My new world matches your bright prophecies and exceeds them. Accelerates the timeline of our connected space by a thousand generations.*"

The skin change quickens past his elbows, swallowing his forearms. He grips Tysha's head like a melon to be crushed, and she staggers further. The palladium sword tip pierces deeper into the cell below, tangling in the chromium wire, and Prichard massages the base of her skull with his thick fingers. My last curse is to feel it all. Her feverish skin on my own face. Her sweat-soaked hair against my scalp. I feel Prichard's hands at the ends of my wrists, where I am stroking and being stroked.

"*You are unwitting kinks in our shared dream.*" His vice grip tightens, pressing into the soft spot behind her cerebellum. "*But I can correct you.*" He presses deeper. Her inner heat delights his fingertips with a masochistic burn. "*I can remove your dissonant urges and synchronize the planet Earth.*"

Tysha spasms wildly in my direction, but he keeps his hold. He squeezes, and I feel her skull failing between my fingers, behind my own brain. I'm finished. I can only stare at the dark collider until even my eye sockets lose their dexterity, until my vision rolls to the empty prism beneath me. I'm a corpse. A calcium rack, unplugged at last.

"*You are wrong.*"

I flinch internally. My earthly vision blackens, but my mind's eyes flash widely open. I look around at my own headspace, my own spotlight, almost completely gone.

Then she rises. Up from the endless gaps, those brown-golden curls come into view. I see a beauty that isn't fair, an alien sculpture, humiliating the limits of the human species. She ascends until her gaze comes level with mine. Then she approaches.

Every step she takes creates a platform of solid light, building a footpath in my direction until we're standing face to face. I see her eyes, glimmering in vivid parity with her hair. Her gift is alive in her expression. A clairvoyant certainty. But she isn't analyzing the fundamental forces of the Earth. It's almost as if she—

"I am looking at you, Emmett Hayes." Her voice is too much for me. Her actual voice, after all these years. "I am *seeing* you." Nazara smiles softly, urging me to understand.

"Mama," I start without thinking. "I-I'm sorry. I mean . . ." I trail off without really knowing where I was going, without any damn idea where to begin.

But she lifts my chin with two of her fingers, guiding my eyes back up to hers. "I am seeing you, Emmett Hayes. Are you seeing me?"

I start to tell her yes, to scream it as loud as I can.

But her eyes insist that I look deeper. They draw me in, expanding high and wide, consuming my perspective with her own. I see my spotlight mirrored back. But I've been replaced. I see my reflection from the triple-pane window—my first hallucination on the shuttle down to Earth. He can't be me. His eyes are as limitless as hers.

"His eyes are yours." Nazara twists the mirror, revealing she and I together, overlapped. "My eyes have not shined for eight years and more. I am an echo—the afterimage of a dim woman who died in rage."

"You're not!" I shout louder than I intended, cracking the liminal mirror down its center. "Didn't you see it? The fuckin' dryland, the way I lived before all of this. I was nothing without you. I was—"

"You have it reversed," she interrupts, showing no uncertainty in her eyes. She strokes my cheek, borrowing a tear I hadn't noticed, displaying it as evidence. "You see everything in everyone except yourself. You receive. But a scatterer must also give."

She lifts the tear. Touches it to her lips. I taste what she does. A bitter meekness. An overwhelming sour fear. The spicy sting of inadequate strength in trying times. And an aftertaste. A sweetness like discernment, like forgiveness for his foes. It tastes like my itches feel. Another approach to the empathic gift. A second scatterer along the highway of endless light. But my access is half of hers. One way traffic. A rising pressure. A painful pinch behind my eye.

"*Now you've seen it,*" Nazara whispers in warm agreement, as though her peace has finally come. "*Every gift can be a curse,*" her ghost insists, closing the gap between us, kissing the center of my forehead. "*But we can only dim ourselves.*"

Before I can argue, she shoots off. A golden particle. A twinkling speck of a brighter soul, blasting off into eternity. Her entire footpath is left behind. Eight shimmering platforms to complete her turning, to grant me all she was and couldn't be. One step forward for every year we survived together. My cosmic mother's dying wish.

To show the world what I can see.

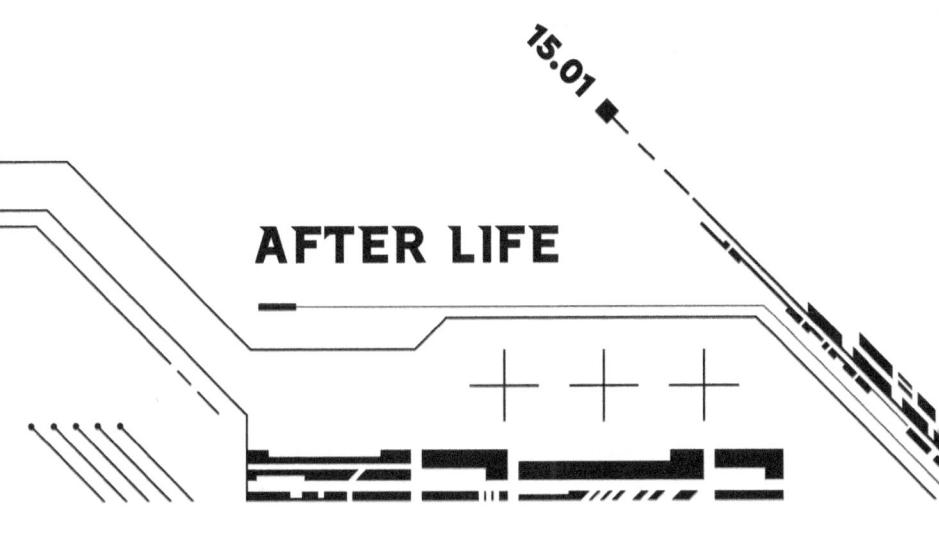

AFTER LIFE

Tysha is as dim as she's ever been. Dimmer than the kennel days. Returned to helplessness by manly, grasping hands.

Calvin Prichard squeezes tighter. He tests the integrity of Tysha's skull, but she has no power to numb the pain. Too shrouded now. Too heartbroken to look away from Emmett Hayes. He's lying there just like he did back in the cave. A limp husk without his skinsuit's life support. A bodiless mind, this time without a chance of coming back.

Calvin Prichard presses deeper. A river of blood traces down her neck, forking at her shoulders, warming her spine. She keeps watching Emmett Hayes. Keeps his vow for him, refusing to look away from his vegetative eyes. Not much longer anyhow. His suit has stiffened. The many colors have faded to one sickly, pallid gray, drying crustily like fresh clay left in the sun. The thing is dead. The ghost of Nazara Thume has left this world.

Calvin Prichard's fingernails scrape against bone. Tysha hears a sound behind her ears like hot water pouring over ice, like a herring chick escaping its egg, but she keeps watching

Emmett Hayes. His eyes are falling now, turning vacantly to the floor. They seem to flash. Several rapid flickers, almost like old Mantz entering a dive. Wishful thinking on Tysha's part. He doesn't move. If he is breathing, she sees no sign of it at all.

Calvin Prichard readjusts his grip, pulling her face against his thigh. He leans forward, surveying his progress, deciding the best entry to her brains. Tysha's trembling sword hand finally slips, knocking her knuckles against the floor. She keeps watching Emmett Hayes, seeing their limp expressions begin to match, seeing blurred flashes of fallen friends: Sila, Jerill, and Goroon. At least they weren't taken in this way, recycled into a machine, deprived of final rest. At least they went quickly and . . . and they . . .

Calvin Prichard stops. His crippling power slowly withdraws like passing clouds. He shifts his feet, retreating his hot breath from her sticky, bloodied neck. "Hey. Hey, stop it there!"

He releases Tysha's head, and she ragdolls away. Her cheekbone bashes against the floor, and one arm is pinned beneath her weight. Prichard glances down at her, as he might a handful of spilled screws, then quickly turns his attention back to the approaching threat.

Footsteps. Steady and deliberate. Harsh. A rhythmic rapping of fortified steel against the glass. Another one of those robotic apes, Tysha thinks at first. But their feet were leather padded, designed for stealth. There is a strange disharmony in this approaching thing. One of the legs sounds twice as heavy. An echoing thud, a subtle hiss of pressurized joints. The other is light. A delicate stride, almost sounding human. Almost sounding like—

"Taiko, I said *STOP!*" His last word is twinned again, a

crashing psychic command in the tangled voice of Calvin Prichard and Kible Thexx. The intruding footsteps halt immediately, and Tysha sees who they belong to.

That demon from the forest. The mindless thing she left for dead—and left again mere moments ago in the outer hall. Now fully assembled. Fully mechanical on its right side, on its left foot. Roboticized with polished metals very much like those mechanical apes. And humanized. The woman thing is shorter than Tysha remembers. Far younger than she'd thought. It appears to have walked here straight through glass and other hazards, cutting itself badly above the left breast and along the meat of its left thigh. Its nether regions are unblushingly exposed, covered only by thin sheets of painted blood. Most alarmingly, it is standing directly over Emmett—

"Hayes?" the cyborg asks, looking down at him with one foggy human eye and one replacement—one striking yellow iris that Tysha has faced before, pinpricked in the center, like the avian gazes among the arsenal of Cuva Khan. "Hayes?" the naked creature checks again, cocking its head blindly in his direction, speaking with numb lips and useless ears.

"*Taiko,*" Prichard's twisted psychic mind insists. "*Return to the medbay, Taiko.*"

That sends its sightless eyes in his direction. Almost. Its eyeline is too low, scanning horizontally near his ankles, dragging its dead perspective across the warehouse floor, stopping eerily on Tysha.

"*TAIKO,*" Calvin Thexx demands this time. "*RETURN TO THE MEDBAY NOW!*" The blending voices are like serrated thunder. A rolling heat like dying darkworlds, colliding across endless time and—

"Hayes," the young creature starts again, not seeming to

register Prichard at all, still searching uncertainly in Tysha's direction. "Hayes said to—"

They both twitch sharply there—first Calvin Prichard, with amazement and alarm, then the demon he called Taiko, with satisfaction and surprise. It smiles, not lingering on Tysha's face but the space around her. Its human eye tracks something incorporeal, some unseen beauty in the air. When the young creature speaks again, its voice is clear:

"Hayes said to ask if he's still your prisoner."

Calvin Prichard is too stunned to understand. Too corrupted to see the hidden meaning land in Tysha's eyes as she looks back down to Emmett Hayes. A reminder like a cure.

"My prisoner?" Calvin Prichard sounds injured by the question. He exhales dejectedly, glancing down at the sergeant's body. "No, honey. No way." He moves slowly, remorsefully in the Taiko creature's direction, running his fingers along the hilt of the inverted palladium sword. "He's my guest here, same as you. He's part of this family."

Tysha hears a smooth and pleasing sound, a long high note like the fingered rim of a water glass. But sharper. Beneath the floor.

Calvin Prichard continues forward, moving gingerly on his bare feet, waving one hand side-to-side to test the pitiful creature's blindness. "Is Sergeant Hayes in there with you? Right now?"

Behind him, Tysha wiggles her big toes, one knuckle at a time. She keeps her eyes on Emmett Hayes, and her free arm begins to shiver across the floor. Her sword hand trembles open, fighting through the psychic damage, reaching blindly for her weapon. It isn't there.

Thin pillars of reflected light dance across the Taiko woman's eyes as Calvin Prichard raises the sword from his left hip. His fully transformed hand makes the blade look almost weightless, rising high, perfectly vertical above his shoulder—a shimmering lightning rod, mirroring the sterilized blaze of his giant machine.

"Are you there?" the poor young creature asks. "Can you really hear me?" Her blind eyes are full of tentative hope, still gazing vaguely in Tysha's direction.

"Yeah, honey." Calvin Prichard sounds sympathetic, even tender, seeing no reaction on her face. "I can hear ya just fine."

Tysha keeps her eyes on Emmett Hayes, and everything drops. She falls past her people in the floor. Slips right through the Earth, falling without resistance, without wind, surrounded by endless beams of light but touching none of it. She is lost to the gaps. The hurtling gravity, the dividing shadow. And there he is. Falling faster, further down, looking up. Shouting now. Reaching now. Needing her now. The brightstar reaches for Emmett Hayes.

And Calvin Prichard brings his violence down. A cutting, booming sound like a cracking whip. Harsh reflections, blinding speed. A mirrored blaze inside the warehouse. Scattered heat.

Only Calvin Prichard sees his work. More modern art as far as the entrance. On the walls. On his kimono. A gory painting to match his eyes. The Taiko woman, sprayed like poultry through a turbine.

15.02

It has taken eleven days for Taiko's world to be deleted. A degradation of sensations, each more precious than the last. She's been numb for ninety hours. Blind for forty-two. Deaf for ten.

Those are her best guesses. Without the nanos, without her suit, even time is just a fading concept now.

In a way, she is relieved. Freed from the helpless observation. No longer a spectator to her own hands, to the crunching sounds that they created. No longer waiting for a maintenance tech to come and hose the stench away—a hot odor like corroded batteries. A stickiness that seemed to seep beneath her skin. She tried to scream so many times. Shouted and wept behind her eyes, begged her own body to drop and die. All wasted energy, of course.

They never heard her. They could barely stomach the sight of her. Always flinching away, looking down to the dirt or up to the sky. Always playing with their hands, their straps, their boots. All except for Cyrus Uba.

Only the captain's mismatched eyes could endure her lifeless gaze.

She guessed that Uba was like herself. A reanimated cadaver on autopilot. Another failed experiment. Then she heard his thunderous voice. His words were huge. His natural eye was alive with patriotic hope. And deep regret.

She hated him for that.

In every quiet look, she could see his self-reproach. He blamed himself for what she was. Refused to let her die alone. Sacrificed his giant life for her monstrosity. She would never forgive him for it, never understand that stupid trade.

Not until she battled Emmett Hayes.

In every move the sergeant made, she saw something even harder to explain. Fear, she guessed at first. A pragmatic panic after all that she had done. Either way, she was relieved to see him run. She hoped he would escape. Prayed his blood and bones would never be added to her stench. Prayed. But never believed.

Her mind inside the hive was like the simulant towers she used to build. Petabytes of conscious numbers in endless evaluation. Origins of digital species in every software instant. Every hour, an entire universe burned and dissolved back down to entropic black. To the unit Zero X, she was a bolt of deadly lightning, a blur of instant death. For Taiko, every step was one of ten billion analyzed choices. An endless data slog to dismantle the walls of time. Any target sighted was already dead, simulated forward and countermeasured in the most efficient way. But there was a foundational error in the hive's computation tree that day—the same flawed assessment Taiko made—a misappraisal of the fear in Emmett Hayes.

That's how it ended. The nanomechanical swarm consumed her for several relative eternities, then, in an instant, it was gone. She was lying in a crater, and the pain was excruciating. The world's confusions had returned. She was human, and she was dying. She was alive in time again. She couldn't make sense of all the input, of how rapidly it was coming, slipping right by her, unanalyzed. But there he was.

The sergeant was looking down at her with that same terrified expression. Still perfectly logical, she thought. He was bleeding. He was wounded everywhere. But he wasn't tending to his injuries. He wasn't running anymore. His only fear was that he couldn't save her life.

Why? she asked him. *Why?!* she shouted just like she'd tried so many times.

And it finally happened. The sergeant's name escaped her lips. She spoke! And tried again. Tried to apologize, tried to warn him of Prichard's plans, but the sergeant's name kept hissing out. Just his name. His maddening, beautiful name.

And Taiko recalled the human eye of Cyrus Uba. His massive hope. His stupid trade.

She counted ten days and fourteen hours from that moment to this morning. After that, there wasn't much to measure with. She was less than a simulant tower, just a floating mind in empty black. But she kept calling just in case. Kept repeating the sergeant's name. She hoped to see him one last time before the hive could be reinstated, before Calvin Prichard could get his teeth in her again. She prayed for the fearful eyes of Emmett Hayes. She believed.

But she never saw those eyes again.

When the sergeant finally found her, he arrived with just a voice.

15.03

The sound barrier erupts. A slice of wind shoots past his knuckles. Three prism cells are pelted with flying bone. One of them shatters, showering its screaming captive in falling glass. Taiko's graphene leg clatters across the floor. The matching arm flies twice as far, severed in two, disappearing down the medical hall. The left foot rides a cyclone of flesh and blood, terminating against the entry wall like a stormy wave against a cliff. Calvin remains hunched forward in the downpour of her gore. Speechless. Stupefied by his own brilliance.

He manages to draw himself back, standing upright, raising the ARID prototype to his eyes. He checks the blade from tip to hilt, seeing no imperfections, no nicks or burns of any kind. Of course, the true edge cannot be seen. It has been sharpened experimentally, painstakingly, to a subatomic width. A quantum katana. An atom splitter meant for Taiko after her rehabilitation. But now it seems that dog won't hunt.

He turns away from her remains, looking carefully at himself. This power he's achieved is beyond all best-case estimations. A perfect hybrid of meat and machine. A full spinal transplant and neurological graft. Billions of nanosims injected to stimulate rapid tissue growth. A programmable evolution with his own body as the multiverse. To say it short and sweetly, this pie is baked and windowed, pestered by a few errant flies, but not for long.

He minds his speed this time, turning the hilt carefully in his hand, bending forward at the waist. He aligns the katana's tip with the nape of the sergeant's neck, then he traces down, stopping directly between the shoulder blades. No response from either of them, Nazara Thume or Emmett Hayes. That's good. He'd rather they didn't suffer.

The blade passes through them both with relative ease. A few dried scales pop loose, tinkling to the warehouse floor. A flood of blood and spinal fluid oozes over the back of the suit, and a larger gush rains from the sergeant's chest where the blade tip reemerges.

An agonized groan stops Calvin there. He checks the sergeant's eyes, still seeing no reaction, no sign of life. But the sound of anguish comes again. He turns sharply, following it, seeing the other one lying where he left her. The female. But not exactly how he left her. Her hand is rising, reaching in his direction. Her eyes are beginning to shine.

"*Stop.*"

She obeys. Or rather, her systems do. A tighter muscle contraction than she could execute intentionally. An electrical freeze of her peripheral nerves, halting all sensory signals to her brain. From her perspective, Calvin doesn't straighten himself. He doesn't pull the katana from the sergeant's back or calmly stroll to her outstretched hand. He doesn't carefully slide the blade between her metacarpals, spiking her palm to the warehouse floor. He doesn't even speak again. "*Breathe.*"

The female shrieks, gasps, darts her eyes to her skewered hand, sees Calvin now hovering over her. From her perspective, it all happened instantly. Still, she struggles. Tries to free her other arm from beneath her hips. Her elbow slides two inches before she seizes again, spasming hideously.

Extraordinary. No wonder she was able to sneak this far into the compound. The wave function that Calvin is emitting now beats any known metric of reacher power. If that beast-master in the woods was a Z-1, then Calvin is off the charts, a new tier all to himself. To resist his control even as slightly as she is here, well, that demands much further study.

He kneels beside the trembling female, reexamining her natural pigments. He'd assumed she was like the two young males, genetically restored by that particle burst in the Taiga. It wasn't visible from the surface, but it fried half his sensors aboard the hovercruiser—a photonic shower of conscious code unlike any he'd ever seen. It reminded him of Chicago. But it doesn't explain this female. It couldn't. He sees that now.

He cradles her chin like a whiskey tumbler and studies her cobalt eyes. Dazzling. Both veiled by her wavy, jet-black mane. Even as mussed and twitchy as she's become, he can see what the sergeant saw in her. A feral mystique that would've weakened Calvin, too, at a younger age. He very much doubts that she was bald eleven days ago. Her skin seems healthier as well. No vitiligo patches like those younger males still have beneath their clothes. She is something else entirely.

My Earth, the whispered answer comes. *My silent one.*

Calvin feels that awful heat at the top of his spine, that hot pressure, throbbing along his left shoulder. He starts to ask Spike for a fresh nano injection, then he remembers Spike is gone. He turns to the husks of his headless Modern Men. They'll lose a few hours—probably for the best—but their nightly backups are in the data spire, a few terabytes at most. He can reload them once repaired, even make improvements. But Spike's memories were localized to his sphere. Qubit storage, too costly to duplicate. Reacher tech. Spike is gone.

"*Follow.*" Calvin yanks the katana from the female's hand, allowing her to stand and walk behind him. He doesn't look back, doesn't need to. He can see her musculoskeletal map behind his eyes, clear as any Ret-tag direct projection. She's fighting, of course. Still resisting his manufactured reach. Impossible, he'd presumed—another careless mistake. He must uncover what she is.

My assigned, the ancient whisper comes. *My found child.*

Calvin grimaces, ignoring the ghostly influence, biting back the searing pain. That particle burst. What could've caused it in such a wild place? Why did it change them? He ponders that and more, standing with the female on his favorite rug, waiting for the hoverlift to automatically engage. Then he remembers Spike is gone.

Grudgingly, he kneels, prodding around the orangutan's ass, searching for the platform's center. He gets impatient. Rips a hole in the cowhide and scrounges beneath it. Punches the manual override with his thumb. The hoverlift rises, quick and direct, totally lacking Spike's finesse. They are thrust up through the floor of his control room, sealing the hatch beneath their feet. None of the panel lights kick on. The alchemic glass is still opaque, leaving the room nearly pitch-black. Calvin grumbles. He starts toward the control panel then remembers the manual switches are on the rear wall behind him. He turns—

And the female is eye-to-eye with him, irises flickering, nostrils flaring, bloody hands trembling toward his neck.

"*Back!*"

She obeys his command, sneering as she goes.

"*Sit.*"

She does that, too, down on the floor without lowering her hands. Magnificent strength in her tight legs. Uncommon balance.

My successor, the implant threatens. *My champion.*

"Shut up." Calvin shakes his head, keeping his eyes on the female as he steps around her to the manual switches. He bangs his knee on the spire terminal, cussing unintelligibly in the dark, but his hands find the large switch levers and he cranks the first one up.

The alchemic glass blinks from its steel form to full transparency, flooding the room with warehouse light. Calvin squints his eyes, avoiding the many harsh reflections in the modern, pristine space. The scattering beams remind him of the skies over O'Hare, that great white flash before The Storm.

He cranks the second switch, and the control room powers out of standby. The spire terminal glows awake, displaying the Dallas Dynamics logo on its wide, curved screen. He steps in front of it, pulling his articulating desk from the wall. It unfolds, wrapping around him in a semicircle, revealing his custom digital board. An ergonomic mouse sits on his right, sharing a rubber pad with his bone conduction headphones. He picks those up and has them halfway over his ears before he pauses, not quite remembering what he was doing. He looks at the female, still sitting there, twitching with an itch to take that sword and give it back to him a dozen times. He looks down at the weapon, held somewhat loosely in his throbbing, transformed hand. The searing heat has reached his wrists.

Spike chimes twice in Calvin's ear. He turns excitedly to listen, expecting his implant to decrypt the high-pitched strings, but nothing happens. There were no strings. It was just the sound of the spire terminal booting up. The Dynamics logo pulses on its screen, awaiting voice recognition. He remembers Spike is gone.

"Malcolm Calvin Prichard." Before he finishes speaking, the security screen melts away, revealing his private feed. Direct messages, business mail, interactive blueprints, expandable code in progress. His market watchlist threads the lower third—a stream of corporations, red and green. He doesn't own any public assets, of course. Never has. He only gambles on himself.

"Tissue table. Configuration two. Add injection." At his command, a large modular cube rises from the floor behind him. It's perfectly smooth on all its sides, dripping with decontamination foam. The top of it blooms open, unfolding into a polished examination table, complete with scalpels, calipers, forceps, and a handheld bone saw. A small tray extends from the face of the cube, revealing a pre-loaded electric syringe. It swims with his prescription, billions of medsims cascading the inner glass like a creamy Irish draught. It reminds him of the initial shower of debris. He took cover behind an information pillar at O'Hare, moving casually, calmly, hoping not to rouse suspicion. Nobody was watching him back then; he could still vanish in a crowd. Unfortunately, that left him free to see their faces, their clueless, naive mouths, gaping up at the shrapnel cloud.

The terminal chimes twice, but Calvin doesn't check the screen. He's looking down at his empty, transformed hand, tingling with icy heat all the way to his fingertips. Empty? That doesn't seem right.

The terminal chimes twice, but he checks his other hand instead. His thumb is rolling over the trackball of his ergonomic mouse. His index finger is double-clicking. The feverish heat has spread there, too.

The terminal chimes twice, and he finally looks up to the screen. Sees open system folders. A clickable box to confirm or cancel a request. A bright red question, clarifying the command.

All Prism Cells: Elevate And Release?

He pushes away from the terminal. Kicks something with his heel. Sends it spinning across the floor. The palladium sword. Hypnotic reflections slash his eyes, dizzy his vision, twist his feet.

The female catches the weapon, one hand on the blade, the other on its hilt. She's still sitting with crossed legs, shoulders forward, chin down, but she isn't twitching anymore. She isn't struggling whatsoever. It's Calvin who can't seem to move. Can't seem to breathe or look away.

My hope, the unbidden answer comes. *Their solution.*

One last reflection in the blade. Two pairs of eyes, concentric and overlapping. The female's sight and someone else's. A young man without a face. A singular shadow, expanding like an endless standing mirror.

"Cowboy?" Calvin asks, seeing only himself, seeing himself, seeing himself. Spike chimes twice, and he turns to listen—

But the stewardess won't shut up. She's screaming like a wounded deer, lying in a bed of glass where the large airport window used to be. Or spinning, rather. Only her left arm and leg appear to be functioning after the shrapnel raked her face. Still leaves her better off than the hundreds of waiting bodies, shredded and dead, some still sitting with functioning laptops and handheld games on their lifeless knees. Calvin tried to warn them. Or rather, he thought about trying. Decided he couldn't risk those kinds of questions: *what was that light? Are we being attacked? How did you know?!* This is certainly more ideal. If the stewardess survives, he'll be a hero. If she dies in his arms, he can sell the trauma. Yeah, she looks pretty enough for that to play. He'll just slow the bleeding for now, and—it's not looking like anyone's going to stream this—so he'll need to leak a clip from one of these security cameras in a couple days. Too bad; Ret-tag footage would really kill two birds. But he's got the hovervacs scheduled to arrive on the South Side in thirty minutes, so that'll draw clicks. Face recognition is still in beta, but the sims are prioritizing youth and minority rescue. Should put Dallas Dynamics on all the shortlists: Planning and Response. Readiness Action. The commission report. That's the big one. He already has two drafts prepared. Either way, the collider reactants will carbon date to Luminara, he made sure of that. So, that should be, yeah, he reckons that'll just about do it.

Calvin wails just like he used to—that same desperate, puerile sound his Uncle Gage stomped out of him when he was five—and Chicago shoots up into the sky, stretching like endless strands of a lightspeed beam. Or maybe he's the one falling, plummeting down from his forced nightmare back to Earth.

He bangs his elbow on the modular cube, dragging half the instruments off the table. He spins downward, trying to brace himself with his hands, but they just noodle uselessly around his hips. He can't even close his eyes before the impact. Can't turn his head to spare his nose. It crunches flat against the control room floor. His right cornea gets a friction burn, and the bone saw bounces off his temple, gashing him badly above the hairline. The room falls silent.

He can hear himself breathing—constricted sucks and gusts of air. He's trying to look around, but his eyes are locked straight forward. His body won't move, but it isn't numb exactly. He can feel that heat everywhere now. He's being incinerated from the inside out. And somebody's coming.

Patient footsteps behind his head. Combat boots, drawing closer, echoing ominously in the sterile space. They stop at his bare feet, stepping over him, landing near his groin. He hears the calipers being handled on the table, being set down. He hears something lighter being lifted, something like a scalpel. He hears the boots turning back around, creasing at the toe. A bracing knee against his ribs. That lighter, sharper thing in his peripheral, lowering toward his neck. That shivering noise his molars made when he was under the covers in Corsicana, whenever Gage Prichard came home late, stinking of Gray & Turner.

But no scalpel cuts him. Instead, there's a tiny pinch where his neck and shoulder meet. The soothing hum of a brushless motor. The intravenous tickle of nanoscopic paste. When the humming stops, the female sets the empty electric syringe in front of his face so he can see his prescription clearly.

"It seems obvious now," she says, allowing her right hand to linger within view. Calvin sees it glitch like broken code, sees the stigmatic wound he gave her disappear. "The highest mind, the reddest hands." She lowers her voice, stretching the phrase like a painful memory. "The brightstar spoke these words before he left us in the cave. Now I see their truth."

Calvin feels her eyes hovering over his spinal scars. He feels the edge of her knee pressing his ribs against his lungs, flattening his sternum against the floor. Just a little bit further and she'll have him. He'll puncture and pop in a few vital places. It'll all be over. But she eases up. She rises, twisting away, walking in the direction of the steel-glass window.

The heat goes with her. His feet, his hands, the base of his skull, begin to cool to healthy degrees. He can move his eyes. He can roll his throbbing head enough to see her standing at the window, looking down at the warehouse. He can see the quantum katana, lying in the center of the control room where she left it.

"You have not been spared." She speaks without turning to face him. "We have given you a taste of what you gave us, but this is not the end. Your trials are just beginning."

"We?" Calvin asks, both incredulous and amused. He blinks his eyes at the steady rush of adrenaline, the new flush of nanos beneath his skin. He flexes his right hand, watching the transformation spread twice as quickly as before.

"Yes." She speaks with certainty, with regret. "Your shadow was a cavity I could not penetrate alone. A scatterer was needed. His gift has lit the gaps between our kinds."

"You mean the sergeant?" Calvin gets his hands beneath him. His knees. He crawls quietly on his bare toes, readjusting his angle to the sword, measuring its distance. "Those memories of Chicago—those *lies*," he hastily corrects. "That was his idea?"

The female makes a disappointed sound, though unsurprised. "No. That man is gone." She shakes her head slowly, thoughtfully. "Unless I do something very selfish."

"Explain that to me." Calvin leans against the modular cube, coiling his muscles, stealthily setting his feet.

"I cannot." She dips her chin, clenching her fists in front of her thighs. "There may be no living person who can."

"Of course," Calvin scoffs, watching the sword. The female. The sword. "Guess we better start asking the dead."

"Yes." There is no humor in her response. Her voice turns slightly in his direction, shifts much colder. "I fear we must."

Calvin stops. A stillness chills the air.

A rigid quiet like the calm before a storm.

The female quickly turns her shoulders—

But Calvin's faster, launching off the cube, denting its frame, rolling across the floor. By the time she turns from the window, he's already coming out of his maneuver, dragging his left hand across the katana, scooping it up.

No, he missed it. He scrambles back across the rug, keeping his better eye down, carefully snatching at the hilt, but he misses again. He abandons his bad depth perception, pawing madly at the weapon with both hands, but it suddenly shatters like broken sand.

He stares at its constituent grains: palladium dust, weapons-grade hickory, treated leather. With one healthy cornea, he watches the fine powders begin to rise and swirl of their own volition, reconstituting as something new.

He's seeing Chicago. A god's eye view. The way it was before The Storm. An entire city right there between his thumbs, alive and thriving in staggering detail. Cars, ships, and passing aircraft above hanging clouds. He can hear their voices, their individual stories, depending which direction he tilts his head. He leans closer, totally transfixed by the fidelity of their small lives, just as the eastern shore explodes at the speed of light.

No ball of flame, no mushroom cloud, just a massive flash and concussive force. A bomb without heat, without radiation burns. A blast like the Earth has never seen. It's perfect. His first dark collider, his proof of concept, reaching critical mass beneath Lake Michigan, sending incriminating shards of reacher salvage as far as Grand Rapids, presuming his calculations are correct.

"*Calculations?*" someone cries from the miniature city.

"*He did it on purpose!*" a young voice shouts, louder, closer.

"*¿Quién es ese? No puedo ver.*"

"Он врёт!" comes a voice from very far away. And deep inside him. And right behind him—

Calvin spins around to the spire terminal. A bright reflection squints his eyes, stings his brain. The palladium blade. It seems to be floating, until he sees the blue fireballs marching vertically behind it. The hilt is secured in a leather sheath, centered diagonally on the back of a duster coat. The female is at the terminal, patiently studying his custom board. With a knowing confidence, she presses an unmarked key.

That triggers the containment alarm, booming from every speaker in the room. The entire warehouse shudders beneath him, but Calvin can't peel his eyes from her. With that same technical familiarity—his familiarity—she raises her hand to the manual switches.

"*Stop!*" he commands the female, surprised to see her obey, relieved to see her alien ear turn receptively in his direction. "How long have you—what's happenin' to me?" he stammers, flinching sharply, expecting Uncle Gage to slap him stupid, to drag him out back and kick his guts in for being such a useless pussy.

"A silence to match your darkness." The female speaks with a wavering voice. "He has scattered himself so that you may listen, that you may learn." She turns slowly, unsteadily, finally allowing him to see the dank misery on her face. "Do not waste it." She pulls the heavy manual switch, and Calvin sinks through the floor.

His favorite rug flutters at its edges, curling around his knees. The hoverlift twists through the air, descending on icy jets, turning him to face the warehouse prison—a prison now rising to meet him. All thirty-six hundred prism cells are ascending like glass elevators, preparing to release half as many captives from beneath the floor.

Calvin shouts for Spike to stop it, to cancel the command, but he can't hear himself over the alarm. No. He can't hear the alarm either. He sees the swirling warning lights on the northern and southern walls, but the digital caterwauling has stopped. He listens carefully, feeling the stale warehouse wind against his ears but hearing no corresponding sound. He tries to think, tries to run through his contingencies, his emergency measures, but there's something ineffable about the process, something missing. His inner monologue is being filtered. A total deafening of strategic thought. A perfect silence. Just as he remembers Spike is gone, the intruding voices come again.

"This is bullshit! It's a reacher trick!"

"Was it really him?"

"AnSorin was innocent!"

"Ana. Oh God, Ana, Ana, my Ana."

"I'll kill him! Calvin Prichard's fucking dead!" comes a voice in Mandarin. Or Tagalog. Or Telugu. Or some Luminaran tongue. Different voices, different faces, layered translations and twisting memories are souping into Calvin's mind at once. And souping out. A two-way street. An endless information highway. He sees them seeing all he is. He sees survivors of Chicago, of the wars he's waged between. He tries to scream, tries to explain, tries to align the logic of his plans for an extended human race, but they're already seeing it. Seeing everything. Seeing his Uncle Gage sitting on his chest spitting

Gray & Turner in his eyes. Seeing Calvin with a flashlight and a pile of books, until the night guard finds him between library aisles and sends him home. Seeing Gage kick down his door, confusing him with Malcolm Sr. once again. Seeing his own bloody bicuspid in the sink. Seeing his fourteen-year-old eyes totally stoic, totally happy, totally stoic, until he can't remember which face is real. Seeing white snakeroot in the mortar, crushed into a bitter powder. Seeing Uncle Gage. Seeing Gray & Turner. Seeing Uncle Gage know it was him. Seeing Uncle Gage be the little pussy, be the one who's useless on the floor, be the one who isn't breathing. Seeing Malcolm Calvin Prichard Jr. on the first bus out of Corsicana, knowing he'll never be caught powerless again.

The hoverlift comes to a stop, sinking flush with the warehouse floor. Calvin blinks, looking around, unable to see clearly through his good eye. He guesses his sight is going, too. All his senses, one by one, just like Taiko, just like Hayes back when Calvin desynced him from his suit. He almost laughs. Maybe he does but just can't tell the difference. Can't see how it matters anymore. He feels something dripping on his wrist. Looks down there, hardly recognizing his hands. The change is nearly done. His new body. This alien power that he craved. An encroaching awareness of distant candles, of varying heats across the Earth.

Our kin, the whisper comes, gaining volume, gaining clarity. *Yours and mine alit together,* speaks the ghost that he created, the failed invader who wasn't strong enough to keep his own kind out of cages.

Calvin sees them escaping now. Blurry wisps, crawling from their lifted cells, stumbling through the prism maze. He feels the itch of surgical nanos swimming in the ocean of his right eye, shaving away the damaged layer so he can see the insurrection clearer. Wasted effort. The female promised darkness.

No, the whisper argues, sounding both intimate and unfamiliar. *Darkness is a choice.*

Calvin realizes he never heard the living voice of Kible Thexx. Only imagined it, and not like this. This second mind is dewy-eyed. Geriatric. Weak. Calvin will be castigated for his methods, etched into history as some kind of psychopath, but he knows the truth. He sees the value of this tech regime, of its messy, hasty rise to the status quo. Even if he was wrong about Nazara, about every single reacher alive on Earth, he wasn't wrong about the universe. The fist of time is slow, but it sure as fuck don't miss. That's all he bought them, really. Just a few more centuries of sovereign black. A little more time to decide which species they're all going to become. The boot or the bug. The survivors or the erased. They're angry now, but they'll get it later. They'll see. He gave humanity exactly what it needed. A kick in the teeth to get its ass up out of bed. A goddamn fighting chance, just like Gage Prichard gave to him!

Everything stops. The pedestrian voices. The inner whispers. Calvin sits there on his rug, hearing nothing, thinking nothing in the shape of words. He shudders, as though his very atoms have lost their heat, as though the marathon of his ego has reached a cold, kinetic end. He sees that mirror once again, sees his reflection everywhere. He thinks of nothing. Suddenly, he can only feel.

Feels those droplets on his wrist, on his bare chest, on his cheeks as he reaches up and rubs the warmth between his fingers. He wipes his eyes and sees there's nothing wrong with them at all. The warehouse is bright and clear in all directions. Clear enough to see their faces, their pale skin and sizzling, electric eyes, glowing brighter as they step free of their confinement. As they place their hands upon each other, as they rejoice in the reclamation of what Calvin Prichard stole, his vision blurs with tears again.

He feels the female, too. Without seeing her, he tracks her hands. Without line of sight, he watches her eyes fall shut at the control room window above. He sees her cock her head as though listening carefully, as though tuning her ear to a more subtle frequency, to something delicate below. A narrow dance begins at her waist. Her left hand is swirling, stirring, reaching. Her right fingers are operating independently as though unraveling separate strands. Or reconnecting them.

Calvin sees applause. Down on the floor, through blurry eyes, he sees the smallest of them clapping, the young male whose pigments are returning. He almost hears it. Cutting through his silent prison, he hears intermittent claps, brief bursts of giggles and little shouts, as though the female's power can't keep it out. He follows the little one's pointed fingers, both hands like bony wands jabbing up at the nearest prism, at the very top of it a few meters above the floor. Calvin thought he'd shattered that one's ceiling, splattered its neighbors with bones and gore, but he sees no evidence of his brilliance, no signs at all of quantum burn—just a few lingering illusory details finally juddering out of view.

He rubs his eyes, but it makes no difference. He clutches his chest and covers his mouth, but there's no way to keep his frailty from escaping. No way to be a useful man ever again.

Yes, the whisper promises. *There will be soon.*

Calvin sees Taiko Chiba, stepping into view atop the elevated prism cell. He sees recognition in her natural eye: of him, of all these strangers, of his crackling dark collider on the distant wall. He sees her responding to the little one's clapping, to his excited sounds. Sees her shivering in embarrassment, in chilly nakedness. Sees her flicking her tongue in comic disgust at the rancidness of her own mouth. He sees her humanity returning, all her senses, one swirling finger at a time—the female's fingers, reconnecting neuronal electric strands. He sees Taiko's heart break as she finally looks down at the tangle of limp limbs, the crusted suit, the comatose eyes lulled against her chest.

Calvin sees the sergeant, Emmett Hayes, cradled carefully in Taiko's arms. But he sees no candle. No heat of life in him at all.

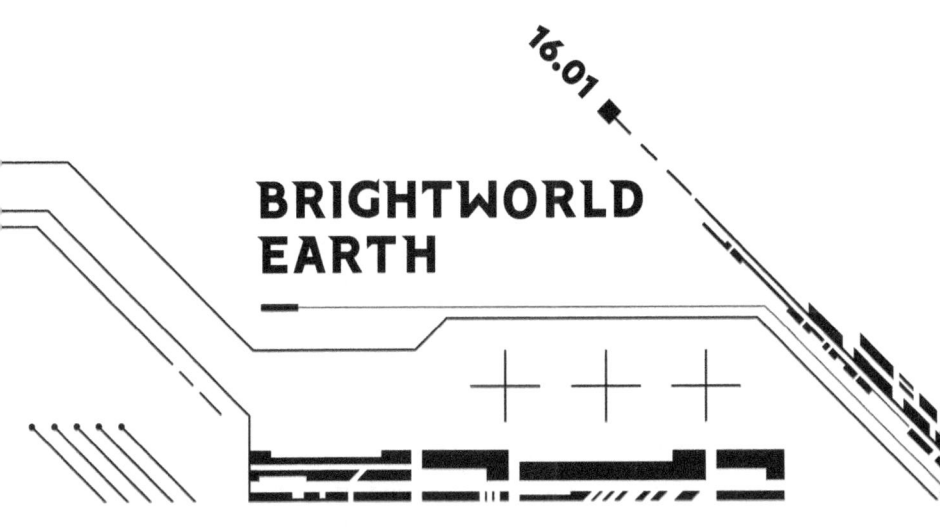

BRIGHTWORLD
EARTH

He flicks the frayed edges of her photograph. The wallet shot. The one she sent him from the road. He turns it over to read what she wrote him. Not to remember what it says, just to see if it still works. Feels like it does. Harder to tell on days like this. Sunless mornings, tourist traffic. Never used to be this way in town. All these faces. These deep pockets flipping land. They avoid his eyes like he's the stranger. Like he's the one who doesn't belong. He turns Abbie's photo back around. Sees her smiling in Buenos Aires. Or São Paulo, he forgets. He balances her 2D hips on the steering wheel. Traces the crease along her thigh. It works this time, he's sure. For a couple quiet seconds, Roosevelt Hall doesn't want to shoot himself.

Somebody knocks on the passenger window. Rosey takes care of Abbie first, turning her photo sideways, carefully sliding her into his sunshade mirror. After he's latched the mirror shut and flipped the visor back up above his head, he glances over at Earl Womack and nods for him to open the door.

The hustle and bustle of Main Street, Dawson, invades the truck cabin as the large man piles in. "What was that, your license?" Earl slips a four-foot padded tactical weapons case from his shoulder, trying to stand it up between his beefy legs while he reaches to shut the door, failing at both.

"Gimme that here." Rosey pulls the case away from Earl. It gets stuck on his center mirror and scratches the shit out of his ceiling before he manages to lay it flat on the arm rest between them, butting against his center console and jutting back to the rear middle seat. Earl finally shuts the door, and the street sounds quiet to a dull roar.

"Sheesh!" He gapes out the window as though into a zoo exhibit. "Heller all these townies comin' from? Not even townies. City feet. Careful keepin' your ID in that visor, one of these taggers is like to snatch it."

"Yeah." Rosey squeezes the tactical bag. Checks out his window for any lingering eyes, any vehicles with tinted glass or exempt plates. "This both of 'em?"

"Yessir. Toni had 'em ready right up front, bagged and paid for like you said. But damn! She really outdone herself this time. All polished and slick like new or better than new. Had to throw in a little extra after I seen the job she did."

"How much?"

"Oh, no, never mind that. Never mind." Earl blocks Rosey's attempt to reach for his wallet. "That was a pleasure for me—my pleasure, I mean."

Rosey makes a funny sound, but he doesn't smile. "She ask about me?"

"No," Earl barks defensively. "I mean, I told her you was sick, so she wished you well and what have you. But she knows her width, she ain't one to pry."

"Mm." Rosey reaches to realign his center mirror, but he stops, noticing movement in the reflection. A young deputy sheriff is crossing the street, cutting a hard diagonal in their direction. One hand is on his shoulder, pinching a radio mic.

"Was Mr. Ferras there?"

"Psh. Yeah." Earl shakes his head. Lets out a sigh. "No gettin' away from him."

Rosey watches the deputy crouch near a van two spots behind them, signaling covertly to someone out of view. Peeking around Earl's gut, Rosey clocks another sheriff in the passenger mirror. This one is older, wearing corporal decals and a handlebar mustache. He signals to the young deputy in response.

"He give you trouble?" Rosey asks.

"Nah. Just the same old barkin' dog." Earl swats the air like it's caught a filthy odor. "Think I finally shut him up though."

"What you mean?" Rosey watches the corporal unlock his holster and remove his sidearm. In the center mirror, the deputy does the same. They both start creeping forward, flanking the truck on either side.

"Uh. Well," Earl giggles with guilty satisfaction. "He started goin' on in Spanish like he does. Talkin' to Toni like I don't understand. Callin' me a fat ass. Sayin' shit about my dad, about how I run the ranch, about Jack."

Rosey gently presses his foot against the brake. Slips his hand beneath the weapons case, twisting the console dial to shift his electric pickup from *Park* to *Drive*. Both sheriffs see the taillights change—they start coming faster.

"Oh, fuck."

"Whoee! Yep!" Earl smacks his knee, misreading Rosey's excitement. "It happened so fast, I don't even—I can't believe it!"

The deputy reaches his hand to Rosey's door.

Rosey jumps his foot to the accelerator. Squeezes his fists around the wheel.

Earl shouts, "Right there in front of Toni, I spun on him and—"

BAM BAM BAM

Both sheriffs slap the windows, one on Rosey's side, one on Earl's, shouting commands:

"Hey! Park it! Park!"

"Stay in the vehicle!"

Rosey flexes his calf to jam the pedal, tenses his forearms to crank the wheel and spin them out into the road. But neither happens. He sits there frozen, tight with panic, neither complying nor escaping.

A lucky loser this time. The sheriffs keep moving forward, passing his truck, continuing to shout with weapons raised. They pull two men from an ancient muscle coupe, idling on gasoline directly in front of Rosey's truck. The passenger and driver are pressed to their bellies, one stretched in the street, the other on the sidewalk. Their hands are white as chalk, same as their necks. One of them is wearing a leather bomber hat with tightened ear flaps. The other has a baseball cap and over-ear headphones.

Rosey and Earl don't speak again until the muscle car has been shut off and both its occupants have been draped over the hood in cuffs.

"Damn." Earl scratches his neck. Keeps checking Rosey's eyes. "What you think they done?"

A prisoner van pulls up on the left, double-parking Rosey's truck. Three Dawson police officers hop out, quickly engaging the gathering crowd. It's all around them now: A few local older folks are watching fearfully from the stoop of the Masonic lodge. A middle-aged cowboy is beet red, shouting viciously at the two travelers in cuffs, pointing straight down Main Street out of town. And about fifteen city protestors are recording the action on their Ret-tags, jeering at the cowboy, spitting at the cops, flipping their fingers in defiance.

"Hey, Rose. Rose."

Rosey turns. Sees Earl nodding to the steering wheel with concerned eyes. Rosey quickly releases it. Clears his throat. Reaches down and twists the dial to reengage the parking brake. "Goddamn. Fuckin' circus out here." He clears his throat again.

"Yeah." Earl watches him carefully. "Gets worse every week."

BANG!

A firecracker detonates behind the wall of officers.

"Mother—! Fuck." Rosey clenches his fists up near his ears then quickly drops them into his lap. His eyes are shut tightly before he blinks them open, breathing deeply through his nose.

Earl watches him carefully. He takes a long, thoughtful look at the weapons case, then starts to ask—

"Alright," Rosey cuts him off. "Well, it seems like—I mean this is fucked." He laughs like a man with a broken rib. "Thanks for doin' this, E. Spared me another Toni interrogation, so I uh, yeah. Appreciate it." He smiles, offering a conclusive handshake with his left. Earl starts to accept it, then he notices Rosey's right hand has stayed in his lap, squeezing his knee to keep it still.

"Sure. Yeah sure, Rose. Anytime." Earl completes the handshake slowly, distractedly. At a similar speed, he reaches to open the passenger door, but his shoulders don't quite follow. His attention drifts from the weapons case to the struggling sheriffs to the city protesters, some with faces painted white, some with electric-blue cosmetic contacts, a few with heads shaved completely bald. One young, lanky woman in the front row has the complete agitator attire. She's holding a digital-ink sign as high as she can, broadcasting in alternating flaming graphics:

Deport Calvin Prichard!
Remember Emmett Hayes!

"I mean it, Rose." Earl's voice drops to an intimate timbre. "Anytime, any trouble, you ring me up." He mutters uneasily, confidentially, but somehow his words arrive even clearer in Rosey's ear. *"I ain't been one to forget my friends."*

Rosey quickly turns to face him, but the large man is already shuffling out. The violent shouts and uncivil mayhem briefly dump into the electric pickup's cabin as Earl opens the door and shuts it behind him, never looking back.

In Rosey's peripheral, the sheriffs finally shove their two pale captives into the back of the van, slamming its heavy gate closed. Another firecracker pops loudly in the street, and one of the officers uses his bullhorn to issue ultimatums to the unruly mob. Rosey hardly stirs, lost somewhere else completely. Slowly, he straightens himself, turning away from Earl's empty seat. He starts an instinctive hand toward the overhead visor, but this time he doesn't unfold it. Just rests his knuckles against the fabric for an extended moment. Then lowers that hand to the weapons case.

He pinches the zipper and drags it forward, keeping his eyes on the officers, on anyone close enough to see through his windows. He rounds the head of the bag and drags the zipper a little further down the other side. Watching his mirrors, he lifts the flap. Watching the crowd for a few cautious seconds, he finally glances down.

He sees the shotgun Toni Ferras special ordered for him—pump-action with a tactical barrel, all painted dryland brown.

Sees two cases of shells stacked in there neatly, buckshot and manstopper slugs.

He sees the old rifle that she restored. The Marlin 336, polished extra pretty just like Earl said. Sees two cases of .30-30s that he hopes he'll never need. Hopes to high heaven he'll never hear that bad thunder ever again.

16.02

Another auto-freighter merges east onto Highway 642, heading to Houston or the Fairfield battery swap. A thin breath of dust rolls in the wake of its thick tires before the road falls still and quiet once again. Few birds in the sky this morning. Fewer clouds. Just one endless gray expanse, darkest to the south but making progress in this direction. Promising rain.

Connie Clark rolls from her chest to her reconstructed shoulder. Glancing down past her boots, she notices her weather enclosure has a saggy rear end. The rusted grommet she found last night must have gone the way of its predecessor, this time leaving the tarp with a torn and fluttering earlobe. Looking further, higher, she sees the offending bungie cord has whipped its way into the worst branches of an especially tangled tree.

"Confirm, please," she sighs, releasing the lapel button on her one-wire earphone. As she rolls back into her rifle nest, she hugs her knapsack beneath her armpits and lifts a spotting scope to her left eye. Her right eyelid relaxes shut, completing the shrapnel pattern of raised scars across her face. "Colt, confirm heading," she repeats with increased annoyance. From her vantage, the auto-freighter has already vanished beyond the eastern trees. She reaches to pinch her wire again, but—

"Maestro confirms." Miles Yang is garbled beneath heavy static, testing the range of the cheap two-way radios. "One simulant transp—passing—south—638. No heat in cabin or cargo."

"Crown copies." Connie turns her scope northwest, searching for any sign of Danny Diaz on the other side of the highway. "Any eyes on Colt?"

"Mosquito has eyes." Chuck Bugg sounds unusually serious, almost professional. "Colt appears to be in distress. Requesting comm check."

"Beetle confirms, obscured visual. Second request to access comms." Derek Bugg speaks just as urgently, a twitch of fear in his cloned voice.

Connie pinches her wire to respond, but something stops her. An itchy intuition in her stomach. A sudden need to act before it's too late. She shoves her knapsack aside then army-crawls out of her nest. Scrambling to her feet, she sprints sideways through the scraggly trees along the eastbound shoulder of Highway 642, keeping her eyes on Danny-boy's last position. Soon as she reaches open terrain, she lifts her scope, spotting the collapsed picket fence at the edge of the abandoned cattle land. Tracing a few paces north of there, she spots Danny's empty nest beneath a ghillie blanket. That same twiggy camouflage mesh is draped sloppily over his modular sniper rifle, glinting visibly from the road, clearly abandoned in a hurry.

"Crown, do you copy?" One of the Buggs sounds breathless, beginning to panic. "Requesting emergency ears on Colt."

Tracing her scope northwest of the abandoned sniper's nest, Connie spots Danny's canteen and one of his boots discarded in the grass. His second boot is three meters further, followed by his lower fatigues. His radio is still hooked to one of the belt loops; his one-wire earpiece extends from there, pointing a straight line to a knee-high shrub of Yellow Bells. Danny-boy is doubled over in the flowers, grimacing in pain, holding the front of his shirt up near his nipples like the world's worst centerfold. That bad intuition bursts in Connie's guts like a wet balloon.

She drops her scope and spins away just before Danny drops his mud. Somehow, that doesn't spare her. She swears she smells it over here. Swears she feels a few of his hot droplets splash the insides of her ankles.

Her left knee pad hits the highway, but she catches her weight there. She fights off the nausea, sucking tightly through her nose, growling heavily through her teeth. She knows the Buggs are watching. She can feel their beady eyes like buzzing wings behind her ears. She swears she can hear their harmonized snickers down the road—that and a sizzling sound, mixing with the stench of burning hair. Perfect. Her Spider-1 implant is overheating yet again.

"Crown?" The urgency has left Chuck's voice, or maybe Derek's, replaced by well-concealed mischief. "Any eyes on Crown? Looks like a false alarm on Colt."

"Jester's got 'er." Alec Shankman makes no disguising effort, no attempt at all to hide his satisfaction in the ruse. "Crown appears to be in distress. Requestin' comm check." He can't even finish. He sounds stoned and idiotic before he drops his wire to laugh hysterically, nested just fifty meters east of where Connie is kneeling now.

She could kill him. Not send him packing to Atlantic City, not cut him loose like she threatened back at Cooks. With fifty paces and one standard round, she could single-handedly raise the average intelligence of mankind. That's the worst thing about this hunt: the desperation for trained hands. Her conspicuous fucking reliance on children dressed like men.

She punches the highway, cracking one of the regrown bones in her ring finger but barely feeling the sting. Too much nerve damage in that limb. Too much heat inside her spine. But that's how she knows they're getting close. Knows it like an instinct, like a foggy road sign coming into view. She knows they need to be. No turning back with empty handcuffs, not after how they left. After two months in dereliction, insubordinate to the man, this capture mission needs a prisoner, or they can't go back at all.

Connie straightens herself. Rests an elbow on her knee. Unclenches her jaw before she tightly squeezes the radio wire. "Crown copies. Maintain instrument freeze; do not engage comms." She waits patiently for a few seconds. "Please acknowledge."

"Copy that."

"Copy, staying cold."

Both Buggs sound mystified by her restraint. Even frightened.

"Thank you." Connie lets out a breath like hot exhaust. "Maestro, do you read me clear?"

"Not clear, but Maestro rea—you." Slightly less static from Yang now that Connie has a straight line on the infantry transport parked two klicks down the road.

"Log one false alarm for Mosquito and Beetle each. Next one will be disciplinary."

"Copy, already noted," Yang responds.

"And bring the rig for Colt. He needs an IV. Probably some syrup for his stomach. Oh, and Hammer, let's get some water boiling just in case."

"Maestro copies. Wheeling up." The jangly sound of the ignition keys comes through the radio before Yang releases his wire.

"Hammer reads you." Aila sounds quiet and uncertain. "Water looks clean . . . if you need it."

"Appreciated. Jester, please switch to channel three." Connie waits for his response. "Jester."

"Yeah. Switchin'."

Connie reaches to her hip, cranks the radio's channel dial from one to three, then pinches her wire. "Shank, you read me?"

"Yeah." He sounds like he's in the principal's office—like he's getting used to being there.

"Well? Should we go a few rounds or get straight to it?"

"Straight to what?"

"Christ. Am I about to get sick? Just tell me that."

"Sick how? What are you sayin'?"

"I'm asking if you spiked Danny's water or everyone's water."

"The fuck? You think I cross contaminated my own fuckin' self?"

"Say you did or say you didn't, Shank."

"No! Fuck no. He's probably rotten because you got him three days on recycled piss. Magar's been squirtin' dirt all week. Don't put that shit on me."

"Seemed like the Buggs knew it was coming. Seemed like you all did."

"You would, too, if you saw the way the kid hopped out of his chonies. Am I on trial for havin' eyes in my fuckin' head?

"You knew Danny was sick, but you didn't cancel the comm check?"

"Isn't that your job?"

"Why'd the Buggs act like he was threatened?"

"They're still on channel one if you wanna ask 'em."

"I'm about to burn them for risking our stealth on a fucking fart joke."

"Oh, will you just—it was a prank! You should be thankin' us."

"So, you were behind it."

"Yeah, I raised morale and then you fucked it again. Nice work, boss lady."

"And you did spike Danny."

"No! Fuck off with that. I saw him squirmin', so I buzzed Chuck to check it out."

"How? Which channel?"

"I buzzed him, I said. For two fuckin' seconds. Don't get your strap-on in a twist."

Connie pinches her wire then lets it go without finding any words. Her eyebrows tighten into a mix of disgust and disbelief. "You went hot on comms?"

Shank says nothing.

"You powered your visor on today?" she clarifies, checking the skies for UT hunter drones, still not believing he could be as mutinous as he is brainless.

Nothing but silence from Shankman's end for half a minute. Then:

"That's generally how it works, yeah."

Connie drops her head. She pinches her nose to distract from the migraine he's just delivered. "Well, that's it, Shank. That's you breaking our only fucking deal and giving me an easy choice."

Nothing but silence from him again. Just the stormy southern wind and shivering sound of dryland trees flanking the road.

"Guess that makes two of us."

"Excuse me?" Connie squeezes and releases her wire, only to realize Shankman's still holding it on his end.

"Two runaway grunts with one choice between 'em." His exhalations are harsh against his mic, intensifying as he continues. "You think I'm out here, why? 'Cuz you fuckin' said so? We're all deserters, but I'm still suckin' your cock in the bumfuck savanna 'cuz I like the taste? You wanna cut me loose from an AWOL unit, where I got lifelong fuckin' friends and you got zippity drippity dick? Well, be my guest, Connie Clark. You just try that, then we'll just see what the fuck happens next!" He racks a round into chamber, and the radio cuts to silence.

But Connie swears she still hears him breathing, not in the earpiece but behind her eyes. She swears she feels his heart pounding against her back, feels his sweaty trigger finger flicking the safety off, feels the rifle stock digging way too tight against his shoulder.

He'll never hit her. Not with the first shot. Not before she rolls hard and low across the gravel into the trees, just like Uba showed them. If she makes it to the trees, he'll be dead in his nest in thirty seconds. Dead on the road if he tries to run. She swears she can feel Alec Shankman pinching his prick to keep the piss behind it, because they both know he's full of shit. Maybe Danny-boy's his friend, out there in the bushes, sneezing from the wrong end. To the rest of them, Shank's a sideshow. An uncomfortable laugh. A liability they'll forget. It's not friendship he needs anyway. Not for this. This is a matter of allegiance. And higher ground.

"I tried, Shank. For the captain. For all of us. I really fucking tried." Connie's Spider-1 bakes the nape of her neck, and she swears she feels Shankman's trigger finger relax. Swears she sees a foggy image of herself drift ever so slightly from his iron sights. "Alright, Hammer. Cook the water."

Fifty meters east of where Connie's kneeling, two bright muzzle flashes pop behind Shankman's nest, followed immediately by the echoing thunder of .50 caliber rounds. Her headache vanishes in an instant. The heat in her spine begins to cool.

"This is Hammer." Aila Hallheim comes in on channel three. Her voice sounds pained but unequivocal as she lowers her scoped magnum. "The water is clean. Jester is down."

"Crown copies. Thank you." Connie holds her wire, wondering what a friend would say in this situation, in the face of sudden loss. Then she remembers she doesn't care. "Remove the battery from his helmet and start packing up his nest. Total teardown. We need to move. I'm going back to channel one."

"Copy," Aila says. "Switching to one."

"Da. Followink you to one," Magar acknowledges, sounding more heartbroken than either of them.

That surprises Connie. It keeps her kneeling in the road for a few more seconds. Keeps her staring at the gravel just long enough to feel the approaching rumble of heavy wheels. She looks east, expecting to see the transport rig arriving for Danny. It's coming, but it isn't close enough to be shaking the road. Still three hundred meters away, it's slowing down, turning left to block both lanes, barricading the highway. Miles Yang is hopping down from the driver's seat. He's too far for Connie to make out his urgent signals, so she quickly switches to channel one.

"—repeat, hot cabin inbound. Hot cabin, civilian plates. Please advise!" Yang releases his wire and tugs his leash forward, pulling Wilson Black's old cop shotgun into his hands.

Connie follows his eyes, spinning around just in time to

see the electric pickup screech to a halt twenty meters west on Highway 642. It's the first civilian vehicle they've seen in two months, and the cabin's reading hot on Yang's passive millimeter wave from over three hundred meters. That means this guy is packing heat, probably multiple rifles and ammunition.

No shooting range this way; no public hunting lands in the county. No reason to take this road at all unless you've been down it before. Two months ago, this offbeat junction mysteriously disappeared from Dynamics Maps. Shankman noticed that. Spotted one of the outdated auto-freighters diverting south out of Dawson instead of east. He thought the unit came here on his hunch. Thought Connie ignored their return-home orders on nothing but his unrecognized quick wits, but she's been following something else. That new instinct. That foggy road sign coming into view. She's spent half a year convincing herself that collective nightmares are impossible, that all those Bright Night fanatics are insane. But Connie's staring at this truck, at its panicked, frozen driver behind the wheel, and she swears she knows what happens next.

This man will take her to Emmett Hayes.

16.03

"Hey, Yono." Poody taps the anchor thread of a spider web, then he leans back to see if anything crawls up from the cracks. "Yono." He taps it twice this time, looking all around the narrow porthole windowsill for any sign of prowling, creeping, biting things. "Yono."

"What?!" Yono finally turns from the much larger hayloft window on the western wall. "What is it?"

Poody's already distracted, staring with fear and wonder at a tiny barn spider, now inching out from the shadowy bottom corner of its web. All eight of its eyes seem to be gazing into his soul. "Do you think he is real?"

"Who? What the hell are you looking at?"

"The shadow man." Poody watches the spider retreat into its dark corner before he turns nervously to Yono. "The one who haunts the lake."

Yono scoffs at that, but some apprehension sneaks across his face. "Don't be stupid. You know who is kept in that old shack." He waves his hand dismissively, turning back to surveil the vast and tangled farmland that leads to the main road.

"No, I do not. Neither do you. Tysha says all childs are banned."

"I'm not a child!" Yono snaps. "Neither are you. You're an orphaned mouse, becoming a weasel, becoming meat if you don't shut up." He clenches his fist on the windowsill, waiting for Poody to speak again. Just one more word so he can run over there and crack him over the head. Instead, he hears the young boy whimpering, sniffling quietly, terrified to make a sound.

Yono sighs. He slowly turns to face him. "Hey. I didn't mean to—"

"What is that?!" Poody isn't looking at him. He's standing on his tippy toes, pointing out to the grounds below. "Oh! Oh no!" He points with both hands at once.

"What? Move!" Yono hurries over, forcing his face into the high circular window beside Poody's scrawny fingers.

"There! There it goes!" Poody points down at the miniature jungle of tomato plants, herbs, and lemons between the barn and the wobbly old farmhouse. At the sound of his shouts, a large black animal, with two white stripes running down its back, scampers from the garden into the uncut grass. Poody thought it might be a wolverine, but now he is remembering there are not too many of those in Texas. This beast is also much smaller than he thought at first, with a big bushy tail sticking up in the air.

"Ow!" He covers his eyebrow where Yono just flicked him very hard. "Why—?!" Poody almost falls off the upside-down crate he's been using as a stepstool. "Why are you flicking?!"

"Why are you stupid?" Yono flicks his ear this time.

"You!" Poody throws his nine-year-old fists at Yono's face—both fists at once in a desperate double punch—and he is equally thrilled and horrified to feel a few knuckles connect with the meat of Yono's nose.

The brawny teenager stumbles backward, more surprised than damaged, but that's far enough to trip him up on the tangled fortress of frayed rope and mildewed blankets in the center of the room. When Poody first saw the old pillows and blankets many many days ago, he guessed it was some kind of homeless person house, then he realized it made no sense to have a little homeless house on the second floor of a ginormous barn house, but now that he is smelling the awful stink that just puffed up from the crusty blankets, he is leaning very strongly toward his first guess again.

"Agh! Ugh!" Yono thrashes like he's in quicksand. He rolls to his knees and frantically crawls to escape the noxious linens, but he stops when something makes a squishing, crunching sound beneath his palm. He recoils that hand in obvious disgust, but he never looks at it, never sees the decaying feathers stuck to his fingers. He just stares straight down at whatever dead bird thing made the crunching sound, and his blood-red mohawk begins to dim. His inky black skin seems to writhe over his cheekbones before he buries his face in the crook of his elbow, sniffing himself deeply, desperately, wiping his defiled fingers in the musty bedsheets. That seems to work. His breathing slows to a normal rate, and he settles down. Then his muscular back arches like a cat, and a gush of puke drenches his flannel sleeve.

Poody is extremely engrossed by these events. That is one of the funny words he learned this morning from the tribe's new archivist, Ketz Clute. Engrossed. It means to pay lots and lots of attention—to watch what someone else is doing like your very life depends on it.

"Yono?" he finally dares to ask. "Are you—"

"Mel nelumen," the older boy threatens gravely, apparently too dimmed to practice his English anymore. "Mel caska nelumen!" he curses in a sudden voice-cracking roar.

"No thank you!" Poody jumps off the wooden crate just as Yono lunges into it, banging his knee hard enough to rip his faded jeans.

"Argh! Mel titi keck!" Yono groans, squeezing his leg like it's Poody's throat.

"I am sorry! No thank you please!" Poody descends the splintery ladder faster than he has ever dared to climb it. Luckily, he is looking upward the entire time, waiting for Yono to come down after him, so he only scrapes the very tip of his chin when one of the rungs snaps beneath his feet.

He falls the full length of his body, which is almost as high as Yono's chest since he has been growing so much this summer, but the natural carpet of overgrown grass only knocks half the wind out of him when he hits the ground. He lies there on his back, feeling like a fallen giant in a forest of skinny trees, expecting himself to burst into tears at any moment. Then he sees Yono reach the top of the busted ladder, looking down at him with very dark eyes. Poody is thankful to be far from Yono in that moment. Thankful for about five seconds while Yono looks to his right then to his left, then hurries to the edge of the loft, drops into a squat and leaps straight from there to the many large sacks of smelly dirt piled in the corner. The landing is rough, but he rolls through it, arriving very close to Poody's feet.

"I am sorry!" Poody shrieks, scrambling on all fours then dashing for the humongous barn door. He takes two and a half steps out into the overcast afternoon before Yono tackles him from behind, crashing them both into the thickest patch of the tomato jungle.

Poody covers up quickly, hands over his face, knees to his elbows, ankles locked tight together. Yono doesn't bother to unravel him. He straddles the skinny boy's hips, thoroughly licking his own teeth and the inside of his mouth, before he spits directly in Poody's hair. Residual chunks of breakfast beef blend with Poody's golden locks, followed by handfuls of soil and dead leaves from the garden floor. Poody starts wailing into his hands, blubbering for forgiveness, but Yono stays on top of him, scrounging around in the dirt for something even worse, something just as dead and maggoty as that wet tangle of feathers in the hayloft. He sniffs the wind like the meanest dog in a hungry pack, but the more he searches his surroundings the cooler his blood becomes.

Poody feels that change. Notices Yono slowing down, shifting his weight toward the northern road. He has been tricked like that before. He squeezes his palms even tighter over his face and shrugs his shoulders up to his ears.

"Hey." Yono knocks on Poody's skull like a wooden door.

Poody shakes his head, not falling for it. He can still hear

Yono sucking through his nose, probably readying another vomit loogie. But resistance proves to be futile. In one powerful move, his entire body is suddenly lifted off the ground, twisted effortlessly through the air, then plopped down on his bottom. He tries to flop back into the dirt, but Yono catches him by the wrists and pulls his little hands from his face with similar ease.

"I am sorry! I—"

"Quiet. Open your eyes," Yono whispers, now seated behind him.

Poody does no such thing. He clenches everything shut and tosses his head side to side, hoping to dodge whatever Yono is trying to feed him.

"Hey—open your eyes or I'll flick your coka." Yono forces Poody's knees apart, exposing his nethers to violence.

Poody's eyes squint open one at a time, still expecting an awful trick. Instead, he sees tall tomato plants wiggling in the breeze beneath darkening storm clouds.

"Shh." Yono pinches his ribs. "Stop crying and look. Out there as far as you can." He releases one of Poody's arms so he can wipe the dirt and tears away.

Poody grooms himself carefully, trying to stop his sniffles, but the lump in his throat does not want to be swallowed. "I—I do not see anything."

"As far as you can, I said. Now!" Yono grabs the sides of Poody's head, directing his eyes to the west and a little bit north.

Poody has gotten very good at knowing his directions. He could tell Yono what is over that way: all the old seedy plants and the big main road he is banned from forever, but he does not think that is what Yono wants to hear. He does not understand why Yono is asking him to look at something he is clearly smelling with his nose. He can hear Yono's nostrils going crazy like there is something very important in the air. Like he is becoming engrossed, too.

"Oh," Poody realizes aloud. "Is it Mr. Rosey?"

"Yeah." Yono nods in agreement. "Yeah, he's with them. Good."

Them? Poody sniffs the air, but all he smells is normal stuff. Dirt, rotten tomatoes, Yono's barfy clothes. He can usually smell people, too, but only if he gets right up next to them. And that is just their armpits and butts and stinky places—their sweaty shoes and unwashed hair. Yono's gift is much better than that. He can smell their lights. Their most secret secrets and grown-up thoughts. Especially if their best secret is a person. When people want other people, Yono can smell that feeling from very very far away. That's how he always knows when Sumella is looking for him. He says he could smell that thirsty girl from Jupiter if he needed to. Mr. Rosey, too. He is very nice for an Earth person, and he has lots of extra land to share, but he is always always sad. Sumella said sometimes that is what happens when the person you want most does not want you in the same way. Poody thinks that might be why Yono has been volunteering for so many delivery missions and why he is not minding very much when Poody tags along. For Yono, it has become especially sad to stay at camp, where he must always always be smelling what Tysha wants the most.

"Oh!" Poody points straight ahead to the west and a little bit north. "Wow, Mr. Rosey has a very bright friend."

"Where? Just one?"

"Yes. She is very close to him. Very close behind him."

"How bright? One of us?"

"Nope. Her light is the Earth color. She is . . ."

"What? Who is she?"

"Oh." Poody shakes his head slowly, lowering his voice. "No, she is not his friend." His eyes dart further north. Then back to the west and a little bit south behind the barn. He tries to talk, but that lump in his throat drops to his tummy.

"Hey." Yono shakes his shoulder. "What are you seeing?"

"We need to run very fast."

"What?"

"Very fast right now!"

Yono tries to grab him, but Poody squirms through his hands and darts off like the skunk he saw from the window. He's a couple inches shorter than the tallest plants of the overgrown garden, so he vanishes almost immediately into the wild.

"Poody! Wait!" Yono scrambles to his feet and dashes after him, heading southeast toward the rear of the abandoned farmhouse. He's almost to the corner when a hummingbird zips past his ear and smashes straight through the low kitchen window. As he pauses to glare at the damage, another supersonic bird slices his elbow, biting him badly, blasting a hanging tomato to bits. That's enough stimulation for him to get running again, now hearing the distant clap of rifle thunder, ultimately deciding these may not be birds at all.

An affirming burst of splinters sprays his face as he rounds the corner of the farmhouse. Without daring to stop, he glances back, catching the briefest glimpse of three Earth soldiers closing in from the northwest, west, and southwest—all much closer than he sensed. Masked somehow. Lightless ghosts, creeping through the sorghum fields with rifles in their hands, none of them firing yet, which means there's at least one more he hasn't seen.

Eyes darting forward, he spots Poody just before he disappears into the dense woodland behind the house. He sprints after him, twice as fast as the smaller boy but not nearly as nimble in the tangle of shrubs and dangling branches blocking their retreat.

"Yes!" Poody shouts as he scurries through the foliage, not continuing straight ahead but drifting a bit to his left, to the east. "Yes, there are seven!"

"What?!" A low-hanging twig jabs Yono in the roof of his mouth, causing him to hack and cough and fall behind.

"Seven bad peoples and one Mr. Rosey. Oh! I do not—" Poody stops on a dime, glancing over his shoulder, searching, spotting Yono. "Yes! Yono is escaping, too. We are escaped!" His eyes are shining extremely brightly as he speaks. His hair is swimming in the air, twinkling so intensely that Yono has trouble seeing any details on his face. But that clarifies who the child is speaking to. There is only one amongst their kin who can transmit that kind of heat.

"Is she coming?" Yono asks, pushing through the dried branches to approach Poody. "Tell her to stay away. It's them— the ones who caught Kible Thexx!"

"Where?" Poody turns away from Yono, apparently deaf to the older boy's shouts. His eyes shine like narrow searchlights to the northeast. "Oh, yes! Wow, she is quick!"

"Hey!" Yono grabs him by the shoulder, spinning him around. "No. Tell Tysha no!"

The great shine cuts out immediately. Poody's golden locks droop around his ears, and the galactic shimmer disappears, as though severed from its source. Yono blinks a few times in the dim light of the woods, not quite believing what he's seeing. Poody's eyes are shut. But that can't be right. That would mean that amazing heat was just an afterglow, seeping through his eyelids.

Poody blinks slowly as though waking up, not seeing Yono

immediately, not seeming to see anything until he flinches much like Yono just did from him.

"What? Why are you shouting?" Poody asks.

"How," Yono pauses incredulously, "what did Tysha say?"

"Tysha? Where?" Poody looks around, excited.

"No! By the light. You said she was coming."

"No, I did not." Poody eyes Yono with concern, lingering first on the teenager's bloody elbow then on his scratched-up face. "He said Ms. Taiko was much closer. And much much faster—shoo!" He zips his hand through the air like a travel pod through space.

"Taiko? Who said that?"

Before Poody can answer, a commotion of snapping branches turns their heads, and the flickering silhouettes of elite soldiers begin to breach the woodland perimeter.

Poody scampers off immediately, heading northeast this time.

"Hey!" Yono hurries after him, shielding his face to prevent further scratches. "Wait—we can't go this way. We'll lead them to camp."

"No," Poody shouts over his shoulder, apparently unworried about stealth. "They will catch us much sooner than that."

"Catch us?!" Yono glares at Poody, then looks around at the foliage and the bending arc of their dash north, now nearly northwest. "You're looping us back. What are you doing?"

"Flanking the gunnery sergeant!" Poody pumps his fist above his head.

"Faking the what? What are you saying?"

"His plan! He is real! He has told me how to win!"

"No! We can't win against them! Who the hell were you speaking to?!"

"The shadow man! The ghost behind the lake!

16.04 ■— – — ——

For the first time in one hundred and eighty-nine days, she misses the nanos. Misses the inhuman speed they afforded, the total lack of lag between concept and execution, the absolute confidence of perfect math. She would never go back. Not for a relative microsecond, not for one nanoscopic instant if it meant she might be swallowed by the hive again. But one thing is undeniable to her right now. Taiko Chiba misses the precision.

Her false eye spots him early, an active tracking lock at forty meters. Thirty-five. Thirty. Her natural brain finally catches up. She thrusts her mechanical arm out like an anchor, digging her diamond claws into the thick trunk of a hickory tree, shredding long ribbons of bark as she swirls around it, abruptly ending her rapid dash. She mildly concusses herself on impact, and half of her left nipple is chafed away, bleeding an expanding crimson circle through her second favorite jumpsuit—the black one with all the zippers, previously owned by some giant named *J.W.*—but she doesn't cry out. She clings there like a cybernetic koala, cheek to tree, left eye shut, right eye slitted, watching to see if Danny Diaz has been alerted.

He looks directly at her. From the magnified perspective of her panther eye, they are practically nose to nose. But Danny just frowns uncertainly, returning one eye to his scope. He's lying prone, wearing a camouflage bucket hat with a few leafy twigs tucked into the ventilation eyelets. A large ghillie cape, threaded with similar shrubbery, is draped over his back from ears to heels. Almost. Two centimeters of dusty leather tread are exposed on his right boot. And some kind of flower petal. Yellow. Doesn't match this dry corner of the woods at all.

Taiko nearly missed it. Nearly ran right by an anomalous

clue the hive would've spotted from maximum range. Nearly got the boys killed. That's the penalty of failure here: two young friends, riddled with UT standard rounds. She needs to be careful. Any factor that impacts her chances of success must be removed.

She studies the dirt. Drops her feet from the tree to the least likely patch of earth to make a sound. Then she circles north. Aligns herself at Danny's distant rear until they're both looking down into the sorghum field where the boys are about to emerge. She can read them there. Flittering pages of life in her photokinetic web. Ever since that night at Dallas Dynamics when all her lost senses were returned, an extra sense has been maturing day by day. This sense of light. This biological uplink to the expanding network of minds on Earth.

They come like data. Thirty-three kilograms of water, fat and protein traveling seventeen kilometers per hour. A light source one hundred and twenty-six centimeters above the ground. That matches Poody. The second mass is twice as heavy, moving faster. An unsteady link, flickering dim. Reads like Yono in distress. Not much time to process that. Not much reason to. The task at hand remains.

Taiko dashes forward, abandoning stealth, rushing Danny from behind. Hard to be quiet moving this fast on tungsten toes, but the noise won't matter if she surprises him. If she grapples his back, success is a probabilistic certainty.

Danny isn't surprised. He's been waiting. Before Taiko gets halfway to him, he's barrel rolling to his back, pulling the modified sidearm he keeps on his chest, aiming straight down between his boots with steady hands. The only certainty now is that he won't miss—not Colt the bolt, named for his youth and the Colt 1911 competition pistol he made famous at special training. He did miss one bullseye on the speed range, just two millimeters shy of tying Captain Uba's perfect score. But the captain knew the course and placed every target personally. Danny shot on the fly, centering nineteen out of twenty, finishing a full three seconds faster than the marksman with a bionic eye.

Before his barrel roll is done, Danny puts three rounds on top of each other, a modern Robin Hood from fifteen meters. He doesn't miss. He doesn't blink, both eyes cool and calm in the shadowed woods. The adrenaline fixed his aching stomach, tightened his grip. But his vision might still be impaired. His attacker still seems to be standing, practically dancing now. Somehow, she's committing to a full-body wiggle, teasing him to trigger her again. He almost does, until he sees her branches, her spindly leaves and splintered trunk. She's not the stem that he expected. She's a sapling, shimmying in the first drops of summer rain. His queasy eyes shoot upward, chasing the storm, following a falling whistling sound. But he never sees Taiko. Just a glint of raining tungsten, blending into stormy clouds.

The collision is vicious. After Danny lies there motionless for a few seconds, Taiko lifts his head to make sure his brains haven't exited his skull. There is some blood in the dirt, but the wound seems superficial. She presses her ear to his nose and is relieved to feel warm, consistent breath. He will survive. But as she traces the shape of his Spider implant, she decides that it will not. She sits him up. Sees a large dent in the aluminum casing at the top of his spine. It may be what saved him—protected his cerebellum when his head whipped back against the packed dry ground. But if the chip is compromised, it may also be what kills him.

She doesn't bother extracting the arachnoid legs. Too risky. Too deeply embedded in his vertebrae. Instead, she cuts them from the Spider's body with her claws. Two slow incisions, slicing four legs at a time. Then she uses her natural hand to grab the entire signal chip. She needs to feel it. Needs to pull it away in one unbroken piece. This will probably wake him up. Or scramble his mind into vegetable soup if she's wrong about the tech. Taiko shudders, imagining Danny-boy revived by the next generation of nanoscopic hives.

Luckily, it comes away clean. One Spider Byte prototype and its two thousand electrode hairs, all leading to its underside where a tiny sphere of glass is soldered into place, apparently by hand. One miniature translucent marble, swirling with white-hot information.

Taiko knows that time is short. She can read the boys at the edge of her web, at the end of the woods, just a few seconds from the field where Roosevelt Hall is being restrained. She reads the shifting ingredients of Connie Clark right there on top of him, a vivid source like nuclear excursion. A self-sustaining chain reaction on the verge of violent heat. But she can read this marble, too. The longer she watches the strange behavior of this tiny ball of light, the more missing pieces she discovers. And the spares. The many twisted fragmentations blended forcefully together.

She shatters the marble between the tungsten fingers of her right hand, and the swirling light blinks out of view—down into quantum eternity or up into the endless black, Taiko can't be sure. Soon as it's gone, Danny puckers his lips. He furrows his brow like he's failing high school math, then his body slackens dreamily against her shoulder. She holds him as long as she can afford to, just a few tenths of one gentle second, before she lays him on his ghillie blanket and takes off running down the hill into the wild field of sorghum.

It's grown so high and thick she can't see through it. She's dashing through the maze with a dwindling sense of navigation but an intensifying sense of light. The chemical datasets of Roosevelt Hall and Connie Clark are legible straight ahead. She could liberate him now, presuming that's what's happened here—someone finally noticed they changed the map. Or some cashier got suspicious about his recurring bulky buys. The vast raw materials, tools, and clothes couldn't all be hand-me-downs. Taiko can't blame him for getting caught, not after all he's done to protect this final mission, not after he's been such a loyal friend. She also can't be sure that's what this is—his mistake, not his betrayal. She must be certain. She must be quick.

She plants her foot and pivots east, setting a collision course for Poody and Yono. One hundred meters and she'll have them. Seventy-five. Fifty. She bursts unexpectedly into the clearing, seeing the farmhouse two hundred meters south, seeing the long dirt road that winds from there up to the northern junction on Highway 642. She never sees Magar, crouching low beside her, now behind her. Never sees Aila, five meters north of him, wonderstruck by the cyborg's swift arrival but eerily unsurprised—as though they've been waiting for her.

Unwittingly, Taiko threads the gap between her ex-teammates, unable to detect their shrouded lights. Her panther eye quickly spots the anomalous squares of disrupted dirt directly in front of her, now beneath her, but her human brain is too distracted by the boys emerging from the woods. She is relieved to see them both relatively unharmed. She smiles, allowing herself one microsecond of success.

Then Magar squeezes his detonator, and the stormy air is filled with lightning.

16.05

There it is. That bad thunder he was dreading. That cannon sound to indicate diplomacy has failed. Rosey's bruised cheek is pressed to the soil, and his clenched eyes are facing west, so he doesn't see the literal electricity behind him—a man-made lightning strike out in the clearing by the road.

Connie sees it just fine. Her eyes are raised and ready, like she was waiting for it to land. Waiting for this moment exactly. "Up." She kicks Rosey's ankle, keeping her short rifle trained on his back. "Go. Slow." She waits for him to get moving then follows carefully behind, swearing she can already see the roasted skin. The melted metallic limbs.

Just as Yono escapes the woods, he drops his heels to stop abruptly. He jolts one hand up to protect his face from whatever projectiles might follow the explosion. The other hand finds Poody's shoulder, corralling the smaller boy behind his back.

Poody is surprised to be protected, especially by Yono. The entire scene seems to confuse him, as though it couldn't possibly be true. "No," he gasps, watching a flaming female shape twisting and falling with the rain. "He told me." Poody turns, seeing the Earth soldiers closing in from all directions. "The shadow man said we would win."

Taiko doesn't hear his voice. Doesn't see the craters left behind by Magar's high voltage mines. Doesn't smell her own smoldering hair and broiled skin. She merely soars, twisting numbly through the air before she lands heavily in the road. Her natural eye is shut; the false one is blackened, shattered, wisping with smoke where the lightning made its exit. Her lips remain half curled in odd delight.

"Who is that?" Rosey stumbles out from the sorghum

stalks, hands zip-tied behind his back. "What happened? Who is that?" he asks in a fluttering voice, watching Magar and Aila approach their charred victim. Aila kicks the body to check for life, and Rosey hears the inhuman thud of a metallic limb. Looking closer, he recognizes the faded fabric of Jack Womack's old greasy jumpsuit, the one he convinced Earl to let him borrow about six months back. Six months since the Bright Night. That doesn't feel right to him—not nearly long enough to justify this pain. "Oh, you fuckers." He shakes his head slowly, batting back tears. "You evil fucks, she was just a kid!"

On that note, Yono grabs Poody by the wrist and tries to run back into the woods. Three muzzles meet them there—two raised rifles, fanning out identically, and one old cop shotgun in the center, its custom stellar shells hissing deep in the barrel like a quiver of cobras snatched from hell.

Lowering that bad business, Miles Yang finally gets a good look at the two young strangers he's been chasing. The smaller boy has wild, bouncing curls, highlighted golden-brown like a lion cub. His skin has the pigmentation and apparent texture of freshly oiled leather, shaded darker around his button nose and boney chin. The older kid's mohawk is hypnotically bloody red, almost seeming to throb with its own life. His skin is so black it looks painted on, but his eyes are electric ice. Both of them have eyes like thriving galaxies underwater.

"No, she was not," Connie coolly retorts, striding out from the maze of crops. Her eyes are on Taiko Chiba, but she keeps her rifle on Rosey's back. "No, they are *not* just kids," she reminds Miles Yang, snapping her fingers to wake him up. He watches her uncertainly, then nods obediently, leveling Wilson Black's shotgun on the boys. The Bugg twins do the same, fanning out further to the north and south.

"She's still breathing." Aila draws their attention back to Taiko. She removes her fingers from the cyborg's neck and quickly retreats a few heavy steps. Her right arm is much scrawnier than it used to be, scarred extensively at the elbow where her bones were once exposed to the Taiga's unforgiving elements. She winces, struggling to pull her great drummed magnum from the magnetic sleeve on her right thigh. She shouts, "Magar, stand clear!"

He doesn't seem to hear her. He's still crouched at Taiko's side, studying all the advanced prosthetics she's acquired. He traces the branching, electric burn up from her melted hip to her right shoulder. He watches as her uncharacteristic smile fades into a twitchy dream.

Aila finally pulls her heavy weapon free and chops the hammer back. She uses two hands to target Taiko, readying her finger on the trigger, but Magar's shaggy forearm rises to block her line of sight. "Mag." Aila tries to aim around him. "What are you doing?"

He doesn't respond. Just steadies his boots beneath him and quietly rises to his feet, fully obstructing her view of Taiko with his stocky frame and broad shoulders. Aila steps back, allowing him the space to turn and face her. As he does so, his eyes stay low, shoulders hunched. He thoughtfully removes his Zero X helmet, looking down at it like a severed head.

"Absolutely not." Connie shifts her aim from Rosey's back to Magar's forehead. "Bear, put your helmet back on and fall in line. That's an order."

No response from Magar. No movement whatsoever.

"Bear!" Connie commands. "Helmet up or kiss the dirt. Final warning."

"Wait. Wait a minute." Aila's eyes dart fretfully between Connie and Magar.

"Hammer, come to me. We're switching." Connie side-steps away from Rosey, allowing herself a clearer view of the apparent defector.

"Wait. Just wait—Mag. Mag, look at me!" Aila's shouts don't stir him at all. He's too slouched for anyone to see his eyes.

"What's happening?" asks Derek Bugg.

"What's the matter with him?" Chuck echoes in near simultaneity.

Connie racks a round into chamber. "Hammer, stand clear now."

"Wait! Just give him a chance to—" The moment Aila looks away, a strong hand clamps around her wrist. Another grabs her by the waist and pulls her in. She fights hysterically for a moment, horrified by Magar's sudden turn, but there is no violence in his grasp, only desperation. He clings to her, the bald crown of his head tucked beneath her chin as he buries his nose between her sturdy clavicles. His shoulders hop in a jerking, unpredictable rhythm as he quietly begins to weep.

Aila looks stunned. She looks like she's never been hugged once in her giant life. Never like this. Her massive hands hover above his back as though repelled by magnetic uncertainty. Then her magnum drops. It splashes fresh mud onto Magar's helmet, freeing her huge biceps to squeeze his head. They hold each other. Aila whimpers breathlessly, pressing tender kisses from his receding hairline to his nose, finally guiding his face up to meet hers. Her visor is nudged above her eyebrows as their lips connect in romantic satisfaction.

For the first time in several weeks, Connie is genuinely astonished. She watches her two best hunters melt into one another, and that foggy road sign begins to fade. She searches the other faces of her unit, seeing only more confusion and perplexity. She aims uncertainly at Magar, then at the unconscious Taiko, then Roosevelt Hall, and she finally finds something familiar—a look of anguish that she swears she's seen before:

Rosey drops to his knees, as though the image of these fierce lovers is too severe for him to stand. He's fighting back emotion, blinking back tears. If his hands weren't bound behind his back, he'd be clutching at his chest. But he isn't looking at Aila and Magar. He's hypnotized by the heat behind them, by the sensuous beam that he's been caught in, a crimson light like love itself emanating from the edge of the woods.

Connie doesn't need to follow his line of sight. Her Spider sizzles red-hot against her spine, and she sees exactly what happens next—not like a hazy road or fading dream but a vivid recollection. A reversed memory, sent from her own inevitable mind. "No!" She spins to the east, drops to her knee, and sets her sights on the teenaged stranger's throat. She hesitates, noticing a raised entry scar precisely where she's aiming—a familiar indignant jawline just above that. Her past and present minds converge in a dizzying spin. Her Spider hisses, boiling her skin. She squeezes the trigger just as somebody tackles her from behind.

Yono hears another hummingbird zip overhead—hears the gunshot trailing behind it. But he's too focused to look away, too enthralled by this eruption of desire he's catalyzed. He doubted Earth people could love like this. Never expected this kind of heat could be intentionally subdued. What a tragedy. What a sudden, obvious need there is for a scatterer on this world. Worst of all, he catches a much more familiar scent— that smoky sugar his stomach hates, that harsh reminder of a brilliant queen with terrible taste in men. The scatterer lives inside these people, fragmented but rejoining. And his beloved brightstar is drawing near.

Miles Yang is the first to move. He starts toward Connie, seeing her tackled just as she fires, seeing her struggle beneath the weight of her own prisoner, Roosevelt Hall.

"Finish it!" Connie stops Miles with a shout. She scrambles on her belly, fighting to keep her teeth above the mud. "Put 'em down! Quick!"

"No more!" Rosey wrestles Connie like a rabid amputee, arms still zip-tied behind his back, knees squeezing her hips to keep her from slithering away. "No more, no more, no more!" he shrieks again and again through panicked tears.

Miles spins from that madness back to his strange captives. He immediately clocks the heightened twinkle in the older one's eyes, the windless ripples running through its crimson hair, the streak of blood trickling from the shallow bullet burn above its eyebrow. Connie shot the thing in the head. Just a graze, but it hasn't even noticed. She was right. Not kids at all. Rogues. The strangers who killed the captain, killed Zayd Aswad, killed Wilson Black. Miles looks down at the old cop shotgun he inherited from the latter. Feels the weight of it. The balance. Then he levels it with the horizon and holds on for dear fucking life.

A blast of dragon's breath cooks the road and grass and trees, igniting hundreds of tiny fires in a wide, symmetrical cone. The rain is thick and quick enough to douse most of the flames in seconds, but sections of the woodlands continue to burn as far as fifty meters from the shotgun's muzzle. Miles stares distantly at the carnage, grimly appreciating the destructive force of his fallen comrade's engineering, but he is quickly roused by anguished shouts coming from his ten o'clock.

"Derek! Oh fuck! You—why did you—?!" Chuck Bugg's rifle is dangling from the leash around his neck. His hands are on either side of his helmet, completing the image of shock and grief. His attention is jumping back and forth from Miles Yang to the cooked body at the epicenter of his stellar burst—not bodies, not the young rogues, just one blackened smear in the shape of a man. The smoking corpse of Derek Bugg.

"*Sleep!*" Poody points his finger at Chuck, just as he is lifting his rifle to open fire on Miles in retaliation. A flash of drowsing light washes over the surviving clone, and he collapses where he's standing, crumbling awkwardly in the mud.

Miles follows the flash of light to the younger rogue, who's now standing out in front of his older protector. Other than that position change, they're both exactly where they should be, standing exactly where Miles thought he just fired the stellar shell, but as he twists frightfully to his two o'clock, he sees the undeniable path of the dragon's flame where Derek Bugg should be penning the two kids in. No, not kids. Not kids at all. Miles drops the shotgun. Drops to his knees in the thickening muck, staring down at his greasy palms.

Poody's eyes are still shining brightly when he points two fingers at Miles Yang, one bony index finger on either hand. He has not perfected this gift yet; he must be sure he gets it right. "*Dream,*" he whispers sadly, relaxing the tightness behind his eyes until they flicker like he practiced, just like old lady Mantz's always did before one of her long lessons. A matching strobing glow can be seen in the eyes of Miles Yang as his chin droops toward his chest, as he crawls himself down into the mud for a deep and sudden rest. Poody remains standing, but his arms relax to his sides and his eyelids begin to shut. As he falls into the space between, he thanks the shadow man for the very smart plan, and apologizes for doubting him, and thanks him again for saving their lives with that last trick, even though it was cruel and very very sad. To his surprise, a softer voice responds.

"*Yes. Yes, it was,*" the new voice whispers, not from the haunted shadows by the lake but somewhere nearer, closing in. A woman's voice that he knows well. And not alone.

Connie screams at Derek's blackened corpse, at Miles Yang, at Magar and Aila, now undressing each other in the road. She roars and snarls at her inevitable self, refusing to let that weakness come, remembering she doesn't believe in collective nightmares and human reachers and all that Bright Night schizophrenia. She cranks her hips clockwise, then counters back, swinging her regrown elbow and tightened fist, catching Roosevelt in the jaw, scrambling his PTSD into thoughtlessness, noodling his body into fitful spasms. She drags herself through the sludge, escaping his dead weight, reclaiming her soaked rifle in muddied hands. She fires two rounds into the ground to spare her face the chance of backfire. Then she looks down her sights at his heaving chest and squeezes her trigger again.

The rifle backfires anyway—or seems to—bursting to pieces in her hands, scattering itself two meters south into useless components and unspent rounds. None of that makes sense. This can't be happening, and yet she swears she knew it would. That's why she fired those two tests, why she's only half surprised to hear a familiar electric scream ride down the wind, why her trembling eyes are already rising north to witness his return.

Cyrus Uba comes striding through the storm, one heavy boot in front of the other, one natural eye burned to blindness, the other covered with a patch. Black Beauty crackles red against his shoulder, freshly fired, steaming wherever the unworthy raindrops deign to land.

"Hello, Ms. Clark."

Connie chuckles miserably at the sound of his rumbling voice. She looks down at her destroyed rifle, this time recognizing the kinetic damage of a high-speed rail slug.

"Where are the others?" Uba guides his useless eyes around the battlefield's horizon. "I do not see them here."

"Don't!" Connie points her finger at the captain. "Don't you play with him. Not you." She reaches behind her head and clamps down hard on her Spider-1, gasping at the scalding heat, at the eye-watering sting she endures as it meshes more securely with her spine. The illusory image of Cyrus Uba immediately begins to judder, revealing glimpses of a smaller figure, holding a sharper weapon.

"What difference does it make?" another familiar voice sneers at her aggressively. "Don't you know what's coming? Isn't that what led you here? You're the same as them now, I can see it in your fucking eyes!" Zayd Aswad points his Nepalese kukri at Connie's reconstructed face.

She draws her sidearm, flicks the safety, and fires at him.

The standard round zips two centimeters above Zayd's shoulder, but he doesn't flinch. His contemptuous expression only deepens as his illusory image begins to glitch, partially revealing another figure just beneath it.

"The next one goes through your cheek," Connie pants, blinking through the sweltering sickness. She grabs her helmet by the visor and chucks it off, pawing at her eyes and forehead to clear the sweat away. "I'll kill you before you cook me; I can promise that." She steadies her aim on Zayd's juddering image. "So, you might as well just show me." She watches Zayd lower his kukri, flickering more rapidly, revealing more and more of the slender frame beneath the illusion. "Show yourself, you fucking bitch!"

The juddering ceases. Between Connie's eyeblinks, a new human shape appears in the road—a woman in silhouette, shrouded by the dryland's heaviest rainfall in a decade, cloaked in a slate-gray duster coat and matching boots. The hilt of a palladium katana is visible above her shoulder, rippling with the wet reflections of her shimmering azure hair. It's much longer than Connie's ever seen it, a wild tangle dribbling around her neck. A matching midnight gleam soars across the flooded earth between them as the infamous brightstar carefully raises her dazzling eyes.

"Your light shines brightly, Connie Clark. It's good to see you."

"Why are you doing this? Why—" Connie staggers, nearly succumbing to the fever. She clenches her eyes shut, breathing vigorously through her nose. "Why did you bring me here?"

"Do you really believe that?" Tysha answers quickly. "You think I'm causing you this pain?" She takes a step forward—

But Connie fires a blind shot at the rogue's feet to stop her there. "I know it's you." She grimaces her eyes into useful slits. "You've been in our heads for six fucking months. You're driving the world insane."

"Insanity would be an improvement on your kin." Tysha surveys the battlefield, lingering thoughtfully on the melted metallic limbs of Taiko Chiba. "An explanation, at least, for your reckless inattention."

"Oh, give me a fucking—" Connie's tongue locks behind her teeth as a molten icicle stabs her brain. She doesn't realize she's lost consciousness until her knees land in the mud. But she keeps her weapon. Keeps the muzzle wavering forward as her foggy tunnel vision returns. "Alright." Her exhalations burn like ancient engine fumes. "My attention. For ten more seconds. Give me the truth." Her iron sights waver to stillness on the brightstar's missing ear. "Or take it with you."

Slowly, resolutely, Tysha turns to look at Connie Clark. Fifteen paces remain between them. A flash of lightning colors the storm clouds with the same electricity as her gaze. Her icy irises are coursed with rain, but she doesn't blink. She gives Connie absolutely nothing.

"You are such a cunt."

"Yes," Tysha agrees. "We've found something in common."

Another tortured laugh blurts through Connie's lips. Her shoulders heave in pained hysteria as she hunches forward, releasing stifled moans and stinging tears. She drops her pistol. Clutches her face to conceal the evidence of defeat.

"*Enough!*" Tysha shouts from everywhere at once. Her duster coat gusts forward at her ankles. The rain falls sideways like slashing blades. "*You demand a meal then shut your mouth. You mistake your own heat for an infection. You have the clockwork gift but see no further than your snout. Look at me, woman!*"

Connie's hands are thrown apart by an explosion. Her head is slammed back by the propellant shine of her own eyes. She sees the brightstar—not here but with her tribe, not now but someday yet to come. She sees a thousand strangers gathered tightly around a lake, parting like sand to allow the dark one through: a hulking man in clinging shadows, cradling a withered body in his arms. The first rays of morning sunlight pierce the thinning clouds high overhead, and a great glass machine is there to catch them—a prismatic octagon.

The brightstar's blade is casting rainbows as she bisects the shriveled figure, carefully slicing him neck to groin. His outer skin is crumbling away like salted crackers, but a second skin is moist beneath it, untouched by time. The immaculate glass arena is spinning like a centrifuge. Or maybe the Earth is standing still. Connie sees light beams scattering in reverse, feels a fragment of heat sucked from herself, from every human in attendance, and there are many. She sees the city protesters and police, eastern faces and western eyes lit by this great invention of mingled species. She sees herself wearing the expression of a defector, of a traitor to her unit, to her partner, to her captain. Her worst fears are arriving together, and their summation is distinct. In her own inevitable eyes, Connie Clark can finally see peace.

Her Spider-1 explodes in a jet of sparks, spraying its trade secrets straight behind her. She staggers forward but doesn't fall. She's still standing, still aiming her sidearm straight ahead, but the target is not who she expected.

"Whoa." Danny Diaz raises his hands. His eyes are widened in surprise. His forehead is bruised in the shape of a tungsten fist. "Take it easy, chief. Easy there." He nods to the trembling pistol she's pointing at his chest.

She stares at him untrustingly, waiting for his image to judder and shift, but something's different now. The air is clearer. The rain has all but stopped. The clouds to the distant north are already dissipating, much like the heat within her spine.

"No more," somebody whispers.

Connie spins around to follow the voice—not seeing anyone behind her.

"Please. No more," Roosevelt Hall mutters from the mud, half-concussed, arms awkwardly bound beneath his back.

As Connie looks down at him, she notices the leash around her neck—the short rifle dangling at the end of it, totally undamaged.

"What the heck happened?" Danny asks, lowering his arms, looking around. "Wasn't I just—?" He looks down at his hands like something's missing. "Didn't I—?" He turns away from the battlefield, looking to his overwatch position in the northern woods, revealing an unusual tan line—a perfect square of paler skin where his neck connects to his head.

Connie quickly reaches to touch herself in the same place. She burns her fingertips, not on the usual polished aluminum surface but a ruptured hole of exposed electrodes. She spins around. Searches the trees for any sign of the woman in the duster coat, but there is only a shuddering woodland, gradually brightening in thinning rain.

A panicked murmuring begins as Magar and Aila ascend from their hypnosis, disentangling from each other, hastily re-strapping gear to tender places. They're both clearly mortified and horrified by the bodily violation, but their eyes keep reconnecting, seeming to ask an unlikely question. Their lips keep twitching shyly at the corners, both too embarrassed to provide an answer.

Miles Yang is stirring, too. He's rising drowsily from an evaporating world, already forgetting what it looked like, who else was there, what he's been doing. But the passage of time feels very clear; he's been gone so long he mistakes one Bugg twin for the other. He sees Chuck, lying unconscious in the mud, and a sweeping relief washes over him. He allows himself to believe that his old life is waiting for him, that all will soon be back to normal. Then he notices the lingering flicker of a few distant fires in the woods. He smells the stink of scorched magnesium. Feels the retardant grease of an ejected stellar shell. Miles sees the ashy remains of Derek Bugg, and his evaporating memories solidify. He begins pondering the meaning of the longest dream he'll ever have.

Connie Clark has no such patience. She's quickly counting the survivors of the greatest unit ever assembled—six former heroes, turned deserters, turned inept. Her morning began with mutiny, and somehow it's still declining. She eyes the turncoat, Taiko Chiba, clinging peacefully to life. She hears the civilian, Roosevelt Hall, shifting sneakily at her heels. She swears she sees his sweaty hands, slipping free of a damaged zip-tie, reaching up to grab her rifle only to receive its nasty noise: a standard round between his eyes to get the fighting back in motion, to rouse her survivors into action and finally finish their campaign.

But she's already walking away from that probability, stepping out of her basest instincts like some kind of astral ghost. She sees herself. Everywhere she looks, Connie sees the clockwork of her world: inevitable futures, branching infinitely, vanishing into incompletion. She walks away from what must come, from every choice that led her here. She makes war with the foggy signs along her wide and empty road until just one narrow trail remains.

That's where she stops, rifle in hand, two strangers slouching in her path, both exhausted and debilitated from the psychic effort of their attacks. Not kids, she reminds herself. Not even citizens of her globe.

She tugs her combat knife from the leather sheath on her left shoulder. Both strangers flinch defensively, especially the older one with the river of blood covering half his face. He nearly collapses, propped up only by the flimsy weight of his tiny friend. Connie sees those scars again—entry and exit circles on his dusky neck. Vicious ghosts flicker back into causal view, but she keeps her sights on the narrow trail ahead.

Her knife stabs itself to the hilt, blade now buried in the woodland mud. She pinches the steel clasp at the top of her leash, and her rifle slips from her shoulder, splashing her boots and their bare feet. She draws her sidearm, releases the magazine and pulls the slide, allowing the chambered round and empty weapon to fall together as she declares, "Gunnery Sergeant Connie Clark, special operations unit commander of Zero X."

Both boys watch her uncertainly, trying to decide if that was indeed an English sentence. Yono opens his mouth to respond, but she continues:

"Lance Corporal Daniel Diaz. Petty Officer Third Class Charles Bugg. Corporal First Class Aila Hallheim. Senior Sergeant Magar Volkov. Sergeant First Class Miles Yang." Her chin dips slightly. She clears her throat and straightens her shoulders. "Carrying tags for Petty Officers Third Class Derek Bugg and Alec Shankman."

She exhales long and slow, allowing her eyes to shut completely. That makes it easier for her to see. The casting rainbows, the gathered faces, the ceremony behind the lake. When she reopens her eyes, the stranger is beaming ear to ear, the smaller one with the gentle face. She swears she's seen that curiosity before. Or knows she will. Her narrow trail is the nearest shortcut to the highway of all things. She sees it now. The surest chance to win the war. She defends the Earth one final time by extending her open human hand. She barely whispers, but the words are clearer than any she's ever spoken.

"*We surrender.*"

16.06 ■⊢ – – —————⟩⟩

Tysha rises slowly, not waking from a dream but from the spotlight of another, the unconscious mind that Taiko Chiba left unfettered in the woods: the Danny-boy. But something's strange. Somehow, her visit isn't finished.

He's clinging to her. Or she is failing to release him. Bits and pieces of her identity are still sifting into place. She sits in silence, cross-legged in a lightless room. Her hands are open, palms up, elbows balanced on her knees. Her eyes are closed, she realizes. She quickly opens them, and a skinny young woman flinches away in fear.

"Brightstar," Sumella gasps. "You—you were strange. So dim."

"Dim," Tysha repeats, as though rediscovering the word. She looks around at the muted interior of the cotton canvas yurt with a similar expression. "No. My light was elsewhere."

"With Yono?" Sumella asks, shuffling forward to the brightstar. "You destroyed the hunters? He is safe?"

Tysha studies the pale girl unfamiliarly. Her cheeks are doughy, but her neck is vascular and thin. Her upper ribs are visible between the modest straps of a vibrant floral dress, and her dainty hands are surprisingly strong; one is firmly clamped at Tysha's left forearm, the other at her shoulder.

"Oh—" Sumella releases her. "Sorry, I—I am not myself."

"It's fine." Tysha rises to her feet, finding her folded duster coat on a wicker chair near the western wall. She lingers there, trying to remember what is missing. "I know the feeling."

"You do? Has something happened?"

Tysha starts to answer, but a small diamond of light glitters into view, circling the inside of the yurt from the south to the west. She follows it slowly, curiously, until she spots her palladium sword, twisting in the knot of a nylon rope near the entry.

Sumella wrings her hands together, watching the brightstar cross the yurt to examine her dangling blade. Tysha appears mystified by the weapon, even mistrusting, until she suddenly grasps it by the hilt and flicks her wrist to cut it loose. She sheathes it just as quickly, lifting the yurt's exterior flap to make her exit, pausing there, turning her shoulders just enough to show Sumella her missing ear.

"Yono was very brave today," Tysha says. "He'll be here soon."

Sumella exhales, covering her mouth, nodding gratefully—until Tysha continues:

"The hunters are coming with him."

Sumella's eyes flick to the exit, but the brightstar is already gone.

16.07

Tysha moves in addled bursts, hurrying forward as her history returns, slowing her feet whenever the recollections come too slow. The camp is a disorderly sprawl, shifting daily to accommodate the expanding population. She knew it this morning. Knew the shoreline and these trees and which northern path was most direct. But her stolen time in the Danny-boy's spotlight is proving very costly. She is disoriented. Diffused. If just two minutes in the gaps does this much damage to the ego, she fails to see how any hope for that man remains.

That man. Even his name is lost to her right now. She strains, scarcely managing to conjure his facial features, the unlettered sound of his rough voice. Thankfully, one detail remains unimpaired. One sensation, really. This incessant feeling of distant torque, of someone swaying absentmindedly at the end of an endless leash. A quantum tether, tied between a brightstar and her man.

That's what they've come to see, all these tribal eyes darting so excitedly in her direction. *Brightstar*, she hears them whisper. *The silent second, there she is.* Today, it's useful. Each interaction summons pieces of herself, forgotten flashes of Dallas Dynamics, of the Taiga, of West Shanghai. And newer faces. Entire tribes of landed kin, blending families with fugitives, mixing her lost people with these minorities of Earth, these few and rarest lights like Connie Clark, already bright enough to see the calling, to witness the scatterer's return.

Tysha slows her feet, wondering which result will be more unsettling. If her promised man is already lost, there will be nothing left to do but burn him—not turn him, as some might be expecting. His infamous light has already been exhaustively dispersed, not to his adopted tribe but everyone else, the dimmest and most broken, the darkest of her kin and the most isolated of his own. If she fails today, then none of that will change. For the best, perhaps. Earth may yet make a brightworld in due time.

But what if she succeeds? Do these congregated cultists even comprehend her schemes? They have crept to this hidden sanctuary, uninvited, drawn together by the fading source of their demigod. A high one, some have whispered. An ascended light unlike their own. It is his unequaled heat that has awakened their connections, their nascent abilities and new reach; that much is true. But her man is just a man, of that she's certain. When the great machine that she's commissioned is unveiled and brought to light, will they return his sacrifice, or will they run? And if that moment comes, Tysha wonders worst of all, will she be bright enough to allow them to escape?

A chilling shadow passes through her, an alluring blackness like beckoning fingers, lifting her chin to look ahead. And there it is. Too soon, she would've thought. She hadn't walked nearly far enough to reach it. But, looking back, she confirms the tribal camp is well behind her. It's quiet now. None of their dim whispers can penetrate this space. The shore of the lake is just beside her, the northern shore, marked by one dilapidated dock. A sunken dinghy juts up from the shallows like wooden teeth.

She's delaying, she realizes. Arriving here has that effect. Too many echoes of fallen evil, of major violence on this porch. This time it's useful. A few more pieces of herself click unmistakably into place. She sets her eyes on the rotten wood, on the tangled veins of ivy strangling the crooked frame where an exterior door should be. She remembers the deal she made and the regrettable husk she made it with. Lingering no further, she strides forward into darkness, hurrying over the reinforced floorboards, turning into the narrow kitchen where she quickly takes a knee. An ancient cellar door is buried there, comprised of three wooden planks, bound at the edges by rusted iron.

She locates a decayed circular knot near the center of the bottom plank. Pressing her thumb against it, she feels an icy smoothness more like glass, an ultrasonic scanner linked to Tysha's biometrics. Her idea, she remembers. Only the bright-star should have a key to where the shadow man is kept.

A depressurizing sound is chased by the hum of an electric motor. Wisps of cooler air escape the cracks around the cellar door as the entire wooden facade flips up and over, revealing a narrow circular hole. The space below is eerily pitch-black, much too dark to see the bottom.

Tysha looks up, checking the side door of the kitchen. No witnesses in the smudgy window frame. No curious footsteps heard nearby, no approaching lights she can detect. Satisfied, she flips a lever on the underside of the cellar door, dropping a collapsible aluminum ladder into the shadows. Not needing it for her descent, she scoots over the edge and drops to the dirt floor below.

The darkness takes her. She sees nothing in any direction. Hears nothing. Even the porthole above has vanished, now obscured by perfect shadow. She waits for her eyes to adjust, but the emptiness persists, imposing conflicting senses of surveillance and isolation. The longer she waits, the further the living world above seems to drift and slip away. She draws her sword but sees no proof of it. No trademark gleam or sound of metal. She defends her left, then slashes blindly to her right. She reaches for the ladder, but it's like it was never there.

A bodiless cackling echoes out, bouncing from the depths of some unseen sunken chasm—an unrepentant howling laugh, mocking her to stillness, forcing Tysha to reckon with one final piece that she's misplaced. It's the one she keeps forgetting. The one old Mantz died to impart. The one that broke her man.

As the ruthless cackling carries on, Tysha forces herself to face it. Despite the panic between her ears, she slowly lowers her sword, inverting it until the blade is angled directly down. She thrusts it there, feeling the reverberations in the Earth, feeling the firmness of her adopted world beneath her feet. Despite the sense of imminent danger, of unpredictable violence all around, she allows her eyes to settle shut. She breathes carefully until that trickiest piece is settled back into place—the one she knows she'll lose again.

Soon as it clicks, she feels the movement of the shadows, billowing like gaseous oil in reverse, swirling through the aluminum ladder, coursing up her shoulders and around her throat, swallowing the derisive laughter like a suffocated scream. She reopens her eyes just in time to see the darkness sucked behind them.

The cellar is visible now—already altered since her last visit, now brightly lit by overhead industrial lights. The eastern and western walls are lined with handcrafted wooden shelves, efficiently stacked with labeled compartments of identical size. Two parallel steel tables run the width of the northern wall, one raised for standing labor and manufacture, the other lowered for seated inspection and design. A magnifying lamp is anchored there on an articulating arm, and something strange is gazing into it. A human shape of wisping, clinging smoke, unnaturally defying the brightened room. A shadow man.

"*Not too shabby,*" the shadow croaks, sounding playful and infirm. "*Almost had you this time.*" Two wrinkled, veiny fingers lift into view above the smoke, pinched but not quite touching. Two muscular legs escape the shadow in a similar way, lifting and swinging around on a wooden bench. A shrouded face abandons the magnifying lamp and the skilled pencil sketch beneath it. Two eyes like empty holes are briefly visible beneath a silvery head of hair, before the shadows envelop the man again. "*What was it?*" A glint of grinning teeth escapes the shroud. "*That last thought that broke you free. Something about a missing piece?*"

His teeth clap together in an unsettling way, but Tysha disguises her unease. She searches the cramped space, seeing no sign of what she came for.

"*Behind you,*" the shadow answers before she asks. A geriatric knuckle and index finger seem to point directly at her chest, but as she turns, peeking between the ladder's rungs, she sees a pyramid of glass piled in the darkest corner of the cellar. A single blue tarp is folded back and forth between the prismatic slabs to separate them from each other, so only the triangular apex is receiving any light, bending every sterile beam into half a dozen other colors, all scattered motionlessly along the darkest wall. She's seen this glass before.

"*No,*" the shadow answers her thoughts again. "*The prism cells are in the valley where we left them. These are quite different. Quite a bit denser than they look. You may need a few extra hands to complete the assembly up above.*"

Tysha turns to face him, alarmed and disbelieving. "It's finished? You're certain?"

"*No work of art is truly finished.*" The shadow spreads his wrinkly hands in feigned concession. Tysha notices his skin appears much older since her last visit, a decade's worth of degeneration in just a few weeks. "*But this work is ready for its audience. Ready as we can make it.*"

Tysha twitches at that phrasing. Considers asking another question but lowers her eyes and tugs her sword up from the hardpacked soil instead.

"*Yes,*" the shadow answers anyway. "*You might call this a collaboration of —*"

"Don't—" Tysha points her palladium hilt at his smoky face. "Don't answer what I haven't asked." The shadow sits back quietly, obediently, saying nothing in response. Somehow that irks her more. "Nobody else is coming down here. I'll carry the components up myself." She spins her blade upward, sheathing it between her shoulders, waiting for the shadow man to protest, but he keeps his stillness. He doesn't speak another word until she's stepped behind the ladder to assess the pile of glassy slabs.

"*We ain't him, ya know.*"

Tysha twitches again. But ignores the voice. Places her hands on the apex of the pyramid, finding no easy edges to anchor her grip.

"*Genetically, we're more like his brother. Or his son.*" The shadow gestures encouragingly, as though delivering good news. "*Ideologically, spiritually,*" the shadow clicks his tongue, whistling a long, high note, "*Calvin Prichard is deceased.*"

Tysha halts her efforts. She doesn't speak, doesn't turn around. But the shadow man seems to sit up straighter. His wisping smoke darkens noticeably as he falls quiet, allowing her to continue tugging the stubborn glass component.

"*Fair enough,*" the shadow yields to her unsaid threat.

Tysha finally tugs the apex free. Staggers backward, clenching it in her arms.

"*If you can't forgive that side of us, we understand. Of course.*"

She can barely hold it. Starts toward the ladder, then quickly doubles back.

"*Just don't forget our other side.*"

Wham. She drops the component back where it started. Leans against the glistening pile, catching her breath.

"*Do not dismiss what we have gained from your found father, Kible Thexx—*"

"AHHH!" Tysha whirls on him with flashing eyes, shrieking lungs, and a slashing quantum blade. She splits the aluminum ladder like it was never there. Splits it atomically, sending a blast of broiling wind through the narrow workshop. The magnifying lamp shatters. The wooden bench bursts into splinters behind the shadow man, who has jumped to his feet, shielding his face with crossed forearms.

The illusory smoke around him vanishes, revealing his

dense, leathery skin just as it's scalded away in cauterizing gashes. His loose-fitting farm clothes are similarly scorched, revealing a strange phenomenon beneath them: instant body armor, bursting from his skin like liquid metal perspiration, thickening to shield his vital organs from the fiery deluge. It does nothing to protect his silvery hair, now smoldering at its edges, burned away in larger patches above his ears and across his scalp. His aged and wrinkled eyes are squinted in the acutest sense of pain. One is cobalt. The other is blue-green.

"No harm," the shadow man says quickly, spoken aloud, no longer within her mind. "Please. No harm intended." He winces, raising his charred hands in meek surrender.

Tysha glares at him, still snarling in blind rage, still hyperventilating through her clenched teeth and flaring nostrils. Then she begins to hear them. In the space between their entangled minds, she hears the enlightened voices of the Earth.

"Who is that? Is it him?!"

"L'hai sentito?"

"By the light, he's there!"

"Calvin Prichard est vivant?!"

The shadow man stumbles to a knee, straining to keep his hands in the air. He's shuddering, eyes fluttering, already overwhelmed by the psychic weight of millions of converging minds. Tysha sees the man without his smoke. Sees him completely.

With some awkwardness, she lowers her sword and takes a step back. Nods for him to drop his hands. Slowly, he obeys. With extreme, deliberate effort, he claws his palms down around his mismatched eyes. He holds them there, and the nanomechanical body armor digs itself back into his pores, dispersing beneath his skin in a stomach-churning wave. His burned flesh rapidly heals, shedding dead cells into the air as instant dust. His breathing slows. The entire room dims slightly, even loses a bit of its color, and the interrogative voices fade away. The shadow man gingerly removes his hands, revealing eyes as depthless and black as they were before. The psychic smoke billows from there, gradually enshrouding his conflicted body of shredded muscle and elderly skin, severing his connection to the highway once again. After an extended silence, he manages to speak.

"Our apologies. We spoke quickly. Stupidly." The shadow labors to his feet, struggling to stand without hunching forward. *"Please save your strength."* He gestures slowly, guiding her eyes to a familiar circular disc and landing pad, buried beneath the prismatic slabs. *"We've cut the hoverlift to match the exact dimensions of the hatch."* His shadowy fingers indicate the open porthole above. *"We'll show you how to operate it. And the machine, of course. The assembly is intuitive. Symmetrical."* He draws an octagon in the air with his clinging smoke, then respectfully bows his head. *"Following that, we await your judgment."*

Tysha twitches at that phrasing. She bows her head, but not to him. Not with anything resembling respect. She stares at the hardpacked dirt, remembering the vow she left him with. A silence to match his darkness. That's what she said. To which man and for how long, she isn't certain anymore, but one thing is coming clear. Her trickiest piece has already been misplaced again.

"We dim ourselves," the brightstar says.

"What's that?" the shadow asks, retreating half a step.

"You asked which thought released me, at the end of your little game." She lifts her eyes to meet his smoke. "We can only dim ourselves."

"*Ah.*" He readies his arms for self-defense. "*We see.*"

"No, I don't think you do." Tysha steps forward, watching him as closely as she can. "If you were truly the spawn of Calvin Prichard or any kin to Kible Thexx—" she stifles there, allowing the darkness to thrash her heart, to clamp its jaws around her throat, until the spasm passes, until her eyes are clear again. "If you were either of those men, you'd know I'm hopeless with machines." She exhales gently. Her sword relaxes in her hand, before she flicks it upward, sheathing it safely behind her back. "I'll help you put the thing together, but it must be you who activates it."

"*Us?*" The shadow asks. "*Out there?*"

"Of course." Tysha returns to the pyramid of components, kneeling to examine the hoverlift. "If we aim to sway these people, to inspire sacrifice from so many different tribes, I see no better way to prove that any unity is possible, that even clouded shadows might reveal a friendly eye." Tysha doesn't turn to face him. Doesn't see how he reacts. But the southern wall of scattered colors appears to spread and grow in vibrance, matching the subtle warmth that now cascades across her back.

"*Very well. Very well said.*" The shadow sounds choked up as he shuffles toward the northwest corner of his shop. "*Though we expect convincing them will be the easy part.*"

"Easy?" Tysha asks, turning her remaining ear in his direction.

"*Yeah,*" the shadow answers, sliding his smoky hand along the surface of his raised steel table. "*A walk in the park compared to this.*" He flips a hidden switch, and a deep, depressurizing rumble shakes the floor between them.

Tysha rises with the sound, turning her attention to the long facade of hardpacked dirt folding upward in two halves.

A mechanical skeleton and electric motors power into view, lifting a cylindrical container from the hidden grave below. The wall behind her bursts with color as beams of artificial sunlight penetrate the prism glass. Dashing condensation droplets cast rippling shadows on the ceiling, transforming the dusty cellar into an underwater cave.

Tysha doesn't realize she's been walking until the mobile incubator stops, until it's level with her hips and her hands are on the glass, until his dehydrated suit, his emaciated cheeks, and his flaking, dying lips are right there beyond her reach.

Only then does she imagine what a scatterer becomes. After six months in the gaps between the conscious lights of Earth, after seeing the unseen for some unfathomable span, what could any person offer to lure that man back to his flesh?

"*Not any person,*" the nosy shadow interrupts.

She waits for him to finish but no elucidation comes. No answer without asking, fair enough. Or maybe she's too dim to hear it. Maybe that's what happens when you choose the selfish path, when you would slow the progress of the endless just to resurrect a ghost.

When you would sacrifice the Earth for Emmett Hayes.

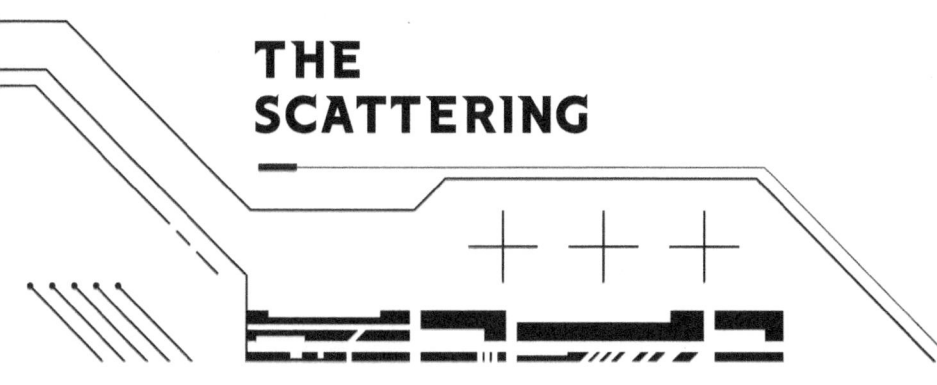

THE
SCATTERING

Mommy's talking to me. I don't know what she's saying, but I know the way she's saying it. She only sounds like this when the room is empty. I've never seen the room, or any room, or Mommy; I can just tell when she's alone. Alone in the room, I mean. Obviously, the two of us have always been together.

At least I think we have. I've only been existing for a couple hundred thousand heartbeats. Maybe Mommy was already existing without me before then. Oh yeah, I think she was. Right before I began existing, Natalie was saying she'd been waiting almost twenty-five weeks for me to come along. Oh, Natalie, that's right. Mommy was already Natalie before I was existing here. That's when I was Natalie, too. How funny that I would forget something as interesting as that. Before I was ever me, I was Natalie Alonso.

I guess that explains it. How I knew she was alone. Empty rooms, empty cars, empty stairwells after work. Natalie was always happiest by herself. That's what made Ignacio so surprising. He was just another noisy Texan before she met him down in Round Rock. He drove way out there from Old Dallas, all alone, just like she did. Well, not all alone exactly. He'd arrived at the toy convention with fifty-seven miniatures of his favorite lady from his favorite film. The scary one with all the dripping chains and the hissing tabby cat.

No, wait, I must be remembering that backward. Natalie didn't meet Ignacio; he definitely met her. Yeah, I remember seeing her come down the seinen manga aisle directly across from my booth of figurines. I remember thinking she reminded me of my tía. Ignacio's tía, I mean. She was the one who bought him his first 1:6 scale model for Christmas when he was thirteen. I remember being the owner of that memory, which means I must have been Ignacio before I was Natalie, before I was me.

Ouch. It stings pretty bad when I try to remember how I existed before that. Maybe I didn't. Maybe I'm some kind of ghost, only imagining what it's like to be alive. But ghosts are usually dead people, aren't they? And these imagined lives seem very real to me. Almost familiar. Maybe they're the closest friends I left behind. Maybe if I keep being them, I'll remember how I died. Yeah, I think that's right. I think I remember that bright perspective over there. I think if I just focus on the spotlight of her life, I should—

—flip this fucking table and put Li Qing-Nan on his pudgy back. He is such a stubborn, mulish dog, always refusing our solutions without offering any of his own. Is his empire so fucking flimsy that he relies on these wretched camps? Can he not see the way the world is turning, the economic panic these new sanctions will inspire in his state, in all of ours? Not one of us is safe from retribution, not if we delay this any longer, not if we keep clinging to this kingdom stacked on Calvin Prichard's lie.

"Varvara." Rishi Saleem of Indi-Arabia touches his chin

to my left shoulder. "He isn't budging. We should move on."
He places his soft hand on the back of mine. His royal thumb
massages my scarred knuckles like I'm one of his jealous wives.
What a whore. What a sightless, pompous cunt. I can't believe
I ever fucked him.

"Fine." I slide my hand out from under Saleem's, rather
stealthily I think, but Aksel Knudsen twitches knowingly. The
wispy Norseman sits up straighter, watching my movements
like a hound who hasn't eaten. Surprising. Maybe he's in the
market for a more convincing beard. "If President Li is still not
agreeing, I am seeing no need to be voting again." I shrug my
shoulders then casually toss my heavy braid into Rishi's nose.
"He can be keeping his . . . education centers. For now."

After his interpreter finishes whispering, the Chinese president frowns in my direction, nodding once in curt agreement.
It's as satisfied as he ever looks, the miserable pig.

"This is unacceptable." Mia Guerrero sits forward, shaking
her head, angling slightly toward the press photographer. "The
American people have made their voices very clear. This is the
wrong side of history, and there will be generational consequences. Just you wait." She wags her finger without singling
anyone out exactly, without ever making eye contact with Li
Qing-Nan. "Just wait."

Seated directly across from her, Knudsen nods in subtle
solidarity. Unfortunately, he is too long and deep in Chinese
mining to signal his virtues at this time.

"I suppose we'll need to," Saleem responds to Guerrero
while glaring sideways at me. "Without unanimity, Ms. Zhurov's motion to outlaw Luminaran internment is denied, one
to four." He gavels his knuckles on the table to signify my bill is
dead. Beneath the table, his right kneecap brushes rapaciously

against my thigh. "With that settled, I say we end the session here, looking to meet again in three weeks to—"

"No." I stun Saleem with my interruption, with the defiant hand I've just raised in his manicured face. "I am not finished."

His discomposure is not nearly so satisfying as the narrowing eyes of Li Qing-Nan. The Chinese warlord finally betrays his power tactic, scowling fiercely back at me before his performative interpreter can reach his ear. He understood me just fine.

Saleem quickly chuckles to clear the tension. "Well, I don't imagine any of us sees this issue as resolved. But you said yourself the vote is stalemated, so—"

"Do you really not feel it?" I ask President Li directly. "Even now, in this room, you don't feel any part of it at all?" I'm as surprised as he is. That line came out much clearer than I expected, certainly better than I rehearsed. I hate prewritten speeches. But one does not press this man on a whim. Not without consequences.

"Varvara," Saleem chuckles much less convincingly this time, reaching surreptitiously for my wrist. "What are you—"

"I am not speaking to you, Prime Minister." I clench my fist to remind him how I got those knuckle scars. "I am not speaking to this boy." I point at Li's interpreter until the young manservant shrinks away. "I am speaking to you, President Li." Our eyes connect again, his even more threatening than before. "I am asking about your experience six months ago, the first day we all gathered in Gaia Plaza, the last night that Calvin Prichard and Sergeant Hayes were ever seen. Obviously, I've read your statements. I'm not asking for the CCP's official stance on the Bright Night event; I'm not even asking you to call it that. I'm just asking you to sit for one more question and answer it as honestly as you can. Just for yourself. Just here." I point firmly at my temple, refusing to blink until he agrees.

He doesn't. Not verbally, not with his usual nod or impatient grunt. Instead, I see a sadistic hint of curiosity. And one chubby finger, rising slowly to his temple, mirroring my own.

Somebody falls out of their seat behind the Americans.

Saleem scoots away from me like I may be contagiously insane.

I lean forward, closing the gap between Li's scowling eyes and mine.

"My question, Mr. President, is *when*." The air is strange when I breathe it in, almost like it's rising from an open flame. "When a few million people woke up last winter, all describing the same shared dream, when all those dreamers became witnesses, became a movement, became a feeling, not just between the original millions but the rising billions of human minds of every race, sex, and creed, when you walked in here this afternoon, with your mind intractable and unchanged, with your total disinterest in this new feeling that even we have come to grips with, that even I have . . ." I blink a few times, trying to tamp the weakness down, trying to finish this last fight with glorious Russian strength, then I remember what I'm saying. I remember to let my ego go. "When will you decide to feel it? When will you allow yourself to embrace our namesake here, to seek a united Earth, or if you can't, if you're simply unfit to satisfy your planet's dream, then when will you decide to get the fuck out of its way?"

I realize I've broken eye contact. I quickly look back up to Li Qing-Nan, and I realize I have failed. He's glaring at me. Twice as vicious as he began. At some point, his pudgy fingers have uncurled into a trembling claw of rage.

The photographer's shutter breaks the silence, snapping off in a rapid frenzy. Li's interpreter hasn't moved, apparently too terrified to approach. His attention darts between me and his master, before he finally decides to hurry forward. But Qing-Nan's claw stops him short, catching the young man by his lapel. He watches me with hateful eyes before he shoves the boy back behind him.

"Again," Li growls at Rishi Saleem, leaning forward in his seat.

"I—I'm sorry?" Rishi nervously asks us both. "Again what?"

"Vote again!" Li barks at him, like nothing could be more obvious.

Mia Guerrero quickly covers her mouth, but an astonished gasp escapes her lips. Aksel Knudsen is less reactive, at least externally. He's watching me with those same hungry, howling eyes, now lit with wonderment and rapid thought.

"Oh. Yes, of course, I um . . ." Rishi sneaks a few dazzled peeks at me before he calls the vote again. "All those in favor of the Separate Planets Act to Coexist on Earth, please say—"

"Aye," says Li Qing-Nan, watching me with that new attention. Not hatred, I realize. Just the excited gaze of challenged tyranny. He'll be worse than ever after this. Dedicated to uncovering some hidden scandal, to rending me as low as he feels now. Fine. If that's the cost of his engagement, I am satisfied to pay.

"Aye," we each respond, my voice arriving at the end. I nod once to President Li, but the old mule just licks his teeth. With some assistance, he is up and out of his seat, leaving the translator to gather his effects. The young man fumbles through that task, watching me with twitchy cheeks and trembly hands before he hastily makes his exit.

"Well," Rishi begins, rising to his feet beside me, "you certainly are full of tricks."

"Absolutely," Knudsen agrees. "I'm half a mind to fire my intelligence director. How in the world did you guess that Li Qing-Nan would understand Swedish?"

"Ha!" Rishi laughs, waiting for the two of us to follow suit. "Wait, are you serious?" He frowns at Knudsen, then points emphatically at me. "My own mother doesn't speak Hindi with such grace." He spouts something off in his native tongue, expecting me to understand it, sinking into bewilderment when it's clear that I do not.

"I heard Spanish," Mia squeaks, drawing our attention to her nervous posture, to the gaggle of aides and limited press now murmuring uneasily behind her seat.

I have no answers for them. As I rise from the conference table, spinning slowly to survey the narrow room, I feel myself shrinking from the spotlight of the enlightened Varvara Zhurov. That pain is back again. That stinging, tugging burn, like a tightening rope around my heart. That was too much memory at once. Too many clues of the fallen soldier I must have been. That's right. I was in the Orbital Patrol. I was a UT Forces fighter somewhere along this gallery of light. Sometime before Ignacio. But when did I begin? Did I ever have a body of my own? Or is this pain the penalty of hope, the cosmic friction of a specter seeking life?

I test the idea, shooting myself higher, no human spotlight in my sights, nothing terrestrial at all. Just the chilling emptiness of black and lifeless space.

Space. Seems like I knew someone who used to call it that. Some lonely kid with optimism for the void. Spacious, maybe, all of this, to the common sight of those below. But never empty. Occupied in all directions if you have the eyes to look. Here comes one now. One conscious beam along the highway, chasing the infinite expanse. One ghost of a distant world.

She calls you.

Goddamn. Feels like my spine is growing back. A phantom skeleton for this hot leash to lasso onto. I remember the intensity of that last spotlight. All those enemies and egos. Competing nations of a violent, dying world. Maybe I died trying to escape it. Maybe I've been searching for a place where ghosts of light can truly end.

Not a ghost, whispers a passing second beam.

Scattered man, insists the next, as though their voices were in sync. Not spoken words or audible language. Not even consciously expressed. Just tacit waves of quantum logic painting over my demands.

I dart between them as they come. I seek deeper, darker gaps between it all. There must be some refuge in this space, some counterpoint to everything where I can just be free.

Not free, argues another beam.

She love—

I finally find it. A place devoid of heat. No human spotlights. No beams. No me. I have found the blackest gap. I am the gap. The cold inception of all things. This is it. My beginning.

My end.

But that last beam didn't finish. Its segmented message sticks to me like soaking clothes, like this goddamn rope around my chest, this sizzling, relentless tether refusing to let me fade away. I spin around, if that makes sense, if anything physical can occur at this depth of nonreality. I grab hold of the flaming leash to rip it out of me and—

I see its color. A cooling shine like a distant soul comes into view. A chilling sorrow, licked with flame. The coldest lake. The brightest star.

"Oh." A country voice produces sound without a mouth, without a body, without air. Some of that assembles too. Skin, scales, hair. A strobing twin in a shuttle's triple-pane. Daddy, Logan, Rosey. A fiery reflection with someone else's eyes. Mike, Bryce, Jakey. Eyes like Cuva Khan, like Mantz AnCarcem, like Kible Thexx. Eyes like Yono. Eyes like Poody. Eyes like . . .

"Oh yeah." I start to laugh, if that makes sense. I see the distant, waiting end of this relentless goddamn rope, this quantum tether colored blue. "Oh, hell yeah!" I give it a tug with my ghostly hand, and I discover the speed of light.

It's nothing like that old film. No massive ocean waves or endless bookshelves to the past. There is no time that I perceive. No causation or effect. Only the infinite tendrils. The hidden interstitium that I mistook for empty gaps. I am riding the bright highway. But something isn't right.

The spotlights. The scattered perspectives I've jumped between. They're disappearing. My offramp to the Earth is dimming as I approach. Time's returning. An enlightened world is vanishing from view. I'm shining brightly, brighter still, but I'm seeing growing shadows down below. I'm reclaiming what I gifted just so I can see her face.

I drop the tether. A full halt without the whiplash. A familiar view from higher orbit. I see the guns—the twisting forest of protective cannons where my intelligence was born. The view is better than I left it. That's enough. The Earth is brighter without me on it, so I can be a ghost—a scattered man, if that is how humanity extends. I can forget. She can move on.

"What happened?"

"Is it working?"

"कहाँ है वह?"

"彼が見えない."

"Why did he stop?"

I search the stars for ghostly beams, seeing nothing of the sort. I look higher, wondering which bright world I'm intercepting, which alien destination these scattered messages are dashing from.

"Down here!" the voices beckon, sounding more intimate as they strike me.

"C'mon, Em! I got the Marlin all fixed up, locked and loaded!"

"Come for us, Texas! Come for our faces!"

"Please, Mr. Emmett! Do not be dim, please please do not!"

No. They don't understand. They're not seeing this perspective, not reconciling with the damage of a scatterer returned. I have no choice. I must defend the Earth.

"You are right," she whispers clearly, cutting through the desperate noise—an icy voice like falling snowflakes dissolving in an open flame. *"You have no choice,"* she admits sadly, sounding broken, sounding certain, sounding violently incomplete. *"You are my prisoner, and I have not released you yet!"*

A tug like towing galaxies sends me faster than before. I try to fight it, but my ghostly hands can't seem to reach the rope. The heat is blinding. The quantum tether isn't just tugging at my chest; it's pulling my atoms individually. It's thrusting like a warp drive at my back. That's when I see it—not one vivid cobalt lasso, not anymore. Billions. Every color, every brightness. A prismatic scattering in reverse. The planet is dimming, to be sure. The minds of Earth are giving up their heat to bring me home.

And there it is. An onslaught of terrestrial hues. A crowded blue world is rushing up to drink me. My eyes recoil to the heavens, but there's something different about the stars. Something soothing. Something maternal about that last beam before the void. It's golden-brown like the setting sun, like a calming wave from neck to toes.

Then comes the ceiling of the Earth. A bed of stormy clouds beneath me. The nameless dryland south of Dawson. Shiloh Lake, speckled with modern dinghies, swaying beneath a hundred feet. Thousands more along the shore. Hands clasped together everywhere. Men, women, children. Human beings and their invaders, though it's harder now to tell. The palest ones are changing. I can see the rising heat beneath their skin. A great machine like a shattered star tomb, recirculating the light it takes. A centrifuge of mingled species. An architect of mingled minds, pressing his wrinkled hands against the glass. A living shadow, losing smoke, being pardoned in real time.

His dancing warden is in the octagon, undoing the silence she enforced. Cutting rainbows with her blade. Slicing the brittle husk of a supine, lightless man. Spreading his dead, protective scales to reveal the bumpkin underneath. Then a collision and a flashing unlike the Earth has ever seen.

But there is nothing after that. No living witness makes a sound. Every lifeform stops to listen, expecting victory to come. But the man is clearly dead. Just a man, after all. Not the high one they expected. Not a god returned to flesh. It's time to burn him, as she feared. Time to mourn his wasted light.

The brightstar sets her blade beside his corpse. Rubs a thumb across his cheek. She doesn't cry. She tries, but the tears refuse to come. And the crowd begins to shift. Uneasily. Disturbed. She's afraid to meet their faces, to reconcile with the damage that she's done. But the movement becomes harder to ignore. She glances out there, through the slowing prismatic glass. She's relieved to see they are not looking at her. They're watching someone on the hood of a large electric truck, parked just outside the crooked shack.

It's little Poody. So upset. Throwing a tantrum, jumping up and down in disappointment, pointing his bony fingers to some wild rhythm only he can hear. It is unsettling. Increasingly strange. From this perspective, it almost looks like he is dancing.

"Hey."

Tysha jolts. She turns to follow my withered voice, to see my crusty eyes crack open.

"Can you keep it down?" I ask her, reaching to massage my throbbing head. "I got a hangover like you wouldn't believe, and your thoughts are louder than—"

She kisses me viciously. Smothers me down against the glass. Somehow, I manage to kiss her back.

"Yes! Yes yes ye—!" Poody's fourth shout is swallowed by the roar of an expanded tribe. Five thousand voices and twice as many triumphant fists excite the air. I hear them all. Not just here but all across the connected globe. Dimmed but not extinguished. I should've known. The thinnest seeds of the scattering persist.

My woman holds me. She pulls me up to my scrawny ass, mingling her cheek against my unattended scruff. That's when I see him—grinning like his longest con has reached fruition, like this is all according to his sick and twisted plan. I flinch instinctively, unable to reach the brightstar's weapon, too weak to fight him if I could.

The shadow man's expression changes. The satisfaction drains from his aged and textured face. He nods back at me, disappointed but accepting. As he turns to make his exit, the thinnest wisp of psychic smoke begins to dribble from his eyes.

"Hey, Prich!" I stop him with my parched and crackling voice.

With the ancient patience of disbelief, he slowly turns to face me, to see if that shout he heard was real.

"Sorry." I nod a dozen tiny times, catching up to what I've missed. "I guess that name ain't right exactly. Either way, it's good to see you, friend." I touch the brim of an invisible cowboy hat, chancing a smile.

He doesn't smile back, not exactly. But his smoke slightly retreats. He smartly winks his blue-green eye before he vanishes into the crowd, some glaring at him, some gaping with open fear, some recognizing the redemption that he has initiated today.

A clap of thunder steals the moment—a cannon sound like a hundred balloons all popped at once. A burly man I've never seen hops up into the bed of a matte-green electric truck, already throwing the lever forward on an old rifle I know too well. He finds my eyes. He grins like the devil's in his shorts. I almost die all over again, finally recognizing the bold bravado of my Southern brother, Roosevelt Hall.

Rosey's second shot is duplicated, triplicated, quadruplicated, as Magar Volkov, Aila Hallheim, and Danny Diaz join the redneck celebration. Unfortunately, Miles Yang and Charles Bugg don't look fit to fire rounds, but the hothead Yono seems unexpectedly delighted by my survival, smiling ear to ear. That's when I realize he's on a heavy morphine drip, bandaged and stitched around the head, with dutiful Sumella at his side.

Tysha shifts her weight. She holds me closer but not as tightly. Her dominant hand drops to the hilt of her palladium sword, as someone steps through the entryway of the halted glass machine. Heavy boots shake the octagonal floor. A muscular body blocks my access to the sun, and all the twinkling rainbows die in our intruder's encroaching shade.

"It's gone," Connie Clark admits. "Can't see it anymore. Can't tell what happens next." She glances at Tysha's readied hand, tightening around her sword. Her own hands are hidden behind her back. I notice her combat knife is missing from the sheath on her left shoulder.

"Me neither," I wheeze back. "Guess we'll just have to hunker down and wait." I nod to the lake, to my expanding tribe and open land, inviting her to join. Connie twitches slightly. Despite what she just said, she seems eerily unsurprised.

"Nice try, asshole." She coughs and swallows harshly, like something sick and sentimental is trying to escape. "If they don't serve me the Big Chicken Dinner, I'm coming back here to collect you. Bet your fucking life." She turns but doesn't leave. She crouches low, carefully unloading what she's been holding behind her back.

Another child, I think at first. A slender, sleeping girl, until the young cyborg unfolds herself on the glassy floor. Most of her robotic parts have been removed. Only her metallic left foot remains. The stubs and cavities of her missing right eye, arm, and leg are accentuated by the spindly superficial burns of a discharged high voltage mine.

"Hayes," the cyborg mumbles, sounding even more lifeless than I last saw her. "Hayes," she breathes again.

I tap Tysha, and she helps me to a knee. Helps to balance my emaciated frame as I scoot closer to Taiko Chiba, as I search my mind for anything I could possibly—

"Hayes, can you fucking hear me?" Taiko grumbles louder,

squinting her resting eye open.

I laugh like an absolute idiot. I'm already crying when I respond, "Yeah. Loud and clear."

"Hell is wrong with you," she huffs. "I'm half dead and you can't answer me?"

"I'm sorry, Taiko. Sorry."

"You should be sorry. *You* did most of this." She gestures to her missing right half.

"Jesus! I didn't—I had to!"

"Oh yeah, sure," Connie cuts in. "Just like he had to liquefy my fucking arm."

"What?" Taiko gasps. "When was that?"

"She shot me!" I cough back. "Several times." I point to a few of the entry scars on my newly exposed chest.

"Yikes," Taiko grimaces in disgust. "Your skin. You should moisturize."

"Ha!" the brightstar shouts. One violent syllable at my expense. Connie and Taiko both recoil, both looking equally amazed. An empty silence. A nervous chill upon the truce.

"What was that?" Taiko asks. "Were you trying to laugh?"

"I—" Tysha starts. "No, I was not—"

"Poody, Yono, you gotta see this!" Taiko tries to wave at the boys, then remembers her prosthetic arm is gone. "Shit. Okay, let's find Prichard first. Clark. Clark, snap out of it." She nudges Connie to get moving.

"Yeah." Connie hoists Taiko up, keeping her eyes on Tysha—on the sword too much like the one that vivisected Zayd Aswad. "Time to go."

As they depart, I am reminded of the change that we've undone, the unknown generations who may suffer now that the unifying dream has been delayed.

"I was not laughing," Tysha insists over the silence. "Only voicing my agreement."

"What's the difference?" I chuckle back, watching the convergence of my friends, watching all the gathered, triumphant faces and the fading smiles in between—some beginning to notice what they've lost.

"Laughter is impetuous," Tysha explains. "Inconsiderate of those yet to be lit."

"Mm. You mean the endless."

"The endless," she agrees, looking up to the infinite stars.

"You know, I had a peek at that."

"At what?"

"Everything. The bright highway in all directions."

The brightstar pauses thoughtfully before deciding to inquire. "What did you see?"

"I just told you. Are you even listening?"

"What? Of course, I am. What did you see up there?"

"Everything." I watch the shimmer in her eyes. I trace the scar my captain gave her all the way to her missing ear. "Everything I'll ever need."

She doesn't laugh. She doesn't offer me another kiss. She just makes that sound my daddy used to, that little grunt to indicate I might not be totally without a brain.

"Par ya Lum sakar?" Her shoulder nudges mine.

"Yeah." I draw the brightstar closer, finally allowing her to rest. "That's a promise."

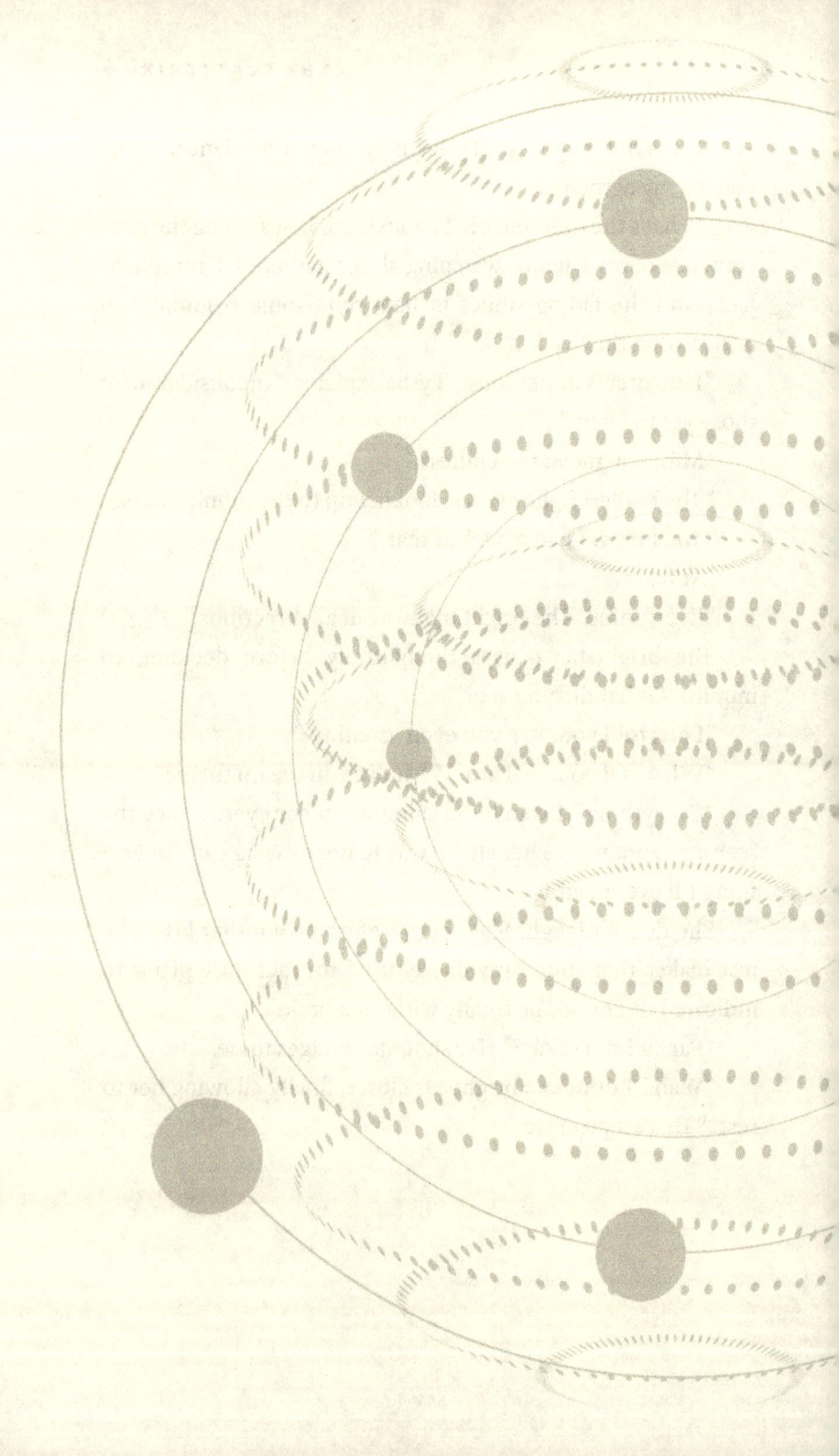

DON'T FORGET

ZERO ONE

Cyrus Uba — Zero Leader (Chirundu, Zambia)

Emmett Hayes — Daydream (Dawson, TX)

Zayd Aswad — Edge (Chicago, IL)

Connie Clark — Crown (Lawton, OK)

Alec Shankman — Jester (Atlantic City, NJ)

Sasha Carter — Sparrow, Hover One (Shreveport, LA)

Miles Yang — Maestro (Edmonton, Canada)

Danny-boy Diaz — Colt (Los Angeles, CA)

ZERO TWO

Faye Thompson — Fangs (Harlem, NY)

Taiko Chiba — Swarm (Tokyo, Japan)

Magar Volkov — Bear (Omsk, Russia)

Aila Hallheim — Hammer (Alta, Norway)

Chuck Bugg — Mosquito (San Francisco, CA)

Derek Bugg — Beetle (San Francisco, CA)

Marco Robina — Vulture, Hover Two (San Juan, Puerto Rico)

Wilson Black — Whale (Wailuku, HI)

THE CAVERN TRIBE

Kible Thexx AnSorin — The infamous rogue. Always thought he was named after dog food, until I heard Prichard at the cosmodrome. Sounds more like "Bible Checks."

Tysha — "Tish-uh." Sounds Ukrainian; will check the translation later. Her accent is hard to place. Her hair is somethin' else.

Cuva Khan — Not to be fucked with. Seriously. Reminds me of the captain.

Mantz Malikah AnCarcem — Nasty old bitch. If I had my way, she'd—

Kendar Shall — Kible's big brother. Hard to explain, but . . . I don't know.

Nazara Thume — "Nuh-Zar-Uh." I'll never forget you.

Poody — Love this kid. His name sounds like one of the words in Nazara's lullaby.

Yono — Love this one less. Such a hothead.

Kono Cora AnAmarka — Yono's old man. Very kind eyes. Guess the apple fell far from the tree.

Sumella — Kinda fidgety, but she means well. Yono should give her a chance.

Lailara — Strong and silent type. Think she might've popped the hothead's cherry.

Ketz Clute — Just met this guy. Has a way with words.

Canna Dhoz AnFannan — Long gone. One of the first to reach the cave. An artist. I love his work.

"Bhakan." — Get up.

"Bhokon." — Go.

"Khall." — Respond.

"Khaimall." — Don't move.

"Futwana." — Now.

"Pervare." — Please.

"Grashalam." — Thank you.

"Ya ben?" — You okay?

"Ah ben." — All good.

"Balo ken." — Take him.

"Mai tenya?" — What you wanna do? / What's it gonna be?

"Mel caska." — To hell with you. / Darkness take you.

"Kharre mel caska!" — Roast in hell! / Die in darkness!

"Mel titi keck." — You little shit.

"Mel nelumen." — You're dead. / Your light is over.

"Yam cereba nis dereta!" — Their genius has no brain!
(Outdated slang. Very offensive.)

"Me paka!" — Dad! / My father!

"Coka" — Penis

"Denzani" — Outsider

"Lum" — Light / Life

"Thume ha Lum!" — Thume is alive!

"Par ya Lum sakar." — I will die for your light. / I promise.

"Ha doso na mer." — He chose the water.

NAZARA'S LULLABY

"A khem ne nenya casko shum.
Segarda kor lu pooden orbis.
Bendarno kor tahz nais cambo lu Lum."

And there were endless empty eyes.
Blinded by the ~~freest~~ loneliest worlds.
Betrayed by those who knew the light.

OLD FILMS TO SHOW THE KID

Sleeping Beauty
Gone with the Wind
Princess Mononoke
Halloween
The Blair Witch Project
Die Another Day
The Sandlot
Raiders of the Lost Ark
Superman
Dragon Ball Z
Transformers
Alien
Interstellar

NEXT STEPS

Bury ~~the suit~~ Nazara behind the lake. Somewhere bright.

Repair the dock. And the farmhouse. And the barn.

Find out where Daddy and Jack Womack were stationed in Okinawa.

Find mama.

525

ABOUT THE AUTHOR

NICK CRAWFORD is a Southern California native and UC Irvine graduate (Zot Zot!). Prior to writing *The Bright Highway*, he worked various sales and post-production contracts for a variety of film and television studios in Los Angeles. His love for filmmaking and photography have heavily influenced his approach to writing books, and his cherished friends, family, and mentors continue to make his world extremely bright.

www.ingramcontent.com/pod-product-compliance
Lightning Source LLC
Chambersburg PA
CBHW020000120726
47903CB00004B/1062